SEAS

All-original stories of the
Valdemar's elite
including a new novella by Mercedes Lackey

EDITED BY
MERCEDES LACKEY

DAW
No. 1840

$7.99 USA
$10.99 CAN

dawbooks.com

EAN

ISBN 978-0-7564-1470-2

5 0 7 9 9

Seasons

Seasons

All-New Tales of
Valdemar

Edited by
Mercedes Lackey

DAW BOOKS, INC.

DONALD A. WOLLHEIM, FOUNDER

1745 Broadway, New York, NY 10019

ELIZABETH R. WOLLHEIM
SHEILA E. GILBERT
PUBLISHERS

www.dawbooks.com

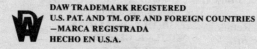

Contents

One Town at a Time
Jennifer Brozek

All trade in the marketplace had ceased. All eyes were turned to the Herald and the two merchant farmers he questioned.

Glad she wasn't in the spotlight, Astrid paid attention as well. It was the only thing she could do as an outlander rope and string merchant. Entertainment, even of the tense variety, was scarce in the Holderkin lands. No one wanted to miss the excitement.

"One and all will see who is telling the truth and who is not," Herald Kalen said, his voice loud enough to carry throughout the marketplace.

The two merchant farmers, one local, one not, stood before the Herald, flanked by a couple of burly Holderkin men. They were rougher toward the outlander than their own man, but they held both fast nonetheless as the Herald began the Truth Spell.

Bowing his head, the Herald chanted half under his breath. He repeated the words—the cadence told careful listeners that he repeated it nine times. As he ended the chant and raised his head, a light blue glow settled about the heads and shoulders of both men. As one, the men acting as guards took an involuntary step backward as soon as the blue glow appeared. Several spectators made warding signs against evil.

"Now," Herald Kalen said, pointing to the outlander, "Is it true that the lamb is yours?"

"Yes, Herald." The merchant farmer nodded vigorously. "I saw my farm's mark on its wool—faint but there. Then *he* shaved the wool, erasing it. He m-m-m . . ." The farmer stopped trying to force the lie and sighed. "The lamb had been left behind because of a lame foot. It wasn't where I left it when I went back. I thought a wolf had gotten it. I had given up on it."

Turning to the Holderkin wool farmer, Herald Kalen asked, "Is it true that the lamb is yours?"

"Yes." The man struggled, words wanted to leap from his mouth, but he pressed his lips together.

"Why do you claim the lamb as yours?"

After another struggle, the Holderkin farmer was forced to speak, "The lamb was abandoned. It is mine by right. I found it. I nursed it to health over the last week. One of my ewes adopted it. It's my lamb."

"No. I tethered it. He stole it," the first farmer insisted.

The Holderkin farmer turned red.

Herald Kalen asked, "Did you untether the lamb from its spot?"

"Yes." The word came out resigned and angry.

Herald Kalen tilted his head as if listening for something. Then he nodded. "This is my judgment: The lamb will be returned to the rightful owner. You may keep the lamb's wool you shaved as recompense for tending to the injured creature."

He raised his voice to address the crowd. "As you are of the Holderkin lands, if there are other punishments deemed necessary for thieves in Crag's Bluff, that is up to the leaders of the town." He paused, "The lamb is to be returned at once."

A mutter ran through the market as both merchant farmers turned away from the Herald. Unease and unhappiness floated on the wind. The Herald seemed to pay it no mind as he returned to his Companion. The large white animal whickered gently.

"Who's to say that's really the truth? How can we trust such magic?"

Though the words were whispered, Astrid heard them clearly. She shifted closer. Such provocative words were worth eavesdropping on.

"What do you mean?" Darbin asked.

His voice was pitched lower than the man he was speaking to, but now that Astrid was paying attention, she could follow the conversation. Darbin was a local baker. She'd found him pleasant but dull—which was more than could be said of most Holderkin. They tended to be suspicious and rude to outsiders.

"I mean, it's *magic*. How do we know that Herald didn't force your kinsman to say he stole the lamb?"

This time, Astrid saw the speaker. Wendel, a traveling merchant like her. Whereas she sold good rope and string, he sold berries. *Probably from Hardorn. Must've crossed Cebu Pass to get to town*, she thought.

Crag's Bluff was the most open town she had encountered in the Holderkin lands. Located on Old Quarry Road near the Border of both Karse and Hardorn, the town saw many more travelers than most Holderkin enclaves. For a single female merchant, Crag's Bluff was downright progressive, with nary a side-eye directed at her. It made for a pleasant change in the mostly insular, patriarchal Holderkin lands. Of course, if she'd had a male worker, things might've been different.

Darbin frowned and watched the Herald talk to the boldest of the children in the marketplace. His job done, he made himself available, but most of the adults returned to work or headed off toward the call of distant drums beating out what sounded like a slow dirge.

A small, satisfied smile flickered across Wendel's face as Darbin walked away, distrust furrowed in the man's brow. She walked to the merchant's side and asked, "What did you mean about the Herald?"

The older man whirled, his eyes wide. They narrowed even as his tension faded and an easy smile appeared as he saw the short, round young woman next to him. "What do you think I meant?"

Shrugging with a side-eye at the loitering Herald and his Companion—a beautiful white horse with blue and white tackle—"I think you meant you can't trust them. But I've been taught that you can."

"Taught by whom?"

"Everyone . . . ?"

He *hmph*ed. "That is dangerous thinking . . . to believe something is true just because 'everyone' believes it's true. I need proof."

"I've seen Heralds save people in danger. They're the personal guard of the Queen—"

"Exactly. In Hardorn, we *know* our King is true. His will is the land's, and protecting the land is his will. If either fails, the other one will, too. We can *see* the King's will. Can you say the same of those white-clad enforcers? Ones who do magic that can force a man to speak with no one to speak otherwise?"

Astrid didn't know what to say to that. It went against everything she'd ever been taught.

"Ah, never mind me." Wendel shook his head. "Maybe it takes an outsider's eyes to see what is wrong. A fish doesn't know it breathes water until it's yanked into the air by the hook."

"Maybe." Anything else she could've said was lost to the approaching drums.

Fair time in the Holderkin lands was unlike any other place Astrid had ever visited. While they acknowledged and celebrated the Harvest Festival, they did so in a restrained and sober manner. The harvest market was as busy as one should be, but it was interrupted twice a day by a solemn procession that wound through the town and the market, gathering all the good Holderkin to walk to the temple to pray. Twice, because it allowed commerce to continue while one partner attended to their souls and the other tended to their stalls; then they switched when the second time for prayer arrived. Holderkin were nothing if not pragmatic.

Astrid watched the procession with respect and veiled curiosity. Were she vending in another city, the procession would be more of a parade, with smiling crowds and cheering revelers. This procession held many more dark looks and few smiles for those who remained behind. The baker, Darbin, joined the procession after one last considering look at the Herald who stood with polite respect next to his Companion as the people passed by, nearly emptying the marketplace as they left.

It took more than five minutes for a new set of customers to appear. Shaking her head, Astrid returned to her cart and began the work of persuading the farmers and townsfolk of the value of her wares.

The tavern wasn't overly busy, but most of the customers were traveling merchants who crossed from country to country to sell their harvest goods in nearby lands. Despite the borders between them, people from Valdemar, Karse, and Hardorn often broke bread together. Borderlands had a way of either softening the differences between the countries or intensifying them. This Fair season showed a more gentle side of the different countries.

Astrid considered Wendel, who was sitting by himself with his back to the wall. It could be said that the man didn't trust anyone at his back. Or, taking a kinder route, was inviting travelers to join him.

She took her drink over to his table and gesture to the chair. "May I?"

He gave her a long, considered look before nodding. "Company is good in a strange town, isn't it?"

"It is." She sat and thought how to start the conversation.

Wendel gave her a shyster's smile. "I know what you're wondering. Aye, you want to know if my thought about the white-clad bastards is true . . . or if it's a trap for the unwary."

Astrid tilted her head and gestured for him to go on. She didn't accept or deny his assertion, but she let a smile grace her face. He could interpret it anyway he wanted.

"Well, it's true. I speak the words of my heart. I don't trust them. I don't trust a land that requires that all children must be taught about the Companions and that if one Chooses them, it is an honor. How do we know those white horses aren't demons? Did you know, dirt won't cling to them? Dye won't stain them? They've been cursed to show their true nature at all times. Why would that be?"

She had her thoughts, but she didn't express them. "I don't know."

"I suspect its some god's curse . . . or a way of protecting people who have the eyes to see."

"See what?"

"That the people of Valdemar are not well served by their monarchs."

Astrid sat back and frowned.

"I see you thinking now." Wendel leaned forward. "When has the crown ever served you?"

She shook her head. "The Waystations?"

"Paid for by you. Your taxes. The military, paid for by you. The Heralds . . . beholden only to the crown . . . paid for by you."

"I . . ." Astrid stopped and shook her head again.

"It's hard to go against what you've been told to believe, I know. But have you ever seen it in action?"

"No," she admitted.

"This is why Hardorn is better. The King lives for the land. If the land suffers, so does he."

"Magic?"

"A blessing. A geas. One our monarch takes on willingly in order to serve the people." Wendel sat back. "Imagine if this land . . . relegated to the Holderkin because none other would have it . . . imagine if it were part of Hardorn. Mud would become fertile soil. Streams would run clear and strong. It wouldn't be this harsh, unforgiving place, but a paradise."

Astrid blinked slowly at him. "Is that true? Could Hardorn's King do that?"

"Yes." He heaved a great sigh. "But we'll never know for sure while the Holderkin lands belong to Valdemar." With a yawn as fake as his smile, Wendel stood. "Forgive me, I need to retire. It's been a long day, and we have an even longer day tomorrow."

:*Is that true? Could Hardorn's King do that*?*:* Kalen laughed in Astrid's head. :*Layin' it on a little thick, weren't you?*:

Astrid laced her fingers behind her head and stared up at the inn ceiling. Solid wood. Simple construction. It did its job. :*I was playing the ingénue, and he ate it up.*:

:*I'll bet he did. That's why I chose you for this.*:

:What's next? He's definitely riling up an anti-Herald sentiment. Arrest him?:

Astrid felt her mentor's disapproval before he answered. *:It isn't against the law to speak badly of Heralds. Our people may speak their thoughts, and I'm more interested in the intimation that the Holderkin lands would be better off under Hardorn rule.:*

Astrid sobered. *:Is that treason?:*

:No. Not if Wendel is from Hardorn. If he is, however, that makes this whole thing a lot more complicated than expected. Anti-Herald thought can be solved by giving the area more attention, more help, more care. Showing that we aren't the enemy rather than just saying it. Having someone from Hardorn encouraging secession, that's dangerous and requires more than just a bit of suggestive talk by a flirtatious merchant.:

:We need proof?:

:Yes, my Herald-in-training, we do. Also, your Companion misses you. She wanted us to pass that along.:

Astrid sighed. *:I miss her, too. I haven't been away from Elsinore for such a long time since she Chose me. You're taking good care of her, yes?:*

:No. I'm letting her starve.:

:As if she'd let you.: They both laughed silently. Astrid allowed her discontent to show through their conversation. *:So, now what?:*

Kalen took a long time to answer. When he returned, his mental voice was filled with determination. *:We find out if he's just a troublemaker from Hardorn who doesn't like Heralds, or if he's something much worse.:*

Astrid watched the marketplace with interest. Being the main day of the Harvest Festival, it was the busiest the area had been. There were even scattered signs of joy and light among the Holderkin. As dour as they could be, they did have their own way of celebrating the little things and the changing of the seasons. Small gifts and much needed new tools. Even a few ribbons here or there. Most of the pragmatic shoppers had already come and gone. Her stock of rope had been depleted. It wouldn't be out of character for her to close for an hour to get a midday meal.

With one last look at the busy Wendel, who proclaimed the wonders of his berries—from fertile soil to kind rains to the fullness of the fruit—to all who would listen, Astrid slipped away.

Most of the merchants stayed in the same tavern. The ones who didn't bunked down in or under their carts. She headed upstairs to the rooms and walked past her door to the one at the end. The door was locked. Not unusual. Not for traveling merchants. But the locks in this place were not much of a match for a skilled woman with a strong knife. It was more of a matter of leveraging the lock open rather than breaking it to get in.

Once inside, with the door closed and locked behind her, Astrid gave the room a long look before she moved, trying to remember where everything was before she began her search. There were two packs in plain sight. If she were attempting to keep someone from finding something important in a room, she'd leave out bait. *Then again*, she thought, *a liar always assumes everyone else is lying. It's possible that Wendel is just what he seems: a Hardorn merchant who doesn't like Heralds.*

No. There was more to him. Astrid skipped the obvious bags and searched the room for something hidden. Something that wasn't where it should be if Wendel were innocent.

With a grin of triumph, Astrid found what she was

looking for: a small, flat leather satchel wedged behind the wardrobe. It was the kind of thing people kept letters in. The paper was as alarming as it was exciting to find.

A quick scan revealed it was a missive from Lord Orin of Hardorn to Wendel of Greenvale, giving him express permission to promise protection, money, and peace to the people of Crag's Bluff, should they be interested in becoming part of Hardorn under his direct rule and the rule of King Tremane of Hardorn . . . which would then give Crag's Bluff, and any Holderkin lands that followed suit, the benefit of the King's bond to the land. For this, Wendel would be paid handsomely.

Astrid didn't believe King Tremane's Earthsense worked that way, but it was not for her to question. This was the proof that they'd been looking for. She called to Kalen. *:I found our proof, and it's way worse than just anti-Herald sentiment.:* She folded the letter and put it back in the satchel. *:You can grab him.:*

As she stood, she heard a step outside the door and Kalen Mindspeak, *:He's not at his stand.:*

:He's here.: was all she had time to send before the door was unlocked and clicked open. Astrid stood face-to-face with Wendel of Greenvale.

Wendel closed the door behind him and threw himself at Astrid. "Thief!"

She didn't waste her breath on an answer. Instead she stepped to the side and swept his legs out from under him. He crashed to the bed but bounced back up just as quick.

"What were you looking for?" Feinting with his left hand, he punched her with his right, then followed it up with a left hook.

Astrid took a glancing blow to the chin, blocked the

second punch, and kicked at his knee. Heart pounding fast, she was scared but exhilarated at the same time. This was what she'd trained hours and hours for.

As he dodged the low kick, she grabbed the nearest thing—a wooden brush—and flung it at his head. It struck him dead center of the forehead.

Wendel reeled back, dazed, then backpedaled even more as Astrid advanced, lunging at him with a knee to his chest. They slammed into the heavy wardrobe, and Wendel collapsed, coughing hard.

She didn't give him time to recover and dropped on top of him with a knee to his stomach. He let out an explosive gasp of air, then went limp, trying to catch his breath as Astrid flipped him over and bound his wrists behind him. She left him on the floor and stood as Kalen burst through the door.

The two Heralds met each other's eyes before turning to the gasping man. Astrid grinned. "I got him." She turned and retrieved the satchel from the bed. "The proof is in there."

Kalen nodded as he opened the pouch and pulled the letter from within. "Watch him."

Astrid stood near Wendel but not over him. She didn't want him to kick or attack her in some other way. She had learned that lesson early on in training. She watched him slowly regain his breath as Kalen read. By the time he put the letter away, Wendel had recovered enough to turn over and struggle into a seated position.

"I was right. You can't trust Heralds. Liars, the bunch of you." Wendel spat at Astrid's feet. "I knew you weren't true." Then he gave a slow, evil smile. "Just wait until the rest of Crag's Bluff discovers that you're here spying on them."

Astrid looked at Kalen. It was true. The Holderkin

would not be happy that a Herald—even one on her first Circuit—was here undercover.

Kalen shook his head. "I think, Wendel of Greenvale, they'll be more interested in the fact that you're trying to draw them into a war between Valdemar and Hardorn with Crag's Bluff at the center of the fighting. And so soon after the Mage Storms." He showed Wendel the satchel. "Do you want to test who is believed more? What they will be more upset at?"

Wendel looked away. "I didn't do anything. It's not against the law to badmouth Heralds. You have to let me go."

"Working for a lord of Hardorn and attempting to get part of the Holderkin lands to secede is grounds for us to escort you back to Hardorn. Or would you rather we make this all very official and arrest you for trial back in Haven?"

Astrid watched Kalen, working to keep her face calm. :*Just let him go? What's to stop him from coming back and doing it again?*:

:*Us. The Heralds. We'll talk more about this later.*: Kalen kept his eyes locked on the Hardorn man's face.

"You can't arrest me. I haven't done anything wrong."

"You're here with explicit orders to entice Crag's Bluff to secede to Lord Orin and King Tremane's rule. What do you think would happen after that? War. By your hand. Now, would you prefer we arrest you and take you to Haven or shall we escort you back across Cebu Pass?"

"I didn't. I just said you Heralds can't be trusted."

"And told me Crag's Bluff would become a paradise under the auspices of your King," Astrid said.

"You advocated war between Hardorn and Valdemar." Kalen put the incriminating evidence into his bag. "Arrest or escort? Your choice."

Wendel scowled and looked away. "I'll return to Hardorn."

No one stopped Herald Kalen as he and Wendel left Crag's Bluff together, though tongues wagged, and rumors sped on the wind. Astrid waited the extra day in town before she packed up her stall and headed west back toward the more hospitable areas of Valdemar. She met up with Kalen, his Companion, Mala, and her Companion, Elsinore, half a day's walk from Crag's Bluff.

Astrid's continued confusion and irritation at Kalen was blunted by Elsinore's presence. The two communicated with emotions rather than words. Once she was back in her Whites and astride her Companion, she felt settled enough to get into it with her mentor.

"Right, why did we let him go? What's to keep him from coming back? What about Lord Orin? What's to stop him from sending other people, more people, to cause problems on the Border for us?"

Kalen rode next to her. He didn't answer at first. When he did, his question surprised her. "Do you want the blunt, unsatisfying answer, or do you want me to ask you a bunch of questions until you figure it out for yourself?"

"If I figure it out for myself, will I still be unsatisfied?"

"Probably."

"Blunt then." Astrid felt Elsinore's agreement. "Blunt is good."

Kalen nodded. "The shortest, most unsatisfying, but truest, answer is that arresting Wendel would've defeated the purpose of our presence there." He held up a hand. "I will explain. We were asked to look into the growing anti-Herald sentiment. We found one reason. One large, complex reason that has a lot of spiky ends that we are not prepared to deal with. This is one for the envoys, diplomats, and spies."

"But we have proof."

"We have a document that appears to make it seem as if a lord of Hardorn wants a piece of land belonging to Valdemar. It could be a lie. Lord Orin may not exist. Lord Orin's enemy may have written the letter. It may be exactly as it seems. All of it crosses the border into a diplomatic territory that neither you nor I should cross into. This is for Queen Selenay and Envoy Elspeth to discuss, then decide if King Tremane needs to know . . . or if more investigation is needed."

"But . . ." Astrid stopped and thought about it. "I . . . that seems awfully convoluted."

"Yes. Court politics often are. This could be nothing more than an attack between Hardorn nobles. At the same time, this could be a lord of Hardorn deciding that he knows better than his King. In both cases, Valdemar cannot officially step in. Now, if it really is as it seems . . . it's still a case for people more skilled than either of us to deal with."

"This is a game, and we are the pieces?"

Kalen screwed up his nose. "I don't like that analogy, but it works. You and I, those of us who ride the Circuits, our job is to help each individual town and the individuals in that town. *We* see their faces. When it comes to matters of diplomacy, trade, and war across borders . . . that requires a distance and a different sort of thought."

Astrid looked away. "You're right. It's an unsatisfying answer. Now what?"

"Now, we get this letter and our report to someone headed toward Haven, and we continue on. We have a different job to do. One that's a bit more on the ground. What we do here, with the people, will grow into the actions and sentiments of tomorrow. We lead by example. We do what needs to be done. It's the best we can do."

"Ride the Circuit and be the Heralds the people of Valdemar expect us to be," Astrid mused. "It's not what legends are made of."

"But it's what Valdemar was built on."

"One town at a time?"

Kalen smiled. "Exactly."

A Midwinter's Gift
Kristin Schwengel

"Please, call me Jo," she said for what felt like the hundredth time. Straightening and rolling her aching shoulders, she glanced from the entry passage into the thronged Great Hall.

Actually, it probably was the hundredth time. Her parents were hosting the first major Midwinter party of the season, and it seemed as though they had invited everyone who was anyone at the Valdemaran Court— and many of those must have accepted. The rooms were packed with nobles and important merchants and courtiers, and her parents had insisted that she stand with them to receive all their guests. It wouldn't be so bad, if her parents didn't also insist on using her full given name—Lady Jhosan Amberdale—which, when pronounced the way they intended, "chosen," made every introduction emphasize the fact that she was clearly not Chosen.

Even when my parents seem to accept that I will not be the next "Amberdale Herald," they still are pointing out my failings. It stung in a deep and bitter way, that even though Jo knew the life of a Herald was utterly wrong for her, her parents felt being a Herald was her only destiny. Nearly every generation of Amberdales for

17

several hundred years had contained at least one Herald, and her parents had been determined that she would be the next one. She had been tutored with that aim, had been a Blue studying at the Collegium for years despite her rank, all to keep her near the Companions, as though proximity was the main thing driving their Choice.

Now that my brother is married and settled, my parents' focus is all on me. Whether that's a good thing or not remains to be seen.

Jo dragged her thoughts back to the party. Lord and Lady Amberdale had just finished chatting with the newest arrivals, and they turned their attention to their daughter.

"I think that's the last of them," Lady Evie said. She smiled a little at the relief that crossed Jo's face. "Yes, Jhosan, you may go find your friends. Just don't forget to come back to us before we move in to dinner." She waved one hand in a shooing motion, and Jo didn't wait for further permission.

It's not as though they're unkind, Jo thought as she maneuvered through the crowded hall to the library, where she was sure her friends would be waiting. *They just don't understand.*

Every corner, every beam, every table of the public areas of the mansion had been decorated for Midwinter. This year, her mother had decided on a theme of ice and snow, even though the actual weather had been unusually mild. Silver snowflakes and glass and crystal icicles glittered, hanging from fresh fir garlands and branches that released their crisp scent as the air warmed. The indoor wintry wonderland effect had elicited many compliments, and Jo had seen several ladies, whose own parties were still to come, studying the garlands as though calculating the costs of replicating them.

Passing through the door into the library, she went

from winter fantasy to solid indoor comforts: plush velvet and warm firelight (well-screened to prevent accidents among the books), and a spicy perfumed air from the incense Lady Evie had used before the gathering.

"They finally let you escape, eh?" As she'd expected, several of her friends had gathered here, where it was quiet and uncrowded. The speaker was a lanky girl in Trainee Grays, Jo's closest friend in the Collegium. Tyria was a distant cousin, and although she didn't have the Amberdale surname, she did have their dark golden hair, where Jo's was a deep nut-brown. Jo was certain Tyria could stand as the Amberdale Herald for this generation, but Lord Jaren and Lady Evie had never agreed.

"The important guests are all here by now, so they didn't see the point in all of us standing in the coldest part of the house any longer," she replied, rubbing her hands together in front of the firescreen.

"Ha, we'll get you warm again!" cried Kosti, and he gave her a handled mug that he pulled from the corner of the firescreen. She lifted it to her face and inhaled deeply of the redolent spice of mulled cider, closing her eyes and smiling. Cradling the warm mug in her cold fingers, she took a sip, then blinked.

"You've put more into this than cider!" she scolded, and laughter surrounded her.

"Of course," said Kosti, his blue eyes sparkling. "It wouldn't be a Midwinter party without a bit of stronger drink!"

"Don't worry," Tyria added, "I poured it myself, so it's not as potent as if Kosti held the liquor bottle! Now, we've got the gameboards all set up, so we can play at Tables until . . ." She let her voice trail off.

"Until I have to find my parents before we go in to dinner. A candlemark or so, I think," Jo replied.

The others nodded, and the six of them sat down at three small tables, where game boards with pegs were already set up. Jo paired with Kosti for the first round, while Tyria matched wits with Geren, and Demi faced Cendro.

"Is Lady Millia here?" Kosti tried to use an undertone, but the room was so quiet as the dice rolled and markers were moved that everyone heard him anyway, and he blushed at the good-natured teasing that followed.

"Yes, she's here, and her father is keeping her close by his side. He knows she'll flirt with every male present if given a chance, and who knows what trouble she'll get into." Jo tried to keep her voice from sounding too irritated. Lady Millia Hereval was nice enough, and Jo was friendly with her, but she was also an attractive heiress and therefore a target for every poor noble in Court—and most of the rich ones, too. The fact that she was a flirtatious featherhead meant her father had his hands full trying to keep her suitors in line. Jo didn't understand Kosti's infatuation with the girl, but she was quite certain it would lead nowhere. Her friend, a younger son of minor nobility, was precisely the kind of partner Lord Delv did not want for his daughter—young and without either influence or wealth of his own. And Lady Millia herself had shown no interest in Kosti other than welcoming his flattery as she did that of every man in her circle.

Several rounds later, Geren was declared the victor for the evening, and Jo left the group in search of her parents. When she didn't find them in any of the decorated rooms thronged with guests, she returned to the entry hall, wondering if there had been some latecomers to draw them away from the gathering. That chamber, too, was empty, but she stood for a moment in one of the corners, enjoying the silence. Even the conviviality of her friends was wearing on her, and she closed her eyes, breathing in the pine scent from a nearby tree, which her mother had ordered cut and brought in from their farm estate just the day before.

"She's a fool, and she'll be shown up for it, right enough." The harsh tone startled her, and she instinctively shifted deeper into the corner behind the tree, tucking her skirt around her and turning her face to the wall, peeking sidelong to the entrance behind her. Two men had entered and stood inside the doorway, just past where they could be easily seen from the Great Hall. They kept their voices low, but she'd always had keen hearing.

"I don't want her hurt." This was a younger voice, one that seemed vaguely familiar to her. A subtle whine inflected the words.

"No, nothing permanent, but her father'll be looking on your suit with favor afterward." There was a slight accent in the deeper voice, but it was neither the throatiness of Karse, nor the lilt of the Tayledras. *Hardornen, perhaps?*

"What must I do?"

"I'll tell you at the Delamers' party. By then I'll have the arrangements made for the Court feast."

The two figures separated, the larger, presumably the older speaker, disappearing out the front door while the slighter man returned to the party.

Jo stood in the entry hall for a few minutes, calming her racing mind. She thanked the gods she had insisted on wearing her dark green gown rather than the silvery one her mother had preferred. Silver was too close to Trainee Grays for her taste anyway, but it would have stood out sorely from behind even this thickly needled tree.

The two men had to have been talking about Lady Millia—her father's determination that she have a wealthy and powerful husband was well known. And no one as young as the whiny man had sounded would have the influence to satisfy Lord Delv, even if he had wealth. But what were they plotting? Not an abduction, nor rape, unless that wouldn't qualify as "permanent damage" in the older man's mind. Scandal of some sort was the only thing that made sense.

Her mind was still spiraling over these thoughts when she decided it was safe enough to return to find her parents, that the younger man had disappeared among the guests and wouldn't notice her emergence from the hall where he had just been. Lord and Lady Delamer were hosting their party in a sevennight, and the Royal Feast, the highlight of Midwinter Holiday, was another sevennight after that. Less than a fortnight, then, to figure out what was going on and what to do about it. Lady Millia might be a silly young woman, but she didn't deserve to have her prospects constrained by a false scandal.

I can't go to the Guard, not with so little as I know, just a fragment of an overheard conversation. Who would believe me? She glimpsed her mother surveying the guests from the other side of the room, a delicate frown barely hinted at in the crease of her brow, and hurried over, her stomach sinking.

"I am sorry I was delayed, Mother," she murmured. "I became overheated in the library and needed to step out for some air." It was mostly true, and her mother nodded shortly.

"Your father is waiting for us outside the dining hall," Lady Evie said, her voice clipped with impatience, and she turned and led the way through the crowd.

Fortunately, Jo was seated between Tyria's parents at dinner, and the two of them kept up a brisk enough conversation that she had only to offer an occasional comment or question and could keep mulling over the overheard exchange. By the time dinner had ended, she had come up with a plan.

She wouldn't tell her friends, at least not yet. Kosti

had never been able to keep secrets or dissemble. Even
Tyria, who was almost a Herald and as such honor-
bound to protect the innocent, would want to get others involved, or go to the Guard, and Jo was back up
against the barrier of how little information she really
had. No, first she would go to all the Midwinter parties
she'd been invited to, including the Delamers', to listen
for that voice and try to at least figure out who the
younger man was. If she was lucky, she'd find out who
the older man was, or what they had planned for the
Delamer's party.

    Then . . . well, she'd figure the rest out then.

The day of the Delamers' Midwinter party dawned
cloudy and cold, gray clouds threatening all morning
until at last, in the midafternoon, the first flakes began
to drift to earth. Jo watched them through her bedroom
window, her breath fogging the glass as she leaned forward so her eyes could follow one particularly fat snow-
flake all the way down to the courtyard below, where it
soon melted on the paving stones. The mild early days
of winter meant that the ground had not yet frozen
through, but all the old gran'thers tucked in the warmest
corners claimed their bones were saying the cold was
coming and that the Terilee River would be frozen soon.

    Jo sighed, idly drawing a pattern in the fog her breath
created on the glass. Never had the chaotic round of
Midwinter parties seemed so exhausting. In years past,
she might have skipped a few of them, or only been part
of the main throng for a brief time before escaping to a
quiet corner with Tyria and the rest. This year, she had
attended every single one she'd been invited to and had
quietly inserted herself into Lady Millia's set of friends.
The Amberdale name was powerful enough that Lady
Millia welcomed her company—indeed, if her older
brother hadn't been married last year, Jo suspected he

would have been a prime target for Lord Delv's ambitions. Jo's own friends were a bit puzzled by her absence from their group, but her frequent visits to the Hereval estate passed without much comment.

One good thing had come from being so involved in the social whirl, though. She was certain that the younger man who wanted to force Lady Millia's hand was Rix Ultare, another younger son like Kosti. Rix, too, hovered around the edges of Millia's circle and was alternately flirted with and ignored, like all the other young men. Only Jo, because she was looking for it, saw the quick flash of anger in his eyes whenever Millia turned away from him. He kept the petulant whining tone from his voice when he spoke, but Jo was positive it was the same one she had heard in her parents' entrance hall.

And Jo had managed to intercept a gift with a message that had been left for Millia during morning visits, tucked in the corner of her favorite windowsill in the Herevals' smaller sitting room. It was a clever carved cat figurine, with a note that read *"With fondest Midwinter thoughts from your admirer, your precious pet."* She had retied the note around the figure and placed it back in the corner just before Millia had entered the sitting room. Jo had noted how Millia's eyes went straight to that windowsill, how they had brightened a little and a light flush touched her cheeks, but she did not move directly to retrieve it. It had been much later that she had gone to the window as though to look out, placing her hands on the sill and subtly pocketing the figurine.

So, Jo thought, retracing the swirls of her finger on the glass, *the plan must be to woo her into indiscretion by luring her with gifts and notes from a secret admirer. I wonder what other nonsense they have written to her, that she responded with a blush.* Tonight, she would be at the Delamers' mansion early, so she might see all of Lady Millia's encounters, as well as watch for Rix and his unknown coconspirator. Not for the first time, she wished she dared take Tyria into her confidence, but even that wouldn't have helped her tonight, for Tyria had not been invited. No, she would have to do it herself, to learn what she could.

"I hadn't heard anything from you. I wondered if you'd given up." It was Rix's voice, with that whine that made the hair on the back of Jo's neck stand up. *How does he manage to keep that tone out of his voice around everyone else?*

"You're almost as much a fool as she is. But she's ready to fall for the bait. I've been sending her presents the last sevennight and more, and she's been blushing mightily over them. She even managed a return message."

Jo filed that bit of information away—it meant Rough Voice must have been watching Millia as closely as she. Or had suborned one of the servants to do so. And that Millia had been an active participant in the written exchange—although she was certain the younger girl didn't know the identity of her supposed admirer.

Jo shifted slightly, leaning toward the hall mirror and patting at her hair, twisting the dark curls into different places and fiddling with her garnet-tipped hairpins, looking for all the world like a flighty featherhead herself, oblivious to anything except her own appearance. But the movement had changed the area of the room reflected in the glass, and now she could see Rix—and the other man.

She was hard-pressed to keep from staring. She had expected to see someone in unremarkable formal garb, but the man with Rix was positively flamboyant, clad in swirls of color lavished with embroidery in an unfamiliar style. She didn't recognize him, but his dark coloring, unusual clothing and accent all suggested he was a foreigner. Perhaps one of the late Consort's countrymen?

There were some who had stayed in Valdemar rather than return to Rethwellan after the Prince's accident. The two were keeping their voices low, but the gentle curve of the ceiling carried the words just enough that she could make them out.

"I've a plan to deliver the last note to her at the Court feast by a page, who will guide her to me in a private chamber, then tell you where to go. After a suitable interval, you will become concerned, seek out her father, and come find us. I'll make sure what you discover will leave her father desperate to unload her onto anyone willing to take her."

"Perfect. My debtors are beginning to be importunate, and this will answer nicely." The smug satisfaction in Rix's voice made Jo's stomach roil with anger, and she forced herself to keep her attention on her reflection in the mirror and maintain her pretense of vanity as the two separated, the stranger again departing and Rix passing behind her to rejoin the party.

Jo's hand nearly shook with fury. This was more than just a passing scandal of sweet-sounding lies and silly notes. What Rough Voice seemed to be suggesting was, in her opinion, permanent damage, and she couldn't believe that Rix was so blinded by his own straits that he would casually agree to be part of it.

In the wine-red folds of her skirts, Jo's fingers clenched into a determined fist. Somehow, Lady Millia must be protected.

Early in the morning after the Delamers' party, Jo did what she had always done when she was uncertain of how to act: she went to the Companions. Although classes at the Collegium were ended for the Midwinter Holiday, and most of the students gone to stay with family and friends to celebrate, plenty of Heralds remained in residence, and students could still come and go as they wished. As she paced along the freshly snow-dusted path to Companion's Field, she recalled the first time she had come here years ago, a ten-year-old girl in Blues, and the sidelong glances the Companions had given her.

"As if I'd try to force myself on one of you," she remembered saying to them. "Even if Mummy and Daddy don't realize it, I know I'm not going to be a Herald."

After that, the Companions had relaxed and approached her, and she would often come to Companion's Field to talk out her thoughts with them. Those wise blue eyes with their silent, comforting presence helped her to think, to filter out the unnecessary worries and focus on the important things.

Even now, as she neared the fence, a white shape drifted out of the snowy trees and trotted along the rails to meet her. She leaned against the fence and scratched under the unpartnered mare's mane, then spilled out the whole story, of Lady Millia and Rix and how the stranger whose identity she still didn't know was going to pretend that he was having an affair with Lady Millia, and probably rape her, so that she could be forced to marry Rix. "And I don't know where to go or who would believe me," she finally finished, and looked up to find that another Companion had joined the first, watching her intently.

"Kantor?" she gaped, incredulous. There was only one Companion who had the build of a warhorse rather than their usual lean, elegant lines. "You think scandal among the middling nobility is important enough to concern Weaponsmaster Alberich?" Kantor tossed his head in an imperious "yes," and Jo turned to face the Collegium, only to see a solid figure in gray leathers moving down the path toward her.

"If the Palace it involves, concern the Heralds it must. Kantor your story has told me," the Weaponsmaster said when he neared her. "Little though you may think it, significant it is, what these men might plot." His piercing eyes softened into a slight smile. "So a plot of our own to answer we will have. But in cold we need not stand. Come." He turned without waiting for a reply, and Jo, stunned, followed him in silence back to the salle.

By the time Jo and Weaponsmaster Alberich had entered his chambers adjoining the training salle, another person was there waiting for them, mugs of hot tea on the low table in front of her.

"Lady Pennory?" Jo schooled her face into a less undignified expression. A few years younger than Lady Evie, Lady Theara Pennory was a powerful and popular fixture of the Court and a frequent guest at the Amberdale mansion. What could she possibly have to do with the Weaponsmaster?

Fortunately, Lady Theara was blinking at Jo with a very similar befuddlement. "Jhosan?"

"Please, call me Jo," she said without thinking, the reply a reflex from years of polite correction.

Lady Theara looked up at Herald Alberich. "Herald-Chronicler Myste said that you needed me for a delicate project. Does Jo . . . ?" She let her words trail off and eyed the Weaponsmaster expectantly.

"Overheard something, Lady Jo has, and the advice of the Companions sought."

"And the Companions very sensibly turned to you."

"And I to you in turn," he finished. "So, Lady Jo, relate all to Lady Theara."

Jo repeated everything that she had told the Companions, from the first overheard words at her parents' party, to the friendship she developed with Lady Millia, to the note with the cat figurine, and then to the conversation at the Delamers'. In Lady Pennory's tightening lips and narrowing eyes she read an anger on Millia's behalf that matched her own. When all was said, she leaned back in her chair, clutching her cooling mug of tea, reassured that they at least believed her and certain that Millia would now be safe.

"I think I have a guess of the identity of the other plotter, although I have no idea of how he came in contact with Rix Ultare, or what he plans to get out of this," Lady Theara said, slowly, and the Weapons-master nodded.

"Fit it does, with what we already know of him. But act we cannot."

"Exactly. He falls under protection, and we have no irrefutable proof."

"But you have to help Millia!" Jo burst out. She still wasn't sure how or why Lady Pennory was involved, but it certainly sounded as though they knew who Rough Voice was but were going to let him alone to do what he would.

The Weaponsmaster and Lady Theara exchanged a look, and the Weaponsmaster nodded, lifting his palm toward Lady Theara in a gesture of encouragement. She turned toward Jo.

"Jo, your family has a long history with the Heralds, so you know better than most what role the Heralds play in Valdemar." Jo nodded. "But there are places the Heralds cannot and should not go."

Jo blinked, considered, then nodded again. "Of course, the Crown must have . . . other means of acquiring information." But what did all this have to do with Millia?

"Exactly so. Weaponsmaster Alberich coordinates many of those . . . means. As do I." At this, Jo simply stared at the older woman, who smiled. "I have trained a handful of young women who move freely about the Court to be eyes and ears where others cannot be." She eyed the stunned Jo appraisingly. "Since you are already a friend to Lady Millia, I think it would be helpful if you

were to aid us in protecting her, rather than introducing
another young lady into the situation. I promise you that
it should not require too much of you."

"Well, I can't leave Millia to face this on her own,
can I? If I know something that can help, I have to."

"Spoken like an Amberdale," Lady Theara replied
with a smile. "I'm surprised you didn't talk to Tyria,
though."

Jo hunched one shoulder into a shrug. "Until last
night, I didn't really know anything, just guessed. And I
didn't want to involve Tyria, or Kosti, or any of the rest
of them, with guesses. And once I knew, well, I didn't
have a chance to see her, so I came to the Companions
instead." At that, she looked over at the Weaponsmaster, who had been silent.

"So," he began, "now, we plan." The three of them
leaned forward over their now-cold mugs, and the conversation began in earnest.

As the dance ended, Jo cordially thanked her partner
and drifted back to the side of the Court ballroom.
Queen Selenay had taken her place on the dais, with
Queen's Own Herald Talamir a pale shadow beside
her. Most of the rest of the Heralds had already disappeared from the formal event, back to their rooms at
the Collegium or joining with friends or family in the
antechambers. Now that the royal feast was over and
the Heir Elspeth had been taken back to her room by
her nurse, the rest of the Court settled in for a long
night of dancing and gossip.

*And I hope not a whisper of the gossip will involve
Lady Millia when the night is done,* Jo thought fervently. Even through the dances she had taken part in,
she kept looking for Rough Voice—Weaponsmaster
Alberich and Lady Pennory had not said who they
thought he was. And she also watched Millia, who had

come to the Feast with an almost frenetic energy about her. The younger girl was clearly taken up with the idea of her secret admirer revealing himself to her at the Midwinter Feast, probably entertaining fantasies of dances and gifts and betrothal.

At last, she saw the dark coloring of the stranger who had spoken with Rix, clad again in elaborate clothing covered with ornate embroidery. *I wonder how many young ladies are wishing they could get that much gold thread worked into their gowns,* she thought while covertly watching the stranger. He leaned over to a nearby page, handing him something and gesturing briefly to her side of the chamber.

Jo, in turn, exchanged a quick glance with a liveried servant standing near her (who was actually a young Trainee not wearing Grays), and he followed her closely as she moved toward the low bench where Lady Millia was seated, surrounded by her admirers. When the page sent by Rough Voice approached, she intercepted him.

"I will hand it on," she said in a low voice. "Where?" She held out her hand imperiously, as though confident the page would give over his task, and he responded by dropping a small wrapped object into her outstretched palm.

"Th-the lower arcade," the boy said, "third door on the left."

Jo nodded in dismissal, and the lad returned to his place while she swiftly pocketed what felt like another figurine. Without turning to look, she sensed the Trainee behind her vanish into the crowd. Alberich had assigned him to shadow her because he had sharp hearing to make out what was said, but he wasn't yet skilled enough in MindSpeaking with his Companion, so he needed to find the Weaponsmaster in person to relate this last piece of the puzzle. She sidled over and sat next to Millia, who freely shared her bench with her. This was the hardest part of it all, to get Millia to come with her.

When the next dance had begun, she leaned over and whispered in the other girl's ear. "Your precious pet is waiting." She hoped that the term, which had seemed so unusual in the note she had seen, would be sufficient to entice her.

A faint blush tinged Millia's cheeks, and she glanced over at Jo. "You know?" she murmured back.

Jo raised one eyebrow and smiled slightly, hoping that her expression appeared lightly teasing. *Vain, silly thing,* she thought, not for the first time. *Well, Lady Pennory will set you straight, if anyone can.* She tilted her head toward the doorway, and Millia nodded, excitement suffusing her face. Arm in arm, they stood and moved out into the halls of the Palace, looking like any two young ladies in each other's confidence, with secrets to share.

Once in the hall, Jo guided Millia, not to the lower arcade, but into the Collegium library. Moments after they arrived, Lady Pennory entered, and the thunderous expression she wore silenced Millia's questions.

"Your vanity, young lady, has almost gotten you into very serious trouble." She held out her hand, and Jo dropped the wrapped figurine into it. Over Millia's protestations, Lady Theara opened it, revealing a small carved dog that looked to be part of a set with the cat. "Hmph. Pretty enough, but there are a thousand like it in Haven."

Millia pouted, but Lady Pennory gave her no chance to speak. "Where was she to go?" she asked Jo.

"The lower arcade, third door."

"Ah. Let's give them another minute, then we can join them."

"Them?" Millia's voice trembled a little, but Lady Theara did not explain further. Instead the three of them sat in silence, listening to the crackling of the logs in the screened fireplace, until the older woman stood and, gesturing, led the two young ladies down a series of side passages that brought them to the lower arcade without passing by the ballrooms.

As they arrived, they saw Weaponsmaster Alberich and two Guardsmen restraining Rough Voice, while a young woman with pale blond hair like Millia's stood nearby, a fierce expression on her face and a dagger in her hand.

"Little bitch," Rough Voice snarled as he was pushed past the girl and out the nearest door. A Captain of the Guard remained behind, moving into the room to wait.

Millia stared. "Who is that?"

"Which? The Trainee pretending to be you, or the man pretending to be yours?" Lady Pennory's voice was crisp and carrying, and the Trainee looked over at her and gave a slight curtsy. "No need for formality, Peri," she continued. "You took no hurt, I take it?"

The other girl came over to them. "No, milady. He did not expect resistance, so I was able to give him a good knee in his bits and get my blade out before the Weaponsmaster and the Guards came in." She grinned, then tucked her dagger back into a boot sheath under her skirts. "If it's all the same to you, milady, I'd like to get back to m'family for the rest of Midwinter Eve." Lady Theara nodded, and the Trainee bobbed her head, gave Millia a pitying glance, and vanished down the opposite end of the hallway.

Lady Theara eyed Millia, whose face had gone pale at Peri's words. "Let's go talk in the library, where we will not be disturbed."

If anything, Millia went even paler at the prospect. Jo found herself pitying the younger girl, just as Peri did. Lady Theara was a redoubtable figure, and an angry Lady Theara was not to be trifled with.

When the three were once more seated in the quiet of the Collegium library, Lady Pennory broke the silence at last.

"Millia Hereval, you are a very fortunate young lady. Did you even give any thought to your supposed admirer's identity?"

Millia had the grace to blush. "I . . . I thought it was Lord Beddoes."

Jo was unable to completely conceal a burst of laughter, and Lady Theara actually rolled her eyes. "Child, you're entirely the wrong type to appeal to Aphrim Beddoes. If you'd had a brother, maybe . . ." Millia blushed even redder at her error.

"I take it you had never met the gentleman Weaponsmaster Alberich was escorting out of the Palace?"

"No, never."

"That was the person who sent you the gifts, not to woo you for himself, but to lure you into his not-so-tender embrace. At which point your father was meant to discover you and hand you off to another gentleman, who had employed this ruse to despoil you and make your father desperate to accept any suitor for you." As Lady Theara spoke, Millia wilted ever smaller into her seat, sinking with the realization of the gravity of her mistakes.

Lady Theara paused for a moment, then smiled gently at the younger girl. "As I said, you have been very fortunate. Lady Jo overheard enough of the plotting that we were able to keep you safe—and in the process weed out from the Court a potential danger to other young women. Now go back to your father and use your head a little more next time!"

Millia wasted no time in fleeing the library, leaving Jo alone with Lady Pennory.

It was not lost on Jo that Lady Theara had still kept unspoken the identities of both of the men concerned.

"Should we be concerned about her being alone in the hallways? What if Rix decides to assault her himself?"

Lady Theara made a dismissive gesture. "Rix Ultare is a sniveling coward. I doubt he'd even try if he was employing *that* one to do his dirty work. If he keeps to his plan, he and Lord Delv should be at the antechamber now, where the Captain will share only that he and another guard prevented a potential assault. Lord Delv will rush back to the ballroom to find a chastened Millia, and Rix will be closely observed by the Guard for the rest of the night. If he's sensible, he'll pray that no whisper of his own role in this will ever get out in the Court."

She leaned back in her chair and studied Jo, who waited in silence. "Would you like to do more of this?"

"My lady?" Jo's mind lurched at the sudden change of subject.

"As Weaponsmaster Alberich said, I coordinate and train several ladies in the Court as observers, to be the eyes and ears and occasionally hands of Her Majesty. Most of the ladies I work with are of lower to middle rank, and often without family, so you would have access to different circles than they. You clearly have a, shall we say, 'Gift' for it, and the Companions seem to have vouched for you."

Jo's pulse raced in sudden anticipation. This . . . this she could see herself doing. She wasn't the sort to travel all over Valdemar, nor the sort to listen patiently to tedious local squabbles, nor yet the sort to stand on the front lines whenever Karse invaded next. She was better suited to stay in one place, to observe from outside the action rather than as part of it. It was the sort of thing she would never have thought of, but now that it was proposed to her, it felt somehow right.

"An Amberdale spy instead of an Amberdale Herald?" She smiled slightly. "My parents might take some time to get used to the idea, but I think I would. Yes, I would very much like to join your ladies, Lady Pennory."

"Please, call me Theara," she replied, and they both grinned at the echo of Jo's own oft-repeated words.

The whirl of Midwinter will never be the same again, Jo thought as the two of them returned to the Court.

Unknowable Consequences
Elizabeth A. Vaughan

To the Dean of the Healer's Collegium, Haven, in the Kingdom of Valdemar,

Greetings,

In Rethwellan, where I was raised, there grows a plant known as wild kandace. To my delight, I have found it growing in abundance here in Sandbriar. The tea eases the aches of the body, and it's possible to make an oil that can be rubbed on stiff joints to aid movement.

Sandbriar was hit hard by the Tedrel Wars, as was all of Valdemar, and is in need of new trade and commerce. I have approached an apothecary in Rethwellan, hoping to establish a new market with him. But it occurs to me that Valdemar may also be interested in my harvest.

I enclose herewith a sample of dried leaves, flowers, and seeds. I will also attempt to send a living plant, but I am not sure it will make the journey intact.

It's my understanding that a syrup can be made as well, but I lack the knowledge of the method for creating it. If you know of such a technique

*and could instruct me, I would be deeply grateful,
and happy to supply the same to the Collegium,
to our mutual benefit.*

In any event, please accept my thanks in advance for any assistance you can render.

        *—Lady Cera of Sandbriar,
in the Kingdom of Valdemar*

:Help us!:

Cera bolted up in bed, her heart racing. Rain pattered against her window. A flash of lightning filled her bedroom for an instant. The room was still, no one was there, but the urgency of that dream—

Thunder crashed, rumbling overhead. The need, the fear exploded in her chest. Cera threw back her blankets and ran for her door, plunged down the stairs, calling for aid. She'd rouse the entire manor if need be. It was irrational and unreasoning, but she pelted out the main door and across the courtyard.

Tents had been set up for the Midsummer Festival due in two days. They'd planned the event for weeks, worried over food and decorations—and now the rain.

But Cera had even larger fears at the moment. She ran to the gates, bare feet slipping on wet cobblestones, as voices raised in response behind her.

"Open the gates," she called to the guard. They gaped at her, nightgown slowly soaking through, her toes bare in the mud. "Open them!"

The voices grew louder now, following her, but that's just what she wanted them to do. The road ahead was dark, thick with rain. No time for words. She pulled a lantern from one of the startled guards, slipped through the creaking gates, and started down the road.

Not far, just out of sight of the gate. A crumpled figure in white lay on the road, curled in on itself. A white horse stood over the body, trembling, its hind foot cocked up off the ground.

"Stonas?" Cera ran forward and threw herself on the ground next to the body. "Helgara?"

Footsteps pounded up behind her, and many hands reached out to assist. They rolled Helgara over. Blood stained her face and her Whites.

"Get her up and into the manor," Gareth was there, calmly directing the others. Cera scrambled out of the way as six of them lifted the Herald and slowly carried her inside.

"This is bad." Young Meron was beside the Companion, looking at the leg in the torch light. "We need Withrin, he knows most about horses."

Someone else went pelting off. Cera shivered in the rain, wrapping her arms around herself.

"You should go in, Lady," Young Meron said. "Catch your death, you will." He sounded like his father.

Cera shook her head, and stepped to Stonas' head to put her hand on his forehead. She'd not leave him, not like this. "She'll be fine," Cera whispered, even though she knew the words might be empty comfort.

Stonas nudged her with his head and then turned to look to the side of the road.

Cera followed his gaze.

There, huddled in the ditch, was a woman, young, her hair plastered to her head. And at her feet, hidden under a cloak, two children peered out, wet and shivering.

"Trine above us," Cera whispered, and she stepped forward, holding out her hand.

The woman flinched back.

"No, no, don't fear." Cera stopped where she was. Stonas nickered and tried to take a step, faltering fast. "We won't hurt you," she offered.

The woman shook her head, pulling the children back toward her.

"What's this now?" Young Meron came up, then stopped dead as the light of his torch fell on them. "Gods above."

The young woman's eyes darted to him, and then to Stonas, then back to Cera. There was no trust there. Cera feared she'd bolt into the woods, taking the children with her.

"Did she harm the Herald?" Meron asked.

Stonas shook his mane and snorted.

"Move back, Meron," Cera said even as she stepped back.

"Aye." Meron stepped back, one hand on Stonas' haunch as he moved. "Withrin's coming."

Withrin was coming down the road on one of the manor's horses at a trot. He was an Ashkevron, known for horse breeding. Cera's relief was dispelled by the grim look in his eyes as he rode up. He dismounted, taking a moment as he waited for his bad knee to support him, but never taking his eyes from the wounded Companion.

"That's not good," he said, staring at Stonas.

"Worse still," Cera said, and nodded at the huddled figures. "I don't think they speak Valdemaran." She caught the woman's eye again and tried Rethwellan. "You're safe here."

The woman shook her head even more vehemently.

Withrin frowned. "Those clothes," he said, and then spoke something harsh and guttural. The woman's eyes went wide as she nodded.

"Karsite," Withrin grunted, even more unhappy than before. "I've a few words, and most of them are not polite. But I can try—"

"Karse?" Meron stepped forward, and then, to Cera's surprise, said something in the same guttural tongue, but the tone was softer, the words more like a chant.

The woman slumped in relief and started weeping. She extended her hand to Meron, and he leaned forward to help her and the children from the ditch.

More voices sounded from down the road; women's voices, probably coming to claim Cera after her mad dash, barely clothed, in the rain.

"I'll see to the Companion," Withrin said. "You need to get to shelter."

Cera put her hand on Stonas' shoulder. She didn't want to break a confidence, but . . .

"Withrin, Helgara and Stonas were in the Tedrel Wars. They suffer—"

"Nightmares?" Withrin said, easing his weight to his good leg. "Not alone in that. We warriors know. I'll see to him, Lady."

Bella ran up, throwing a cloak over Cera. "My lady! What were you thinking? And who is this?"

Cera meekly accepted the scolding she was due as they all stumbled back to the manor house and into the kitchens. Fires were being lit, and the manor roused.

Athelnor, her aged steward, stood by one of the tables, wrapped in a warm robe, looking tottery. Emerson, Cera's tapestry weaver, was hovering beside him. Cera wished they hadn't woken the old man, but he took his duties seriously.

"They've taken the Herald to her usual guest chamber," he said. "Marga is with her, and she's summoned those with healing skills." Athelnor blinked at her with tired eyes. "How did you know?" he asked as the women fussed around the newcomers.

"Strip," Bella commanded, holding up a blanket to shelter her. Cera obeyed, shivering as the cold, wet nightgown fell at her feet. Bella wrapped her in the blanket, warm and soft against her skin.

"I don't know. I—" Cera paused before she answered Athelnor, trying to remember. It all seemed like such a muddle in her head suddenly. Bella used a towel to dry her hair.

"I . . . woke," Cera said slowly. "And I just *knew* something was wrong. Next thing I remember, I was out the gate and down the road."

"We need to clean the mud from you, and the newcomers." Bella gathered cloths and called for hot water. "What were you thinking, not even wearing boots?"

"I wasn't," Cera said from under the towel.

The other women were seeing to the young Karsite woman and the two children. The little ones already had mugs in their hands and milk foam on their lips.

"And who is this?" Athelnor asked.

"I don't know," Cera admitted. "Withrin said they are from Karse, but I—" She glanced around, looking for Young Meron.

"Karse." The steward's voice hardened. Cera looked up to see hate flare in his old eyes.

"Athelnor—" she started but was interrupted when the kitchen back door swung open and Young Meron appeared with his father, Old Meron, in tow.

Why had he roused his father? Cera frowned as she stared at the wizened man with his withered arm. *No need to wake him for—*

Old Meron took a stool across the table from where the young girl sat. He spoke in those same guttural tones as his son had earlier.

The young woman looked up, her face alight with relief, and started spewing words out, her hands fluttering, talking quickly.

Old Meron lifted a hand to slow her. He said something, and she nodded and turned back to the children, urging them to eat the bread and butter that had been placed before them. "I told her to see to the little ones, then we could talk." Old Meron said. "And I'd do with a bit to drink myself, as to that."

"You speak Karsite?" Cera asked.

"Aye," Old Meron said gruffly. "And before you go making something of it that it isn't—" he glared at Athelnor, "—let me tell you that back in my day that wasn't the shame that it seems now. My parents brought me over when I was not much older than that one," he nodded at the small boy. "My folk said we were of Valdemar now, and we'd be of Valdemar, and become of Valdemar, and learn the tongue and live their ways. But we kept to the old faith and kept the old prayers in the old tongue."

He looked around the room. "But being of Karse grew less and less something to be proud of, and we let it fade. Young Meron here knows little but the old prayers."

"They are from Karse," Athelnor said flatly. "Nothing comes out of Karse but bandits and bad weather. You know that, Meron. They are strangers and—"

"So was I," Cera said quietly.

Athelnor blinked at her, looking confused, then dropped his eyes. "Milady, you are Rethwellan, yes, but . . ." he sputtered a bit. "You have proven yourself to us."

"As will they," Cera said, smiling to soften her words. "Once we know them as I know you and you have come to know me."

Gareth strode in then, wet and mud covered, his spear in hand. "The Companion is in the stables, and Withrin is seeing to him. Do we have any idea who attacked the Herald?"

Old Meron leaned forward and started talking softly to the young woman.

"Withrin is in the barns?" Emerson fidgeted. "I'll go see if he needs anything." With that he slipped quickly out the door.

Old Meron spoke. "Her name is Katarina, and the children are her brother and sister, Lukas and Greta.

She says they fled Karse, and the Herald helped them, but as they traveled, they were attacked on the road."

"By Karsites?" Gareth demanded.

Meron asked a few more questions and Katarina answered quickly. "She says no. They spoke our tongue and were tattered, misshapen," Meron and Katarina exchanged more talk. "Ah, ragtag. Armor did not match weapons, no uniforms, and the Karsite words they used were rude ones."

"Bandits," Gareth said grimly. "I'll need to increase our watch." He took a breath, looking older to Cera's eyes. "After the Festival, we will have to deal with this in force. This was much too close to the manor."

Katarina grew more agitated, talking, her eyes starting to tear. Old Meron shushed her, shaking his head.

"She says the Herald took hurt protecting the little ones. She feels at fault." Old Meron spoke again, his voice gentle even as the sound of the words grated on Cera's ear.

Katrina started to nod, wiping her eyes.

"Why did they flee Karse?" Cera asked. "The war is over, isn't it?"

Old Meron looked at her from under his shaggy brows. "There are other things to fear in Karse, Milady."

Marga swept into the room. "Helgara is as comfortable as we can make her. The worst seems to be the head wound, but the rest is cuts and bruises, easily seen to." Her voice was confident, but Marga's face had a pinched look. Her gaze fell on Athelnor, and her brow furrowed deeper. "Right now, we should sleep if we can. There is much to do, and guests will start to arrive tomorrow."

Old Meron spoke to Katarina. The little ones were yawning, their eyes drifting shut. "You've guests coming, and every room accounted for." He started to struggle up. "They can stay with us. More than enough room for this night, and already warmed."

Katarina rose and lifted Greta onto her hip. Young Meron took Lukas up onto his shoulder.

Cera rose as well, keeping the blanket tight around herself. She waited as the others filed out, and Athelnor was on his way out the door. "How is she, really?" she asked Marga.

Marga and Bella exchanged glances. "Come," Marga said.

They went to the guest area, and Marga opened a door. The room was lit with candles, and one of the women sat by the bed.

Helgara lay there, still and quiet, nearly as white as the sheets she was under.

"She did not waken as we cared for her injuries. It's a bad head wound, Milady," Marga admitted. "She may never wake. Even if we sent to Haven for aid, for a true Healer, it might not be in time."

Cera nodded. She'd written to the Healer's Collegium weeks ago about the wild kandace and had yet to hear back. "What if we sent Helgara to Haven?"

"Like as not, she would not survive in a cart," Marga said. "Perhaps if her Companion could travel, but I fear—" Marga pressed her lips thin and shrugged. "I'll sit with her this night, and we'll see what the dawn brings, shall we?"

Cera sighed and said good night and headed up to her chambers. Her feet felt like lead on the stone steps. All their plans and hopes for the Midsummer Festival seemed empty now. Frivolous. Helgara was more than the Herald on Sandbriar's Circuit. She'd become a friend and confidante, as had her Companion, Stonas.

Cera stopped dead, her breath catching in her throat.

Stonas.

* * *

Cera eased the barn doors open quietly. She'd had
sense enough to dress and pull on boots before she'd
snuck back out of the manor house. She could see light
and hear voices coming from the large box stall along
the far wall.

In the pens on both side were sleeping *chirras*. One
opened its eyes, flicking its large ears, huffed, and went
back to sleep.

"Withrin?" she called as she drew closer.

"Here, Lady Cera," came his familiar voice.

The box stall was open, with Stonas standing in the
center, drinking from a bucket of water. Withrin was
using a rough towel to get the worst of the muck off his
legs. Emerson was sitting on a bale of hay, a pile of
tapestry straps at his side.

"It's a bad sprain," Withrin said softly. "I was thinking a rope sling, to help him take the weight off the leg.
Emerson came up with a smart idea to use straps. More
comfortable, we think." He looked up at her. "How's the
Herald?"

Stonas stopped drinking, but he didn't lift his head
from the bucket.

Cera put her hand on the Companion's warm neck,
his hair damp under her fingers. "She's resting com-
fortably, but Marga says it's a bad head wound. All we
can do is wait and see." She hated being this honest,
but it was best. Besides, given the links between Herald and Companion, Stonas probably already knew the
worst.

Stonas rattled the water bucket, then started on the
grain.

Cera sat on the bale, reaching to help Emerson, but
he shook his head. "Lady, you need your rest. Tomorrow your guests start to arrive, and you'll give the for-

mal welcome. Then you'll need to walk the Fair before the dancing starts."

"Guests." Cera sighed. "You mean suitors."

"Those too." Emerson flashed her a grin. He'd arrived in the guise of a suitor, when in fact he had no interest in anything but her support of his weaving.

"Your parents are some of those guests," Cera pointed out. That wiped the grin off Emerson's face.

"Father's forgiven me . . . I think." He shuddered. "Mother, on the other hand, might not be so understanding . . ." His long fingers nervously plucked at the strapping. "She tends to stay angry for a long time."

"You have been writing her?" Cera asked.

"Well, yes, of course."

Which meant no. Cera shook her head. "You're right, though. I should get to bed."

"We'll stay with the Companion," Withrin assured her. "See to him as best we can."

"The best we can." Cera rose. Stonas lifted his head, and reached out to bump her chest with his head. Cera stroked that soft neck. "It's the best any of us can do."

The next morning the rain had cleared, and the day looked to be glorious. Sellers arrived early to set up tents along the road to the manor. Gareth had already arranged rotating patrols so that all could both keep safe and enjoy the celebration at the same time.

Cera had little time to do more than eat the morning meal and check on Helgara, still lying quiet and still. "Where there's life, there's hope," Marga said as she led Cera out of the room.

Hopeful words, Cera thought, *but with little real hope behind them.*

Marga took her down to the Great Hall to stand before the hearth. Athelnor was waiting for her, as was her handmaiden, Alania. She hovered close, ready to escort the guests to their rooms.

"Where were you last night?" Cera asked softly as everyone got into their places.

Alania blushed, and glanced away, toward the main doors. Cera followed her eye.

Ager was standing there, looking handsome and fit.

"Ah." Cera smiled. "Never mind." She raised her voice. "Let us greet our guests!"

One by one the families came in, bowing and introducing themselves. Athelnor announced them loudly, then kept his voice low as he reminded her of their holdings. They'd gone over the list in the weeks before, totting up the potential economic benefits of every potential suitor.

Benefits to Sandbriar. Not necessarily to Cera.

"My Lady," Athelnor droned on, "May I present the Merchant Petros, his wife Gretchen, and their sons Alonz and Alfred."

"Welcome to our Midsummer Festival." Cera smiled as they bowed. The boys were both young and pimply, and she mentally crossed them off the courting list.

"Our boy Alonz is much taken with you, My Lady," Petros smiled.

Cera didn't let her smile falter. "I look forward to the dancing," she said. They bowed, and Alania took them in hand.

So it went, a seemingly endless procession of lords and ladies and merchants and craftsmen from her lands and the surrounding areas. Cera's smile started to hurt.

"My Lady," Athelnor droned yet again. "May I present Lord Cition and his Lady Parissa."

Cera's smile warmed. "Lord Cition, so good to see you again. Lady Parissa, I am glad to meet you at last."

It was clear where Emerson got his tall, thin frame.

Cera reached out her hand to greet them. Lord Cition's smile was warm, but Parissa seemed a bit cool as she spoke. "And where is my errant son?" she asked, scanning the room.

"My Lady," Athelnor spoke again. "May I present Master Craftsman Falor, and his sons Felix and Fenton."

"Come, Parissa," Cition took his wife's arm. "We'll no doubt find Emerson at his loom."

Cera turned to Master Craftsmen Falor and offered her greetings. His sons towered over her like trees. He was extolling their virtues when a ruckus started by the main doors.

"Out of my way!" a loud piercing voice crackled. "I'll see the Lady Cera now, thank you."

A tall, handsome man with a scowling face strode down the length of the hall, focused on her. Cera caught her breath; for the briefest moment he looked like her late, unlamented husband. But Sinmon had been suave and polished, and this man was barging in rudely and was all dressed in green. Cera wrinkled her nose, trying to remember what exactly that meant. Heralds wore white, Bards wore red, and—

The man stormed up. "Are you the Lady Cera?" he demanded. "We've come to see—"

—Healers wore green. Cera caught her breath. "You're a Healer," she gasped. "A true Healer?"

The man glared at her. "Of course. I'm a Master Healer, do you think I'd wear green otherwise. An idiot would know that."

A man popped up behind him, shorter, chubbier, wearing plain homespun but with a smile and a shrug of apology. "Lady Cera, this is Master Healer Xenos, from the Collegium at Haven. Please forgive—"

Cera grabbed Xenos' arm. "Come with me," she commanded.

Everyone started talking at once as she dragged the

complaining man away from the Great Hall and to Helgara's bedside. "A Herald," she explained. "Helgara, Chosen of Stonas. A bad head wound," she started, but Xenos yanked his arm away.

"Yes, thank you, but I will see that for myself. Foul's the day when laypeople attempt to tell me how to—"

The chubby man appeared by Cera's side. "Perhaps, Xenos, we should leave you to work," he said, starting to usher everyone else from the room. "I'll be outside if you need aught."

"I suppose this room is adequate," Xenos approached the bed. Cera hesitated to leave, but then she saw him place a gentle hand on Helgara's forehead.

"Come," whispered the other man, and Cera left, pulling the door closed behind her.

The corridor was filled with Athelnor and Marga and Alania, with both anxious and shocked looks.

The chubby man heaved a breath. "Now that Xenos has managed to offend everyone, please let me introduce myself. I am Master Jebren, an apothecary, traveling with Master Healer Xenos at the behest of the Healers' Collegium."

"You are very welcome, Jebren," Cera said.

"Master Xenos is really very rude." Marga sniffed.

"Oh, yes, I am afraid he is all of that. But for all that he is loud, abusive, and demanding, he is a very powerful Healer." Jebren gave them all a sympathetic smile.

"Thank the Trine you have come." Cera ran a hand over her hair. "We feared Helgara would waste away if not tended to soon. How did you know of our need?"

"We didn't," Jebren said. "We—"

The door behind them opened, and Xenos appeared. "A bad head wound. Other injuries, but their treatment was adequate. Barely."

Marga huffed at that.

"We need food and drink and someone to see to our

mounts," Xenos demanded. "And a cushion for the chair, since I will be spending hours of my time at the Herald's side."

"She is awake?"

"I am a Master Healer, not an avatar working miracles," Xenos snapped. "Only a fool would expect results that quickly. And don't be making inquiries, either. I will send word when there is word to send. Jebren, don't just stand there. See to it."

The door closed before anyone could reply.

Jebren sighed, then gave them all a hopeful look. "Shall we be about it?"

Later, Cera had a lighter heart as she walked through the Fair, Gareth at her side. She'd managed to convince him not to carry his boar spear. He had settled for sword and dagger.

The Fair was not the finest, or the biggest, but it was her first in Sandbriar, and she meant to do right by her people. This was not just a day of dancing and celebration. Her father had long taught her the need to go out and talk to merchants, traders, and craftsmen. To learn what the markets would bear and what the people had a need and interest in. "Knowledge brings trade," he'd told her, and she was her father's daughter.

It aided her that Gareth was well-known, being Athelnor and Marga's grandson. He received a lot of attention, and pinches of his cheek. "How like your father you are," many a granny said. "Almost a man!"

It embarrassed him to no end.

Cera kept her eyes open to any and all possibilities for her people. She admired the local wares and praised any she thought worthy, trying not to play favorites. She made certain to stop and talk to foreign merchants as well. Anything that would encourage the health of Sandbriar's fortunes. Her former home, Rethwellan, held promise. Karse was a close neighbor, but Cera hesitated to even broach that subject, given Athelnor's feelings. Still . . . it bore thinking on.

At one of the tents displaying needles and wooden frames for embroidery, she found Lady Parissa making a purchase.

"Lady Cera." She nodded. "May I speak with you for a moment?"

"Of course," Cera said. She looked back to see Gareth looking over a knife-maker's display, and getting his cheek pinched yet again. "Did you find Emerson?"

"Yes," Parissa shook her head, clearly exasperated. "At his weaving, as Cition said. As glad as I was to see him, I have not forgiven the boy. He deceived his father and me as to his purpose in coming here. And he never writes."

Cera smothered her chortle. "I don't think your son has any real interest in me," she said gently.

"No," Parissa agreed. "Who is this 'Withrin' Emerson keeps talking of?"

"Withrin Ashkevron," Cera said. "Of Forst Reach, to the North. He came with the *chirras* that I hope to breed to replace the old herd."

"Of that family?" Parissa looked interested and thoughtful. "Good prospects, then?"

"I hope to see him settle here, although no final decisions have been made yet."

"And why not?" Parissa demanded. "Why do you hesitate?"

"Well, we'd put off decisions until after the Festival," Cera said. "It has nothing to do with Withrin's abilities. But I fully intend to—"

"Good. He will need lands sufficient to be able to support Emerson." Parissa walked on, glancing at the wares in the booths around them. "And earn an income. That is a war wound, yes? Does he have skills beyond those of a warrior?"

Cera stopped dead, letting the people flow around her. "Lady Parissa, are we bargaining for their dowries?"

"Yes, of course. Emerson has skills as a weaver, and his tapestries may be potentially marketable. I admit that is yet to be seen, but—"

"But they haven't—" Cera stopped talking, nonplused. "They're still dancing around one another like—"

"Lovesick fools? Yes." Parissa nodded. "But Withrin will be your man, and you are the Lady of Sandbriar. Cition has told me that you are a merchant's daughter. I expect you to look after his interests as I will look after my son's. After all, is that not what we do? Protect our own?"

"Yes," Cera said. "We do."

"Left to their own devices men are idiots." Parissa rolled her eyes. "Adorable, loving, trusting, impractical idiots."

"Well," Cera started them walking again. "I insist that we wait until they make up their own minds."

"Or someone makes up their minds for them." Parissa snorted. "Another thing, about those *chirras*."

Cera perked up. "Yes?"

"The wool of the old herd was notorious for not taking dye well," Parissa said. "I have a new dying technique that seems to work on stubborn cloth. I would be interested in a sample of their wool to try to work with. Perhaps we can come to an arrangement."

"Well, we are weathering them at the present, to see if they can survive the late summer heat," Cera explained. "But let me get you some raw wool from their combing. I would be very pleased to open talks if your results are good."

"Excellent." Parissa nodded to her again. "There's more to you, Lady Cera, than your looks."

Cera blinked, then smiled. "The same, Lady Parissa."

The sun was setting, and the vendors were closing their tents for the night, in anticipation of the dancing. Gareth had patrols both outside the gates and in, just in case.

Cera returned to the manor house to change into her new dress and slippers. The dancing area had been festooned with lanterns and candle lights and flowers. There were benches and chairs on the outside, and tables loaded with food and drink.

Cera found a quiet spot just outside the barn where the *chirras* had already been settled for the evening.

Jebren found her there. "May I?" he asked, and at her nod settled beside her.

"How is Helgara?"

"Xenos is still working on her," Jebren assured her. "He told me to stop bothering him and to leave. It's usually a good sign."

Cera leaned back against the barn wall. "Yes, well, for all of Xenos' talents he lacks certain . . ."

"Courtesies?" Jebren chuckled, nodding in agreement. "Which is why the Dean of the Healers' Collegium finds reasons for him to travel out of Haven as often as he can." He shook his head. "Xenos knows his abilities, and he doesn't suffer fools. And he considers us all fools. But highborn, you know." He shrugged. "For all its pluses, it has certain minuses too."

Cera nodded, remembering her dead husband's arrogance. "I know that well. Makes me feel an inch tall."

Jebren nodded. "Yes, Xenos breezes in like a superior whirlwind, hits you with uncomfortable truths, then smugly sits back and basks in his own perfection.

But he's not perfect. Skilled, with a powerful Gift, I will grant him that. And dedicated to his art. But lonely. I feel sorry for him." Jebren lowered his voice. "He has a nickname in the Collegium. One of the instructors was overheard telling him that he shouldn't be so acerbic. But a student mis-heard, so now they call him 'Acid breath.'"

Cera snorted and coughed.

Jebren's eyes twinkled, then he looked over toward the manor house. "But that there"—he nodded—"is why, for all his flaws, we put up with him."

Cera caught her breath. "Helgara," she called, and jumped to her feet.

Helgara was walking, dressed in clean Whites, supported by Xenos. "Don't knock her off her feet," he warned as Cera came close. Jebren moved to take Helgara's other arm.

Helgara gave Cera a smile, then grimaced. Her eyes were oddly wide and distant. "Stonas," she whispered.

"Yes, yes," Xenos said. "All you damn Heralds are the same, get a bit of healing in you and its 'have to do this' or 'need to do that.' You want to sleep in a barn, you'll sleep in the barn even if you needs crawl there." Xenos frowned at Cera. "Where is the damned horse?"

"This way," Cera smiled, and she led them to the box stall.

Young Meron was sitting with Stonas, with Katarina and the children. Lukas and Gerta were playing at Stonas' feet. They all sprang up when they caught sight of Helgara, crying out a welcome.

Helgara stumbled forward and clung to Stonas's neck, pressing her face into his mane. She shook, they both shook, and their quiet joy filled Cera's eyes with tears.

Outside, the players had started tuning their instruments, launching into a joyous tune. The *chirras* started to hum, and Lukas and Gerta started to dance, holding each other's hands. Meron twirled Katarina around, and they both laughed out loud. Jebren and Cera exchanged quiet smiles.

"I suppose you want me to heal the horse, too," grumbled Xenos.

"YES!" they all chorused.

Cera returned to the dancing area with a lighter heart. Athelnor was seated close to Marga, holding her hand. He gestured to Gareth, who drew in a deep breath. "Let the Festival begin! Dancers, to the center!"

Cera grabbed Gareth's hand, and they started in, a wonderful circle dance with partners changing at every twirl. The music was rough but spirited, and those not dancing clapped in time. Children laughed and ran through the crowd to join in the gaiety.

But after that, Cera had to face the suitors.

And it honestly wasn't that bad. She had dreaded it far longer than the actual dances took. And there were quite a few, and all of them nice enough in their own ways, but all had a feeling of desperation, of trying to meet a goal.

She smiled and danced a few dances, then begged off another, taking a seat between Athelnor and Marga. Marga shook her head, but she allowed it.

The dance floor was overflowing, and various children were running in and out, some dancing with adults, some just so giddy they burst with energy, laughing and clapping and chasing each other. Cera was pleased to see that Lukas and Gerta had joined in the fun.

Beside her, Athelnor heaved a sigh. She gave him a questioning look, and he leaned in to her. "You asked, the other night, why they would have fled Karse," he said, nodding toward Lukas and Gerta.

Cera nodded.

"There are things you should know," Athelnor said. "About Karse. There are also things that I should remember. Innocents get caught up in times of trouble. We will talk about it, later, you and I, after the Festival." He gave her a smile. "But not this night. Tonight is for joy."

Cera smiled, and turned back to watch the dancing.

It was odd—she should be happy. The pantries were filling, the house was full of guests, her people were celebrating. They'd survived the winter, and with hard work and a bit of luck they'd flourish in the next, praise the Trine. Helgara healing, joyful faces all around, and yet her sadness and loneliness settled on her like a heavy cloak.

Even as she danced and twirled, she couldn't help but think. Her late, unlamented husband has been charming, witty, a splendid dancer. At least until the doors to their chambers were closed, and the abuse began.

Cera glanced at Athelnor and Marga, seated side by side, happy and joyful, watching the dancing. They had been married long years, and that seemed like something to dream of, to desire.

But how could she ever trust again? Trust another? Trust herself? She'd thought she'd loved Sinmon and that he had loved her, but it all turned to ash in her mouth. How could she believe her heart again or even know—

"Are you well, Lady?" Jebren was standing before her, concern in those eyes. "You look like you just sipped some bad ale." He sat close, sharing her bench, easing down carefully next to her.

Something in those warm eyes made her blurt the truth. "They make me feel like a prize," she said glumly, gesturing to the men hovering at the drink table, watching her.

Jebren gave them the once-over. "But are they not supposed to be the prize for you? To bring some benefit to you? To Sandbriar?"

"Would they?" Cera asked glumly. "Not one of them can even shear a sheep."

"Well, that's quite the criterion to have to live up to," Jebren tilted his head and gave her a serious look. "Do you offer classes?"

Cera saw the teasing twinkle in his eyes and burst out with a laugh.

"Well, I can't shear a sheep, but I can fend off some of your suitors and offer you a dance." Jebren rose and offered her a hand.

"I would be delighted," Cera said.

He surprised her. For a man of his size, he was a lovely dancer, with a firm hand on her waist and a gentle lead in the dance. Cera relaxed and decided to enjoy the moment.

She did catch a glimpse of Emerson, sitting off to the side, watching the dancing with the oddest expression on his face. Withrin sat beside him, and, yes, Lady Parissa was watching both of them like a hawk.

She also caught a glimpse of Ager and Alania, dancing, heads together.

The music ended and Jebren led her back to her seat. "Can I get you an ale?" he asked and she nodded as another tune rose and the dancing started again.

Xenos appeared from nowhere and thumped down beside her. "Has he told you yet?"

Cera braced herself. "Told me what?"

"Why we are here, of course," Xenos sniffed. "I knew he didn't. Jebren has odd ideas about courtesy."

"Which you don't share," Cera said dryly.

"Jebren won't tell you that he is a Master Apothecary, and even better at his craft then I am," Xenos said. "He won't tell you that because he thinks of it as boasting, when it is just the plain truth. And he won't tell you that—"

"I won't tell her what?" Jebren stood before them, bearing two brimming mugs.

"Why we are here," Xenos reached out. "I'll take that. Too much ale isn't good for you."

"It could have waited a day," Jebren said firmly, putting the mug out of reach. "I am drinking this. Go get your own."

"Fine," Xenos said. "Apparently the reward for work well done is—"

"To go get your own ale," Jebren said. "And to get out of my seat."

Xenos rose, and while Cera didn't think he could actually flounce, he did leave in a snit.

Jebren handed her one of the mugs and resumed his seat.

"I thought you came for Helgara," Cera said, taking a sip of the cool ale.

"No," Jebren said. "We came in response to your letter to the Collegium. Well, I was sent. Xenos was an afterthought by the Dean. A happy one for the Herald, mind, but not the real reason we are here." He'd turned serious. Cera watched him as he took a drink. "We've been on the road for quite some time."

"Why, then?" Cera asked. "I expected a letter back, true, but not more."

"Lady Cera, you are of Rethwellan. The plant you sent, which didn't survive, by the by, since none of the carriers thought to water the poor thing," Jebren rolled his eyes. "That plant goes by a different name in Valdemar. Thanks to the Tedrel Wars, it is in short supply. We didn't know it grew this far to the south." He hesitated. "It eases pain, yes, but it is also an ingredient, you see. For a potent mixture that you would know by the name of 'argonel'."

"But that's a poison," Cera stared at him, horrified. "Are you saying that I've poisoned—"

"No, no, it is part of the mixture," Jebren reassured her. "In and of itself, it is mild and beneficial. Argonel can be deadly, but so is a sword, My Lady. It all depends on the usage. In the hands of a skilled apothecary, it is a blessing to those in need."

"A skilled apothecary like yourself."

"Like myself. And the Collegium will take all that you and I can produce, under better terms than others can offer. I am here to check the quality and train your people in making the syrup."

"And the oil?" Cera asked hopefully. "I've had no luck trying to make it."

"Using enfleurage? The cold or hot method?" Jebren asked.

A throat cleared, and they both looked up to see Marga frowning at them. "My Lady—" she started.

Cera sighed, rose, and handed her ale to Jebren. "I know, I know, my suitors." She stood and shook out her skirts. "We'll talk later. On the morrow, Master Apothecary?"

Jebren saluted her with both mugs. "On the morrow, Lady of Sandbriar."

> *To the Honorable Apothecary Reinwald, Capital of Petras, Kingdom of Rethwellan,*
>
> *Dear Reinwald, I fear that I am going to have to rescind my prior offer for this season of wild kandace. The Healers' Collegium in Haven has made demands on Sandbriar for all that I can provide and on very generous terms.*
>
> *I will have more at the next year's harvest and will then be in a better position to open talks with you. Although I will warn you that the prices you have offered previously do not compete with*

theirs. While my fondness for you is strong, the needs of Sandbriar, and Valdemar, are stronger still.

With all respect and deep affection,
—Lady Cera of Sandbriar,
in the Kingdom of Valdemar

The Price of Friendship
Dayle A. Dermatis

The town of Malm looked like a fairy tale, nestled in a valley surrounded by mountains.

At the top of the pass, Syrriah and Mieran and their Companions paused to admire the view.

Lush green grass filled the bowl, blooming with butter-yellow and snow-white flowers. Syrriah breathed in cold, clear mountain air, but she could imagine the flowers' sweet scent. The sky above was blue with just wisps of white clouds traveling through. The small city, with red-roofed buildings clustered cozily together, couldn't have looked more inviting.

The mountain passes would be open for only a few more weeks at most. It was two days past Harvest Festival. Syrriah was sorry to have missed the celebration, but their previous stop had taken longer than they had anticipated.

The main purposes of Harvest Fairs was to give merchants a final chance to sell their wares before winter drove them into their workshops to create more goods, and to give farmers a venue to sell the last of their harvests. Additionally, it allowed everyone to stock up for the coming winter, as well as see friends and family who had gathered from surrounding areas.

That said, Harvest Fairs included entertainment—jugglers and musicians and dancers and more—as well as excellent food. She would have enjoyed the festivities.

More importantly, Syrriah and Mieran would have been there earlier to investigate the disappearance of a fourteen-year-old girl, the information brought to them by a messenger on the road.

On both sides of the road, the scrubby bushes were dark green with dots of red berries. The chill air bit Syrriah's cheeks. Below, she could see trees turning colors, crimson and pumpkin and gold, and her heart lifted.

Autumn: a time of celebration, bonfires, and love both young and new. (Well, the latter was true at most celebrations.)

But this harvest time had brought something darker.

As they descended into the valley, the clear mountain chill faded into a crisp, still cool breeze. The last of the flowers stubbornly held on to their colors, purple-blues and honey-yellows. Malm was primarily a mining town, but it also had goats that produced the sweetest milk, legendary throughout Valdemar. They grazed on the lower hills, the bells around their necks clanking as they bleated and tore the last of the green grass with their blunt teeth.

"We'll talk to everyone, but we won't pass judgment until we have as much information as we can gather," she told Mieran. "The most important thing is finding the girl, safe and unharmed."

Mieran nodded. "Safe and unharmed is our goal, but we have to be prepared for the worst."

Mieran was about the same age as Syrriah's eldest son, who was also a Herald, along with her eldest daughter; her other two children were Herald Trainees. Would they have such a bleak outlook? Mieran wasn't wrong, but Syrriah chose to focus on the best scenario, not the worst.

"We have procedures in place for any eventuality," she said. "But it's best to show a positive front. Even when we're called to pass judgment, it is our duty to look at the background and reasoning."

"If reason is even involved," Mieran said.

Syrriah felt the weight on her shoulders. Finding a missing girl, keeping up hope that she was alive and, if so, unharmed. Training a new Herald. And being a Herald in her own right, called late in life, at a time when some Heralds stepped back from riding Circuit and found work at the Collegium.

But being Chosen after her husband had died and all four of her children—all Chosen in their own right before her—drove her to continue on Circuit, as all new Heralds did.

She didn't want special treatment. It had been awkward enough doing her Trainee Circuit with Joral for a year. Almost everyone they met assumed she was the Senior Herald based on the fact she had been a good twenty years older, despite her wearing Herald Trainee Grays. At least now she was the Senior Herald, supervising her own trainee.

Mieran was a fox-faced woman with a pointed chin, pale skin, and startling blue eyes. Her mind was as sharp as her features. She was thin, tiny, but with wiry strength, especially with a bow (Syrriah's own strength) but also with a sword. She wore her long, straight black hair in braids looped around her head like a crown.

Syrriah had her own hair, brown shot through with silver, cropped short, both for ease and age. She never understood any Herald, male or female, who stuck to the conceit of long, flowing hair or even dangling plaits—not only was care on the road difficult, but more importantly, in a fight, it was a clear disadvantage. Mieran, although choosing to keep her hair long, at least had it safely out of the way.

When they arrived at the outskirts of the town, the vestiges of the holiday were apparent. Trampled grass showed where rows of stalls had stood, livestock had clearly been penned in certain fields as evidenced by the churned-up mud. Gourds and garlands were still strewn by the roadside, and as they passed a scatter of bruised apples that had dropped from someone's basket, Cefylla turned her head.

:*They would be sweet,*: she said wistfully in Syrriah's mind.

"You'll have better food at the stables," Syrriah returned. "Leave them for the animals who don't know where their next meal is coming from."

Cefylla snorted, sounding more horselike than Companion-like. :*You are so wise!*: she teased.

"I was wise before I met you, but I'll grant you've taught me a few things, dearheart."

Syrriah, Mieran, and Lord Parr, who oversaw the city, stood in a field dotted with the remains of Harvest Fair bonfires. Rings of stones curled around gray ash and charred black logs. The scents of smoke and livestock still permeated.

"You know how it is on Fair nights," Lord Parr said. "The cider flows freely, and lovers are encouraged to sneak away for trysts. Jonquil came with her friends—I've spoken with the lot of them—and they never saw her leave. It was only when the celebration waned that they noticed she was gone."

"Was anyone else gone by then?" Syrriah asked.

He squinted, thinking. He was a sandy-haired man in his forties, with skin tanned and ruddy, showing he spent time outdoors. Stocky but fit, he wore well-fitting but un-

adorned clothing. Syrriah had the sense he worked with
the people of his town, rather than spending time in his
manor and sending others to do his bidding. "A few said
they had left earlier. I have their names. One in particular stands out."

"How so?" Mieran cocked her head.

"Everyone says he had an interest in Jonquil, although almost everyone also says she didn't return his
interest, at least not in a romantic way," he said. "Although he denies it, it stands to reason that he might
have wanted to prevent Jonquil from leaving Malm."

Syrriah frowned. "Was she considering leaving?"

Lord Parr scrubbed a hand through his hair. "Oh,
that. I'm sorry, I thought you knew. Jonquil had been
Chosen. Her Companion is in our stables, but my understanding is that Jonquil refused to speak with him."

Lord Parr's stables smelled of fresh hay and oiled
leather. A horse nickered, and another answered; the
only other sound was that of doves cooing in the raf-
ters. Syrriah and Mieran had already dismounted,
their Companions walking at their sides down the
wide, sawdust-strewn dirt row between the stalls. Lord
Parr clearly cared for his animals.

:Mori is eager to speak with us,: Cefylla said.

Indeed, Mori met them at the end of the row, stepping
out from his stall. Companions didn't need to be con-
fined. If they decided to leave, it was for a good reason.

Mori explained the circumstances from his point of
view. He had arrived a few days before Harvest Festival
to Choose Jonquil, only to have her refuse him. She
hadn't broken their bond, but she was strong-willed and
had shut him from her mind. He could only vaguely
sense where she was, but he knew she was alive.

He would know if she died.

"Did she give any reason why she rejected you?" Syrriah asked.

Through Cefylla, Mori said she'd simply said she didn't want to leave Malm. She'd seemed distressed, he added.

"Because of her romantic interest, who might not have been as unwanted as she said?" Syrriah asked, although she wasn't really speaking to anyone in particular, human or Companion. "Or for some other reason?"

"Young love is a wayward thing," Mieran said. "I've watched many of my peers turn themselves inside out over a crush."

Mieran was young, as were her peers. Syrriah remembered her youth through the pleasant haze of years. Had she been that foolish when it came to matters of the heart? Her husband, Brant, had filled her life so completely, she wasn't sure she accurately remembered any previous relationships. She trusted Mieran's assessment.

"So Jonquil wanted to stay for love?"

"It sounds so," Mieran said. "Girls of that age . . ."

"But she professed not to like this boy." As soon as the words were out of Syrriah's mouth, she saw her own narrow thinking. "Which might be exactly the opposite."

The boy, Settel, lived with his family in a small but tidy house with a vegetable garden and two cats prowling the perimeter. His parents, who expressed their concern for Jonquil, were wool merchants.

Settel himself had deep brown eyes, the beginnings of a tall, broad-shouldered physique, and a crooked lower front tooth. Sitting across from Syrriah and Mieran, he clasped his hands together and admitted he had left the bonfires shortly after Jonquil had left— because, he said, he wasn't interested in staying if she wasn't.

"She's beautiful," he said of Jonquil. "I . . . don't understand why she doesn't like me other than just a friend."

"I don't know you, and I don't know her," Mieran said before Syrriah could speak. "I know only myself, and I can tell you this. We love who we love. Some people are friends, some are more, some are less. It's usually not anything to do with the other person; it's about who *we* are, not who you are."

He frowned. "So what am I doing wrong?"

"Nothing," Mieran said, and now Syrriah, impressed, let her continue. "You and Jonquil might not be the right partners for each other. Love is . . ." She turned to Syrriah, hands palm up in a gesture.

"Love is impossible to predict," Syrriah said. "It is without reason, without logic. Beauty fades. If you base your relationship on that, it likely will fail. It's about compatibility."

Settel scowled now. "Of course we're compatible. We grew up here together; our whole lives are here. I'm handsome, she's beautiful."

He was young, and fixated on Jonquil. He was unlikely to hear what they were saying and understand in a short time—time they didn't have to waste.

"Maybe she just hadn't seen that yet," Syrriah said to placate him. "The question is, when her Companion arrived and Chose her, how did you feel?"

He spread his hands, his eyes wide. "To be Chosen is the greatest honor. My heart breaks, but of course she must go." He glanced around, then leaned closer to them, lowering his voice. "And when I'm old enough, I'll follow her, which will show her my devotion."

"Settel is obsessed with Jonquil, but I don't think he had anything to do with her disappearance," Syrriah said as they exited the house. She breathed in the pure mountain air. It felt like a drug, filling her senses.

"I agree," Mieran said. "Despite everything, he supported her being Chosen. With any luck, the time apart will allow his unhealthy obsession to fade."

They had discussed his fixation on Jonquil with his parents, who already knew and had been keeping an eye on him. Jonquil's friends had always been encouraged to tell Settel's parents if his behavior concerned them.

"She ran from being Chosen," Syrriah said. "Now we have to figure out where she went."

"And if anyone helped her," Mieran said. "Friends . . . who might have been more than friends."

Syrriah raised an eyebrow. "You still think it's about romance?"

"There are all kinds of love," Mieran said. "She may not have loved Settel, but there could be someone else she loved enough that she didn't want to leave."

Jonquil's parents' reactions were unsurprising. Her mother's face was swollen from weeping and she begged them to find her daughter. Her father, grim and stoic, put a hand on his wife's shoulder, but she flinched away, not wanting his comfort.

Syrriah and Mieran sat down with Jonquil's other friends, asking about how she felt about being Called, about Settel, about anything else they could think of.

One boy, Arald, flushed to the roots of his red hair so completely, his freckles nearly vanished. He was on the small side for his age, fourteen like the others.

Without intruding on his thoughts, Syrriah opened her mind and reached inside herself for her Gift of Empathy.

He was nervous or concerned about something. Which made sense; Jonquil had been his friend. But was his concern something more?

"I didn't see her leave the bonfires," he insisted.

"There were so many people around, and it was so loud, and . . . well, the cider. We all assumed her parents had found her and she'd gone home with them. I left soon after to find the privies and then decided to go home myself."

The other children had relayed the same basic story. From what Syrriah and Mieran gathered, none of the children in Jonquil's circle of friends had had too much to drink, although they were technically old enough. But anything could happen in a crowd of drunken adults, including accidents and poor decisions.

Other than Settel, there was no one who would have reason to take Jonquil. Including Arald. He was upset, but all Jonquil's friends were to varying degrees.

Syrriah and Kieran were given rooms at Lord Parr's manor. Syrriah's night was fitful as she pondered what to do, where to search for Jonquil, if there were anyone else they should talk to.

The next morning, the questions increased.

Arald had gone missing.

And another Companion had arrived—searching for Arald.

Lord Parr's stables were abuzz when Syrriah and Mieran arrived. Syrriah had a mug of tea, barely sipped, and Mieran stuffed the last of the flaky pastry she'd grabbed into her mouth as they reached the wide-open, large double doors.

The horses were restless, rustling the hay in their stalls as they paced and snorting as they tossed their heads. No doubt the presence of four Companions in the middle of the block had something to do with that. The stable master and a girl dressed for riding were leading horses out to the paddock to let them run out their energy.

It was a crisp autumn morning, early enough that the

sun's angle hadn't reached all of the frost on the grass. Syrriah hoped finding the missing children didn't take too long; if there was an early winter storm, the passes out of Malm could get blocked.

:*Naschenie is looking for the boy called Arald,*: Cefylla told Syrriah, nodding at the newest Companion arrival.

"As are we now," Syrriah said. "A message from his parents arrived only a few moments before you called me here. He left home after we spoke with him yesterday and hasn't been seen since. He didn't sleep at home. And it's not the first time, apparently. The night of the bonfires, he came home just before dawn—not early like he told us."

"I can't imagine he's involved with a kidnapping if he's been Chosen," Mieran said. Her black hair was in her customary braids but not yet wrapped around her head. The trailing plaits made her look younger somehow. "That's not an action befitting a Herald-to-be."

"I agree," Syrriah said, as Cefylla and Frind, Mieran's Companion, obviously shared that thought with the other two. "But it's probable that the two are together. Two children running away separately in the span of a few days seems unlikely."

"So how do we find them?" Mieran asked.

Syrriah didn't know. She had reached out last night, but she determined that Jonquil was too far away for her Empathic Gift to reach. That meant they weren't in Malm. Jonquil might have made it to a pass, but unless Arald had stolen a horse, he couldn't have gotten that far.

She relayed as much to Mieran and Cefylla.

:*Naschenie says she sensed something that she believes was Arald in the hills to the west,*: Cefylla said. :*But then she was cut off. She came from the east, so when she realized we were here, she came to us first.*:

"Then we go west," Syrriah said. "Naschenie can get us as close as possible to where she sensed Arald, and between us, we should be able to find both children. Or if they've moved on, hopefully we can find their trail."

The group made a sight as they proceeded through Malm, with the four Companions' white coats shining in the morning sun. Hearing the bells dangling from bridles, families came out of their houses to watch them pass.

Syrriah and Mieran nodded to the onlookers, and thankfully no one tried to stop them to answer questions or let the little ones pet the "pretty horses," as young children often referred to Companions (much to the Companions' gentle dismay).

The sun's arc through the sky brought some warmth, but the air as they ascended grew more chill. Fallen leaves scuffed beneath the Companions' hooves, sending up the scents of loam and decay. Soon they were beyond trees, into the scrub land, and then nearly above that.

Syrriah and Cefylla paused, and the others followed suit.

"Roads leading off from this one," she noted.

Mieran pulled out the map of the area Lord Parr had provided. He had offered them an escort as well, but they felt another person, especially one on a regular horse, would slow them down.

"The road we're on is the main one leading to the pass," Mieran said, pointing up in the direction they were heading. "The others lead to mines."

There was no visible traffic on the roads. The mines hadn't officially closed for the winter, but work had stopped for the Harvest Fair and would be low from now until winter came.

:They could be in one of the mines,: Cefylla suggested.

"But they'd run a real risk of being found if they stayed after work resumed," Syrriah said. Then a thought struck her, and she turned to Mieran. "Are there any closed mines? One that aren't producing or were shut down due to hazards?"

"The map doesn't say why mines were shut down, but it does show three in this area that are no longer operational," Mieran said. She looked up from the map. "Am I right that we're checking those first?"

"I have a feeling you're not going to be a Herald Trainee very long," Syrriah said.

The first mine was a complete cave-in at the mouth of the mine. Jonquil and Arald's Companions strained to catch a mental glimpse of their Chosen, to no avail.

"We just have to hope this collapse is old and this isn't the mine they're in," Syrriah said. "Let's move to the next one."

The next one was clear, and they ventured in as far as they felt safe. But no amount of calling, whether by voice or other means, produced replies. While the children could be refusing to answer, the Companions would have had some sense of their presence.

They emerged into the afternoon light. The sun was dropping behind the mountain range, bringing an early dusk. The temperature was dropping as well. They donned their wool cloaks and began the journey to the final possible closed mine.

"If we don't find them at this mine, what do we do?" Mieran asked.

Syrriah had already been pondering that. "We didn't bring supplies to stay out overnight, although we could manage. But I think we should return, and organize a larger group to search in the morning."

All three mines had wooden structures at the mouth of the entrance, sturdy wooden uprights and cross beams. At this mine, boards blocked entry, and painted wooden signs had been hammered into uprights, warning that the tunnels and shafts were unstable and cave-ins were likely.

Syrriah dismounted and, in the dying light, peered at the boards blocking access. She pulled at one, and it swung down; the nails on the right had been removed, and the gap she'd created was big enough for two teenagers on the smaller side to squeeze through. Mieran might even fit.

Mieran crouched next to her and cocked her head. "I think I smell woodsmoke."

"Let's go get them," Syrriah said. She had already reached out with her Empathy and felt fear.

What did they have to be afraid of, really? Jonquil had run away, as best they understood, because she had been Chosen. But the connection with a Companion was a beautiful, magical thing.

If Arald loved Jonquil, then he might fear her leaving. But the arrival of his own Companion would have changed his future, too.

Syrriah and Mieran lit lamps and leveraged more boards loose so they could enter.

However, although the tunnels might have been big enough for adult males and the mules that hauled the wagons of ore, they weren't exactly Companion-sized.

The four Companions looked ghostly against the hills in the dark gray just before full night. Cyfella's tail swished.

:*Keep yourself safe, my dove,*: she said. :*And bring the children out safely.*:

"I will, dearheart," Syrriah said fondly.

She and Mieran squeezed between the boards and headed into the tunnel proper. Inside, the farther they went, the blacker the tunnel was, and their lamps felt inadequate. Even in the daytime, she mused, it would be darker than night.

Despite the mine being closed, their passage kicked up dust. Syrriah knew she'd be washing this set of Herald Whites soon. She had heard them described as "Oh, shoot me now," because they made Heralds easier to spot. Between that and the way dirt showed, she wondered why impractical white had been chosen.

The tunnel curved slightly, one way and then the other, with side tunnels snaking off at regular intervals. The scent of woodsmoke grew, and the darkness seemed less complete.

"Jonquil, Arald!" she called out. "I'm Herald Syrriah. You're not in any trouble, but your families—and your Companions—are worried about you."

No reply came.

"Please let us know you're safe and unharmed."

Again, no reply.

She sighed, and they kept walking. A few minutes later, around a long, shallow curve, they came up on what looked to be a cave-in, rocks large and small filling the tunnel from floor to ceiling.

In front, a ring of smaller stones held the still-glowing embers of a hastily extinguished fire. Two blankets and several canvas sacks sat to one side.

There were no children in sight.

Syrriah crouched and looked in the sacks. Food, probably hastily grabbed when each children ran. Apples, dried meat, crumbs that indicated the remains of honey oat cakes. Not enough to survive on for very long. Either the mine was intended to be a temporary residence for them, or they hadn't had much foresight—or, most likely, a combination of both.

"They couldn't have gone that way," Mieran said, gesturing with her lamp at the wall of rubble. "And they didn't sneak past us."

"They must have come back toward the entrance but

ducked into a side tunnel before we passed it on our way in," Syrriah said. Hands on her hips, she turned and surveyed the way they'd come in. "I don't know that we have time to search every tunnel, and anyway, if we're in one, they can duck into another. But none of us have a map to this mine, and eventually someone—or everyone—is going to get lost."

"Or hurt," Mieran added. "What do we do?"

They began the trek back. "One of us should stay here in case they come out," Syrriah said. "The other should go back and organize a search party, ideally made up of people who know the mines."

"You should go back," Mieran said. "As Senior Herald—"

Syrriah held up her hand. "Did you hear that?" she whispered.

Ahead, a scuffling noise, then silence again.

The children were ahead of them, probably in the main tunnel.

The Heralds picked up their pace while still moving as quietly as possible.

The tunnel straightened out of a shallow bend, and the entrance came into view, a smear of black slightly lighter than the blackness of the tunnel. Syrriah couldn't see anyone ahead of them. Her heart sank. The children must have ducked into another side tunnel, and she and Kieran had hurried right past them.

But then, outside, the jingle of bells, a cut-off shriek of surprise, and what sounded like a scuffle of hooves on the pebble-strewn ground.

As one, Syrriah and Kieran broke into a run.

When they burst outside, Syrriah's concern turned to a laugh that she fought to keep from bubbling out.

The Companions had things well in hand. They had surrounded the two children, preventing their escape.

Her Empathic Gift let her clearly feel the children's frustration, which had temporarily overtaken their fear.

:*They don't dare duck beneath us,*: Cefylla said, also sounding amused.

Now, Cefylla and Frind each stepped aside, opening the circle and revealing the children inside.

Dust smeared their faces and clothing, darkened the tips of Arald's red hair and streaked through Jonquil's, which was pale yellow and wisping free of its plaits. He had his arm protectively around Jonquil's shoulders, even though she was a few inches taller than him.

"Hello," Syrriah said. "You've led us on quite a chase. I'm Herald Syrriah, and this is Herald Trainee Mieran. Our Companions are Cefylla and Frind, and the other two I believe you've already met."

The children glanced guiltily at the Companions who had Chosen them.

Then Jonquil raised her chin in a gesture of defiance and widened her stance, causing Arald's arm to fall from her shoulders. "I'm not going with him," she said, her eyes flicking back at her Companion. "I'm staying in Malm."

"I am too," Arald said, reaching out to grip her hand. "I won't leave her."

Syrriah raised her own chin. "Well," she said, "if that's your choice, it will be honored. But you owe it to your Companions to explain why you are rejecting them. When a Companion Chooses, a bond is made. To break that bond is like breaking a heart. If you do this, both you and they will be scarred forever."

Syrriah and Mieran stepped away, as did their Companions, leaving the children to face their own Companions in relative privacy.

Syrriah believed the children would make the right choice. A bond with a Companion was magical, unlike anything else. It was finding a part of yourself you had never known you lacked and a relationship that would support you unconditionally. You would still feel fear and sadness, but you would never be alone with those feelings again.

After a while, the sound of hooves kicking pebbles made her and Mieran turn around.

The children and Companions had stepped forward, each Chosen standing with a hand on their Companion's shoulder.

Jonquil had been crying; her tears had left pale streaks through the dust on her cheeks. Arald had clearly tried to stay strong, but he was swiping an arm over his own face.

They had obviously chosen to be Chosen.

And now, the truth was finally revealed.

Jonquil feared for her mother's safety. Her father's temper meant he frequently shouted at her mother and sometimes hit her; Jonquil didn't want to leave her mother alone with him. The only other person who knew was Arald, her best friend, who had pledged to defend her and her mother.

So, Jonquil had run away and hidden from Mori in the hopes that he would return to Haven without her. Arald had followed suit.

"I know your mother may feel ashamed, possibly believing it's her fault," Syrriah said gently. "But none of it is her fault—that lies with your father. We have laws in place about this, laws that will be enforced. Your mother need never fear your father again."

They rode down to Malm, the Companions surefooted even in the darkness, and went straight to Lord Parr's manor house. Messages were sent to the children's parents.

By the time they had their Companions unsaddled, groomed, and fed—Jonquil and Arald both doing a fine job with Syrriah and Kieran's assistance—all four parents had arrived.

Jonquil's mother burst into tears and gathered her filthy daughter in her arms. Jonquil's father stood near them, a hand on his daughter's back, his expression unreadable. Arald's parents took turns hugging him, and then his father—who clearly had shared his coloring with Arald—kept ruffling Arald's hair, sending up little puffs of dust.

Lord Parr's chatelaine would be displeased with the gray marks smeared on the furniture, too, but it was too late to change that.

Syrriah and Kieran explained how Jonquil and Arald had been Chosen and what that meant for them, just in case they didn't understand the deep importance. All the parents seemed delighted—even Jonquil's father said he was proud of her.

Because of the questionable weather ahead, the children would sleep in their homes tonight and would have only the next day to say their goodbyes. The four would leave before dawn the day after that, in order to get through the pass and down to the first hamlet where they could rest for the night.

Before everyone left, however, Lord Parr asked to speak privately with Jonquil and her parents. They went to another room, the door closing behind them.

When they returned, Jonquil's mother looked shaken and scared, and Jonquil's father wasn't with them. Jonquil and her mother left the manor with their arms around one another. Arald gravely thanked Lord Parr before he accompanied his parents home.

They took the eastern pass, Malm shrinking behind them as they climbed, then disappearing as they started their descent. The children were alternately excited, nervous, and then silent, although whether they were listening to their Companions or lost in their own thoughts wasn't clear.

Several days later, they parted ways. The children headed to Haven while Syrriah and Mieran had more places scheduled on their Circuit before they would return for the Midwinter celebrations.

"I wonder if their friendship will grow into something more," Mieran mused, watching the newly Chosen ride away.

"Does it matter?" Syrriah asked. "There are so many forms of love, and a friendship like the one they have is priceless."

The Gift of Love
Anthea Sharp

Twang! The unmistakable sound of a gittern string breaking echoed through the Bardic Collegium's wood-paneled rehearsal room, accompanied by youthful laughter.

Bard Shandara Tem kept her smile on her face despite her exasperation, and she glanced to her left, at the soprano section of the Bardic Trainee Ensemble.

"Would you like assistance tuning, Jaya?" she asked the red-faced girl sitting up front.

"I know how to tune up," the girl said. "Honestly. I think the string was just weak. But, if you could help me put on a new one?"

Shandara nodded and took the gittern. Like most Bards, she had a solid acquaintance with most instruments, though her main proficiency was on the harp.

Quickly, she restrung the top course of Jaya's gittern and handed it back to the girl. Already, the babble in the room was growing louder. Too long an interruption, and the two dozen members of the ensemble would veer into cheerful chaos. Many of them were of an age where teasing denoted signs of affection, and with the Vernal Equinox approaching, the intensity of their young emotions was almost overwhelming.

"Trainees!" Shandara pitched her voice to cut through the noise. "Focus, please. We only have a week before the performance."

She hadn't chosen to lead the ensemble's rehearsals, but the Bard who directed the Trainees had been called away on a family emergency.

"You're best suited to take over," her mentor, Master Bard Tangeli, had said with a brief, sympathetic smile. "The Trainees have been working hard for their performance at the Spring Fair this month. We can't disappoint them."

Or their families, of course. Parents of the Trainees often made a special effort to attend the Fairs and cheer their offspring on. Seeing their students perform was a high point, and it was up to Shandara to make sure the ensemble was at their best.

Given the general disorganization in the rehearsal room, however, Shandara wasn't sure her charges were equally dedicated to their upcoming performance. The amount of foolery and shenanigans she'd witnessed in the past two weeks was impressive, even for Trainees with an overabundance of romantic longings.

In addition to suspiciously regular incidents of instruments going awry, the tried-and-true practice of switching sections to fool the new director (it hadn't taken Shandara long to sort them all back out again), and sheet music getting ridiculously shuffled, the sopranos had managed to fall an entire measure behind during the last rehearsal, and the piece had dissolved into giggles.

The main instigator seemed to be a boy named Edwold. The moment Jaya's string broke, he'd bent over with laughter. With an inward sigh, Shandara turned to him. "Edwold, I think we should go over your solo section."

In her limited experience, she'd found that nothing

was better guaranteed to settle young spirits down than putting them to work. Edwold was one of the two soloists chosen for the performance. His high, clear voice was perfectly suited to the descant lines in the closing ballad of the performance.

The grin fell from his face.

"I don't feel well, Bard Shandara," he said, a slight shake in his voice. "Can't we do it next rehearsal?"

She studied him. He'd gone pale, and though she knew he was a consummate actor, it seemed as though he was telling the truth.

"Very well," she said. "I'll hear you tomorrow. Now, everyone, let's try 'The Sparrows Aloft.' Jaya, the first chord, if you will."

The girl strummed a tuneful chord, the Trainees settled, and soon the strains of the celebratory piece filled the air. Shandara kept a close watch on Edwold, but he remained perfectly well behaved for the rest of the rehearsal.

She had no doubt that on the morrow, however, he'd be back to his mischievous ways.

"I don't know what I'm going to do about Edwold," Shandara said, taking a thoughtful sip of tea.

She and her friends, Healer Tarek and Trainee Lyssa, had gathered in her rooms for dinner and were companionably seated around her small, round table. A cozy fire crackled in the hearth, taking the cold edge off the air as they finished up their meal.

"He's just a boy," Tarek said, mopping up the last bit of sauce on his plate with a hunk of bread. "Probably sweet on that girl Jaya, and worried about embarrassing himself at the Spring Fair. He'll settle down."

"I hope that's the case. But I can't help feeling it's something more."

Lyssa shot her a glance, her sweet face concerned.

"My Empathy is getting stronger as my training progresses. If you'd like, I could come listen to the rehearsal tomorrow—and pay special attention to Edwold."

"Would you? I'd appreciate any insight you might have." Shandara reached over and squeezed her young friend's arm.

Lyssa was a Mindhealer, a rare Gift. If anyone could ferret out what was at the heart of Edwold's trouble-making, it would be her.

"Speaking of the Spring Fair, is there anyone you're planning on attending with, Lyssa?" Tarek gave her a wink.

The girl made a face. "All the boys my age are silly. A group of us girls are planning to wander about together."

"Wise," Tarek said. "I don't blame you in the least. I was impossible at that age."

"Only a handful of years ago, as I recall," Shandara said, teasing him.

Tarek put a hand to his chest. "Me? Never. You're thinking of my friend Ro. Who, as I'll remind you, is now happily wed."

Lyssa cleared her throat and gave Tarek a significant look. "Married. And he's your age."

"He finished at Collegium before I did," Tarek said. "Besides, the expectations are different for lordlings."

Shandara noted the tips of his ears had reddened. She, too, was a little uncomfortable with Lyssa's not-so-subtle urgings toward matrimony. While Shandara was very fond of Tarek, they were both young yet—and he was still finding his footing as newly minted Healer. For now, she was content with their relationship. If, in the future, they were ready for more, well, they would face that decision together.

"After the Trainee Ensemble performs, I'll be free

to wander the Fair with you," Shandara said, glancing at Lyssa and then Tarek.

"I wouldn't want to interrupt the cooing of you two lovebirds." Lyssa gave them a smug look. "Besides, Tarek, you're a lordling, too."

"I'm a Healer first," he said, his voice clear with conviction.

Shandara sent him a warm smile. He'd had his own difficult journey, and she was glad to have been able to help along the way. Lyssa, too, had struggled with her Gift.

"Come with us after the concert," Shandara said, turning to the girl. "Spring Fair is about celebrating all the connections between people, don't forget. Friends and family count just as much as romantic interests."

Tarek gestured with his piece of bread. "Absolutely. And speaking of family, you can use us as an excuse to escape yours, any time."

"Thank you." Lyssa's tone turned serious. "You two know you're my *real* family here in Haven."

Shandara leaned over and squeezed the girl's shoulders. "We know."

"She's just angling for us to buy her a half-dozen pocket pies at the Fair," Tarek said, his grin showing he didn't mean it.

"Well, of course." Lyssa blinked innocently at him. "Isn't that what families are for?"

The next afternoon, as promised, Lyssa arrived at the rehearsal room as the Trainee Ensemble was gathering. She took a seat in the far corner and opened a book. A few of the young musicians glanced at her, but since she was clearly there with Shandara's permission, her presence was noted, then dismissed.

Wondering what the day's mischief might be, Shandara called the group to order.

"Let's start with the 'Ode to a Companion,'" she said. "Are you ready for your solo, Edwold?" Might as well begin with putting the lad in the spotlight and see what happened.

"Yes, Bard Shandara," Edwold said, jumping up.

He took his place at the front, a light in his eyes that boded trouble. Shandara caught Lyssa's gaze. The girl glanced at Edwold, then back, her brow furrowed. Clearly something was afoot. Ah, well, the only way to uncover it was to forge ahead.

"Jaya, the chord please," Shandara said.

The girl complied, and Shandara was glad to see that at least the instrument was behaving today. Even if there was a spate of muffled giggling from some of the boys.

She counted off, and the ensemble began. The song was a lovely composition about the bond between a Herald and her Companion—perfect as a finale for their Spring Fair performance. The full choral parts softened, and Shandara gestured to Edwold.

He opened his mouth for the first bars of his solo.

Croak. The unmistakable sound of a bullfrog sounded from somewhere about his person. Probably the pocket his hand was tucked firmly in. Shandara narrowed her eyes.

A half-dozen answering ribbits and croaks sounded from the back of the soprano section. The music dissolved, the melody lost under shrieks of laughter.

"Edwold." Shandara kept her tone stern, though she had to admit it was an amusing prank. Amusing—if they didn't have a performance looming in two days. And if it weren't abundantly clear that Edwold was trying desperately to keep from performing his solo. "Please show me what's in your pocket."

The boy pulled out his hand. He held a fat brown

frog with a green head, its long legs dangling down on either side of his palm.

It croaked again, blinking at the sudden light. For such a small creature, it produced an astonishingly loud sound. Again came answering noises from some of the other boys. The Trainees started to giggle again. Shandara waved her hand for silence, keeping her gaze fixed on Edwold.

"I'm sorry," he said, with false contrition. "I was out in the meadow before lunch with my friends. The frogs must have crawled into our pockets somehow."

"Somehow," Shandara said dryly. "Perhaps you and your co-conspirators can take them back to their preferred habitat. Now."

With a broad grin, Edwold nodded. "If you say so, Bard Shandara."

He jerked his head, and three other boys rose from the back of the ensemble. Their trousers were all muddy at the knees—no doubt from their frog-catching efforts.

"Ribbit," one of the boy's pockets said.

"Go." Shandara waved at the door. "When you return, we'll run the Ode again."

"Of course, Bard Shandara." Edwold gave her a jaunty wave and led his crew out of the room.

"Come back right away!" she called after their retreating backs. She had the sour suspicion they'd dawdle until rehearsal was over.

Drat. She shouldn't have said they'd practice the Ode.

From the back of the room, Lyssa gave her an eloquent look, eyebrows raised. Clearly, the girl had sensed something. Shandara could hardly wait to find out what it might be.

But first, they had the remainder of a rehearsal to get through.

"Trainees, while we wait for Edwold, let's run 'The Sparrow Aloft.'" Shandara raised her hands.

With the worst miscreants gone, the ensemble quickly settled. Soon, the sweet strains of voices interwoven with gittern and flute filled the room. They were a talented bunch. When they focused.

As she'd suspected, Edwold and his friends timed their return to coincide with the end of rehearsal.

"I'm sorry," he said, sounding completely unrepentant. "The frogs got away outside the Common Room, and we had to chase them down."

"Hm." Shandara stared at him a moment, then looked to Lyssa. Should she ask the boy to speak with her?

Lips compressed, Lyssa gave a slight nod. Clearly she'd sensed something. Edwold's behavior was more than just boyish pranks. Whatever was amiss, it was high time they uncovered the problem.

"I expect dress rehearsal tomorrow to go smoothly," Shandara said. "It's our last scheduled practice. And I'm sure the rest of the Trainees would be unhappy to give up their free morning at the Fair because I had to call an emergency rehearsal the day of the performance. Do you understand?"

Edwold gulped, the smile falling from his face.

"Yes, Bard Shandara," he said meekly, dropping his gaze—but not before Shandara glimpsed something that looked like panic in his eyes.

"Good. Please see me in my rooms in fifteen minutes." She turned to the rest of the ensemble. "Don't forget the work we put in today with dynamics, everyone. And tenors, please go over your parts, especially the exposed sections. I'll see you all tomorrow."

She turned back to Edwold, but he was already gone, slipping out with his friends ahead of the rest of the students.

The last of the Trainees filtered from the room. Lyssa tucked her book under her arm and came to stand beside Shandara. The petite blonde's head barely came up to her shoulder, and Shandara blinked at the reminder of the girl's youth. Lyssa carried a maturity beyond her years, due in large part to the burden of her family's expectations, as well as her Gift.

"We should talk in your rooms before you meet with Edwold," Lyssa said.

"Certainly."

Shandara led the way through the halls of the Bardic Collegium and tried not to worry. Whatever was wrong with Edwold, they had a mere two days to set things to rights.

"You're right," Lyssa said, settling cross-legged in one of Shandara's upholstered armchairs and propping her chin in her hands. "My Empathy was definitely prickling during rehearsal. Edwold is distressed at the thought of performing his solo. That's why he's been doing everything he can to avoid singing it."

"Distressed? In what way?" Shandara paced before the window, unable to settle. "Can you tell, specifically, what the problem is? Stage fright?"

Lyssa shook her head. "I didn't get a sense of fear. More like an immense sorrow . . . and guilt. I think he *wants* to perform—he's proud of being chosen for a solo—but an even bigger part of him is swamped with sorrow at the thought."

Shandara let out a deep breath. Failure to prepare the Trainee Ensemble for the Spring Fair performance would reflect badly on the entire Bardic Collegium— which meant she had to get to the bottom of Edwold's troubles as soon as possible.

"Is there anything else you can tell me?" Perhaps the boy had lied somehow in order to gain the solo— but that didn't make sense.

The students were hand-selected for the honor, and Shandara had heard Edwold sing before. He was talented, with a clear, sweet voice that hadn't yet deepened—a good choice to sing the part.

Perhaps that was it. "Do you think his voice is changing, and he's afraid to admit it?"

Lyssa firmed her lips in thought, then slowly shook her head. "I don't think so. His reaction felt . . . older, somehow. Not recent."

"Well, thank you." Shandara gave her friend a weary smile. "You've helped give me a direction to go, anyway."

"Of course." Lyssa jumped up. "Good luck talking to him!"

"Stay for a cup of tea?" Shandara went over to set the kettle beside her small hearth.

"No—Edwold will be here soon, and it's better if you talk with him privately, I think."

"You're right." Much as Shandara would have liked Lyssa's support, they didn't need to outnumber the boy.

Shandara gave the girl a hug as she left, then went to fix herself a cup of tea. And one for Edwold, too. As she was pouring hot water over the minty leaves, a soft knock came at her door.

"Come in," she called, setting down the kettle.

Edwold peeked around the oaken planks, anxiety clear in his expression. "You wanted to meet with me?"

"Yes." She gestured for him to come in and take a seat. "Tea?"

"All right." He took the cup she offered, then perched awkwardly on the edge of the same armchair Lyssa had inhabited. "I haven't done anything wrong."

"I didn't say you have," Shandara said mildly. "Although the frogs were a bit much, I think. And I'd prefer the instruments to stay in tune."

Edwold swallowed and glanced down at his tea, but he said nothing in his own defense.

"You're a talented singer," Shandara continued, trying to feel her way forward. "I think Bard Alvee made a good choice, picking you for a solo, and I look forward to hearing you actually sing it. Are you ready for the dress rehearsal?"

At that, Edwold looked up, and she saw that same flash of panic cross his face.

"I . . ." His voice choked, then fell to a whisper. "I want to sing the solo. But I can't."

"Why not?" She kept her voice soft. Her Empathy was humming sympathetically with the force of his distress.

He shook his head, his expression miserable. "I just can't."

"Please, tell me why." She leaned forward, trying to project reassurance. It wasn't the first time she'd helped a young Trainee face what seemed an insurmountable problem. "Maybe I can help."

Edwold closed his eyes for a moment. When he opened them again, they were filled with the shine of sorrow. With a ragged breath, he set his cup aside, then clasped his hands tightly in his lap.

"My . . ." He glanced at the floor, then back at her. "My family will be at the Spring Fair. They're coming to Haven from our village on the coast. And I can't sing in front of them. I thought I could, but . . ." He blinked furiously to keep the tears back.

Had Master Tangeli been aware that beneath Edwold's cocky exterior, the boy was struggling? It would explain why the Master Bard had appointed her to take over the ensemble.

She studied Edwold, trying to get to the heart of the matter. "Why can't you sing for them?"

"It . . . wouldn't be right!" he blurted out, his voice catching. "My brother was supposed to be the Bard— not me. He was going to come to the Collegium, and be amazing, and make everyone proud. I stole his place. He should be here, and instead, I am—"

He broke off with a choked sob and scrubbed his forearm across his face. The misery rolling off him made her heart catch with mirrored sorrow.

"How old are you, Edwold?"

"Twelve." He cleared his throat. "I mean, next month."

"And what happened to your brother?"

He sniffed and looked away, out the window toward the view of the Companion's Field. Shandara didn't press him. She leaned back and took a sip of tea, letting the silence lie easy in the room.

Several minutes passed, and Edwold seemed lost in his unhappy thoughts.

"When I first came to the Collegium," Shandara finally said, "everyone had such high expectations of me. Instead, I felt like I was moving backward. All my yearmates got their Scarlets, and I was still waiting for my Gift. For quite a while, I believed I was here by mistake."

"But I am!" Edwold turned to face her. "It was supposed to be Kendry."

"There's no rule that says siblings can't attend the Collegium together," Shandara said gently. "I've heard you sing, and you're very good. I'm certain you have the other talents necessary to become a Bard, as well. We don't admit people who don't belong here."

"Kendry was better," Edwold said. "And now, because of me, he's—he's dead."

Shandara blinked. Not what she'd expected the boy to say. No wonder Edwold was filled with guilt and sorrow.

"What happened?" she asked gently.

"Two years ago, the spring before Kendry was going to come to the Collegium, we were playing by the sea—

we live near Kelmskeep—and the cliffside fell." He gulped, then continued. "We were down at the beach, and Ken noticed it first. I was closer to the cliff, and I wasn't paying attention. He yelled at me to run, but I didn't hear. So he . . . he ran in and pushed me out of the way of the rockfall. And it crushed him."

Tears were rolling down the boy's face, and Shandara couldn't keep her own eyes dry.

"Oh, Edwold. May I give you a hug?" She opened her arms.

He nodded and scooted closer, letting her squeeze his shoulders. "Kendry was the best singer I've ever heard. My parents and sister are coming to the Spring Fair for the first time, and when they see me, when they hear me sing, they'll remember that it's supposed to be my brother. That he died because of me. They'll hate me for it!"

The boy's grief was tangible, and Shandara had to draw several breaths before she found her own balance. Surely everyone had told the boy it wasn't his fault and that his family didn't hate him, but emotions didn't listen to reason.

"It's tragic that Kendry died," she said. "But it doesn't mean you have to deny your own Gift. Do you really think he would have wanted that? Or that your family blames you?"

"It's not fair." Edwold looked up at her, guilt shadowing his eyes. "I shouldn't be happy when he's gone. And I don't want my parents to think I don't care about . . . what happened."

"Is the anniversary of your brother's death during the Spring Fair festivities?"

He nodded mutely, and Shandara felt another pang for the boy. The Vernal Equinox was supposed to be a time of joyful celebration of all the bonds of love. But maybe, despite the tragedy of his brother's death, she could help Edwold see that act of heroism for what it was.

"Why did Kendry push you out of the way?" she asked.

"To save me." He looked down at the floor.

"Yes—but why?"

"Because he was supposed to watch out for his little brother?" His hands were squeezed together so hard that his knuckles were white.

"Plenty of people are supposed to take care of others but don't. Kendry made a choice to save you. I think he must have loved you very much."

Edwold sniffed, then glanced up at her. "He shouldn't have."

"Shouldn't have saved you or shouldn't have loved you?" She tightened her arm around his shoulders. "He did both. Do you think he would have been able to sing after watching you get crushed by a falling cliff? To go off to Collegium carrying the knowledge that he'd failed his little brother, failed his family?"

"I . . ." Edwold pursed his mouth.

Shandara waited, letting him work through the ramifications of her question. Her heart hurt for him, for the whole family, but refusing to shine wasn't the answer to the darkness of sorrow. It never was.

"We both should have lived," the boy finally said.

"Of course you should have." She gave him a sorrowful smile. "But that's a perfect dream of something that didn't happen. Kendry didn't save you so that you could be sad all your life."

Edwold drew in a shaky breath and then bobbed his head. "I guess . . . I understand."

"Will you be able to perform the solo, or should we try and find someone else?"

"I think . . ." He bit his lip. The grief in his expression slowly faded, replaced by worry-tinged resolve. "I think I can do it. I'll try."

"No more tricks to avoid singing?" She raised her brows at him.

A faint smile tugged the corner of his mouth. "They were good ones, though."

She shook her head. "Very creative, I'll give you that. Now, go practice. I'll see you at dress rehearsal."

"Thank you." He leaned in, gave her a squeeze around the middle, then rose and headed out the door.

Slowly, Shandara finished her tea. She wasn't entirely sure she'd helped Edwold enough—the boy had been carrying a heavy burden, and that couldn't be easy to set down, even taking into account the resiliency of youth.

They'd know soon whether he'd be able to put aside the guilt and sorrow, stand tall, and let his voice ring out. She hoped, for all their sakes, that he was strong enough.

"Is your ensemble ready?" Tarek asked as he and Shandara strode out of the Collegium gates toward the Spring Fair.

"Maybe."

Shandara adjusted the carrying strap of her harp and squinted at the bright pennants hung around the perimeter of the Fair. The day was chilly, but the sunlight carried a welcome warmth—which would help keep the instruments in tune once the Trainee Ensemble took the stage. One less thing to worry about.

Delicious smells from the food vendors wafted through the air, and the sound of laughter rang over the babble of the crowd. Many of the attendees wore ribbon-bedecked love tokens in their hair or pinned to their clothing, and the mood was merry.

The gaiety only underscored Shandara's anxiety.

She hadn't gone into detail with Tarek, but the dress rehearsal had been less than ideal.

A bad dress rehearsal means a good performance, she reminded herself, trying to believe the old adage was true.

It wasn't just Edwold's shaky solo that had her concerned, though that was the pinnacle of her worry. He'd had to stop halfway through 'Ode to a Companion,' his voice choked with tears, and his tension had infected the rest of the ensemble.

Tempos were all over the place, despite Shandara's keeping time at the front of the group. The flutes squawked, the tenors missed their entrance, the altos were flat. The entire rehearsal had been altogether dreadful.

She'd ended it with a bright smile and words of encouragement she didn't quite feel. Especially not at this moment, making her way to the large stage set in the center of the Fair. Her stomach knotted as she saw the members of the Trainee Ensemble milling about at one side.

"You brought your harp." Tarek nodded to the instrument she carried.

"Yes." Moved by an impulse she didn't quite understand, Shandara had grabbed her lap harp on the way out the door. "We didn't practice with it though, so . . ." She trailed off in a shrug.

"Don't worry. I know the performance will go wonderfully." Tarek gave her a smile so full of confidence, she didn't have the heart to contradict him.

They reached the stage, and Shandara was surprised to see Lyssa waiting there among the other Trainees. Edwold stood beside her, a shadowed look in his eyes.

"Hello, Lyssa," Shandara said. "Is everything well?"

"I think so." The girl gave her a crooked smile. "I've been talking with Edwold."

Shandara glanced at the boy.

"She said maybe she could help," he said, shuffling his feet. "If you don't mind, Bard Shandara."

"Not at all." Shandara's tension eased down a notch. She wasn't sure what Lyssa might be able to do, but just having the girl there was a relief.

"I told Edwold I'd sensed he was having trouble, during rehearsal," Lyssa said. "With his permission, I'll be standing by to lend my support during the performance. Maybe my Gift will be able to help."

"I hope so," Edwold said fervently. He jerked his chin to the front of the stage. "My family is right there, front and center and I . . .." His expression folded, and it was clear he was battling back tears.

"I'll be right here," Lyssa said. "You'll do fine."

On stage, Master Bard Tangeli was thanking the previous group of Bards, who had showcased a lively set of dance tunes from the Rethwellan border.

"I know many of you are especially looking forward to the next performance," Master Tangeli said. "The Bardic Collegium is pleased to present the Trainee Ensemble!"

Amid cheers, the students mounted the low stairs and filed onto the stage. The instrumentalists, including Jaya, took the chairs in the center, while the vocalists ranged behind them. Edwold stood in the front row, his face pale.

Tarek squeezed Shandara's shoulders. "Good luck," he whispered.

She gave him a tight nod, then strode onto the stage. A quick glance into the crowd showed her a dark-haired couple standing up front, with two younger children who bore a marked resemblance to Edwold. They wore cautious smiles, and the littlest girl waved excitedly as she spotted her brother.

Turning to her Trainees, Shandara gave them a heartening smile.

"Let's give them our best," she said, her voice pitched for the ensemble's ears alone. "I know you'll make your families proud."

Her gaze landed on Edwold, and he gave her a faint nod. Still, she saw the misgivings in his eyes.

Before the group could give in to their restless nerves, Shandara lifted her hands, nodded to Jaya for the opening notes, and launched them into "The Sparrows Aloft."

Despite a shaky start, the ensemble rallied, and soon the joyful chorus filled the air. Bright trills from the flutes and a lovely run from Jaya's gittern embroidered the melody, and Shandara felt her heart lighten.

The second piece, an instrumental with wordless choral accompaniment, went equally well. The audience applauded and shouted encouragement, and Shandara's smile to the group widened.

But "Ode to a Companion" was next. As the instruments checked their tuning, Shandara watched Edwold with concern. The boy's eyes were shadowed, his face tense.

Shandara pulled her harp from its case and went to sit by Jaya, ostensibly to tune up, but also to be near Edwold.

"You *can* do this," she said to him.

He swallowed and couldn't meet her eyes.

"Ready?" Shandara called to the group. "Follow me from here, please."

The whispering Trainees quieted, the silence spreading in ripples out into the crowd until they sat in the center of a hushed expectancy.

Shandara nodded to Jaya, then joined her on the intro. As her fingers plucked the harp strings, she concentrated on breathing with the music, on infusing the notes with assurance and directing it at Edwold.

The singers entered on cue.

Edwold blinked rapidly, swaying.

"Unlock your knees," Shandara whispered urgently to him. He couldn't pass out now.

The chorus softened, holding their note. Edwold opened his mouth.

No sound emerged.

Sing! Shandara thought at him. *You can, I know you can.*

Still he stood there, paralyzed. Another second more and the piece would fall apart.

Unless . . .

Hoping the ensemble would follow her, Shandara began to play loudly, ringing the notes of the melody line to give Edwold more time.

There was a stuttering moment as some of the singers followed her, and some didn't. Then the piece settled, and Shandara was suffused with gratitude. No matter how fractious and silly the Trainees could be, they were true musicians at their cores.

Indeed, as she wound the melody around and back to the solo's starting point, the ensemble coalesced, sounding even better than at any point during their practice.

A bit of color returned to Edwold's cheeks.

This time, when they hit his cue, he opened his mouth and sang.

Clear and high, the verse soared above the crowd, telling of the connection between Companion and Herald. The audience listened, riveted, and Shandara sat back in relief.

A relief that was short lived.

Edwold reached the second stanza and shot her a panicked look. Too late, she realized that *this* section was the danger point. The verse about how the bonds of love could transcend even death was next—and Edwold was breaking.

His voice cracked.

He dragged in a fresh breath and tried again, but his voice fell short of the high, soaring melody. In the front row, his parents looked on with stricken expressions.

A faint sense of misery began to permeate the air, and the crowd began to whisper.

Then, suddenly, Lyssa was there. She knelt on the stage before Edwold and grasped his hands.

"Sing," she commanded.

Shandara nodded and played a ringing chord, pulling the fragmented ensemble back onto the beat. They could do this. They *must*.

Desperately, Edwold tried again. This time, a surge of warmth followed. He reached the first note. Then the second.

Shandara could not quite sense Lyssa's outpouring of confidence and healing, the support that she lent Edwold, but it was there—visible in the straightening of his spine, in the increasing strength of his voice.

Once again, the ensemble rallied. Shandara led with her harp, her voice, keeping the chorus quiet enough that Edwold's solo could soar.

They reached the final verse, and, with searing poignancy, Edwold sang—straight at his family.

> *Whatever else remains below,*
> *We carry on, we carry on,*
> *Remembering what is above.*
> *We carry on with love.*

The music swelled, the final chord holding, holding . . . until Shandara lifted her hand and swept it to the side.

The ensemble cut off perfectly—not a single straggler or missed note.

A moment of awed silence followed.

Shandara looked at Edwold's parents, their faces shining with tears. With approval. With love.

Then the audience broke into riotous cheers and applause. Lyssa slowly rose to stand, her face soft as she looked at Edwold.

"You did it," Shandara said to him—to the whole Trainee Ensemble. "I'm so proud of you."

She beckoned the boy to step forward and take his well-deserved bow. He did, his eyes bright, his smile wobbly about the edges.

"Thank you," he said to her as he went back to his place.

Lyssa held her hand out to him, and he took it, the gesture all but lost as the other soloist took her bow, and the rest of the ensemble followed suit.

As they left the stage, they were already turning back into rowdy youths. Several of them stopped to congratulate Edwold, some by mussing his hair, others by offering to buy him sweets.

"Thanks, but I'm going with Lyssa to the pie vendor," he said, a wash of pink across his cheeks. "After I see my family."

Edwold's sisters and parents rounded the corner of the stage, and there was no mistaking the gladness in their eyes. His mother went straight to him and enfolded him in her embrace.

"We are so very proud of you," she said. "And I know Kendry would be, too."

Edwold cleared his throat. "I sang it for you. For him."

"We know." His father's voice held a somber note, but his expression was tempered with joy. "You honor his memory."

He leaned over, drawing his whole family into his arms.

Shandara turned away, eyes pricking with tears, to find Tarek waiting for her.

"Nice work, Bard Shandara," he said softly.

"Thank you." She let out a breath. "For everything."

"I bought you this." He held out a white-ribboned token embellished with strands of silver. "It made me think of you—and the brightness you bring into the world."

She did start crying then, as the emotions of the day overtook her. Tarek pulled her into a hug.

"I feel silly," she said, the words muffled into his coat as she leaned into him.

"You can be as silly, or as strong, as you need to, Shan," he said. "No matter what, I'll be here for you."

"I know."

She snuffled a bit more, but the tears passed quickly. By the time she straightened and smiled at Tarek, she was filled with lightness.

"I'll gladly wear your token," she said. "As long as you'll let me buy you one in return."

He smiled down at her, the corners of his eyes crinkling. "Nothing would please me better."

"Ooh," a girl's voice broke in, "does this mean you're handfasted?"

Shandara glanced at Lyssa, who stood just within earshot.

"Don't you have a pie date?" Shandara asked archly. "I noticed you and Edwold holding hands."

Lyssa grinned. "Exchanging pocket pies doesn't mean anything. Not like *love* tokens."

Tarek swatted at her, and she nimbly danced to the side, then went to join Edwold and his family.

Shandara watched her go, with a fond shake of her head.

"I could use a bite to eat," she said, turning back to Tarek. "Let me just tuck my harp away."

"Then we shall wander the Fair together." He extended his arm. "My lady?"

She made him a curtsy, then threaded her arm through his. "Indeed, my lord. Indeed."

No Place for a Proper Kyree

Ron Collins

Nwah hated Haven the moment she smelled it—which had been earlier this morning, back when thick woods still lined the road Kade, Winnie, and she had traveled to arrive here. First had been the acidic tang of hot steel from the smithy shops that raked the back of her throat, followed closely by the overpowering stench of human refuse that clogged her snout. The dense scent of burning wood brought up primal fears from places she'd rather not consider, and finally had come the rotting smell of discarded food soon to be slopped to pigstock or just tilled back into the ground.

It was the last one she deemed the worst.

The woods she'd grown up in took care of its meat well before it rotted; the bulk eaten by crows, red-beaked buzzards, or other, bigger scavengers, the rest left for ants, beetles, and bore worms. The idea of purposely throwing food away became more distasteful the closer they got to the city.

:Are you all right?: Kade had asked while they padded over the hardpacked road.

:I'm fine,: she replied, knowing even then that Kade could feel her lie.

To his credit, he didn't call her on it. Not then, anyway.

Regardless, it wasn't Nwah's fault that the fur around her neck stood on its end, and it wasn't Kade or Winnie's fault that they couldn't understand that a city like Haven was no place for a proper *kyree*.

By late afternoon, however, the three of them had journeyed through the rings of the city to stand at a trellis gate that led to the Collegium.

For Nwah, the raw stillness of the street was disquieting, but thankfully so. The trek through the outer rings of Haven had been hard, and she was as tired as she was dirty. She wanted nothing more than a quiet corner where she could catch her breath and take care of her matted pelt.

Then, perhaps, could come a full belly and a languid sleep.

But there was still this to do, and she was still anxious.

The city grew tall and tight here, the buildings, pushed together, seemed to press on her, and what alleys lay between those buildings were paved with rock and tiles such that there was no bare ground to walk on. The gate was fancy, clearly wrought by a smithy of high quality, its sharp reliefs painted over in thick black coats that reflected the afternoon light. At least the year was nearly in autumn, so the air was cool and the sounds of the Harvest Fair celebration thankfully distant.

"What is it?" the guard said as he approached the gate. Nwah caught the scent of malted drink, though not as heavy as with most in the outer areas of the city.

"He'd like to apply to Healer's College," Winnie said.

The guard's response was as much laugh as grunt. He turned to yell at his partner, "Hey, Harve! This grimy sod thinks he's a Healer!"

:*I don't like him,*: Nwah said.

:*Don't judge,*: Kade replied. :*It's—*:

:*Harvest Fair,*: Nwah snapped, knowing she was being too sharp, but not caring. :*I know.*:

As if a festival should make a difference.

Even after years with Kade, humans were hard to understand.

The two of them, Winnie and Kade, had jabbered incessantly about Harvest Fair for the past several days, though, saying it was a time when people came together to enjoy being part of the city and give thanks for their bountiful summer. Kade said even his parents, who lived a good distance from others, celebrated their crops with pies, music, and prayer, and Winnie exalted over market places in Tau that had been full of everything from handcrafted tools to exotic roots. She babbled on about music and parades. There would be parties, she said, and rituals. Plays and concerts would be held. Much gaiety would ensue.

Haven was the capital city, after all. Anything could happen.

Winnie even laughed at Kade's expression when she said they might dance.

Nwah was from the forests, though. To her, community meant curling against the weight of her mother in the warmth of their den, or the aura of safety brought by the pack. Or, in those rare moments she let herself recall the magic she'd used to bring the animal horde together, Nwah recalled how the presence of each animal felt in her casting, unique and individual while making the whole.

Maybe that was what Harvest Fair was, she'd thought at one point.

Walking through the festivities, however, Nwah decided this was most definitely *not* what Harvest Fair was. Instead, the festival seemed nothing more than a reason for the entire city to go wild as a flea-bit boar.

Just getting through the outskirts had frayed her nerves.

Traversing the maze of alleyways and gates that

followed laid a stifling sense of confinement onto her already overwhelming mess of anxieties.

She couldn't imagine how people lived like this.

Each step of their way toward the Collegium made it feel more and more as though they were walking into an inescapable labyrinth, which, of course, caused her mind to race over even more horrible probabilities.

What if the guard detained them?

What if they shackled Kade rather than accepted him?

What if none of them could get out of Haven, or worse, Nwah thought as they stood at the trellis, *what if Kade was accepted and they had to stay here?*

What would Nwah do if she had to choose?

They'd been together so long. She couldn't imagine leaving him.

The taste of magic in Haven was disconcerting, too.

Nodes and the lines crossed the place like an invisible cloud, their bittersweet scent tangling in her senses. They seemed fresher than others, perhaps younger, but that didn't make sense to her, and the uncertainty made Nwah even more aware of what she didn't know about her Gift.

As they'd walked, she found herself daydreaming in their mix without any conscious thought.

Which was something else to worry about.

What if she made a mistake?

What if she lost control?

The second guard glanced up, took in the road grime covering the three travelers, and broke out in deep laughter. "Looks more like a ditch digger to me."

"And, yet, I've come to apply to Healers' Collegium," Kade finally spoke up.

"He's got the Gift," Winnie added, extending her jaw as though she was looking for a fight.

It had been her idea that Kade come to Haven. *"It's*

the best college in Valdemar," she'd argued. *"It's where you belong."*

The guard's muscular arms crossed over his chest, and the glint in his eyes grew as sharp as the dagger sheathed in his thick belt. The dusty blue tunic of his dress uniform seemed to rise.

"I'd say the mutt's the only one of you that knows how to heel," he said, glancing at Nwah.

The fur on her shoulders ruffled, and she fought an urge to leap at the gate.

"She's a *kyree*, sir," Kade said.

"I *know* what it is," the guard snapped back. "Regardless, I think Dean Teren has better things to spend his time on."

"How's about a little test?" Kade said, motioning the guard. "Give me your hand."

The guard frowned.

"The nail's ingrown, isn't it?" Kade said of the thumb as he motioned the guard to extend his arm.

"Fancy findings don't make you a medicine man," he replied.

Still, he put the hand through an open gap.

:*I could give him a good clawing if you really want something to work with,:* Nwah said.

Kade's lips curled upward, but he just lifted the guard's thumb to get a better look.

"It's going to burst to gangrene if we don't take care of it," he said, running his finger over the red skin.

Kade removed a folded leaf from a pouch on his belt that contained the paste of lavender and rosemary he had concocted on the road.

"This will soothe the pain," he said, rubbing it in and letting his Gift carry farther. "But you'll need more than I can do simply standing here. You should see an apothecary before it gets out of control."

The guard flexed his thumb.

"I'll be damned," he said, moving it without effort.

The gate opened with a squeal.

"Just the young man," the guard said when Nwah and Winnie stepped forward to join Kade.

"But they're with me," Kade replied.

"Staff's thin enough with the festival on," the guard said. "If you're making the application, you're making it alone."

Kade looked at Nwah, then Winnie. His confusion struck Nwah deep in the bones his Gift had once knit together. He wanted to be a Healer more than he could express, yet he didn't want to leave them behind.

"Go on," Winnie said.

:Winnie's right,: Nwah said. *:You're too close to stop now.:*

Kade smiled, relieved.

:Come and get us when you've passed,: Nwah added, hoping Kade felt her confidence. Kade was a true Healer. He would pass whatever tests they could give him.

A moment later the trellis slammed shut, and after the guard retook his post, Nwah stood alone with Winnie.

The sensation was like dead air.

Sounds of footsteps and conversation seeped in from the distance, and the early fall breeze still moved, but with Kade now delivered to the Collegium, Nwah wasn't sure what to do next.

Winnie bit her fingertip. "I hope he makes it."

:Of course he'll make it,: Nwah snapped, touching a ley line to enable their MindSpeak. *:Why wouldn't he make it?:*

Winnie shrugged and looked up at the tightly packed buildings where nobles lived.

A child scampered across a rooftop, carting messages to the elite.

:You're the one who drove him to come here,: Nwah said, suddenly angry. *:Now you don't believe in him?:*

She glanced past the trellis gate where Kade had disappeared.

:I know,: she said. *:I'm not really worried . . . it's just that he's so . . . different.:*

Nwah gave a disgruntled chuff. It was a sound that other *kyrees* would have taken as something like "get away," which wasn't quite right, but which seemed to say what was needed. Human language was so limited.

Winnie wasn't wrong to fear for Kade, but the problem wasn't that he was different so much that he was too trusting.

Nwah saw something more then.

She saw it in the lines drawn on Winnie's face.

Winnie was worried for herself as much as she was for Kade.

She clearly loved him in her way, but she had given up her place in Tau in order come with him, and now she was alone and waiting to hear the verdict on the young man she'd fallen for.

Nwah saw that.

And in one way she understood—hadn't she, just a few moments before, worried about whether she could stay in Haven if Kade was accepted?

Still, to doubt Kade was to betray him.

If Winnie couldn't see that, she didn't deserve him.

:I know what his Gift is,: Nwah said. *:He will be accepted.:*

"Yes," she said aloud. "But sometimes who you are is more important than what you can do."

:That makes no sense,: Nwah said.

:I know,: Winnie replied.

A collection of three Adepts approached the gate, clearly having come from the festivals. They chattered rapid-fire as they neared, their footsteps scraping the pavement with pedestrian monotony.

Nwah and Winnie stepped aside as the guard opened the gate.

:Come on,: Winnie said, breaking their silence. *:Let's see the Fair.:*

Then she briskly stepped back along the path they'd come from.

Nwah grumbled, but followed. Kade would kill her if anything bad happened in the city.

A few minutes later, they found themselves back in Nwah's worst nightmare.

The streets were clogged with people who talked and danced and moved so fast she had to clench her muscles just to keep from jumping. Boots kicked too near her nose, and countless legs swung too close by her flanks. Skirt hems swished in blazes of color. Carts drawn by cattle pushed through the crowd, their drivers calling out warnings, their spinning wheels clattering close enough that Nwah was constantly pulling her tail tight and skittering left and right in self-defense.

Wine and ale flowed like water.

Voices called from so many directions and in so many languages that her ears couldn't swivel fast enough, and never-ending strains of horns and lutes played in crescendos that made it impossible to tell where anything was coming from. The banging of drums pounded in her head. Odors of incense and roasting meat assaulted her nose.

There'd been a game of hurlee playing in the distant fields that brought loud cheers and seemed to incite fisticuffs and foul tempers. The game itself made no sense to Nwah, but Winnie had been so interested it caused her to be unable to walk straight.

Without warning, a clanging bell pealed nearby, and Nwah nearly jumped out of her skin.

Survival in the woods had taught her that any tiny movement or nuance of scent could be the difference between life and death, but now everything that happened was like a hammer blow to some part of her.

:I need to find a nook so I can work on my coat,: she said as Winnie led them into the morass of humanity.

Winnie ignored her, of course.

Winnie was a good woman overall, but she was young and often thoughtless. Throughout their trip, ignoring Nwah was sometimes Winnie's strongest gift, and now that they were at the Harvest Fair, that gift was in full force.

"Ah, damn!" came the ragged voice of a man who, out of nowhere, nearly tripped over Nwah. He saved himself but sloshed hoppy ale over the lip of his tankard to spill on her back.

Nwah growled and unfurled a claw as he stumbled away.

"Calm down," Winnie said, laughing as Nwah shook liquid from her fur.

But, as the man disappeared, Nwah felt anger build.

She took the moment to clean the claw and felt a tingle of magic flow over her shoulders. She'd wanted to strike. Wanted to feel the release that came with sinking claws and teeth into flesh.

Her heart pounded hard as she imagined the taste of blood until, with a nervous shiver, she stopped herself.

It would have been so easy, she thought.

So easy to lose control.

For a fleeting moment, she recalled an image of Maakdal, the *kyree* male she'd paired with prior to this trek, standing firm and bold on a barren cliff, his body musky and strong. She sensed firm forest peat under her feet then, and the feeling of the moon above, felt the sharpness of nighttime air in her chest.

"Isn't this the most amazing nightshift?" Winnie said without notice as she flitted to an open-air tent across the way. She held a swath of golden fabric across her midriff and spoke in the breathy way she had when she wanted to attract attention.

The weaver gave Winnie a sideways glance that brought Nwah's immediate appreciation.

Winnie left the garment and stepped to the next stall.

"Aren't these the ripest melons you've ever seen?"

As if any melon could make a reasonable meal.

"Ooooh, look at those carvings!" she squealed as she held her hands to her cheeks. "It's like they were cut by Master Mohan himself!"

Nwah quieted another instinctive growl.

She remembered Mohan's shop from her time in Tau. He wasn't that good.

Suddenly, the crowd parted, and a gleam of pure white drew Nwah's attention. *It's a horse*, Nwah thought, but she knew immediately it was like no horse she'd ever seen. It was tall and muscled, pure white with eyes that burned in hues of cerulean depth. Its gait came to her then, a clopping ring as clear as river water, its timing as perfect as the wingbeat of an owl in open sky. Nwah felt a bend in the magical net around her, a pull firm like the press of a sun-warmed rock against the nodes.

Atop the horse was a rider, a young woman of clear complexion and wearing a spotless white tunic embroidered with silver patterns at the collar. Her hands were long and thin, the expression on her face calm and patient as the festival crowd parted before her.

A Companion, Nwah thought, her mind stunned.

A Companion ridden by a Herald.

As they made their way, the Companion turned her crystalline blue gaze to Nwah, and it felt as though time stopped and she'd been laid bare. Her sense of magic froze in her throat, and every hair in her pelt was suddenly vibrating in an invisible way that made it seem as if nothing existed but the two of them.

The Herald patted her Companion's shoulder, and the Companion turned away.

Slowly, as the rider headed toward the city proper, Nwah's senses returned.

"Did you see that?" Winnie asked.

Nwah hesitated, uncertain what she was feeling.

As their reputation had grown within their Pelagirs homeland, Nwah had heard people talk about her and Kade as if they were Companion and Herald, usually with a sense of irony or caustic wit—as in, who do they think they are? But, regardless, that idea was ridiculous. A Companion's bond to a Herald was something of legends, steadfast and pure. A Companion, she'd always heard, chose a Herald, and, if anything, it had been Kade who had chosen Nwah back when he had pulled her dying body from under the bramble briars.

:She was beautiful,: Nwah finally said.

:They both were,: Winnie replied, giggling at first but then actually noting the state Nwah was in. *:Are you all right?:*

:I'd heard stories of Companions,: Nwah said. *:But this is the first one I've ever seen.:*

:Ah,: Winnie said. *:That makes sense then. Don't worry. It gets easier.:*

Nwah didn't reply.

As ripples in the nearby magic lines echoed in her mind, a wave of embarrassment passed over her.

Somewhere deep inside, she'd been proud of those comparisons, because, unlike whatever Kade and Winnie had, she could always fall back on the strength of their connection, could always comfort herself with the fact that she could feel Kade's thoughts so strongly she sometimes thought she could hear them. It was something special they had. She knew Kade in ways she knew no other person. Yet, until now she'd never really let herself see how their bond itself made her feel important.

The strength of the Companion's presence and the gentle grace that passed between Companion and Herald had changed that.

They made her feel smaller. Weak.

That sensation of connection gave her a sense of just how limited her relationship to Kade was.

The Companion was more than beautiful, Nwah realized then. She was overwhelming and otherworldly. She was *awesome* in the full meaning of the word. Recalling the intensity of the Companion's gaze brought Nwah a fresh burst of discomfort about everything from her mere existence to the state of her coat.

I could never be like that, she thought to herself. *I could never be that strong.*

Without realizing it, she thought about Kade then.

Tried to imagine what it would feel like to talk to him now.

How deep is deep? she thought.

How strong is strong?

She pulled on magic that lay in the nodes around her, and by reaching across the city, felt power pool in her solar plexus as she separated from her body and soared over Haven's huts and clay buildings, over its open firepits of roasting beef and pork, and over fields of dancing people, laughing people, and drinking people holding games and rituals and all the other things that thankful people might hold.

Finally, after Nwah crossed walls and streets, and twisted through windows and around doors, she found him.

Kade stood before a board of haggard-looking regents whose faces showed they were unhappy to have

received his application when they could be out celebrating Harvest Fair. Their faces were drawn and lined.
Their robes and tunics of green and gold were pressed
and clean despite the time of day.

She felt the tone then, too.

Disappointment.

Shame.

Loss.

They were Kade's emotions. Kade's reactions.

He had failed entrance. He wasn't going to attend
Healer's college.

For a moment Nwah's heart gave a selfish leap. *We
won't need to live here,* she thought, and was immediately ashamed of herself.

As she listened to the council's edict, she saw what
was really happening.

To the people at the Collegium, Kade, standing before them in rags worn from the trail and with a face
still too young to take seriously, was just a straggler. A
nobody of less-than-commoner birth. He had no spon-
sor, no one to care. The faculty saw him as nothing but
a wayward urchin, dirty from the road.

Sometimes, she remembered the low timber of Winnie's voice, *who you are is more important than what
you can do.*

Anger boiled inside Nwah.

She smelled disgust and tasted revulsion.

It's not fair, she thought.

Then she was back in her body, panting and shaking
amid the rancid smells and fervid motions of the Harvest Fair crowd.

She was suddenly both very tired and very hungry.
Her head hurt, and she was so sensitive she felt the
weight of every whisker in her body. She felt horrible,
sad, and incredibly angry.

Her hackles rose with involuntary rigidity.

A distance away, over the din of the festival, a drumming and a general roar of voices rose.

People turned to the ruckus.

An amplified voice rose to call a gathering.

"Come on!" Winnie said, reaching to pull Nwah along. "It's a show!"

Nwah couldn't shake her anger, but she followed Winnie anyway because there was nothing else to do.

They took a position at the front of a crowd that developed around two performers—a robust woman in bright greens and blues and a thinner whippet of a man who had taken a place against one of the outermost walls that encircled the city and who was dressed in tight-fitting apparel of equally gaudy red and green.

An acrobat, Nwah saw. And a barker.

The acrobat was a young man, lithe and graceful in his body suit. He raced across the grounds, then bounced, jumping and flipping several times before finishing with a flying cartwheel and a somersault from which he bounded upward to a pirouette and a bow.

The flowing routine brought great cheers from the crowd.

"Ladies and gentlemen, and everything in between," the barker called. "The Great Marten flies through the sky for you now, unaided by magic or mind spells, unprotected by either net or any sense of caution!"

Cheers rose again, and the Great Marten, flashing a toothy grin, climbed like a cat up the side of a high-walled wagon, whereupon he did a back flip to land on a bare patch of ground.

Cheers came again, this time accompanied by wild clapping and a round of raised tankards.

The barker, cheeks reddened to match the color of her curly hair, removed a hat from her head and passed it around as, this time, the acrobat ran directly toward the city wall and defied gravity by climbing up the sheer surface with a motion that was half leap and half sprint. He managed three heights of a man before he grabbed a hand rest and flipped himself the rest of the way to the top of the wall, where he teetered precariously, drawing gasps that Nwah saw were earned more through showmanship than any real danger.

Then the acrobat seemed to catch his balance and rose up.

As he stood, arms outstretched and with a flamboyant expression, the people around Nwah began to clap a steady beat.

Clap . . . clap . . . clap . . . clap . . .

"Jump!" one man yelled.

"Jump!" a young girl beside him called.

As the people clapped, Nwah's senses settled again.

The heartbeat of the communal rhythm grew inside her, and in a flash, she finally understood how a moment like this could serve to bring people together. Their fear was shared even if some understood the game that was being played. Their enjoyment was universal, their encouragement combined. *There is something here,* she thought. Something she needed to understand better if she wanted to truly know Kade.

Her gaze went to the faces around her, all tilted up to the acrobat, and she thought about Kade.

She felt a niggling on the ley line then, the gentle pull on a node.

The disturbance was faint, yet there.

Coming from somewhere nearby.

From the woman, perhaps?

From the acrobat?

She didn't understand what was happening, but she'd heard the barker's claim that no magic was helping the acrobat. Yet her heightened senses told her that magic most definitely *was* here.

She focused on the sensations.

She opened her nostrils and hunched her shoulders as she touched a ley line, and magic, tasting sweet like grass, flowed to pool in her mind.

On the wall, the acrobat bent, then leaped, twisting his body as he turned in the free air.

The people gasped a collective breath.

Nwah touched the magic the barker had been casting and saw it wasn't there to protect the acrobat from a fall, nor was it magic to make him fly true. Instead of being designed to pass fakery over the audience, the spell was there to blur the acrobat's thoughts, there to hide the existence of something else.

As the acrobat hit his apex, Nwah peeled the spell away.

As the acrobat fell toward the ground, she found the unprotected core of thought it had been shielding.

Images and memories flooded over her. Remnants of conversations, snippets of agreements made, and payments given. The layout of maps, and a plan hatched to enter a chamber and pour poison into a nightstand cup. She couldn't see the intended victim, but part of Haven showed outside the window in this forethought.

The man was an assassin.

He was planning to kill someone.

Surprised at Nwah's intrusion, the barker gave a start, and the acrobat, in midair, suddenly lost control.

The crowd's fearful call rose to a fervor as the man hit with a sickening crunch.

Then the sound faded to silence, and no one moved.

The accident was clearly bad. One of the acrobat's legs was shattered and an arm was bent underneath him.

Finally, he moaned in the ugly tones of someone who knew exactly how badly he was hurt, and Winnie, her fingers drawn to her lips in concern, moved forward to help.

Another person screamed, and others followed.

Amid the early chaos that broke out, a few gawkers came forward to help Winnie.

"Stop!" she called as one of the men tried to move the acrobat, but the sound of her voice faded as Nwah focused on the portly barker.

Rather than go to the acrobat's aid, when she regained her composure, the barker unleashed a bolt of energy at the mangled acrobat.

Nwah instinctively threw as much magic between the barker and the acrobat as she could, deflecting the bolt to wildly scorch the city wall, and she raced toward the portly magician, understanding now that the barker was trying to kill the acrobat to protect their plan.

She leaped with a wild yowl that carried all the day's frustration and anger. Her body crashed into the woman, and they tangled as they fell hard to the ground.

The barker managed to press her hand against Nwah's flank and unleash another bolt that made her freeze in pain. But even knowing she was badly wounded, Nwah managed to sink her teeth into the fleshy part of the magician's shoulder.

The taste of blood came sweet and metallic against her throat.

Her back claws raked her foe's legs as her foreclaws pinned the woman to the ground until the magician used her girth to roll away.

Nwah tried to twist away, but the woman reversed her, and had her pinned.

Unbidden, Nwah's magic broke free.

It flowed inside her, powerful and pure, filling her with its presence.

As the barker nearly suffocated her, Nwah called out. As the battle raged between her and the barker, birds came forward, and cattle, and market monkeys, and stray cats and dogs, and boar, and chickens and turkeys. All answered Nwah's call, all leaping on the woman as she screamed, all biting, pecking, stamping until, finally, the barker struggled no more.

The animals faded into the background then, and, indeed, as Nwah lay damaged in the grime, it was only the presence of buzzards still circling in the sky above her that made Nwah certain her horde had even come at all.

Shocked gazes fell on the bloody body beside her.

She explored her wounds and found her flank burned and glistening, her pads torn and bloody.

She tried to rise, but collapsed in pain.

Her gaze went back to the humans surrounding her.

They were afraid of her now, and they wouldn't understand what had happened. Perhaps they would wait for the guard to take care of their fears, but eventually they would sense her helplessness, and they would come for her. She saw it etched in their expressions. It was only a matter of time.

Across the way, Kade appeared, his face ashen.

:Are you all right?: he said, rushing to her side.

Her vision wavered, but she saw his face take a stern set.

:You need help,: he said.

Some in the crowd warned Kade to stay away, others urged him to kill her.

Instead, Kade put his hand on her side and suddenly Nwah once again felt the power of his gift. A closeness dripped into her. A golden heat brought her the smells and images of the family farm where he'd been raised, and the sound of his voice as he'd once sung to her in the barn he'd chosen as her sickbed.

His healing slipped into her as it had before, removing her pain, or maybe not so much removing it as overwhelming it.

:I'm sorry about the college,: she said.

Kade nodded, but continued working.

Yes, she thought as pain flared inside her again. It was Kade's concern that overwhelmed the flare, not the flare that fell away.

:That's your real Gift,: Nwah said weakly.

:What's that?: Kade replied almost as if he wanted her to keep talking more than anything else.

:That you care so much,: Nwah said. She sent a smile into his mind.

:Only for you, you silly mutt,: Kade snapped back.

:I'm not a mutt.:

:I know exactly who you are,: Kade replied with such clarity that she thought her heart would burst.

Perhaps their connection wasn't that of a Companion and a Herald, but they *were* connected, and that made all the difference.

A moment later he backed off.

:Can you stand?:

Nwah gathered her strength. *:I think so.:*

She stood, shaking but firm enough.

"Kill it!" the acrobat screamed with raw throat as he lay bleeding and unable to move. "You saw what that beast did to Shaval!"

Winnie, who still knelt beside him, punched the acrobat on the jaw, and he fell silent.

Some in the crowd turned to her.

:The acrobat is an assassin,: Nwah said, passing images to Kade.

:I see,: Kade replied. *:I recognize the maps. He's from Ancar.:*

:I don't know what that means.:

:I don't either,: Kade replied.

As the crowd suddenly hushed, another voice replied.

:It means the Queen is going to want to speak with him.:

From the direction of the city, almost as if she had

simply appeared in the area, came a Companion, as strong and as pure as the Companion Nwah had seen earlier. This one, however, was alone.

She came forward, her mane almost silver in the evening gloaming as it fell over her forehead, stopping as she stood before Kade.

Through their link, Nwah felt the Companion take him in.

She felt Kade's confusion.

When the Companion glanced at Nwah, admiring Kade's handiwork, the lines of magic bent around her, and a dread rose inside Nwah that was deeper and more terrifying than anything she'd ever felt.

No! she thought. *Not Kade!*

Limping forward in her weakness, she stood between Kade and the Companion and bared her teeth.

:There's no need for that, little kyree.*:*

:Yes, there is,: Nwah said. *:If he leaves me, I'll die.:*

:Of course you would,: the Companion replied. *:The two of you are Lifebonded.:*

Nwah's gaze narrowed, and she felt her energy falling.

:But there can be room for three of us,: the Companion said.

:Three?:

:If you can manage it. Things will be different, though, and not all creatures are strong enough to share the focus of their love.:

As Nwah paused, the word *Lifebonded* settled over her. It felt right, and for a moment she was pleased merely to know there was a term for it.

Everything was still too confusing, though. Happening too fast.

She didn't know what to think.

The Companion used the break to return her attention to Kade.

:Troubles are coming, Kade of the Southern Lands,:

the Companion said. *:And your Gift is clearly strong. I am named Leena, and I Choose you as my Herald-in-Training.:*

:Choose me?: Kade said.

:Are you deaf?: Leena replied.

:But I was rejected at the—:

:The Collegium is known to make occasional errors in judgement.:

Kade swallowed, then looked at Nwah. *:She has a Gift, too,:* he said.

Leena glanced to the remains of the barker's body.

:I've seen as much,: she said. *:And, since she has no self-control, we've all felt as much, too. I'll be interested to learn how a boy Healer and a* kyree *with nature magic came to be in such a bond, but probably no more interested than Darkwind will be to have a* kyree *in the Mages Collegium.:*

:She can study here, too?: Kade said.

:We couldn't leave her as she is, now, could we? Otherwise she'd be far too attractive to any BloodMage she ran into. I'd say you can blame only luck that you haven't fallen prey to one already.:

:I don't think I can live here,: Nwah replied, catching on to the argument.

:It will be all right, little kyree. *The Queen has some very quiet corners, and you won't need to stay in Haven throughout your studies. You'll have plenty of time to take care of that coat.:*

Nwah sat back, so tired her forelegs still shook, her body aching from everywhere at once. The idea of staying in Haven was still crushing. And, yet, an offer to study magic with a true Mage was something that felt right. And there was Kade, of course. He was Chosen now. She understood what that meant. But Leena knew Nwah's bond with Kade was real. If she could find a way to stay here, she would not have to lose him.

She felt his hand on her shoulder and knew her answer without speaking it.

:*My name is Nwah,*: she said to the Companion.

"What's happening?" Winnie said as she came to Kade's side.

Kade looked at Leena and shrugged.

"This is Winnie," he said to his Companion. "I love her, too."

:*And she has a Gift of her own*,: he added. :*Or at least a calling.*:

The Companion blew a damp-sounding breath from her wide nostrils, and, as Nwah, Kade, and Winnie stood together, Leena's tail gave a twitch that was large enough to qualify as the first break in composure Nwah had seen from a Companion.

:*I suppose all families have their complexities,*: she said, pausing again to take them in. :*We'll work them out. In the meanwhile, it's time we take this man to the Palace. Nwah needs her rest, and the Queen will want to hear what you have to say.*:

An Omniscience
of Godwits

Elisabeth Waters

"All the animals on the property are tattling on me, aren't they?" Keven winced as he set his crutches to one side and sank into bed.

"If by 'tattling' you mean reporting to me on your progress in learning to walk again, they thought I'd be interested," his wife replied from her dressing table where she was brushing out her hair. "They're right; I am."

Lena and Keven were still virtually newlyweds; they had married in Haven and escaped (both of them agreed on the description) to the nearest of the estates Lena had inherited. As the last surviving member of her family, she had several estates and enough wealth to make her an attractive target for fortune hunters. It was, therefore, ironic that in fleeing from Keven's brother and their ambitious father, she had met Keven in the quiet, out-of-the-way temple where they had consigned him to obscurity after his injury.

"Are you still thinking of offering land here to the Temple of Thenoth, Lord of the Beasts, so they'll have someplace to keep more of his animals?" It was something they had discussed during their journey here. With the special saddle Lena had given him for a Midwinter gift, Keven could ride, but the pace was necessarily slow.

It would have been slower with baggage wagons, but both of them had pared their luggage down to what could be carried by horses.

"I'm still thinking about it." Lena laid down her hairbrush and started to braid her hair for bed. "I'm concerned about the game warden here."

"Why? What's he like?"

"I haven't officially met him yet; he's gone to spend the Vernal Equinox with his mother and sisters."

"That's more than my father would do," Keven said. "He's ignored my mother and sisters for years; he even leaves them in the country while he spends Midwinter Festival at Court." After a few seconds' thought he added, "Of course, they may prefer it that way."

"I don't know what Algott's family prefers," Lena said, finishing her braid and tying it off, "but I'm afraid that his departure may be due less to filial piety and more to a desire to avoid me. He probably thinks I'll stay here for a week or two and then be off to the next estate, and I'm sure he has comrades in the village who will send word to him when I'm gone."

"Are the animals saying bad things about him?" Keven didn't share Lena's gift of Animal Mindspeech, so she had to relay anything she wanted him to know.

"The animals aren't saying much, but the Steward here tells me that Algott got his job because he was a friend of my brother's."

"I don't really know much about your family. How bad is that?"

Lena climbed carefully into bed next to him. Keven was wonderful, and she, unlike his father, didn't think less of him because of his injured leg. She *really* wanted to be a good wife and make him happy—or at least not cause him unnecessary physical pain.

"It's pretty bad," she admitted. "My parents died when I was about four, so I don't really remember them.

Markus became my guardian because he was my only living relative. He died about five years later. I wasn't there and don't know all the details, but apparently he made up his own religion, used it to steal and blackmail people, and died at a hearing in front of a good portion of the court, the Prior, and my friend Maja, who says the gods struck him down for his crimes."

"Did they really?" Keven asked, fascinated.

"I don't know. The Healers said it was his heart, but he wasn't even 30 years old. Anyway, he was cruel to me, my governess, and my animals. I had a charm of finches—"

"A what?"

"A group of finches is called a charm, the way a group of puppies is called a litter," Lena explained. "Some of us at the temple keep a list of odd collective nouns—did you know that a group of vultures is a wake?"

"How appropriate. So you had birds . . . did any of them come with us?"

"I'm sure quite a few crows did." Lena sighed. "The finches have all died of old age now. At least none of them died from being used for target practice by Markus and his friends, though one of them got a miniature sword through her wing, which is how we wound up at the Temple of Thenoth. The Temple Healers made me leave her there, and Markus took me home, but I snuck out early the next morning and never went back." She smiled reminiscently. "Dexter was my first friend at the temple."

"Maja's raccoon?"

"Maja's friend who happens to be a raccoon, yes," Lena replied. "By the time the Prior realized I was there, they knew I had Animal Mindspeech, my brother was dead, Maja had unofficially adopted me as a little sister, and I petitioned to stay there as a Novice."

"But you were a child, weren't you?"

"I was ten, I was Gifted, and I had no living family. The King became my official guardian, but he gave me into the Prior's custody while I was a child. As I got older, I had to spend some time at court, and after I turned seventeen last summer, the King said I had to participate in the winter social season—and we know how that turned out!"

"Do you . . . regret being married to me?" Keven asked cautiously.

Lena laughed. "Of course not, but I didn't have to go to court to meet you. I might just as well have stayed at the Temple and been spared the misery of fortune-hunting suitors."

"And my brother's attempt to force you into marriage."

"To be fair to your brother, the rape was your father's idea."

"And which one did you jump out your bedroom window to escape?"

"The important thing is that I *did* escape, you and I are married, you are legally part of my family and not your father's, and if Thenoth is good to us, we won't ever have to deal with your *ex*-family again."

"Amen to that," Keven said. "So is your game warden here one of those friends who uses birds for target practice?"

"Yes," Lena said grimly.

"Well, if he's off to visit his family, let's enjoy the Spring Festival in his absence. We can ride into the village for the festivities, eat ourselves sick on sweets, and do all the things we never got to do as children."

"That sounds like a great plan," Lena said, curling up next to him with her head on his shoulder.

Lena was surprised when, two days after the Festival, the crows told her that Algott had returned. She walked out to the front garden to meet him and waited on a bench there. His demeanor was very different from the last time she had seen him, but she was no longer a child, and he wasn't drunk, which probably accounted for a great deal of the change.

"Would I be correct in believing that you want to keep your position here?" she asked bluntly.

"Yes, Lady Magdalena," he replied, "but first I owe you an apology. I treated you badly, and I treated your birds worse."

"By which you mean you didn't throw knives at me."

"I certainly hope I didn't," he said. "I wasn't at my best that day, and you ran into the room suddenly."

"That's true. I suppose we were all lucky that the damage wasn't worse."

He shuddered. "Having a position that allows me to spend more time with my mother and sisters has given me a new perspective on the way I behaved then. I suppose 'young and stupid' doesn't serve as an excuse when I was older then than you are now, but I like to think I've matured since then. And the way your brother died . . ."

"Were you there?" Lena wasn't sure who had been, aside from the King, the King's Own, a few Heralds she knew, the Prior, and Maja.

"No, but it was all over town that the gods struck him down."

Lena shrugged. "That's one theory, and I suppose it's possible."

"It certainly is," Algott agreed. "Is it true that you have Animal Mindspeech? And that you can talk to birds?"

"Yes," Lena replied. "Why do you ask?"

"Your godwits—they're wading birds that live in the wet section of grasslands at the north edge of the lake— are disappearing. About a dozen of them went missing last summer, and the ones I've seen since then seem unusually skittish."

"Last summer, as in during the time they had their summer plumage? And none of them have vanished since?"

"No. I can't imagine why anyone would want to kill them; there are plenty of animals that would provide more meat if someone was starving—and no one in this area should be that desperate for food. This estate produces more than enough food for everyone, and the Steward makes certain it is distributed to the needy."

Lena sighed. "It's because you're a man."

He frowned. "That does *not* mean I don't know what it is to be hungry."

"No, it means you don't notice the fashion for hats with orange feathers, which are a specialty of the local milliner. I must have seen ten of them in the village during the Spring Festival, but I didn't realize someone was killing the birds instead of merely collecting shed feathers. I'll talk to the godwits, and then you and I can go have a chat with the milliner's son."

"He's a child, and he's simple," Algott warned her. "If you charge him with poaching, which I admit you have every right to do, it's likely to upset people."

"I'm not planning to drag him off to jail or have him executed," Lena said. "And I'm not going to do anything until I'm absolutely sure. If he's the killer, I will explain, slowly and using small words, why killing animals for their feathers is wrong. And if his mother still wants orange feathers after she finds out what her child has been up to, I can ask the godwits to drop them where the boy can pick them up without having to go near the birds."

"That sounds like a good plan," Algott said. "And if he is guilty of poaching, I can do what I do with all the local poachers."

"What do you do?" Lena asked curiously. The answer would help her determine what kind of a man Algott had become.

He grinned. "I put them to work in the fields for a few weeks. There's always somebody who can use extra hands and doesn't mind supervising a new worker."

Lena grinned back. "I've always liked constructive punishments." She stood up and headed for the house. "I have to meet with the Steward now, but I'll try to find the godwits this afternoon. You can continue your regular duties."

Lena and Keven rode down to the lake together that afternoon. *Keven may not have Mindspeech,* Lena reflected, *but he's really good with animals, and I need these to stay as calm as possible.*

She dismounted alone at the edge where the wetland met the lake, stood quietly with empty hands in plain sight, and sent out a mental call, along with a visualization of a godwit in winter plumage.

Soon a bird with predominately silver-gray and white feathers stood near her. The bird's head came to well above her knees, and it had a very long sharp beak, so Lena didn't want to annoy it. As she tried to think of a good way to broach the subject, the bird spoke to her.

:*Is he a new killer?*: it asked, looking at Keven.

:*No, he's my mate, and he won't harm you. Please don't harm him.*: The bird was a female; Lena could tell by the length of the beak.

The bird looked up at him, and several more godwits appeared out of the tall grass but did not approach. :*If he's your mate, why doesn't he stand with you?*:

:*He was injured and has trouble walking.*:

:*He should try it in the water.*: The bird probably wasn't serious, but it occurred to Lena that it might be a good idea. The water would help support his upper body while providing resistance for his leg muscles to work against.

:That's a good idea; I'll tell him to try it. Meanwhile, would you please show me what the killer looked like. I need to know so I can make sure he doesn't bother you again.:

Lena's mind was filled with images of a boy from various angles. In some of them she could see the slingshot he was holding. Her lips tightened. *:I know who he is:* she assured the godwits.

As they rode back to the house, she told Keven what the godwit had suggested about walking in the water.

Keven thought for a moment and said, "You know, that's really not a bad idea."

Lena and Algott were sitting on the bench the next morning discussing the deal he had made with the milliner and her son. The boy was doing field labor to atone for the murdered godwits, and he would do more of it to pay for any feathers his mother wanted in the future. Everyone had agreed that feathers would be gathered after the godwits had shed them, not from the birds themselves. Lena was certain the godwits would be happy to drop their shed feathers in one spot away from their territory in exchange for being safe and free from harassment.

When a godwit flew to them, Algott looked at the beak and fell backward over the bench getting away from it. Lena just asked what the problem was.

:Come quickly! Your mate can't breathe water.:

Lena whistled and Mindcalled her horse. She was mounted, albeit bareback, and heading for the lake before Algott could get to his feet.

She arrived to discover two things. First, Keven, being the considerate soul he was, had chosen to try his experiment on the far side of the lake from where the godwits nested. Second, the godwits had crossed the lake, dragged his head out of the water, and were holding him in place by his hair.

Lena, thanking all the gods she'd ever heard of that she wasn't wearing fancy clothing, shed her overdress and boots and waded into the lake clad in stockings and a shift. By the time she got a good grip on Keven and dragged him ashore, she was soaked to the skin and her shift was indecent, but there was nobody to see her but the godwits and her husband . . .

. . . and Algott, who had taken time to saddle a horse before following her. Lena quickly pulled her dress over her wet shift. She looked at Keven, who was busy coughing up the water he'd swallowed, and called to his horse. It hadn't gone far, but it had found some tasty grass to occupy its attention.

"Next time, Keven, let's do this together. I think the godwits have enough of your hair to make *themselves* new hats."

"I'd be embarrassed to be rescued by a bunch of birds," Algott muttered. He kept his voice down, but Lena had excellent hearing.

"These aren't a bunch of birds," she said, remembering the lists of names she had studied at the Temple. "They're an omniscience of godwits."

Keven groaned. "The animals around here really *do* know everything."

Going Home
Louisa Swann

Liana put her hands on her hips and stretched, willing away the ache in her lower back. The fragrance of meadowsweet mingled with the tang of lemon balm and thyme drifted up from the flower-filled basket at her feet.

She studied the broad meadow, the morning sun glistening like jewels on dew-moistened leaves. Dazzling white daisies with yellow centers the color of the sun and bluebells as true as midday skies sat amid other flowers she had no names for, the reds and oranges, pinks and blues painting the meadow in vibrant colors.

The people of Haven were strange. Not only did they wear odd clothing, their language made no sense to her.

And they *loved* flowers, especially at Midsummer's Eve.

Liana had brought flowers back to the Tedrel tent once and had earned a beating. Picking flowers now took every ounce of courage she had.

But pick flowers she did. It was the only way she had to earn coin.

Midsummer's Eve was scarce a day away, and she had only filled one basket, albeit a basket large enough to bear a sleeping toddler. She glared at the empty basket sitting next to the full one and swallowed a sigh. Picking flowers was child's play compared to the life she'd suffered before coming to Haven, so why did the task seem so difficult?

She was young—just turned fifteen—and the struggle wasn't physical. Not really.

She was worried.

A slight dimple at the edge of the meadow, just inside the border of knee-high grasses showed where she'd left the twins sleeping beneath an oversized shawl. Liana studied the tall grass for signs of trouble and gnawed on her lower lip. She had wandered farther than expected during her first foray into the meadow . . .

It would take time to check on the babes—

Liana sighed. The abuse she'd suffered at the hands of a Tedrel mercenary had left her weak-minded as a worm—jumping at her own shadow, waking from nightmares that the children she'd birthed had transformed into two-headed monsters, each determined to make her life miserable. In the Tedrel camp, she'd been too numb to worry. Now it seemed she worried about everything—her babes turning into Tedrel monsters being the least of those worries.

Who would care for the twins if she took sick and died? Liana's room and board had been paid for by the Herald who had brought her to Haven, but eventually she'd have to earn her own coin for food and shelter, wouldn't she?

With a shudder, she slammed the thoughts—and nightmares—into a hole deep within her mind and buried them. Other than weeing on their poor mum— Reneth II being a better aim than his sister—there was nothing monstrous about the twins. Neither one had inherited their father's *disposition*, though they could be a bit ornery at times.

She glared at the empty basket, chewing on her

thumbnail, then sighed. She'd just take a quick look at the twins, then get back to cutting.

Quickly, she slid the slender knife back into the sheath at her waist, hoisted the filled basket, and waded back through the grass, straining to catch the slightest hint of something out of place where the twins were hidden. Bees added their soft buzzing to cheerful birdsong. Butterflies of all colors danced with the bees, briefly alighting on one flower, then flitting away to another.

No sign of trouble while she was approaching the twins. No sign of trouble as she set the overflowing basket to one side.

Feeling absurdly relieved, Liana lifted the shawl covering the babes, a shawl that doubled as both sling and blanket.

And discovered that she had somehow managed to lose a babe.

Belani stared up at her, blue eyes wide in wonder. She turned her tiny head toward the empty space where her brother had lain. Her tiny face crumpled, and she started to cry.

Liana watched her sobbing daughter, unable to believe Reneth was gone.

Yes, she had worried—that the twins would wake while she worked, that they might cry themselves sick or kick off the blanket and get burned in the sun . . .

She never imagined one would *disappear*.

"No, no, no, nonono!" Liana frantically shook the shawl, but no babe tumbled free. She floundered through the tall grasses, frantically parting the tallest sections and peering at the ground as though she were searching for fleas instead of a babe as her sense of foreboding threatened to explode into mindless panic.

A critter likely got 'im while ye had yer back turned.

Any attempt to think fled as the notion rapidly ballooned into a conviction that took over her mind. She thrashed through the grasses, filled with dread at what she might find. If a critter had dragged her babe off, there would be traces. Drag marks or spots of blood.

Her motions became more and more erratic as the world blurred around her. Her stomach churned, her heart squeezed in a painful knot, and she couldn't seem to catch her breath.

Liana kicked a particularly stubborn clump of grass, welcoming the pain that shot through her toes. She deserved the pain, didn't she? Good mothers didn't lose their babes.

Then again, good mothers didn't leave their babes untended while she wandered around picking flowers.

The aroma of torn grass filled the air, sending her into a fit of uncontrollable sneezing. Lianna fell to her knees, caught between a sneeze and a sob. She drew a deep breath, attempting to bring the world back into focus.

And failing.

Beyond the impossible images of Reneth crawling or waddling away, beyond the horrifying thought that something had carried him off, lay a sense of utter and complete terror.

Had the Tedrels found Liana at last? Had Grunt— the man who'd abused her and fathered the twins— taken the babe in retribution?

"No." Liana swallowed against the terror threatening to choke her. Grunt was dead, killed in the Tedrel wars. She couldn't give into the fear again. Couldn't let the monster win.

Thoughts of Grunt triggered memories she'd thought locked away. His greedy, pig-eyed stare as he watched her moving about the camp—hauling water, washing his dishes, scrubbing his clothes . . . The predatory grin on his scarred face as his enormous fists struck her—

Something brushed against the back of Liana's head,

startling her out of the memories. A black shadow slid along the ground and a raven croaked somewhere close by.

"Grunt ain't here. Grunt ain't here," she reminded herself, repeating the mantra several times—

Belani wailed. The heart-rending sound tore the air, slicing through the dread permeating Liana's soul.

He's back!

"No!" Liana screamed. She shoved to her feet and stumbled blindly toward Belani, tripping on the trampled grasses, certain she was once again too late. She fixed a glare at the spot where she'd left Belani, expecting to see someone running off with her child.

Except for the bees and butterflies flitting like dust motes in the sun, the meadow was empty.

Liana staggered to a stop, heart freezing in her throat.

The meadow was empty.

She couldn't breathe. Couldn't move.

Couldn't find her daughter.

The raven croaked somewhere behind her, and she spun around, gulping air as she scoured the meadow, seeking signs of her daughter, besieged by the emotions buffeting her mind—

There.

Relief washed the world in a blanket of darkness as her knees threatened to buckle. There was no time for relief. No time for weakness.

She forced her feet to move. To carry her back to Belani's side.

She needed help—they needed help.

She had to find her son.

Feeling as though her feet were mired in mud, Liana forced her way back to Belani. Blinking back tears, she scooped the babe, reduced to sobs and hiccups, into her arms and took off at a jog, prompting more cries from her daughter. She should slow down and reassure

Belani, should tell her daughter everything would be all right.

But it wouldn't be all right.

Nothing would be right.

Not until she found her son.

"We got ta get help," she whispered, clutching Belani to her breast as she ran. The babe heaved a broken sob, the sound echoing the pain in Liana's heart.

Even the softest sound can tear at a person's soul.

Liana couldn't remember who had whispered those words in her ear. Her mother—a woman she scarcely remembered—most likely. She hadn't really understood the words.

Until now.

The entire world felt as if the sun had slipped behind a veil by the time Liana reached the cottage. She stumbled inside, her panic spilling like water over a fall.

"Taken he is," she gasped to whoever happened to be in the room. "Help to find him we need."

It took a moment for her eyes to adjust, the room as dark as her mood. She drew in deep breaths, struggling to slow her breathing and her heart, and stared down at Belani who stared back, tiny blue eyes accusing.

"We'll find him," she promised, though she had no idea how to fulfill that promise. A foreigner in a strange land, without coin, without friends—

"Who is taken?" A chair scraped on the wood floor. A moment later, Belani was lifted from Liana's arms.

She immediately snatched her daughter back, clasping the babe to her breast as if Liana could pull Belani back into her body, could keep her safe. Her heart threatened to burst, and she couldn't swallow for the dryness in her mouth. Even though she knew there was only one person in the room who would so blatantly take her child, her mind was filled with that moment of panic when she'd discovered her son missing—

"Take a deep breath and tell me what happened."

Liana squinted, her eyes confirming what she already knew. The speaker was Danelle, the woman who had taken Liana into her home. Stocky, with streaks of gray in her dark hair, the woman reminded Liana of granite cliffs. No matter how hard the rain fell or the wind blew, Danelle refused to budge—or panic.

"Reneth." Words tumbled from Liana's mouth like wild water over rocks. She realized halfway through her explanation that she was speaking Karse and switched to Valdemaran, which only made the task more confusing. She continued talking until she felt gutted and drained.

"Stef," Danelle told one of the boys standing nearby. "Go fetch the Watchman."

The boy disappeared out the back door.

Danelle reached out her arms, and Liana reluctantly set Belani into them. The woman settled herself at a plank table set near the back wall of the main room. Belani started to cry, and Danelle hushed her, efficiently rocking the babe, holding her in one arm while she straightened a pile of wicks sitting to one side, ready to be made into candles.

"When the Watchman comes—"

Liana wasn't waiting. Belani was safe with Danelle. Now it was time to go find her son.

"Tell them you will, please. Seeking the Herald I am," Liana said. She turned and headed toward the front door.

"Sit. The Watchman will need to talk to you." The woman's words were a command, not a request.

Commands were always to be obeyed. Always. That lesson had been beaten into Liana, body and soul. Her footsteps faltered, dragging to a stop as surely as if she'd become mired in stone. She glanced over her shoulder at Danelle, sitting so calmly at her table, and gnawed on her thumbnail.

"The Watchman will find your little 'un," Danelle said, shifting Belani to her other shoulder.

"Talk ta Herald Reneth is what I'm needing," Liana said. The Herald and his Companion Bolan had rescued Liana from the Tedrels. They would know what to do. She frowned as the coppery taste of blood coated her tongue. She'd nibbled her thumbnail down to the quick again.

"Tell the Watchman your story." Danelle nodded at a shadow darkening the open door.

"Not a story," Liana grumbled as she stepped forward to greet the newcomers.

Two men wearing the uniforms of the Haven Watch strolled into the room. Liana's steps slowed. One of the men was old enough to show gray at his temples and was smaller than the other man. The way the smaller man chewed on the ends of his mustache reminded her of a nervous weasel. The younger man's head nearly brushed the ceiling. His square head and burly shoulders put her in mind of the monster she had fled little more than two months ago.

"This here's Liana," Danelle said as the two men stopped before the stone hearth opposite the table, ignoring the stools and rocking chair. "One of her little 'uns has gone missing."

The air of authority surrounding the men brought a chill of fear to Liana's belly. She pulled herself up straight and looked the smaller Watchman in the eye even though her insides quivered like spoiled milk. She kept her gaze from the bigger man and worked hard to assure her words were clear, though she stumbled now and then when she couldn't recall a Valdemaran term.

Something kindled in the Watchman's eyes as she

spoke. Anger—the realization shot through Liana like an iron spear. He was angry with her.

He isn't going to help me, she thought. But why? Because she was from Karse? Because she was young—

Danelle must have shared her concern. When Liana finished speaking, the woman slapped her hand on the table and glared at the Watchmen.

"I told her you'd find her little 'un. You get yourselves out there now and prove me right."

A loud thud sounded from the kitchen and caught everyone's attention.

"What now?" Danelle rose to her feet, handed Belani back to Liana, and stomped into the kitchen.

"The Watch has been alerted, and I've sent a runner to the Heralds," the older Watchman said. "A Herald is on his way."

Everything was taking too long. She should just leave. Start the search where she'd left off now that Belani was safe.

Years of struggling against authority, being beaten when she'd tried to rebel, was the only thing preventing her from dashing out the door.

Liana bit her lip, wanting to scream her frustration into those complacent faces.

Only they weren't complacent. Not really. Both men's faces were lined with concern.

Besides, screaming was another thing that brought on the beatings.

So she stayed quiet, restlessly shifting from one foot to the other, her insides threatening to leap out of her throat.

"You'd best feed that little 'un afore you get yourself gone. It appears our milk supply is greatly diminished." Danelle called.

Liana ground her teeth until they hurt. The itch to be moving, to be doing something, drove her toward the bathing room just off the kitchen. Once in the bathing room, she laid Belani on a small table near the metal tub, removed the soiled diaper, and gently sponged the babe's tiny body, no longer feeling as clumsy and inept as she had following the twins' birth. She wrapped the babe in clean swaddling and stood, putting Belani to her breast. Eager lips went to suckling as Liana headed into the kitchen.

She found Danelle mopping up what looked like a pond of spilled milk, a boy barely out of diapers standing next to an overturned milk can, guilt plastered on his young face. The aroma of simmering stew started Liana's stomach roiling. If she stayed here smelling that stew, she'd be sick. She didn't need to eat; she needed to find her son.

"Finding the Herald I am when done this one is." Liana's broken Valdemaran was made worse by the panic threatening to sweep her into despair.

She turned away before Danelle could protest.

Bolan and his Herald had promised help if she should ever need it.

All she had to do was find them.

Liana didn't know whether or not to feel relieved when a Herald showed up at the door just as Belani finished nursing. She studied him from her perch in the doorway between the main room and the kitchen.

The Herald wasn't Reneth, but all Heralds were supposed to help, weren't they?

The Watchmen waved him in, and the three began conversing in low tones. She straightened her shoulders and stepped into the room, fighting the urge to run.

Conversation stopped, filling the room with awkward silence. Liana swallowed, trying to moisten her suddenly dry mouth. Then she raised her chin and took a deep breath. Beating or not, she had to find her boy.

"My son you are finding?" she demanded.

The Herald gave her a nod, his short blond hair glistening in the firelight. "You are the mother of the missing boy?" he asked in almost flawless Karsite.

He must have noted her bewilderment. "Our Weaponsmaster is from Karse. He taught me your language, all the while threatening to beat me to a pulp if I didn't learn it perfectly." The Herald's blue eyes twinkled, then grew serious. "I am Herald Nikko."

"We have ta go find him," Liana said to Nikko. "Now."

A vacant look crossed Herald Nikko's face, then he nodded. "Rufina, my Companion, agrees."

"A'course she agrees!" Liana said with a scowl. "Companions be smart where babes is concerned."

Danelle stalked into the room and held out bundle of dry diapers. "Just in case."

Liana handed Belani to the woman, nodded her thanks, and awkwardly tucked the diapers into her waistband. "An eye on the little one, will ye keep?"

"Of course." Danelle glared at the Herald, then the Watchmen. "Take care of her. Take care of them all."

Liana pressed a hand against the reassuring presence of the knife at her waist and headed out the door.

Once outside, she led the way back toward the meadow. There had to be something there, a clue of some sort she had missed. She would not miss it this time.

A shadow moved into the street behind them. Liana's heart leaped into her throat, then settled back where it belonged when she recognized Jedren.

"I'm comin'," Jedren, the oldest of six Tedrel orphans who'd been placed with Danelle, said. The boy looked like he'd been stuck on the rack and stretched until the top of his head almost reached Liana's shoulder. Skinny as a stork, he moved like a smaller bird, darting here and dashing there. His carrot-red hair was as stubborn as Liana's, refusing to be tamed, and the number of freckles on his face matched his curiosity—that boy was curious about everything.

The smaller Watchman shook his head. "We don't need—"

Jedren held up his hand. "Heard from Luka, who heard from Cliffer, who heard from someone so high up the ranks no one down here knows 'is name, that more'n one babe's gone missin'."

More'n one?

Looks like Haven ain't as grand as folks claim. Liana felt a wave of guilt at the thought.

Herald Nikko's face grew dark. He drew the Watchmen to one side and spoke to them in a low voice.

Why weren't they moving? Why were they staying so calm? Wasn't anyone worried about the babes? This news should make them move faster, not stop and chat.

Liana bit her thumbnail for a moment, then turned and walked away. She kept her steps quiet so she didn't attract the men's attention, not because she didn't want their help but because she was afraid they might try to stop her.

And no one was going to stop her.

Panic had turned to determination, a feeling she could handle. In the Tedrel camp she had been determined to survive.

Now she was just as determined to find her son.

Jedren stalked beside her, his freckled face wrinkled in a dark scowl.

"Why?" she asked him, keeping her voice low and their conversation in Karse.

"Why what?"

"Why are you coming with me? He is not your child."

"They're not just taking your babe. Whoever is doing this is taking others. Why wouldn't I want to help put a stop to something like that?" He looked away, seeming uncomfortable. "'Sides, I like baby Reneth. He deserves to be safe. All the babes deserve to be safe."

He didn't need to add, "Just as the rest of us are now safe."

Safe.

Jedren had been rescued by the Heralds just as she had been. Did he actually feel safe?

Liana picked up her pace. She thought she'd felt safe, but today showed her just how shallow that feeling had been. Constant beatings while enslaved by the Tedrel mercenaries and other . . . abuses . . . had drained her of the ability to believe in anything, leaving behind only the husk of a girl who had once dared to dream.

Then a raven had led her to a Companion and his Herald. They had saved her life and those of her twins.

But what did she really know of these people?

A thought seized her mind in vicious jaws, refusing to let go. She stared at Jedren in horror. "What if this Midsummer Eve festivaling is jes' like our Feast 'o the Children?" she whispered. "What if they took little Reneth 'cause 'e got some kind 'o magic?"

Do they burn the magic ones here?

Liana squeezed her eyes tight against the vision of babes lying alone in a shed, waiting for someone to light them up.

"Cain't be the magic," Jedren whispered back. "They'd've taken Celia that were so. She been healing since we got 'ere. Danelle said they'd send Celia to Healers' Collegium once she's old 'nuf. 'Sides, Luka said the babes was taken from folks down here. 'Spawn 'o the rabble,' he called 'em, even though he lives right next door."

Liana's panic gave way to growing anger and she picked up the pace again. Spawn 'o the rabble, indeed!

"Babes're babes, no matter the loins they spring from." Her voice sounded more like a low growl than a whisper, but she kept her voice down. "That's what Bolan says, and Herald Reneth agrees."

She hadn't agreed with them, not at first.

Her twins had been sired by a man so violent, so monstrous, she had been certain the babe growing in her womb would be born a two-headed monster.

But Bolan had shown her otherwise, allowing her to feel the babe's innocent spark.

And the other spark—just as innocent—growing alongside the first.

Jedren's scowl deepened, wrinkling his nose so the freckles sat side by side, forming a solid mask beneath his eyes. "I been wondering—why'd only the boy get taken?"

He studied her curiously as another nightmare vision plunged her into darkness—the Tedrel mercenaries had forced young boys into "Boy's Bands" to train them up "proper." She'd witnessed firsthand the misery those boys were put through—near starvation, beatings, forced to steal, and punished if they were caught.

Some died from wounds suffered during training with real blades; others died from broken spirits.

Those who made it through training became monsters.

Just like Grunt.

"Do ye know if the folks what lives in Haven take boys fer . . ." She had to force the next words out. "Fer trainin'?"

Jedren's face went so pale she was afraid he'd keel over. "Never thought on that one," he said with a gulp. "Some of us orphans got took fer trainin' soon as we got 'ere—"

"The training here in Haven is nothing like the so-called training in the Tedrel camps."

Liana's heart jumped back into her throat. She spun on her heel, hand going to the knife in her waistband. Jedrel spun with her, his face as startled as hers.

Herald Nikko stopped, hands in the air as if trying to convince them he was harmless. "My apologies. I did not intend to startle you."

At least the Herald remembered to speak in Karsite. Liana dropped her hands and resumed walking, picking up the pace. "Took you long enough."

The Herald nodded. "I needed to confirm the boy's statement. There are, indeed, other babes that have gone missing. Some last evening, some—like your babe—only this morning. The two Watchmen say the entire Watch is befuddled. The Heralds have been notified and—"

The sound of feathers slicing through the air halted Liana midstep. She held up a hand to quiet the Herald and scanned the skyline as a raven croaked close by.

Afternoon sun glinted off tiles as she scanned the nearby rooftops and doorways, finally spotting the feathered culprit perched atop a stone lintel.

"What be ye after?" she asked the raven, unable to keep the frustration from her voice. Not frustration at the raven—at the delay.

For as long as she could remember, animals had been Liana's true friends. She held a memory of her younger self, laughing and playing with only the forest animals as her friends. She never got lost. Never was scared.

A raven had led her to Bolan and helped her escape the Tedrels—

She almost choked at the sight of something dangling from the raven's beak. Afraid to breathe lest the object turn out to be something other than what she suspected, Liana held out her arm.

The raven dropped from the lintel, swooping onto her arm.

Then it dropped a blue bootie into her other hand.

Liana turned the bootie—Reneth's bootie—over in her hand.

"What is that?" Herald Nikko asked.

"Is that—" Jedren started.

The raven launched into the air with a cry that sounded more like someone dragging a sword over rough stone than something uttered by a bird. Liana hurried after the bird, forsaking all thoughts except one.

The raven had found her son.

Black wings took to the sky, and Liana took off at a run, not looking back to see if either Jedren or the Herald followed. The raven led her past houses and down twisting roads, around corners and through streets that stank of piss and rotting food, the streets shrinking in on themselves until she found herself in a dark alley.

Liana tried to calm her racing heart and catch her breath. The Herald stopped close behind her, Jedren not far behind.

"What is it?" Herald Nikko asked. Liana took absurd pleasure in hearing the Herald was slightly out of breath.

She held up the blue bootie. "Reneth's."

"You believe the raven's found the babe, then?"

The answer died on her lips. Had Reneth been found? Or was the bootie simply a clue?

A shush of wings and the raven landed on her right arm. Liana's belly clenched as a sense of danger flooded through her. She froze at the sound of boots on stone.

Not the steps of a drunkard stumbling home or—

Herald Nikko's hand fell on her shoulder and gently guided her back several steps into a shadowed doorway.

She didn't want to hide in a doorway. She wanted—no, needed—to follow that clue. Find where the bootie had come from.

Get her son back.

"We need to see who comes and where they go," the Herald whispered. "Then we can form a plan."

He was right. She knew he was right. But little Reneth was out there somewhere . . . The yearning to hold her son grew so strong, Liana's legs threatened to dump her on the ground. She sank to her heels, raven shifting restlessly on her arm, and blinked hard against the tears threatening to spill from her eyes.

The sound of footsteps resolved into two distinct sounds—one much heavier than the other.

Liana almost leaped out of her skin as two men entered the alley. One of the men wore an ugly, scarred face all too familiar to her.

Grunt.

Talons tightened on her arm as Liana willed herself not to move. She bit her lip, choking back the scream demanding to be released. The coppery taste of blood added to the roiling mess of fear, loathing, and despair churning in her belly. She drew in a shaky breath.

It's only a nightmare. Not real. Can't be real—

Liana didn't recognize the man following the Tedrel mercenary. The man put a hand on Grunt's arm and mumbled something she couldn't hear.

Grunt seized the other man by the tunic and slammed him against the wall.

"What d'ya mean ya only got one?"

"I were feared she'd see me, see. And the babes were fussing somethin' fierce."

Grunt spat in disgust and stomped to the end of the alley, stopping in front of a battered door. She leaned forward in time to see light spread across the alley as a door opened—

And the sharp cries of babies echoed off the walls.

The color drained from Liana's face as the door closed, leaving the alley empty. She sprang to her feet, overcome by the need to rush in and snatch her son from Grunt's monstrous grip, a grip she knew all too well.

The raven launched itself awkwardly from her arm, scolding her softly as it rose to the rooftop across the alley. Before she could take a step, Herald Nikko took hold of her arm.

"It's the ogre—the monster what kept me a slave," she hissed, baring her teeth as if to bite the hand that kept her from going to her son.

"The mercenary?" The Herald's face went dark. "One of the Tedrels?"

Liana glared at him. "The very same."

The cries she'd heard when the door opened echoed in her mind. With Grunt in charge—if the monster . . . the ogre . . . was in charge—the babes would have been fed only enough to keep them alive. No one in Grunt's company would care if the babes were changed or soothed.

Anger burned deep in her belly. She tried to tug her arm free of the Herald's grip, but Nikko refused to let her go. His face had the distant look that meant he was communicating with his Companion.

They needed to do something, though Liana didn't know whether to charge in or toss up what little remained in her stomach from breakfast.

"Hold tight a moment," the Herald said. "Rufina?"

The back of the alley filled with a graceful white figure that glowed in the sunlight. Liana caught her breath.

"Is that a—" Jedren started.

"My Companion." The Herald nodded. "I'll introduce you later."

His face went distant again, then he blinked. "Rufina says there's a door that opens on the next alley over. She set someone to watch both that alley and door and summoned more help."

Liana started toward the door, but the Herald shook his head.

"You two stay here. Give a shout if anyone slips out."

He strode down the alley to the door, his step light though purposeful. He rapped twice, waited a moment, and rapped again.

The door opened a crack.

The Herald lashed out with his foot, smashing the door back on its hinge. Someone shouted. A hand showed where the door had been. Herald Nikko blocked the hand with his arm and disappeared inside. Voices raised in angry protest as something crashed to the floor.

Liana raced down the alley, Jedren close on her heels. She slipped through the splinters of jagged wood that used to be a door. The room inside was lit with lanterns on every wall.

There was no one in sight. The Herald had disappeared through another door and the sounds of fighting came from a room deeper within the building.

Liana tore through the room, peering into alcoves and cupboards, frantically searching for her son.

She almost missed him.

He'd been tucked into a pile of blankets in one of the alcoves. She pulled him free, careful to protect his head and neck.

"Reneth sweet," Liana cooed. "It's all right now. Mum's here."

Her son didn't move.

She shook the babe, gently at first, growing more and more frantic when he didn't respond. "Reneth?"

Forcing herself not to panic, she laid her cheek to his and almost sobbed in relief at the warmth against her skin—

A rough hand grabbed the back of her neck in an all-too familiar grip.

"There ya are, ya little whore!"

Liana released her grip on Reneth before she was lifted off the floor. Agony lit the muscles of her neck and shoulders on fire ...

And suddenly she was back in the Tedrel camp ...

Fear struck her so forcefully, she momentarily lost control of her body. Her legs and arms dangled as uselessly as a puppet without strings. Any moment, she might wet herself as thoroughly as her babes—

"Let her be!" Jedren's young voice—laced with anger and fear—ripped through the air.

There was a sound of a scuffle and the grip on Liana's neck was gone. She caught herself on one knee as she tumbled to the ground, bruising her elbow when she stopped her momentum just short of rolling into Reneth.

Out of the corner of her eye she saw Jedren fly through the air, slam against the far wall, and crumple to the floor.

Grunt loomed over her, his pig-eyes gleaming. A scar glistened on his forehead and his leering grin exposed a gap in his teeth that hadn't been there before. "Ya think it was bad before? Now yer gonna find out just what runnin' away gets ya."

There was a time when those words would have turned her into a puddle of wet mush, unable to protest, unable to move. If he had stopped there. If he had let those words be his only threat, she would have been his again. Not from any desire to please him. Because she had known no other way.

"Then," Grunt continued, "I'm takin' my son and teachin' him what it means ta be a real man." His cracked lips widened into the evil grimace that still haunted her nightmares. "And I'm findin' my daughter and teachin' her what it means—"

"No!" Liana screamed and launched herself at his face, fingers curled like claws. Despite the difference in heights, she managed to leap high enough to sink the nails of her left hand into his cheek.

Grunt roared and grabbed her by the throat, a move Liana had expected. He liked to choke her nearly unconscious, then claimed he'd "given her back her life" before having his way with her.

He would never have his way with her again.

He would NEVER have his way with her children.

She fumbled her knife clear from her waistband. Stars twinkled at the edges of her vision and she sucked air into her lungs through the crushing grip on her throat. She had to delay the darkness she knew would come next. She squirmed as if trying to wriggle out of his grip.

The monster liked it when she struggled. Liked to gloat over his so-called superior strength.

Grunt pulled her closer, eyes glinting at her pain—

Lightning flashed behind her eyes as Liana swung the knife up—and plunged the blade through the monster's eye.

Somewhere in the far distance Liana thought she heard a horse scream, then she felt herself falling . . . falling . . . into a bottomless pit of darkness.

A baby's cry penetrated the darkness, yanking her back into a world filled with confusion. She coughed, the searing pain racking her throat echoed in her left arm and hip. She blinked—

And found herself lying on her side, staring into Grunt's unblinking eye.

It took a moment before she recognized the knife protruding from his other eye.

Liana rolled to her knees, scuttling away like a frightened bug.

And backed into a pair of legs.

Stifling a scream, she lunged forward and yanked the blade from Grunt's eye. Growling, she whipped around, blade dripping, and faced her new opponent.

Herald Nikko slowly lifted his hands. "No need for that, m'lady. The evildoers have all been—" He glanced at Grunt's still form, "disposed of. Your son is safe."

Liana stared at the Herald, struggling to remember just who he was. Where she was.

Memory swept over her, driving her back to her knees. She dropped the knife and scanned the room until she located a pile of blankets. A sob stuck in her throat as she crawled to the blankets and lifted Reneth's limp body in her arms. Swallowing a scream, she rocked back and forth on her knees, stroking the tiny cheek, willing his eyes to open.

"He should be fine." The Herald kept his voice low and quiet, the tone one might use to calm a frantic horse. "Rufina says the babes have been drugged, but only enough to help them sleep."

Drugged. Not hurt.

Liana drew in a deep breath, battling the urge to cough. She gently laid her son back on the blankets and pulled the bundle of diapers from her waistband. Her nose confirmed her suspicions—he hadn't been changed.

"I'll check the others," Jedren said.

"Rufina's called for assistance," Herald Nikko said. "A wise idea, considering you just saved twenty infants."

"Twenty?" Liana stared at the Herald. "How—"

Herald Nikko raised his hands. "Seems the Tedrels' goal was to 'collect' enough babes to pay for the children 'stolen' by Valdemar."

Liana shuddered. How long had Grunt been in Haven watching her, plotting how to snatch the twins?

"He ain't gonna bother ye nor the twins again," Jedren said. "Ye done made certain 'o that."

Liana nodded.

Then she threw up, turning her head just in time to avoid splattering the babe.

:Good,: a voice said in her head. *:I was hoping you'd react that way.:*

The only other time she'd had a voice in her head had been in the Waystation with Bolan.

But Bolan wasn't here—

:Rufina?:

Why was the Companion speaking to her?

:Not Rufina. A friend. Perhaps we'll meet some day. Just remember—your ogre was indeed a monster. Taking a life should never be easy or pleasurable. Sometimes it is necessary, but it should always make you feel just the way you feel right now. Sick.:

:Who are—?:

:I told you. A friend. Now take care of your son. He needs you.:

And the voice was gone. She could feel the emptiness left behind, a sudden loss that felt as though something had been torn from her.

Reneth started to cry, chasing away the sense of loss and emptiness. Liana gathered her son close, relieved to hear him take a deep breath and bellow his protest at being held so tightly.

"Ye be safe now," she assured him. "Yer sister's safe. We all be safe."

Around her she became aware of other babes waking, some sniffling, some sobbing, some erupting in loud screams.

"Hush now. You're going home," someone said to one of the babes.

"Going home," Liana whispered. She thought of Danelle and the other children. Of Belani—waiting to be fed.

And for the first time since escaping the Tedrel camp, she knew those words were true.

Holiday Reunions

Dylan Birtolo

The central bonfire in the small village had just begun. The flames licked at the large logs, charring the outside as the heat grew. By nightfall, it would be an intense blaze causing any onlooker to squint if they looked at its center. Eventually the woodsmoke would overpower the musty scent of an oncoming storm. But every raging inferno starts as a few sparks and a lick of flame.

Paxia held that lesson close to heart as she thought of the path laid out before her. This was her spark, her small tendrils producing smoke to herald the forthcoming cleansing.

The nagging sensation at the back of her mind heightened and she squeezed her eyes shut against the pressure. She could see them now, the Vrondi watching her. Pulling her cloak tight around her did nothing to dull their attention.

More had gathered since she approached the village, a clear indicator of a Herald. They would continue to gather. She wondered how long she had before she forgot how to use her Mage Gift. According to one of her tutors, it was inevitable. No one could remain within the boundaries of Valdemar and retain their magic.

Even if she forgot her magic, she would never forget her hatred for the Companions and what they did to her.

Dropping deeper into the woods, Paxia hiked back to her band of followers. They came from all over, acquired during her travels. Warriors from Karse, bandits from Rethwellan, and even a couple of mercenaries from Taymyrr. They followed her because they believed in her cause and her power.

Paxia picked up the large warhammer resting against a thick trunk and slammed its head into the earth. Few men could heft her hammer, let alone use it well, but years spent in front of a forge gave her the strength to wield the weapon. She had created it herself as she'd earned her keep crafting all manner of weapons and armor in her travels. It was a far cry from her previous requests for horseshoes and shovels, but it was work she plunged into with an intense fervor.

The men and women gathered in front of her were dressed in traveling clothes with small patches of hardened leather and the occasional metal plate. Speed and stamina were far more critical when operating in enemy territory. They all gave her their complete attention, and she took the time to make eye contact with each one before speaking.

"Tonight it begins. I promised you we would strike at Valdemar. Our target lies just beyond the edge of the tree line. We will start small, but these ripples will start a wave."

She wasn't much for speeches, but even that tidbit was enough to whet the appetites of her company. She saw more than a few grins and hands tightening on weapons in anticipation as they leaned forward. If the enemy presented itself right now, she doubted she could hold them back.

"When do we sack the village?" Brathe asked, one

of the more bloodthirsty members. His grin managed to be more unsettling than his battle cry.

"We don't," Paxia said. "We have a single target. A Herald."

The statement caused several murmurs. More than one person stepped back, and a few weapons lowered. When she passed her gaze over her men and women, about a third refused to meet her eyes. She expected as much.

She reached for the current of magic underneath her, seeking reassurance with its presence. Even that small act caused the stares to bore into the back of her skull with renewed intensity. She snarled as her fingers tightened around the haft of her weapon. Picking it up, she slammed it into the tree beside her hard enough to make the bark crack.

"You all knew this was our path. You knew the Heralds were our target. They're the lifeblood of Valdemar, its spirit. Taking them out will make the whole structure fall. They and their Companions have forced their will over others for too long!"

She had their attention, but they still looked hesitant. Only the most aggressive of her company seemed ready to follow her. The others held back, shoulders hunched, feet turned away. She recognized the stance, the fear.

Horns sounded from the village, indicating the Sovvan hunt had begun. Soon the most capable would leave the village in an attempt to bring back prey worthy of the great feast. Each village had their own traditions, but she grew up here. She had been to the Sovvan Feast in this town as a teenager.

If her plan was to work, she needed to act now, and she couldn't do it alone. They needed to fear her more than they feared the Herald.

Tapping into the current of magic, she threw out her

hand. Lightning answered her call, arcing down from the storm clouds overhead to strike a tree a stone's throw away from the gathering.

The flash of light made them jump even before the crack of thunder echoed through the forest. People gripped their weapons, some in shaking hands, but she didn't care. They knew the plan and would do their part. All that mattered was getting the Herald. Any damage done to the morale of her company could be dealt with later.

As she turned away to take her position, she swung at one of the Vrondi lurking near the edge of her vision. Her burst of magic brought a small swarm of them down on her, but they danced away from her blow. They continued to stare, making her almost wish they spoke, even if it meant a maddening jumble of voices in her head.

Brathe stepped up next to her. She kept him close to keep an eye on him and make sure he didn't get too enthusiastic. Over the months of their partnership, their proximity resulted in a measure of respect and turned him into something of a confidant. Praxia trusted his judgment, if not his restraint.

As they crouched on the hunting trail, Brathe tugged at his dark beard. His other hand remained on his blade, and he was too professional to draw his eyes away from the trail, but Praxia could almost hear his mind churning.

"Out with it," she snapped.

"You didn't need to do that," he said, his voice little more than a whisper. "They woulda come, just a bit nervous since it's a Herald and all. Probably thought we were starting smaller."

"There's no point. The Heralds are the target, and just the Heralds. If I had my way, no one else would get hurt."

"And what if someone stands between you and this Herald?"

Paxia didn't hesitate. "Then we cut them down."

That brought a grin to Brathe's face, and he rolled his neck from one side to the other. Despite her purpose in being here, Paxia meant what she said. She didn't want harm to come to the innocent townsfolk, some of whom she might recognize. What had happened to her wasn't their fault. They didn't put her under constant watch, make her ostracized and an outsider, all the while pretending she didn't exist. They didn't knowingly make everyone forget what she could do and make her question her own sanity.

What did the Companions make her forget?

Paxia drew in a deep breath and growled as she exhaled through her nose. Her magic. They forced her to forget about her magic. And now it was happening again. For the last couple of years, that had been her identity, and now it was being wiped clean. The atrocities committed by the Companions continued.

She recited the mantras taught to her by her first tutor, moving her lips without making a sound as she went over the words, hoping to use them to reinforce her mind. It reminded her of being on a splintering raft and snatching at pieces, hoping it stayed together until her journey finished.

Hooves pounding against the dirt forced her attention back to her surroundings. She crouched down, using the trees and foliage to hide as the hunting party rode past. As the group of eight reached the next bend on the hunting trail, they pulled up short in a wild collection of whinnies and curses as the rest of Paxia's crew barred their passage. Paxia stepped out into the middle of the trail behind the hunters, Brathe at her side. The pair formed a wall across the road leading home, a barrier made all that much more formidable since there were only two of them.

The villagers on horseback carried bows with arrows

held against the grip. Several of them dropped their weapons as they wrestled with their mounts. When the chaos settled, they noticed the ring of bandits with crossbows and bows of their own. A few of them twirled their mounts around, looking for any sign of escape or weakness in the ambush.

"Happy Sovvan-night to you," Paxia spoke, calling their attention. "Those of you still holding onto your arms, drop them now. We have no interest in harming you."

They exchanged a few glances, but it didn't take longer than the space of a few breaths for them to comply. Once they were disarmed, Paxia continued.

"We came for the Herald." Paxia would have been more delicate with her language, but she had no time for such pleasantries. Each second she lingered, her skin continued to crawl.

"What do you want with the Herald?" one of the younger men challenged.

She walked over to the man, carrying her hammer at her side in one hand. The hunter nudged his horse forward, taking the position of leader with the recklessness of untested youth. He even went so far as to pull his shoulders back as she stood at his knee. She looked up at him, waiting for him to speak. When he opened his mouth, she reached up, grabbing his jerkin and yanking him out of the saddle. She threw him into the ground with enough force to drive the air from his lungs and cause his horse to scamper sideways. Paxia picked up her hammer and dropped the weight of it on his chest. His entire body jerked from the impact, but the weight of the weapon kept his torso pinned.

He reached up to the hammer, so she kicked his arm away and pushed down on the haft. When he continued to squirm, she lifted it off his chest and dropped it back down. The thud of it made the other villagers wince, but she made sure not to crack his chest with the blow. She hoped the demonstration would be sufficient. She didn't want to do any lasting harm, but this youngster could probably use a lesson in humility.

"Anyone else want to question me?"

Only the hoot of an owl answered her.

"Get off your horses and go stand by that tree," she gestured to where Lark stood with a bundle of rope.

Paxia stepped off the young man, lifting her weapon so he could get up. One of the other village hunters came over to help him up. He yanked a dagger from his belt and lunged at Paxia. She lifted a hand between them, fingers splayed, and his weapon struck an unseen barrier before deflecting to the side. His eyes widened and he dropped the dagger into the dirt before shuffling back to his companions. None offered any more resistance as they went to Lark and allowed her to restrain them.

By then, Paxia, Brathe, and six others mounted the horses, leaving a small number of their company behind to stand watch. Not that it would be necessary. The villagers still stared at Paxia with wide eyes and held their breath if she so much as glanced in their direction. They might not understand what happened, but they knew when they were outmatched.

The group rode back to the village on the stolen horses, taking the trail the original hunting party had followed. Before it came into sight, Paxia caught the scent of woodsmoke. The bonfire had to be well on its way. She had fond memories of Sovvan-night, but now the wariness of the dark would be given flesh. With her cloak flapping wild behind her as she rode, she imagined she could pass for one of the spirits the villagers feared.

As they approached the village, she heard the music and saw the silhouettes of people moving around the bonfire, preparing for the feast. The people gave them no notice with the darkening skies. After all, they anticipated the return of their own hunting party.

Standing in the center of it, overseeing the entire ceremony, was the silhouette of a man and his horse. Even with the light behind them, there was no mistaking the Companion for an ordinary beast of burden. The animal had a magnificence in shape and form, standing with a pride and confidence not even the best warhorse could imitate.

Seeing the Companion made Paxia's lip curl, and she spurred her horse faster. The others followed suit, maintaining their formation as best they could as they ran toward the village. Despite their best efforts, they fell behind. It was as if the horse underneath her could sense Paxia's urgency and rage.

The Companion was the first to react to their charge. Its head came up and around, and Paxia felt the creature's stare even through the constant weight of the Vrondi. Paxia let the hammer drop a bit, sliding her hand to the bottom of the haft and holding it next to the horse's side. She might only get one opportunity.

She was still several strides away when the screams and shouts started. The people scattered, running away from the oncoming cavalry. The Herald rushed to his Companion, grabbing the saddle and jumping into it in a smooth, practiced motion.

And then Paxia was on him. She swung her hammer in a big sweeping arc as she charged past, aiming for the Companion. The animal dropped to the ground on its side, making her weapon clip its shoulder rather than crushing its neck. The Herald cried out as the Companion's full weight crushed the side of his leg, but the animal sprang up before he had a chance to fall out of the saddle. The Companion stumbled, blood trailing from its front shoulder, stark against the pristine white coat.

Paxia whirled around, fighting her mount to come back for another attack. In that pause she got a good look at the Herald. His head was shaved, and he was athletic without having the toned muscles of a fighter or laborer. He carried a Healer's pouch and brandished a thin blade in her direction.

"Adouin." Paxia shook her head. "I told you I'd come back when you banished me!"

She kicked the sides of her mount hard, making it jump forward. She had to reach down and grab the saddle, but still managed a hammer swipe. The Companion sidestepped, but she wasn't aiming for her. The head of her weapon slammed into Adouin's sword, ringing out as the two pieces of steel struck each other. He held on to his weapon, whipping it back around to keep the point on her, but winced as he rolled his shoulder.

By now the rest of her company rode into the square.

"Brathe!" she barked out as he turned toward the tavern.

His attention snapped back to her and the Herald.

"Right. You remember the command," he shouted at the others.

His reminder held them on course and they spread out to surround the center clearing. The Herald paused for a moment, eyes unfocusing as he listened to a voice no one else could hear.

"You didn't come for them," he whispered, looking around the group working their way around.

"Take him!" Paxia screamed.

The others rushed forward with as much order as one would expect from novice riders on mounts they never rode before. In comparison, the Companion and Herald moved as a coordinated team, slipping through the gaps and getting to the outside of the circle without so much as breaking a sweat. Once they were on the outside, they fled, taking off at a full sprint.

Growling at Brathe, Paxia charged after the Companion. Her mount heaved and panted, foaming around the bit as she continued to urge it forward. She didn't want to lose sight of the Herald. The Companion couldn't maintain this pace forever.

"This is madness!" Brathe shouted when he caught up to her, the wind whipping around them and drowning out most of his voice. "It'll be full dark soon, and we can't catch a bloody Companion!"

The pressure in Paxia's head mounted as hundreds of judging eyes weighed on her, measuring her failure. She lashed out with her hammer, smacking Brathe in the shoulder. The blow glanced off, but he twisted in the saddle and sucked in air through his teeth.

"We're not letting them get away! Not after the years they stole from me! The Companion's injured. She can't run long."

She glared at him, eyes wide and burning with fury. Brathe ducked his head and dropped back, forming up with the rest of the pursuers and not offering further challenge. He rubbed at his shoulder, wincing as he did so.

The road they followed seemed familiar, something about it itching at the back of Paxia's memory, but the invisible eyes buried it too far to recover. The unseen judges were always there, pressing down on her until all she wanted to do was scream. She couldn't remember a time before them, when they weren't around. The only thought piercing through the haze was that the Companions were to blame. They did this to her, and nothing mattered beyond getting her vengeance.

The sky darkened to the point where pushing the horses was dangerous, almost impossible, but still she rode on. As she crested the next hill, she saw a flickering blaze on the horizon. They traveled far enough to reach the next village, and the glow had to be their own Sovvan-night celebration. The Companion must've taken refuge there. It was the only trace of civilization around for hours, even at this pace.

She headed for the beacon, leaning forward until her chest touched the horse's neck. The heat radiating off it made Paxia sweat, but she remained in position. The animal panted and snorted with every flying step. It wouldn't last much longer, but it didn't need to, and soon it would all be worth it.

The glow might have originated from the bonfire, but it had spread to engulf a two-story building lining a city center that made her face scrunch in confusion. People formed a line to the river as best they could, ferrying buckets of water in a vain attempt to douse the blaze. A young man charged at the doorway, stumbling back as a fresh gout of flame blossomed forth.

The weight on her continued to press against her skull, letting her know her quarry was close.

A man ran up to her, forcing her to lift her hammer and prepare to strike. He held up his hands in a surrendering gesture and then pointed at the burning building behind him.

"Please, would you help? Someone's trapped inside!" He looked strong and healthy, and something about him was familiar, but his stubbled face didn't cut through her singular rage-induced focus.

"Have you seen a Herald ride through here? Answer me!"

"Paxia?" he whispered.

The use of her name made her pause. She squeezed her eyes shut as she tried to force her mind to obey. Flashes of memory came tumbling through. The forge . . . An eager assistant . . .

"Reynaud?"

"It is you! Please! Tessa's trapped inside the trading house."

The rest of her group pounded up behind her, stopping at the edge of the city center. The horses snorted and panted, exhausted from their sprint. Paxia smelled their sweaty stench heavy on the air.

The Companion had to be close. The pressure bearing down on her was proof of that. This was her best, and possibly only, chance.

But she remembered Tessa. The young girl who came to her forge and watched from the wall. The one who listened to her stories with wide eyes and a disarming smile.

The pounding in her head continued, making it difficult to sort through it all.

"Please. For Tessa!" Reynaud called out as he rushed back to the line and picked up a bucket to join in the line.

Paxia leaped off her mount, taking long strides to the front entrance of the trading house. Seeing her destination, the other members of her company hesitated, glancing at each other before settling on Brathe. Paxia lost sight of them as she stepped through the entryway, pushing back the flames with a force she didn't understand.

The heat still reached her, and she imagined she dropped into a cooling bath in a forge, complete with red-hot worked steel. A timber above cracked and dropped from the ceiling in a shower of orange sparks. Paxia lifted her hands, catching the beam and deflecting it to the side, the force of the blow dropping her to her knees even though her hands never touched the wood. Forcing herself to her feet, she passed deeper into the trading house.

The heat waves played with her vision, making shapes

waver and become indistinct. It did nothing to help her memory, which scrambled to sort through what she saw. Reaching up, she wiped her sleeve across her brow, but salty water still dripped into her eyes. Her cloak caught on something and she had to jerk it free, ripping the fabric around the clasp in her rush to remove it.

"Help!"

The shout came from farther inside the main room, punctuated with several coughs. Paxia used it as her guide, as the smoke killed any visibility. Flames licked at her skin, making it blister and filling the air with the acrid scent of burning hair.

When she saw a small figure crouched under a counter, Paxia reached out and grabbed the child's wrist. The girl wrapped her arms around the woman's waist, but the grip was weak, more like the arms were put in place than any attempt to hold on. Paxia ran toward the entrance, stumbling in her blindness.

She needed a path. Somehow she needed to see where to go, but flames and thick smoke choked off the air in every direction. Calling forth reserves she didn't understand, Paxia thrust her hand out and screamed at the flames. It was a shout of pure unbridled rage and anger, too raw to be given words.

The flame and smoke swirled and billowed out through the entrance, creating a path. Paxia glimpsed the outside world. She ran forward, holding Tessa tightly to keep the child pinned to her side.

When they broke out into the night, Paxia fell to the ground. She heaved and coughed, her lungs full of soot no matter how much she tried to expel it.

The townsfolk rushed forward, checking on Tessa. They moved to give the same courtesy to Paxia, but her companions held them at bay with their presence.

Brathe snatched a pail of water from one of the

townsfolk and handed it over to Paxia. She scooped up handfuls, swallowing the first few before dunking her entire face in the bucket. When she came up, her lungs still burned, but the heat faded from her face.

"You saved her. You came back and you saved her," Reynaud said.

He stepped forward, crouching down into a squat while he was still a few strides away. He looked up at Brathe, the bandit grinning as his fingers danced over the hilt of his blade. If Reynaud considered coming closer, he reconsidered.

Paxia took a few breaths, experimenting to see how deep she could breathe before the coughing resumed. She lifted an arm, and one of her companions helped her stand up. She turned away from Reynaud, walking toward her exhausted, stolen mount.

"Wait! Please, stay!" Reynaud stood up and reached out.

Brathe stepped into the man's path.

Paxia paused and twisted her head so she could address Reynaud without looking at the young man.

"You should forget about me."

"But, Paxia . . ."

Paxia turned and walked away. She squinted her eyes against the mounting pressure in her mind. She needed to get out of Valdemar. She didn't know why, but she knew it was the only thing that would help. The Companions would have to wait.

The villagers stood and watched as Paxia and her companions mounted, riding out of the village at an easy pace compared to their arrival. The weight of their eyes was meaningless compared to the other pressures Paxia experienced.

Brathe came up next to her. "Gave up the Herald for a girl? Don't seem like good business. Troops'll be pissed."

"It was the right call," Paxia snapped.

She would not be like them. She would not give up on others' lives because doing otherwise was inconvenient.

No matter how far she was willing to go, some prices were still too high to pay.

Cloudwalker
Michele Lang

Life is not about the calm, it is about the storm.

Sparrow found it hard to remember this essential truth, sometimes. Or, even, to accept it. After all, she was lucky enough to live with her family, her beloved heartmate, the Herald Cloudbrother, and their son, Thistle. Together, they had made their home in the beautiful oasis of K'Valdemar Vale, where storms appeared to be more of an illusion than a reality.

In the Vale, Sparrow could almost pretend that storms and sorrow had become a fable of distant legend, rather than an unavoidable aspect of life itself.

Almost.

But times like the Summer Gathering drew her out of her personal paradise and back into the larger world of Valdemar. And Sparrow knew a great reckoning was waiting for her outside the safety of the Vale.

Summer in the Vale was, if anything, even more lush than in all the rest of the year. After the intense growth spurts of spring, the Vale settled into a glorious sequence of blooming, flowering, fruiting, repeating. Sparrow had grown up in the stony northern village of Longfall, her childhood punctuated by ice storms and heavy snows. Now, she marveled at the temperate bubble that was K'Valdemar Vale.

The Vale's heat and abundance, so easy and overflowing, thrilled Sparrow every summer. Intoxicated by the heavy floral perfume of the multicolored canopy blooming overhead, waking to the rising chorus of exotic, intensely plumed birds, warmed by the languid heat, she walked more slowly, smiled more often, took naps in a hammock out back in the heat of the afternoons.

The Vale was her home. But while Sparrow much preferred the peace of her calm and anonymous life in the Vale, the storms of the world outside her ekele reminded her how precious her life with her family was, how fragile.

She turned her mind away from such huge, overbearing thoughts, and instead concentrated on setting things to rights in her own sphere of being. Her comfy ekele, snug at ground level, seemed too small of late. Mostly because of her rapidly growing son Thistle, who was undergoing his own intense growth spurt.

At the moment, Sparrow concentrated on polishing her best serving bowls. She sat in the shade outside her front door on a wrinkled old blanket as she scrubbed away, the beaten copper of the largest one singing under her fingers. A gentle, cooling breeze caressed the back of her neck.

After the Gathering, she expected at least a few members of her heartmate's clan, the Cloudwalkers, to stay in the Vale with them for an extended visit.

First, they had to get through the Gathering. But Sparrow had to keep her thoughts close to the ground, snug and safe in her nest.

It had been years since Cloudbrother's adopted family had ventured so far south, and Sparrow welcomed the opportunity to offer hospitality to the people who had saved her heartmate's life long ago, when he was a lost, desperately ill little boy.

Even smaller than her son Thistle was now.

Thistle was six going on seven. The baby smell at the base of the back of his neck had faded, and instead when she grabbed him to hug him, Sparrow gratefully inhaled his salty and peppery scent, just as intoxicating in its own little boy way.

Tis was a creature forever in motion. He had lost his baby chubbiness, and now, wiry and dark, he busied himself about the ekele like a never-resting, darting shadow.

But Tis was wise beyond his years . . . as if there were an invisible sage walking behind him, whispering disquieting truths in his ear. Deep down, Sparrow knew with rock-solid certainty that her boy would soon be Chosen, just as her husband had been.

This was the world's way.

And, while she was deeply proud of both heartmate and son, sometimes Sparrow felt a little wistful that their talents would sometimes take them away from her.

Suddenly, as if conjured, Tis materialized in the front doorway, interrupting her thoughts, balancing on the threshold on the tips of his toes. In his outstretched hands, a small, jade keeryn climbed and danced, its wide golden jaws open in a toothy smile.

He squinted down at the little scaled thing, his face a study in fierce concentration. "Urtho, the Silent Mage, was the father of this keeryn."

That was an interesting way to put things, to say the least.

Sparrow set the copper bowl down on the old, patched blanket where she was sitting. She massaged her aching fingers as she looked up to focus on the boy and his keeryn.

If Tis had named it, he had never told his mother. A

part of her didn't want to know, didn't want to intrude
on his inner world. But the secret of the keeryn from
Iftel weighed on Sparrow's mind.

Almost five years ago, Sparrow and Cloudbrother
had traveled on a Herald's mission to the remote, closed
land of Iftel in search of an antidote to the drought that
raged there. In return for Cloudbrother calling the rain
back into the land, the grateful ruler of Iftel had bestowed the gift of this little enchanted keeryn.

Sparrow and Cloudbrother had hoped the little
keeryn, creature of fire and water, could provide the secret to healing their own corner of Velgarth: the Forest
of Sorrows, dangerously imbalanced once again and
suffering, in need of healing.

So far, that hope had remained unfulfilled. Cloudbrother had taken the little keeryn to the Council at
Haven and offered it to the Crown as a possible antidote for the troubles in the north, but the Council in its
collective wisdom insisted that the keeryn was the
Herald's, that he and his family were the rightful care-
takers of the gift.

They were instructed to transport the gift right back
home to the north, to the country of the Forest of Sorrows. And so they had obeyed, and they stayed in their
home in the Vale, knowing that a day of reckoning
would come, someday.

Deep down, Sparrow knew the Gathering was the
place, the time. The battle was going to be joined, for
once and for all.

The shining silver claws of the jade keeryn scratched
faintly against Tis's skinny, outstretched forearm. It
scampered up the length of his arm and nestled in the
hollow of his collarbone.

Despite her deep and unremitting worry, Sparrow
couldn't keep from smiling. Such beauties in the world!

"Yes, indeed, Urtho's green jade child," she said. "Agreed, our little keeryn is a most amazing and generous gift. Do be careful with it. Keep it safe."

Tis met her gaze, and, as usual, his intensity half amazed Sparrow—and secretly half frightened her. How could such a small, compact body contain so much fire?

How could he know the dangers they faced now?

"I want to bring him to the Gathering, Mama." He paused. "Please."

She kept her gaze level, even as her heart started pounding, hard. "Why?"

His expression didn't change, but his lips began to tremble.

"Because," he said, his voice tentative. Suddenly, he sounded exactly like the little boy he still was. "I know it is a jewel. I know it is a treasure we need to keep hidden. But . . . I just have a feeling."

Sparrow nodded slowly, swallowing the big lump that had formed in her throat. Tis was just a boy, but he knew, as well as she did, they were all soon walking into a crucible.

"Me too," she said. "Keep him hidden, but bring him." Sparrow hesitated, then decided to say what she was thinking. "I think we might need him."

The following morning, the day dawned hot and dry, and they prepared to leave for the Gathering.

Cloudbrother, dressed in white trews and tunic, embroidered with the intricate and brightly colored patterns of his clan, sat astride Abilard, his Companion, tall and slim on his mount. His eyes were closed, sealed shut by a near-fatal childhood fever, but otherwise he looked so agile and gallant on his mount, like a Shin'a'in warrior.

Sparrow stood in the doorway, watching her heartmate

and his Companion whirl in the clearing outside the ekele, unified in motion. A light breeze blew, and a white and pink cascade of blossoms rained down on them like aromatic, fluffy snow.

"Handsome devil, your fine heartmate," Roark said from behind her.

Roark always made Sparrow smile. She kept watching Cloudbrother and Abilard as she replied, "He's my handsome devil, all right."

She turned then to take in the sight of Roark, half-hidden by the cool shadows in the back of her home.

The fact that her best friend in the world was a bossy hertasi usually didn't give Sparrow any pause. But this morning, perhaps because they were riding once again, away from her daily, everyday mundane life, the sweet absurdity of their friendship brought tears to her eyes.

"Sure you don't want to join us?" she asked, her voice light and teasing, her heart absolutely serious. Because, deep down, Sparrow was terrified she was never coming back.

Roark laughed, a deep throaty croak of a laugh. His amber eyes shone, and his dewlap stretched out, revealing the rainbow iridescent scales so often tucked away while he worked. "No Gatherings for me, dear little bird. I am made for the hearth, for the tidy hole, for the quiet and warmth. You go fly away, into the bright sky. You will come back to me."

Sparrow caught Roark's gaze, which did not waver as they looked at each other for a long, lingering minute.

She swallowed hard. "You sure? You sure I will come back?"

"My darling, I promise you. You will return to me, and we will have tea and scones in the gardens, and we will listen to the bondbirds singing. Until then, celebrate. And remember, love is bigger than the world."

He blinked his eyes then, slowly, his lower eyelids

closing up over his enormous amber irises. Roark opened his eyes again, bowed to Sparrow with a flourish, and withdrew into the shadows of the cool storeroom in the back of the ekele.

She and Roark had an unspoken rule—never say goodbye. Roark had not broken their pact, but he had come pretty close.

With a great effort, Sparrow turned her attention away from the ekele and back to where Cloudbrother sat tall astride Abilard, waiting for her to emerge.

And Tis sat in front of her heartmate now, dark and quick and tense, his fingers buried deep in Abilard's glorious, silver-white mane. His face, still and intense as always, was tilted up toward the sky, taking in the sun like a turning sunflower.

"Mama," he said, his imperious voice brooking no more delay. "We've been waiting for you. I'm . . . All. Packed. Up."

And he looked down then, wiggled his eyebrows meaningfully at her, his expression so deadly serious that she had to restrain a nervous laugh.

"It will be so wonderful to see our family once again," she replied to him, and to Cloudbrother, too. "It's been a long time since we simply celebrated the season."

Abilard drew near, his silvery hooves flashing in the loamy dirt, and Cloudbrother reached his long, strong arm down to her.

"Let's ride, my love," he said, his voice easy, warm, and free from fear. "It's going to be fun."

And then he whispered into her soul, his Mindspeech a gentle caress. *:Don't be afraid,:* he said. *:What will be, will be.:*

And her beloved's courage sent strength and peace flowing through Sparrow's own body. If he could be brave, then she could follow his lead.

She clambered up onto the craggy rock near the

front entrance of their ekele, the one she used as a mounting block, and Cloudbrother pulled her up to sit behind him. She snuggled up close to his back, Tis no longer sheltered between them, but riding in the vanguard, up front.

But all of them knew, outside of the protection of the Vale, the Forest would be looking for them. And they would have to face the malevolence that had sickened the Forest and almost claimed Cloudbrother's life, time after time.

The Summer Gathering had already begun in the Great Clearing located between Longfall and the K'Valdemar Vale. Midsummer was still a couple of days away, so the zenith of the festival was still building. Tis was beyond excited for the festival, as it was the first one he would attend.

The Forest of Sorrows hummed with life. Outside of the Vale's protection, the forest was sticky and humid instead of hot and dry, and clouds of gnats, thorny thickets, and boggy patches impeded their progress.

Abilard forged ahead, his wise, far-seeing eyes picking out the safest pathway through the damp, spongy forest floor. And as they rode, the four of them considered the problem they were riding into.

Long ago, when Cloudbrother was a five-year-old Longfall boy named Brock, a wraith had enticed him into the forest, and he was sickened with a strange and deadly malady. He was discovered by the Cloudwalker clan, who had saved his life but at the cost of the life of Silver Cloud, one of the clan elders and a wise Adept.

Sparrow hugged her heartmate closer as Abilard broke into a canter. She had met Cloudbrother's clan before, and they had always welcomed her with open arms. But Sparrow, deep down, always felt a little awkward in their presence. They all knew that Cloudbrother still owed his clan a life-debt.

Even his name was a reminder of what it had cost to save him. Thanks to the intervention of his clan, Brock had survived, but he had lost his sight. Instead, he had gained the ability to fly high above the ordinary plane of existence, into the elemental realms where spirits and energy fields reigned. His clan had renamed him Cloudbrother, since he lived in the clouds more than on the plane of the living.

All of this changed when Abilard had Chosen him and brought him to Sparrow for the healing only she could bring to him. Sparrow, who had no Gift, could still bring Cloudbrother back to earth, just as he could lift her spirit into the realm of the clouds. Together, they could range from the upper vault of the heavens all the way to ground.

They had fought the Forest, and the malevolence that had sickened it, to a draw. In the course of this struggle, Cloudbrother had grown from a sickly and blind Trainee to a powerful Herald, one renowned in the far-off land of Iftel as Cloud Born, the Herald who had called the rain down upon a drought-stricken land.

Now it was time for Cloudbrother to heal his native country. And finally free himself from the debt he owed both his clan and the Forest itself.

But he could not do it alone.

:Our adversary has claimed air and earth,: Abilard Mindspoke. *:To heal the forest, we must bring fire and water.:*

His words sent a healing peace through Sparrow's body, as always. And despite the dangers hunting them, in Abilard's company, as always, she knew they could all depend on the Companion's strength, his love for them all.

Could a Companion Choose a whole family?

Sometimes, Sparrow liked to think it was so. Cloudbrother's Companion, Abilard, had Chosen him before
he and Sparrow had become lifebonded, but from the
moment Sparrow had encountered Abilard and Cloudbrother in the Forest of Sorrows, the Companion had
treated her with immense gentleness and welcome.

And, to her forever gratitude, despite the lack of a
Gift of her own, Abilard could Mindspeak into all of
their minds. So he was able to fully communicate with
all of them, Thistle, Cloudbrother, and Sparrow herself.

Now they rode to the Summer Gathering as one
family.

:I brought the keeryn,: Tis said, his voice strong and
steady. *:He will help us, he is both fire and water.:*

Sparrow could not reply in Mindspeech, and she
didn't want to speak of the keeryn aloud . . . it seemed
as though the Forest itself was listening to their passage through the trees. The dark dappled shadows
under the trees vibrated with an uncanny energy.

The Forest was hungry. But for now it waited before
it pounced.

Cloudbrother replied, speaking the words that echoed
in Sparrow's own thoughts. *:The* keeryn *may be the key,
the Council said. But I'm not sure how he can help us.
Do you know, Tis?:*

Sparrow could sense her son's frustration as a tension between her shoulder blades, even more than
through his words. :It is a puzzle, Papa . . . I don't have
the training to solve it. But don't you know? Don't
Heralds know everything?:

Cloudbrother laughed out loud at that, his easy, ordinary laugh, the one that Sparrow loved the best.
:Don't I wish! But, no. This is Urtho's mystery. The

*Council didn't know what to do either, so it's not just
me. This is untrodden ground, Tis. Let's explore it together. Maybe my brothers the Walkers will have an
idea.:*

Sparrow nestled closer along Cloudbrother's back.
"I hope the whole clan is there," she said. "I know they
can't all make it. But we've only been back to visit up
north the one time. Sometimes . . . do you ever wonder
what your life would have been like if you had never
left them at all?"

Her heartmate didn't hesitate. "My life up there
would have been pretty short, Sparrow. I was pretty
sick. You're the one who kept me from floating into the
clouds forever."

She rested her cheek against his strong, slim back,
her sun hat slipping off the back of her head and resting
by its strap across the back of her shoulders. "I'm glad
you came," she said. "What would I do without you?"

The Forest rose up all around them as Abilard cantered along, the firs and oaks surrounding them all
alive and dark and scary and beautiful. The Forest of
Sorrows was full of secrets and magic, and while Sparrow, a daughter of the northern reaches, always main-
tained a healthy respect for the dangers, she had always
loved the Forest, too.

From far away, hidden in the trees, rose the faint
sound of singing.

The Gathering.

Sparrow peeked out from behind Cloudbrother's
shoulder, and that's when she saw them. Didn't hear
them, because despite their multitude they never made
a sound.

Over their heads, darting from branch to branch, an
enormous murder of crows.

An honor guard? Or messengers of danger?

*   *   *

Within a candlemark, the little procession, family on the ground, great flock of crows in the sky, reached the Great Clearing where the Gathering was taking place. A huge, rolling meadow, surrounded on all sides by craggy forest and protruding boulders and stones like prehistoric keeryns' teeth. The fairgrounds were dotted with dozens of round white tents, some for visiting clans, some for merchants selling spices, dyes, fabrics, and regional culinary delights.

It was not an ancient site. Once a small meadow, the Clearing had only been expanded once trading between the northern clans and the isolated northern villages, like Longfall, became steady and significant every year. The Midsummer Gathering outside Longfall had grown from a simple summer festival, to a trading fair, to the full-blown celebration of life that the Gathering had become.

Now the Clearing had come to life, with tents, horses, clan members, and local villagers all celebrating the fullness of summer in northern Valdemar. A great roar of music, singing, chanting, and chatter filled the air, echoing among the trees.

Longfall kites swooped through the humid air, their long, rainbow-colored tails a striking contrast to the dull, bluish gray homespun the northern villagers wore, down on the ground. Sparrow's heart leaped up at the sight of them. They reminded her of the Longfall kite festivals of her childhood.

As Abilard drew closer to the Gathering, Sparrow scanned the clustered white tents, looking for the Cloudwalker clan. Before she could find them, Abilard's pace quickened.

"There's Liros," Cloudbrother said. "Do you see him? I sense him. He is with his children, way at the end."

Abilard whinnied and broke into a gallop. Sparrow couldn't stop herself from grinning.

Liros was Cloudbrother's closest friend, a singer and Adept who often met Sparrow's heartmate on the elemental plane. Sparrow hadn't seen him since Thistle was a tiny baby.

He stretched to his full height, his jet-black hair long and straight to the waist, hair flecked with silver now. Liros' trews were embroidered with fantastical, intricate designs of twining vines, birds of paradise, and smiling hertasi.

Here, in the midst of this multitude, it was hard for Sparrow to maintain her fear and sense of high alert. Instead, she relaxed in this sea of teeming humanity and realized that if danger struck, she was connected and protected by a clan that had claimed her little family for its own.

Liros saw them and raised his arm in greeting.

Abilard drew close, and his silver hooves danced as they arrived outside Liros' tent.

"Welcome!" Liros called to them. "Welcome, brother Cloudwalker. How you walk in beauty! Come in with your family, we have a great midday meal afoot, inside, out of the heat of the day."

And then he saw the crows, and he paused. At least fifty of them, flying in a lazy, swirling column over their heads, as if they feared to alight on the open ground.

Liros bowed to the birds swooping in flight. "And welcome, messengers of the sky. You have come once again to escort my sister. You bring tidings."

Abilard's long, strong legs stilled, and the three of them slid off his richly caparisoned saddle. Tis took Cloudbrother's right hand, and Sparrow held his left. Abilard led the way to where Liros and his three children waited for them.

They all embraced in turn, Liros hugging Cloud-brother first, then Sparrow. He smelled of spices and cook smoke.

"And who is this great warrior?" Liros asked, crouching down so he could meet Tis's gaze at eye level.

"My son, Tis," Cloudbrother said. "He is growing fast and strong now."

"Of course," Liros replied. "I remember you from when you were a tiny littling, my friend. Welcome! Many friends here for you to meet. These are my brood . . . Mila, Tantos, and Harmony. Are you hungry? Eat, then explore the fair. We do not dance until tonight."

Tis was bashful, Sparrow could see, but he mastered his nerves and offered his hand for Liros to shake in greeting. "Thank you, sir," he said.

"Liros is one of the greatest song healers in our clan," Cloudbrother said. "You will see, tonight. It's going to be great, Tis!"

Together, they followed Liros and his three children, the comely Mila and her little brother and sister, Tantos and Harmony. Abilard left them at the entrance to the tent, so that he could explore the Gathering, and they agreed to meet at dusk for the Great Dance.

Until then, it would be feasting, reconnecting, and, if Sparrow was lucky, some afternoon napping.

Sparrow squinted up at the crows before she entered the tent. She and the crows could not speak to each other; she knew that from the other times they had appeared to her. But she waved at them now, as if to say she was fine and that they knew where she was.

This seemed to satisfy them, and they whirled into the air and flew back to the forest, suddenly cawing in unison as they went. She watched them go, wondering at their visitation and appreciating the mystery of them.

And then she slipped into the tent with all the others.

* * *

Her dream of an afternoon nap came true. Liros's heartmate, the slightly round and pacific Angheli, offered her a sleeping mat well inside the tent after their feast.

"Tis will roam with my brood," she said. "And we can rest in the heat of the day. Long night, tonight!"

Sparrow deeply appreciated Angheli's generosity. "You all can catch up while I take a rest."

Angheli nodded, smiling and patting the white linen cushion. "I can get things set to right myself. You've had a long ride, please, rest."

Gratefully, Sparrow sank into the cool white linens. And fell backward into a deep, soft dream.

The keeryn appeared before her, his golden and silvery whiskers quivering as they spoke together in the clouds. In this plane of being, the keeryn was huge, and his jeweled eyes sparkled with kindness and fire.

"There is fate, there is destiny, but there is also love, Sparrow," the keeryn said. "Greater than all of these is love."

Sparrow considered his words. "Keeryn, you speak true, but why do you remind me of this now?"

"Because, my dear friend, Cloudbrother's destiny was to die, as a boy, long ago."

In this place of heightened sensation, the keeryn's words pierced Sparrow's heart with a physical pain. "But he did not," she whispered.

"No," the keeryn said. "Love saved him. The love of the people who found him and healed him, and your love too, Sparrow. Never doubt the power of love."

"Cloudbrother is in danger, then."

"Do you doubt it? Yes, he is. We all know it, and the power of love might not save him this time. But that does not mean that the love does not exist."

"What do I do? I can love him, but I can't save

him . . . I'm not a warrior or a Mage or even a Healer. I'm just his heartmate."

"Without you, Urtho himself couldn't save Cloudbrother from his fate. But love is beyond fate."

The keeryn bowed and grinned, his curving dreamteeth much longer and stronger than those in his jade statue form. And gigantic, webbed silver and gold wings unfurled behind him, and her little keeryn shot into the sky over her dream-head, filling the sky with his green, gold, and silver presence.

He opened his mouth wide, and fire reached across the cloudy gray sky of her dream. It lit up the clouds from above, turning them from ash to a shifting, multi-colored glory, like an upside-down sunset.

Sparrow struggled to wake, to flee from the intense, overwhelming beauty of the dream. She lay in her shadowy, quiet corner, heart pounding, the sweat streaming down the back of her neck.

She made a distinct, conscious decision not to worry. And the fear that had been stalking her since her conversation with Tis faded away and disappeared.

That night, the Great Dance celebrating the Midsummer Night began.

At dusk, the dancers linked their hands and began to snake through the temporary village of the Gathering. Drummers were dotted throughout the Clearing, their separate rhythms combining into a complex and intricate trance beat.

Sparrow and Cloudbrother held hands tightly, and Liros held on to Cloudbrother's other hand while Sparrow interlaced her fingers with Angheli's. Tis and his little cousins from the Cloudwalker clan ran free through the fading light.

Sparrow surrendered to the dance, her body connected to the long chain of people, villagers, folk from different northern clans, traders from far away, all coming together into a single connected celebration.

Far above their heads, the stars began to emerge. The clouds of earlier in the day had dissipated, so the dancers below were granted an undisturbed view of the heavens.

First one, then another, then a profusion of stars dancing in the sky as the people danced below. A song rose from the people, split off and disjointed at first, then gaining cohesion and becoming a single, breathtaking melody:

Star-Eyed!
Star-Eyed!
Star-Eyed!
Greet your Beloved from the Heavens!

Their song thrilled Sparrow, saturated her with happiness.

She stamped her feet in time to the rhythm of the drums and the harmony of the rising song. She loved to dance, but this dance in the night was something very different.

The whole Gathering drew together in a collective trance, a hypnotic train of consciousness. Like a keeryn, the human chain twined and twisted among the tents, the ground all but shaking under their stamping feet.

The Forest vibrated, and Sparrow sensed the consciousness of the Forest fixing on them all. She had encountered the spirit of the Forest years before, in a struggle that was one of the most terrifying of her life.

But, hidden within the human keeryn dancing in the starlight, Sparrow could face the pain of the Forest without flinching, without becoming lost in it.

She loved the Forest now, loved it as a child loves, with openness and a revealed heart. She loved it as the place where she had made her home, human habitation gathered up against the wilderness, but depending upon it too.

She reached for Abilard with her mind. She could not Mindspeak, but she sent him love and gratitude, her heartmate's dear Companion, the one who had Chosen him for life as she had.

And Abilard responded to her search, with a soft caress inside her mind.

:No fear,: he Spoke. *:Love is greater than fear.:*

And as he Spoke, the truth of Abilard's words soaked into Sparrow's heart. The song of the dancers became a prayer of healing, and she and Cloudbrother danced the healing dance of the Midsummer Night.

Gently, almost imperceptibly, she and Cloudbrother slipped out of their bodies, and even as they kept dancing, deep in trance, they flew together above the great Midsummer Gathering, into the elemental plane above.

They danced among stars.

The Forest of Sorrows joined them.

:I've come to heal you,: Cloudbrother said. *:Me and my brothers and sisters.:*

:A dance is not enough,: the Forest insisted. *:You rootless ones all dance every year. But still my pain increases.:*

This time the Forest was not filled with rage or murder. But with sadness, separation, sickness. Wistfulness.

Even here, Sparrow had to speak aloud. But the effect was the same as Mindspeech, up here. Everybody could hear her fine.

"Your air and earth is ruled by pain," she said. "But we have brought you fire and water. By these, the balance is restored."

At this moment, the demon Zeth joined them.

This was the demon who had hunted Cloudbrother and almost killed him as a boy. It was the demon who had given the Change Adept Emptiness the power to enthrall and almost destroy Longfall. And it was the demon who had sucked the life out of the land of Iftel.

It was the demon. Tis had called him out by name.

Even now, Sparrow was free from fear. She understood now, that in the moment of the storm, fear is a luxury, an indulgence she could not afford to take.

Fear did not serve her. It was a tool of her adversary. And she was glad to let it go.

Instead, she accepted the force of the storm. And stood in the face of it.

It might well sweep her away, but fearing the possibility would not prevent it.

Tis joined them. On the plane of the elemental, the boy possessed a native power.

He and the demon stood face to face. Zeth was a creature of energy, a clot of static that ripped a hole in the place where he manifested. He looked like a man bear, a moss-covered ball of dirt, with small, cunning eyes and restlessly moving hands.

Zeth belonged to the abyssal plane, where he and his kind spawned and grew. How had he ascended to this place?

"Go home," Tis said. "You don't belong here. You can only harm yourself here."

Zeth laughed. It sounded like a snarl, coming from his long, bearlike snout. "I could harm you. I could suck your life force out of your marrow and grow even more powerful."

Sparrow wasn't afraid, but she took a sharp breath in. Here, Tis was more powerful than her, but it was still hard to let him go, to fight.

Tis didn't answer the demon. His keeryn joined them then.

On this plane, the keeryn loomed even larger than

in Sparrow's dream. He came across the plain of stars, and his eyes shone like stars; he was as huge as Haven.

"Zeth," the keeryn breathed. "Go back where you came from."

Zeth growled, snuffled. And with every bellows-like breath he took, he grew.

He grew to the size of the keeryn. And the two giants began to wrestle in the sky. They twined together, writhed like a single frenzied being. Danced their own heavenly Midsummer Dance.

The air of the demon fed the fire in the keeryn, and the earth of the demon drank the water of the keeryn. Their energies evenly matched, there was no way for the battle to be won by one side or another.

The heavens rang with their war, and Cloudbrother gathered Sparrow and Tis close to him. They combined their energy, and Sparrow sensed the raw power of her heartmate and her son, surrounding and protecting her.

From far below, the song of the dancers in the Gathering rose. And the crows broke through the clouds at their feet, circling the fighters.

They landed on Zeth's shoulders and back and skull, and they called and pecked at him. One of the crows broke away from the melee, swooped to where the three of them stood.

He hovered in the air, his flight more like a hummingbird's than a crow's.

He nodded at Cloudbrother. "Sire," he said, his voice clear and soft. "You will have to intervene."

Cloudbrother sighed.

"Such is the way of a Herald," he said, his voice soft and sad. "I've owed the debt since I was five. It's high time I paid it, Crow. Thank you."

And he kissed the top of Sparrow's head.

And walked away.

Sparrow watched him go, and even now, even at this moment she had feared from the time that he had first disappeared, she was free from fear.

Because Cloudbrother walked in love, not fear.

He walked across the carpet of clouds, his hands open and outstretched. His Gift was flight, not spells. But here, Cloudbrother had the power to command.

"I send you to your home, in peace," he said. "Zeth, farewell. Thank you for the Gifts you had bestowed on me, no matter your intentions."

Without her heartmate to hold her in the elemental plane, Sparrow knew she did not have the Gift to stay. She held on to Tis, told him, "Be careful up here! If the keeryn tells you to get out, well, then . . ."

Before she could get the rest of her sentence out, Sparrow tumbled back to earth, to her own body.

She knew the matter was already finished.

Sparrow woke to the gentle song of bells.

Abilard stood over her. *:You fainted, but somebody always does during the Midsummer Dance,:* he Spoke. *:It is dawn. The dance is ended.:*

"Is Cloudbrother . . . gone?" she asked. The effort of speaking sent a wave of pain shooting through her body.

:No: Abilard said, but his voice, usually filled with a reassuring warmth, was full of concern for his Chosen. *:He is down from the clouds now. I fear, forever. Please, comfort him. He has done a great deed, this day:*

A surge of hope rose in her, and Sparrow struggled to rise. "Take me to him."

She stood unsteadily on her feet, threw her arm over Abilard's mighty flanks. Gently, he nuzzled her shoulder, and his soft, sweet breath brought her back to her senses.

Dawn had just come, barely displacing the dark of

night. The dancers had dispersed, to their tents, to break their fast with honey cakes and morning mead.

Abilard took her to Liros' tent. Cloudbrother was there, thank the Mother, and so was Tis.

Tis was in tears. "My little keeryn," he said. "It broke. I'm sorry, Mama, it's my fault."

Tis was a great Mage in potential, but at heart he was still a little boy. He held the broken shards of jade in his hands, crying for the life force Urtho had breathed into the little figure, the life force that had gone away now.

Sparrow gathered Tis in her arms, hugged him close, stroked his straight, jet black hair until his sobs slowed. "He's in the clouds now, watching over the Forest," she said. "It's all going to be fine."

Cloudbrother rested on the same sleeping mat where Sparrow had slept. He was alive, breathing easily. A part of Sparrow couldn't believe it.

"How are you still alive?" she asked, blurted really.

"It was the keeryn's sacrifice," he said. "His life restored the balance to the Forest. He and the demon are gone to the abyssal plane. And I . . ."

Sparrow waited for him to finish, held her breath in anticipation.

"I think my Gift is ended," he said. "It was called out by the demon, I think. Without the threat of the demon, the clouds will not call me anymore. Heralds don't really retire, but they can get new postings when their missions are done. I think I'm going to be that kind of Herald."

Sparrow swallowed hard.

Then smiled, in gratitude.

"There are a lot worse fates than that, my heart," she said. "We will be fine. Plenty of life to live, right here on the ground. If you were to ask Roark, this is where all the best stuff happens anyway."

Cloudbrother sighed, relaxed back down onto the

mat. "Roark is right. But part of me was made for the storm. And now the storm in the Forest is past."

:*No fear, Chosen one. Every storm must have its end. We will go to Haven, your victory will be celebrated,*: Abilard said. :*And we will present Tis to the Council. It is time for him to receive his training. Soon he, too, will be Chosen.*:

Preparing for the Worst
Brigid Collins

It was times like this, when he was standing in the breakfast chamber of the lady of the hold and hoping to change her mind, that Dreyvin truly wished he still had his right arm. Holding his left hand respectfully behind his back became that much harder without its right counterpart to clasp.

"Lady Areshinn, I don't think we ought to send every fighting man in our hold out on the Sovvan hunt. The Treehill gang is going to see it as an open invitation to attack."

Lady Areshinn smiled and waved at the second chair beside her breakfast table. "Sit, Dreyvin. You know very well I won't have you stand in my presence. Have you had any more letters from Simen lately?"

Dreyvin clamped his teeth against the inside of his cheeks, awkward as always with his Lady's mothering affection toward him since she became aware of the relationship between her son and himself, but he complied with her request. His leather jerkin creaked with the stiff motion. "Simen is an avid correspondent. He sends his love, along with the latest piece he wrote for his coursework. I think it's a Sovvan Feast ballad, but I'm not the expert on these things."

"Well, give it to Temara, and she'll let us know if it's fit to sing at our feast tonight. The men will enjoy hearing something new after we hunt."

Dreyvin dug his fingers into his knee under the table. "My lady, please consider leaving at least a small contingent behind to protect the women and children."

Lady Areshinn's smile remained in place, but the hardness in her eyes brooked no argument. "I appreciate your concern, but there's no reason for it. The Treehills are going to be licking their wounds from last week's scuffle for some time. They didn't even manage to carry off a single bushel of grain from our shipment to Haven."

Her voice rang with pride, and Dreyvin couldn't help feeling an echo of it in his own chest. He'd been drilling some of the younger fighting men in defensive tactics for months now, ever since he recovered enough from the loss of his arm to make himself useful. Their victory defending the shipment last week was his victory, too, despite him not having been there.

The death of Lord Areshinn five years ago might have weakened Areshinn Hold's defensive edge against the various bandit gangs that roved the surrounding hills, but with rigorous training they were rebuilding their strength and gaining ground little by little, one shipment at a time.

But it might all be undone in a single night if the fears that had Dreyvin's missing arm tingling with phantom itches were justified. The hold couldn't bounce back if the Treehill gang decided to act on the opportunity the Sovvan hunt would present to them. All the fighting men gone? Only the women left behind to prepare the feast for when the men returned in the evening? Even bandits still nursing bleeding wounds wouldn't hesitate to try it.

"I still think we ought to be prepared for the worst," he said.

"The worst," said Lady Areshinn. She didn't even twitch her eyes toward the corner where her fallen husband's armor was displayed, but the lines of her face drew tighter. "Our hold has been prepared for the worst for years now. It is a lifestyle that puts a heavy strain on those who live it. My husband and I used to talk about our responsibilities to our people often, of how our duty did not stop at making our people safe, but continued ever onward, driving us to ensure our people's prosperity and, perhaps most importantly, their happiness. There's been precious little happiness in our hold these past few years, Dreyvin. Will you deny any of your men the chance to earn themselves a bit of well-deserved luck through the Sovvan hunt?"

"Not by choice, my lady. But if the Treehills should attack—"

"We cannot always be looking for the next attack, lad. And we couldn't have asked for a better chance to relax our guard as we have now. You should listen to more of the men's boasts from last week. They aren't all exaggerations for the kitchen girls!"

Her laugh flowed easily, her head thrown back and her eyes crinkled now with mirth. Simen looked the same when he was at ease with his joy.

Dreyvin bit back a sigh. If Lady Areshinn was so confident of their momentary safety, then perhaps he was being over-defensive. But it was hard quieting the tactical part of his brain when he'd been relying on it near constantly for the past two years. Even when he was delirious with the pain of his severed arm, he'd been working out lines of defense from his bed.

Maybe her point about the strain of their harried lifestyle had some merit. "Very well, my lady. I trust you still mean to ride with the men?"

"Of course. I want some of that Sovvan hunt good

luck, too. And who knows, if I do well, perhaps Lord Areshinn will honor me with a visit from beyond."

Now her gaze turned to her husband's armor. The autumnal morning sun slanted in through her windows to glint off the burnished edges, giving it an ethereal look that made Dreyvin's breath catch.

There wasn't a day that went by that he didn't feel the absence of the man who had, for a time, been like a father to him.

"If we could have him back even for a moment," he said, "it would go a long way to alleviating the melancholy of the hold."

"It would indeed," said Lady Areshinn, before lightening her attitude again. "As would Simen's return, if he was able to escape his classes at the Collegium for the festival. Tell me how he's doing, Dreyvin. He never writes such long letters to me as he does to you. Is he making more friends since that Herald Trainee went on her internship?"

Dreyvin recounted what he could from Simen's latest letter, though he kept some things to himself. His lady didn't need to know how her son had waxed poetic to him about what a perfect hideaway the forest behind the Companion's Field made, or about the detailed fantasy Simen had described of the two of them making use of it.

Areshinn Hold was a different place without the menfolk around. Even though Lady Areshinn did much to help the women under her protection feel at ease, there was no denying the fact that most of the kitchen girls kept their thoughts to themselves while the men might hear.

They'd gotten used to Dreyvin hanging around since his injury made him too much of a burden to accompany the fighting men, though. And, if he was honest, he enjoyed the few times he'd been left completely alone with the kitchen girls. They were less worried about making him feel the loss of his arm.

"Teela, pick up your pace, girl! Old One-Arm has peeled more apples than you in the last ten minutes, and that's just disgraceful."

The girl sitting beside him at the prep table, Teela, stuck her tongue out at Temara, the woman who had berated her. "That's because he's not distracted like I am. I'm trying to think of the best way to get Gerren's attention tonight. Do you think he'll look my way if I wear orange leaves in my hair? It worked for Sira last year."

"I think he'll look your way if the applesauce is perfect. Imagine the look on his face when he finds out Dreyvin's the one who made it so sweet!"

Peals of high laughter mingled with the sweet and savory aromas throughout the kitchen, and Dreyvin didn't bother hiding his own smile. He reached across the table for another apple to affix to his peeler.

"By the way, Temara," he said when the giggles died down enough. "Simen sent me another song. Lady Areshinn wanted you to see if it was fit to sing at the feast tonight."

"Have you got it with you?"

"Of course." Dreyvin carried one of Simen's letters everywhere with him. It helped him feel the distance between Areshinn Hold and the Collegium in Haven just a little less.

He pulled the letter from a pocket inside his shirt, an easy motion as he had removed his leather jerkin. Getting out of even the scant armor he usually wore around the keep was helping him stay in the "relaxed" state of mind his lady had suggested. He had to admit, losing the tension in his shoulders was a nice change of pace.

He separated the song from the rest of the letter—
taking a moment to silently preen over the improved
dexterity in his left hand—before handing the song to
Temara.

Temara had studied music for a time under a master
before Lord Areshinn's death, but as she lacked the
Bardic Gift, she had never gone to study at the Collegium. But she knew how to read music, and it made her
an indispensable member of the hold, beyond her strong
skills at running the kitchen.

She hummed softly as she read through Simen's song.

"This is good," she said when she finished. "Haunt-
ing, melodic. Really brings out the spirit of the season.
He's branching out these days. I'll have to change my
lute's tuning before the feast."

"I'll be sure to tell him he's given you a challenge
when I respond."

"Oh, I didn't say it would be a challenge," Temara
said with a grin. "And get back to peeling. The sauce
won't cook itself."

"Just giving Teela a chance to catch up," Dreyvin
said. Beside him, Teela huffed and picked up another
apple.

A clamor rose outside, loud enough to be heard over
the chaos of the kitchen. Dreyvin's hackles were immediately up, and he'd half-risen from his stool before the
door leading out to the yard flew open and the stable-
master's daughter stumbled in. Her cheeks were flushed
from running, her braids coming unwound in wisps.
Dreyvin had put her with the small group who were to
watch from the walls until the men and Lady Areshinn
returned.

"Movement on the south hill," she said, panting.

The lady and the men had gone hunting to the west.
South could mean only one thing.

Dreyvin reflexively went to draw his sword, only to

recall too late that he never wore one anymore, and that the arm he was trying to move no longer existed. A sour wave of grief, unwanted and unhelpful, cascaded down his throat as he swallowed forcefully.

To their credit, the women of the kitchen didn't set to wailing or crying, though they were clearly frightened. They turned bright eyes toward either him or Temara, wringing their hands, but otherwise awaiting their orders.

They'd been harried too many times by the Treehill bandits to waste time with useless tears.

The picture of calm, Temara turned to him. "How long until the hunters return?"

Too long, he thought but did not say. "They won't ride for home until after dusk falls. That's still an hour away."

"Have the girls bar the gate, light the watch fires. Make it look like we've got men on the wall. You've still got sparring weapons in the practice yard, right?"

"Yes, but subterfuge won't help. The bandits know the calendar as well as we do. They know we're undefended."

Dreyvin regretted the words as soon as they were said. The women began whispering among themselves, and a few moans underscored the miasma of fear.

But there was no time to berate himself. "Temara, take the women to the cellars and barricade the door from the inside." The cellar door was made of stone, so the bandits would have a hard time burning the women out if they discovered the hiding place. There was enough food put away in storage to last at least a few days, if not a whole week. With Temara's good management, they'd be able to hold out until Lady Areshinn could mount a counterattack to retake the hold.

He turned the situation over in his mind a few times, until he was satisfied that he'd prepared for the worst.

That left only the question of what he was going to do with himself in the interim.

As if she'd read his mind, Temara frowned. "I think I see where you're going with this, but you can't mean to simply let the bandits in without any resistance, can you?"

"I don't see how I can fend off even a small faction of the Treehills," Dreyvin said, shrugging the shoulder that still had an arm attached and grinning with grim humor. "I'm a bit short-handed."

Nobody laughed at his joke. Beside him, Teela rose from her stool. Gone was the daydreaming kitchen girl; in her place stood a woman with inner steel to rival that of Lady Areshinn herself.

"I don't want to let those bastards take our hold," she said. An answering murmur of assent rose from the gathered women.

"I commend your bravery," said Dreyvin. "But you are none of you trained to take on the dirty fighting tactics these hill men use."

"If they're going to fight dirty, we'll fight dirtier!" cried a woman by the butcher block. She pulled a knife from the collection and brandished it. It was clean, unused yet today as the kitchen awaited the bounty of the hunt to prepare the main course for the night's feast.

Other women were taking up the cry, picking up kitchen implements and tying their aprons tighter about their waists as if that would help them fight more effectively.

Dreyvin felt his control of the situation slipping rapidly away. If he put up much resistance, he might well find himself locked in the cellar while the kitchen girls took matters into their own hands. He couldn't think of a surer recipe for disaster.

"All right, all right!" he yelled, holding his hand up to quiet the women. "All right. Those of you who would prefer to defend the hold may do so, but 'fight dirtier' is not a viable plan of attack on its own. We need some way to stretch our defensive power as far as we can."

He glanced at Temara, hoping to find her, at least, prepared to be rational. Maybe she could even convince most of the girls to go down to the cellars.

But he found her wearing a positively wicked grin. She held the page with Simen's Sovvan Night song written on it between two callused fingers.

"I have an idea. You said yourself the Treehill gang know their calendar as well as we do. I think, with your cooperation and a little borrowing from the lady, we can give them a Sovvan Night they'll never forget."

A chill ran down Dreyvin's spine at the dark look on her face, and it tingled all the way to his extremities. The itch was strongest in the missing fingers of his lost sword hand.

If Temara noticed the effect she'd had on him, she gave no indication of it. Instead, she turned to the woman who had pulled the butcher's knife from the block. "Go and fetch a chicken. I'm afraid we'll have to break tradition and slaughter a domestic animal tonight, but I think our hold's spirits will forgive us the transgression."

The dark blush of dusk was creeping up from the eastern horizon, and a heavy scent of cook fires laced the crisp air above the yard.

From his hidden vantage point on the roof of the Areshinn manor, in the shadow of the south tower, Dreyvin could watch the approach of the Treehill Gang toward the hold's southern wall. He had a fine view of the scattering of ladies down in the yard, too, as well as the pots, pans, and other kitchen devices they had moved outside in order to receive the bounty of the hunt as soon as the men arrived. Temara was waving her arms, directing four of the strongest women of the hold in arranging the long tables for the feast.

Dreyvin's palm itched with nervous sweat. His real one, not the phantom of the one he'd lost. That one, for once, was quiet, as dead and gone as the once-mighty lord of this hold. He hoped it wasn't a sign that Temara's plan was not appreciated by the spirits on the other side.

He tried desperately to shut off the part of his brain that incessantly prodded the plan for weak points. There was no time for revision. The dark shapes in the hills were nearly upon them. He had to be ready to play his part to the best of his abilities.

His left hand twitched awkwardly around the tinder box he held. He felt clumsy, and naked without a shield on his arm, despite the armor he wore.

His first job was to signal when the bandits came close enough to disappear behind the rise of the wall. The moment he lost sight of the first of the dark shapes out there, he wet his lips and blew a fair imitation of a white-faced stable owl, an appropriate call-signal for a Sovvan Night scheme.

In the yard below, Temara perked at the sign and began to sing.

Dreyvin had never heard her voice sound like this before. It was sharp, keening, and yet the falling tones of the song gave her a mournful sound, as if she'd lost someone who made her life worth living. The lyrics heightened the image. It sent cold fingers walking down Dreyvin's spine to hear.

Simen wrote this, he thought. He couldn't picture his bright, happy lover sitting in a fancy room at the Collegium and putting these notes, those words, on the page.

Other women had joined their voices to Temara's now. The song twisted through the yard just like the smoke from the fire pit, until Dreyvin was ready to see ghosts in the writhing mists.

But he had no idea if the tune was creating a similar effect among the bandits as they drew closer, closer, close enough to storm the unbarred gate any moment now.

Dreyvin couldn't help scanning the darkening eastern forest one last time, hoping for even a small sign that Lady Areshinn and the men were returning. He got nothing.

A great crash and a splintering of wood had him tensing for action. The bandits had struck at the gate.

The women set up screaming, some tripping over their skirts as they ran for the shelter of the manor.

It set Dreyvin's teeth on edge to sit back and do nothing as the Treehill gang swarmed into the heart of Areshinn Hold, but he made himself do it. His fingers gripped his tinder box so tight they went numb.

As Temara had had to wait for his signal to begin singing her eerie song, so now he must wait for the next signal.

He quivered, bowstring-tight, and kept out of sight as the chaotic cacophony came up to him. He could no longer tell whether the high screams of the women were genuine or put on for the sake of the plan.

May Lord Areshinn's vengeful spirit slay me if I've made a horrible mistake, he thought. May Lady Areshinn curse my Havens-be-damned name.

At last, the clamor died down, and the Treehill bandits began to gloat over their victory.

"Get your hands off me!" came the clear, youthful voice of Teela. There was a masculine grunt of pain, and Dreyvin smiled to imagine one of the self-assured bandits doubling over with a sudden affliction in his groin.

Teela heaped more abuse on her captors. "A lot of filthy hill dogs you are, and cowards to boot! Oh, you think I'm only spitting words, do you? Well, we'll see the color of your bellies soon enough, oh yes. You interrupted our Sovvan Night ritual, but we'd nearly completed it anyway."

She drew a breath, and Dreyvin pictured the dramatic way she must have thrown her head back.

"Oh, spirits of Areshinn! If ever you loved your home and your people, come now in our defense. Find these mongrels a worthy sacrifice."

That was it, the signal. Dreyvin's heart thundered like always at times of action, but his left hand remained steady as he managed to strike a spark one-handed into the brazier he'd dragged onto the roof. He knew that at the same time, the hold children were doing the same at each brazier along the hold wall, all keeping out of sight so as to make it appear as if the fires were springing to life of their own accord.

"What the—"

"The fires!"

"What have you done, woman?"

The bandits continued their questions in gruff voices, but Temara had taken up Simen's Sovvan song again, and the other women joined in one by one, until the eerie sound filled the yard.

Dreyvin checked the sky. The dark band of dusk had spread over halfway across the sky, and a sprinkling of stars winked in and out from behind a shredded curtain of clouds and smoke.

It was as perfect as he could ask for.

He almost forgot to take the time to empty the bowl of chicken blood over the front of his armor before he rose from his hiding place, but he remembered at the last moment.

Lord Areshinn's armor had been enshrined in the lady's room in exactly the same condition in which it was last on the lord's body. A great rend in the breastplate showed the line of the fatal strike which the lord had taken as he himself cut down the previous leader of the very gang of bandits who had hounded the hold ever since.

It was a little big on Dreyvin, but Temara had insisted that the cobbled-together effect helped forward the idea that he was Lord Areshinn's vengeful spirit returned to defend his keep once again.

Dreyvin rose to his full height and planted one foot firmly on the downslope of the roof. He let the heavy crimson cloak bearing the Areshinn crest flutter in the smoky breeze, but he ensured that it continued to hide the fact that his right epaulette and gauntlet hung empty at his side.

He was in full view of the women and the Treehills now. Some of the women wore expressions of fierce victory despite the bruises and mussed hair from the rough treatment the bandits had given them.

The bandits stared slack-jawed and glassy-eyed up at him. For a few thudding heartbeats, Dreyvin saw in his mind's eye what they must see: a figure wearing the armor of their once-defeated enemy, cape flaring and embers flying about him as if conjured up by the deepest rage of the afterlife.

He gripped the hilt of the sword that hung at his right hip and pulled it out with what he hoped, hoped, hoped looked like the practiced ease of a warrior lord and not the fumbling of a one-armed man about to lose his balance.

Dreyvin pitched his voice as low as it could go. "I am the Lord of Areshinn Hold! I loved my home and my people. I come now in their defense. And I find these mongrels a worthy sacrifice!"

One of the bandits shrieked, flung his weapon to the ground, and fled toward the broken gate.

The others looked around, perhaps for assurance

from their fellows, but found instead the women whom they had thought pacified holding an array of butcher's knives, meat forks, or heavy cast-iron pans, pulled from where they'd been hidden in the their skirts. The flickering light of the burning braziers all around the hold reflected like ghost fire from the makeshift weapons.

And from the darkness of the eastern forest came the baying of hounds, the pounding of hooves, and the trumpeting of hunting horns.

The bandits turned tail. Some of the women gave chase, Teela among them brandishing an apple peeler like a dagger. Temara led a cluster of kitchen girls in heading off a few escapees. Everywhere, the sound of Simen's Sovvan Night song rose in scraps and shreds.

Once again, chaos reigned below Dreyvin. His body hummed with the desire to go down there, to join the fight, to make himself useful as he used to when he was whole.

But he held his place on the roof, keeping up his spectral appearance both to intimidate their enemy and to embolden those who fought to defend Areshinn Hold.

Outside the walls, the hunters who had returned just in time to rout the fleeing Treehills made short work of mopping up the stragglers. Lady Areshinn's clear, commanding tones rolled like thunder, keeping the men from celebrating a victory too early, but she couldn't quite mask her own elation as she rode through the broken gate and into the yard.

The lady of the hold tilted her face up to the roof, pure awe and hope nakedly displayed for Dreyvin to read.

He saw the moment she registered his true identity and the way her brow drew downward in pain.

Feeling self-conscious and ashamed of having hurt his lady, he lowered his borrowed sword. The muscles in his arm thanked him for it. He'd never get used to holding a weapon in his left hand. He would just have to find some other way to continue to be useful to his lady, provided she still wanted him to be useful to her.

But Lady Areshinn showed her grace and shook the confusion away with a twitch of her shoulders. "I suppose you're entitled to say, 'I told you so' now, Dreyvin."

"And yet, so could you, my lady," he called down. "We don't seem to have needed the fighting men on hand to get rid of the bandits, after all."

Lady Areshinn surveyed the yard from atop her horse, taking in the efficient way the kitchen girls were cleaning up the mess of the fallen bandits. Over by the splinters of the gate, Teela was flipping her suspiciously stained apple peeler and smiling at Gerren as he rode through. At some point, a scuffle had affixed a tangle of twigs and orange autumn leaves into the mess of her braids.

"Let us simply say the spirits of our hold have smiled fondly upon us on this Sovvan Hunt," said Lady Areshinn. "Now, how many times do I have to say I won't have you stand in my presence before you comply with it? Come down here and let's have ourselves a feast."

My Dear Drey,

Imagine my little Sovvan song playing such a pivotal role in the defense of our home! Your description of the skirmish, though admittedly a little lacking in poetic flourishes, puts me in such a state of mind as I fear I'll rush off to write ten more such pieces the moment I've finished this letter. Next time you write me, you must include a more detailed explanation of your own role in the scheme. I would have loved to see you all fitted up in my father's armor. If only my Herald friend Marli had been able to peek in on you at just the right moment! But speaking of when I'll see you next, I'm working on a little scheme of my own. I won't say more now, but just you stew over it, won't you?

All my love,

Simen

His heart full and warm, Dreyvin carefully folded this latest letter back up, removed the previous one from his breast pocket, and slipped the new one right in.

Just now, he meant to spend some time preparing for the best.

The Rose Fair
Fiona Patton

The morning sky was a brilliant blue, the sun beating down cooled by a breeze just stiff enough to keep the pennants on the iron market entrance snapping without tangling about the poles, the air redolent with the scents of flowers and the trilling of songbirds. It was as perfect a MidsummerEve as could be . . .

"What game d'you think yer playin' at, beak! Our family's been sellin' at the Rose Fair for decades, an' our stall's always been right here next ta the main entrance!"

Straightening from the small wagon he'd been trying to help maneuver through the gate, Sergeant Hektor Dann of the Haven City Watch kept his expression as neutral as possible in the face of the small, angry flower-merchant shaking her fist at him from behind a load of rose boxes.

"Yes, ma'am," he said. "On that side." He indicated the space to the left with a careful nod of his head; Pansy Barrow was well known for her matchstick temper, and she'd never cared for pointing. "Basil's stall's always been on this side, remember?"

"Basil's stock's caught the mold!" she retorted. "He ain't comin' this year."

Hektor glanced up the street to where Basil Greenfields was waiting patiently to bring his fully laden
wagon inside the market grounds.

Pansy followed his gaze with narrowed eyes, but her
only concession to his silent point was an explosive
snort.

"So, uh, where's Jem?" he asked carefully. "Isn't he
supposed to be helpin' you set up this year?"

"He was," she growled. "He's chasin' after some
girl, no doubt. A body could fall down dead in a ditch
afore some grandsons'd lift a finger to help 'em. And
don't think he'll inherit a thing neither. That farm an'
all that goes with it'll go to his cousin Marnie. See how
he likes them apples," she added loudly as a young man
ambled over to them. He bent to kiss her cheek and
received a mild smack for his trouble. "Where've you
been?" she demanded.

"Helpin' Ellan wi' 'er ma's stall," Jem replied with
an easy smile.

"Ellin's ma has enough family to set up three stalls
at once. Get workin' on mine or you'll get no supper!"

"Sure, gran." He gave Hektor an evil grin. "Where'd
ya want it?"

Eyes narrowed, Hektor pointed silently toward the
left of the entrance, then tried to regain the sense of
peace he'd somehow managed in the midst of Iron
Street's Midsummer preparations. But it was no use.
With a sigh, he returned his attention to the line of
merchants waiting outside the grounds.

Traditionally a time when Valdemar's youth showed
off its physical prowess; the Midsummer festival was
held outdoors; in the countryside on the village greens
or the common lands, in the towns on whatever bits of
open ground that could be spared. In the capital, the
wealthier neighborhoods, those that contained green
spaces within their walls, erected large, colorful tents

where the older citizens could take their ease with a glass of wine or cider while the younger contested with the bow, quarterstaff, and sword. In the vendor and trade districts the well-to-do merchants sponsored skittles, bowls, or stoolball competitions, and even the poorest streets managed a foot race or a shinty game during the day, with the more adult pursuits of fighting, dancing, and drinking in the evening. Betting was fierce and neighborhood pride fiercer. All manner of prizes, from money to sweetmeats to simple bragging rights, were handed out, but at the Iron Market, renamed the Rose Fair for the duration of the festival, the traditional prizes had always been roses, for Midsummer was also the traditional time when the flower sellers descended on Haven en masse. The best went straight to the Palace and the wealthier houses, but enough of the smaller ones crowded into the Iron Market to cause a yearly sweet-smelling and colorful headache for the Watch.

"Sleepin' on the job, eh, Sergeant?"

Once again, Hektor dragged himself up from the sense of peace he'd struggled to maintain to find Fair Master Linton Kray grinning at him.

"Jus' thinkin'."

"Bad idea. Causes ya to miss things." Linton jerked his head to where Constable Marcher was trying to broker a peace between two elderly brewers arguing over the placement of their individual stalls.

"Clay's managin' fine."

"If by managin' you mean managin' not to get his head knocked in by a walkin' stick, I'd agree with you, but managin' to get all the food an' drink vendors set up by tonight, I dunno." He turned before Hektor could answer. "Mornin', Pansy. You got my order?"

"Who else would have it? Twenty of the finest yellow roses in all of Valdemar."

"Twenty? You're gettin' generous in your old age."

Hektor's older brother, Aiden, laughed as Linton turned an indignant scowl on him. "You do like to sneak up on a man, don't cha Corporal?" he retorted. "Gonna get yourself into hot water one of these days. As it happens, besides the heavylift and the hammer throw, I'm sponsorin' the littles' stone toss. Got a grandson enterin' for the first time."

"All three of those sites are already set up," Hektor pointed out. "So, did you actually want me for somethin'?"

Linton shook his head. "Nope. Just wanted to let you know that the tug-a-war ditch is all set up too," he answered. "Nice an' muddy. Just waitin' for a line of smiths to send a line of watchmen tumblin' into it just like they do every year."

"Not this year," Aiden retorted. "This year we've got Lance Constable Barrons to anchor us."

Linton made a mock show of considering the other man's words seriously. "Yep, yep, that might do the trick for you, unless, of course, we got Benj Gransil's nephew, Ted, to anchor for us."

Hektor's eyes narrowed. "Thought Ted was a butcher."

"He is, but as it turns out, he served a full apprenticeship under Benj afore he took over at his da's abattoir."

About to say something he was sure he'd regret, Hektor was spared incurring the undying wrath of Haven's leading blacksmith by a shout of warning from one of the wagoners. All three men turned to see the youngest Dann brother, thirteen-year-old Padreic, pelting down the street toward them at high speed.

"He ain't half fast, your Paddy," Pansy noted. "Guess I'll be bettin' on his gameball team this year."

"Hek! I mean Sarg!" Paddy skidded to a halt in front of Hektor, straightening the front of his Watch House runner's uniform as Hektor gave him a stern look.

"You gotta come quick," he panted. "The Cap'n's gone an' gutted the tug-a-war team."

"What, why?" Hektor kept his gaze on his brother's face, ignoring Linton's suddenly wolfish grin.

"Dunno. But he's got most of 'em on shift tomorrow at dusk. He's written it on the staff chart by the Duty Sergeant's desk an' all."

Aiden's eyes widened. "There'll be a riot."

"Constable Marcher!"

Clay came at the run, drawn by the urgency in Hektor's voice.

"Take my place here. The flower an' honey sellers all know their sites." He waved a distracted hand at Pansy's snort, and for a change, she allowed the familiarity to pass. "If there's any problem with the food an' drink vendors, get Linton to sort it out."

The Fair Master's grin became a full out laugh.

"You wanna concede our win now, Sergeant Dann, or wait till tomorrow dusk?" he asked.

"Not a chance."

"An' when we win," Aiden added, "any of you smart enough to lay your bets on us'll clean up."

Linton's retort went unheard as the three Danns turned and ran for the Watch House.

The place was in an uproar when they arrived, but as yet, no one had mustered the courage to confront the Captain, sitting peacefully in his office with the door open, either unaware, or unconcerned about the chaos he'd created.

Aiden shoved his younger brother unceremoniously inside.

"Sir?"

Captain Travin Torrell, closed the ledger he was studying and looked up, an expression of mild inquiry on his face.

"Ah, Sergeant." He glanced past him. "And Corporal. Do come in."

Hektor schooled his own expression to one of neutral respect as they entered. Ordinarily it was the responsibility of the Day Sergeant to post the shifts. The Captain had the right to have his . . . opinions listened to, but he rarely interfered with Hektor's decisions. And he'd never arbitrarily rewritten the staff chart. Until today.

"What do you need?"

"About the new staffing for Midsummer's Dusk, sir. It's just that you've put Pat an' Jamie across from the Awl an' Tongs."

"I did." The Captain leaned back. "Last year, with so many Watchmen attending the tug-of-war competition, we saw far too many incidents of public drunkenness and brawling in and around the local taverns." He laid his hand on the ledger for emphasis.

"Yes, sir, which is why I doubled the Watchmen in those areas. Already. Without your . . . help," Hektor added silently.

"I noted that. However, Lance Constable Barrons has the height and Constable Farane the girth to create the necessary impression to promote order, which Constables Spotsworth and Cooper lack."

"Yes, sir." Hektor took a deep breath. Might as well leap into it. "But we need Pat an' Jamie to beat the smiths, Capt'n. Without 'em, we don't stand a chance."

Behind him, he felt Aiden bridle, but he ignored him.

"From what I'm given to understand, the Watch has never stood a chance as it were, Sergeant," the Captain replied. "That we have never, in fact, beaten the smiths in the history of the Rose Fair. And I'm not so sure that having the entire community see the Iron Street Watch covered in mud year after year promotes the proper degree of respect and confidence necessary to maintain the peace. We have a reputation to uphold, after all."

Hektor cast a swift sideways glance at Aiden. From

anyone else, this outlandish speech would have generated aggressive disdain, if not full out derision from his older brother, but Aiden had a tightly controlled expression of polite neutrality on his face. To be honest, the Iron Street Watch covered in mud was what most of the community came to the Rose Fair to see on Midsummer's Dusk, but since most of the Watch were their sons, grandsons, and nephews, it hadn't ever seemed to erode respect, confidence, or their reputation all that much.

"I am aware that the tug-of-war is a time-honored tradition," the Captain continued, "Which is why I have put in a request for reinforcements from a few of the other Watch Houses. If they arrive in time, we may have enough men to keep order and field some kind of a tug-of-war team at the same time."

Hektor and Aiden shared a look of deep apprehension.

"Um . . . no disrespect intended, Sir," Hektor said slowly, feeling his way around the delicate subject of the Captain's Breakneedle Street past, "but Iron Street's awful' proud of its own, an' they don't take too kindly to . . . um . . . outsiders tellin' 'em what to do."

The Captain raised an eyebrow. "You don't say. But I think I've got that problem solved as well."

"Aiden! Hektor! Where are you hidin', boys?"

"Uncle Daz?"

As the two Danns spun toward the familiar voice, Captain Torrell smiled slightly. "Ah, good. That will be Lieutenant Browne now. Captain Hutton's letter said he would be arriving today."

"Lieutenant Browne?"

Like most cities, Valdemar's capital was made up of many small, insular districts, some no more than a single street long, each with its own history and traditions.

There was very little movement up, down, in, or out, and generations of families lived and died within a few blocks of each other. Their mother's twin brother, Dazen Browne, had done the unthinkable. He'd accepted a position at the Cheese Court Watch House on the other side of Haven, taking his wife, children, and aging parents with him. They might as well have moved to another country.

"So, you're an officer now, huh?" Once Aiden had extricated himself from their uncle's bear hug, he gave the insignia on his uniform a suspicious look.

"Well, there was an openin', an' what with gettin' older, I figured I might need a bit more authority to keep the younger fellas in line."

"Uh-huh. What does retired Sergeant Grather-Preston think of that?"

Daz chuckled. "Not much," he admitted. "Had a few choice words for his youngest son."

"I'll bet he did. Somethin' about nothin' carryin' more authority than a proper sergeant's voice."

"Word for word. You developed that voice yet, Hek?"

"Workin' on it," Hektor answered as Aiden snickered. "You come by yourself, Uncle Daz?"

"You mean besides the five Watchmen I brought from the Cheese Court nick to show you lazy louts how it's done?"

"Yeah, besides them."

"Emptied the house. Your ma hasn't seen our youngest yet, an' the rest haven't seen their auntie nor their cousins in ages. Came up the river way with Deem first thing this mornin'. Already dropped most of 'em off at your place, but Hamil an' Prest walked up with me." He jerked his thumb behind him to indicate the two very large young men in Watch House uniforms standing by the duty sergeant's desk. "Oh, an' Shanda brought a pile of littles hopin' they could earn some fair money cleanin' out bird cages for Kasiath. Hey there, little Bird Speaker!" he shouted as Hektor and Aiden's fourteen-year-old sister came pelting down the stairs to throw her arms around a girl only a few years older than herself. "Messenger Bird apprentice, eh? Yer Granther Thomar woulda been proud."

Shanda returned Kassie's hug before they were both engulfed by a crowd of children all talking at once. They slowly moved across the floor and up the stairs as one, the sound of their chatter slowly receding.

"So, you were saying, Sergeant?"

Hektor blinked. "Cap'n?"

"About outsiders? Are these men close enough to suit the street?"

His tone was mild, but Hektor thought he could see an unusual flash of humor in the older man's expression.

"Yes, Captain."

It didn't take long to get Hamil, Prest and the other three Watchmen partnered up with Iron Street veterans; then Hektor and Aiden returned to the market grounds with their Uncle Daz in tow.

Since it was for the most part sponsored by merchants, on Midsummer's Eve the Rose Fair predominantly involved selling in the daytime and revelry in the evening. Most of the flower, salt, and honey sellers were in position by noon, and, not to be outdone, herbalists Sue and Bill March had a stall next to Pansy's, selling kellwood and sendlewood oil lotions and wheat smut tinctures. Several potters had tall, thin ceramic vases for sale to hold the winning roses, and the posy-makers were doing a brisk business in the small maiden's hope bundles popular with young lovers. Although no livestock was allowed on the Iron Market grounds, the Temple of Thanoth had special dispensation; it had a wide area fenced off with various domestic animals available for deserving families only, a table for selling whistles and small carved animals, a bin for food and cleaning donations, and a small iron box for monetary offerings.

The serious drinking and dancing wouldn't begin until dark, but the scrumpy and summer-wine sellers were already in place in the very center of the grounds. As the three men ambled slowly through the growing crowds, they kept a careful eye out. Clay had already arrested three pickpockets, a smash-and-grab artist, and two Tyver boys for tossing stench beetles into Holly Poll's ribbon cart.

"I mostly hauled the littles in to keep her from braining 'em," he'd confided to Hektor.

And Jez Poll was on his way off the grounds, escorted by two of the larger Watchmen, for picking a fight with Hektor's father-in-law, Edzel Smith. Of an age, the two men were equally matched sober, but as Jez was already reeling and Edzel never touched a drop, the retired blacksmith had sent his old schoolmate flying into a sweetmeat stall with one punch.

"We arrested Jez on account of his language around the littles," Corporal Kiel Wright told them. "That and for the chaos he caused sendin' all those treats scatterin' in among 'em. He can come back this evenin' if he can dry out a bit."

Along the far west side, the food vendors were already busy, and the odors of frying onions, fish pies, and pescods reminded Hektor that he hadn't eaten since early that morning. He shared half a dozen pickled eggs and a huge cheese toasty from Nanny Agga's pie stall with Aiden and Daz, then led the way back toward the entrance.

As they passed the bookmaker's stall, the man waved them over.

"Is it true the watch is concedin' the tug-a-war?" he asked, eager for some first-hand information.

Aiden's eyes narrowed. "No, it ain't true, Lee. Who told you that?"

The bookmaker shrugged. "It's all over the fair. I've had to set the bettin' at four to one what with Pat an' Jamie off the team an' all. I know yer the Captain, Aiden, an' the Danns have always been big, strong lads," he added with an attempt at an ingratiating smile, "but really, it hardly seems worth it without them two, don't you think?"

"Pat an' Jamie are not off the team," Hektor retorted.

"Thought your Cap'n put 'em on shift. He take 'em off again?"

Hektor made to reply, then just turned away, shaking his head.

"Nothin's settled yet, Lee; not by half," Aiden growled as he turned to follow.

"So, they're still on shift then?" Lee persisted.

Neither Dann bothered to turn around.

"You need to talk to the Cap'n," Aiden said as they headed back to the Watch House, their Uncle Daz wisely keeping his thoughts to himself.

"I know."

"Soon."

"I will."

"When?"

"When we get back to the nick."

But when they arrived, Paddy informed them that the Captain had gone to take an early dinner with Captain Rilade of the Breakneedle Street Watch House, and before the Captain returned, Hektor got called out to handle a botched shoplifting-turned-street brawl in Spud Lane. By the time he got back, with the four Watchmen he'd had to call, the shoplifter, his accomplice, and the three grocers who'd objected to their behavior, the Captain had left for the night.

"Why'd you bring them in?" Hektor's old partner, Kiel Wright, asked, jerking his thumb at the indignant grocers.

Coach of the tug-of-war team Corporal Hydd Thacker turned on him with a furious snarl. "Because you don't bring a punch-up into the street!" he shouted. "That's why we're missin' Pat an' Jamie in the first place! Get 'em all downstairs!"

As cowed as the grocers were now, Kiel obeyed.

By the time Hektor and Aiden got off shift, the wall chart still held the names of Lance Constable Barrons and Constable Farane at the Awl and Tongs on Midsummer's Dusk.

"You have to talk to him," Aiden said as they took the tenement steps up the Dann flats, two at a time.

"I will."

"When?"

"First thing tomorrow, all right?"

"We're not on shift tomorrow," Aiden reminded him.

"I'll go in anyway."

"An' if the Cap'n won't change his mind? What are you gonna do then?"

"I'll think of something."

"It better be a good somethin'."

Hektor closed his mouth on what would have been a profane answer as their Aunt Alana and Aiden's wife, Suli, met them at the door to her and Aiden's flat. Suli thrust a large pot of stew into her husband's arms, and their seven-month-old twin sons, Thomar and Preston, into Daz's.

"Everyone's at your ma's for dinner," she told them. "Hektor, can you help Jakon and Raik with the chairs, please? Bring all of 'em. How many are you here?"

"Just us. Hydd Thacker took the other Cheese Court men home with him," Aiden told her.

"Well, at least that's three less. If the littles sit on the floor an' Granther Preston's in Granther Thomar' old armchair, we should have enough seatin'. If not, Rosie's folks have offered to lend us theirs."

"Comin' through!" The two middle Dann brothers pushed past them, carrying two chairs each, then headed up the stairs at a run.

"When you're done with that, the plates need bringin' up," she called after them.

Daz laughed. "Just like old times," he noted, "happy chaos."

"It is that," Alana agreed. "Entertainin' any thoughts about movin' back, husband?"

He smiled over the heads of his two nephews. "Maybe."

"Good."

Half an hour later, fifteen adults, seven youths, including Paddy's sweetheart, Rosie, and Kassie's best friend Laryn, six children, and eight babies all sat down to dinner together.

The next morning, heading for the fair in a crowd of family, Hektor shot his brothers a look that banned talk of the tug-of-war. He'd said he would handle it, and he would handle it, although he was still completely unsure of how. Adult conversation was impossible anyway as Aiden's four-year-old son, Egan, holding court high above them on his father's shoulders, kept up a constant, high speed explanation of the fair for the benefit of those cousins who had never attended before.

"Cost a pennybit to get in, but babies are free. All the sweets are a pennybit too an' so's the cider."

"The soft cider, little jaybird," Aiden interjected.

"Uh-huh. Ma says we gotta keep together an' that we gotta do what Kassie an' Shanda say. Ma say's that if we're all real good we can stay at the fair for supper. I'm gonna do the littles long race an' the short race. Gus an' Jacy an' Emma can do those too, but Ben an' Bryan are too young. They can do the littlest stone toss an' the beanbag throw."

"Me too!" Squirming around in her cousin Shanda's arms, two-year-old Leila gave her older brother an egregious scowl.

"Maybe. You might be too little still."

"Me too!" Leila began to cry, and Aiden tapped his son sternly on the knee.

"But she might be, Da!" he protested. "It's not my fault!"

"We'll find a game for you to do, cousin," Shanda assured her. "Maybe we can team up together for something."

Comforted, Leila settled down, and Egan continued to sort out which family members were to enter which competition and who was going to come away with what prizes.

"Da is cap'n of the tug-a-war, so we're gonna win that a course, and take all the roses there an' make a HUGE bunch on Gramma's table!" He threw his arms wide, almost flying backward off his father's shoulders. Hektor caught him at the last second, and the boy gave him a beatific smile in response. "Thanks, Uncle Hek. The Danns an' the Brownes are gonna take all the prizes, right?" he added as he righted himself.

"Hope so."

Aiden shot him a look but said nothing.

As they passed The Awl and Tongs tavern, Hektor turned to see the publican, Helena Rell, and her four children lifting the shutters off for the day's trade. With the clear weather holding, they had several tables outside already under an awning, and he paused, an idea beginning to grow in his mind. "I'll meet you later," he said, striding across the street. "Don't let anyone talk about any kind of conceding until I get there."

By the time he reached the fairground it was midafternoon, and the place was crowded with people from Iron Street and beyond. Egan ran up to him, bubbling over with news about the family's triumphs. Jakon and Raik had placed second in the junior relay race, but Paddy's gameball team, the Watchmen, had destroyed their rivals, the Chandler's Row Wolves, by a score of five to nil. Aiden remained the unbeaten senior wrestling champion for the fourth year in a row, and Kassie had taken the junior ring toss and junior horseshoe throw both, winning two roses and a twisted wire bracelet. He himself had come in third in the littles long race, behind Tawny and Hassa Tyver, and second in the short race to Ebony Poll.

"There's still the stone toss an' the three-legged race; I'm gonna do that with Jacy, an' then there's team tag! After that, we're all gonna watch the tug-a-war an' eat sweets!"

Still chattering, he led his uncle to where most of the family, babies in their arms and at their feet, were taking their ease beneath a small tent within sight of the children's games.

As he came up, he was surrounded by the rest of the littles, all shouting at once to make themselves heard.

"How come you didn't race today, Cousin Hek? Da said you was the fastest ever when you was a little!"

"You gonna buy us all sweets at the tug-a-war, Cousin Hek? Egan said you might!"

"I lost a tooth bitin' a treacle pie; wanna see it?"

"I'm gonna be in the stone toss, I've been practicin' all week!"

"How come there isn't a littles' tug-a-war; we'd win it for sure!"

"Ben barfed behind the sweetmeat tent 'cause he ate way too many at once an' then spun 'round and around and around!"

All six cousins and at least eight friends of Egan's began spinning about in a circle until them all fell laughing to the ground. Hektor admired their technique for a few moments, answered questions, and exclaimed over winnings until Kassie and Shanda scooped them up to prepare for their next events. Then he threw himself down next to Jemmee and Ismy, accepting his own sons, five-month-old Ronnie and Eddie, onto his lap. As Jakon and Raik presented their mother with their winning roses from the long jump, he looked over at the ceramic vase of flowers already sitting by her side.

"Shouldn't there be more?" he asked.

Jemmee shifted her new niece from one arm to the other as she gave him an unimpressed look. "Well, you weren't here to add to my hoard this year," she scolded. "An' Kassie gave most of hers to her Granny, as she should," she added in case Elinor might think she was finding fault with that.

"What about Paddy's?"

"Ah, yes, well," she glanced over to where Paddy and Rosie had already found themselves a seat on the makeshift bleachers beside the tug-of-war pitch. "Who'm I to stand in the way of young love," she said with a fond smile.

Hektor followed her gaze, counting the flowers clutched tightly in both toung fists. "Looks like they did about the same. That's good."

Uncle Daz glanced over their heads. "I see there's no bonfire pit again this year."

Hektor shook his head. "Not since the fire two years

ago. Just didn't seem right what with the deaths an' all. We may never see another on Midsummer's Dusk now."

Daz nodded. "I miss your Da. He was a good friend."

"When I was a young man, we didn't have no Midsummer's Dusk," Preston noted. "Jus' Midsummer's Eve. All the games were packed into one day. The tug-a-war was at sundown right before the bone-burnin'—the bonfire, that is. The butchers made a killing all through the springtime, what with folk buying an' drying bones to add to it. The whole street built it, not just the woodsmen like nowadays." He scratched at his chin. "Somethin' to do with raisin' of healthy crops or the chasing off'a bad magic. Can't remember. There was fire jumpin' too. In yer great-granther's day it were only maidens that did the jumpin', but by my time, it was boys as well as girls. That was a sight. An' I was pretty good at it too, could jump to the moon back then. When I was seventeen, I leaped straight over the top to impress yer granny."

Aiden glanced over at Granny Elinor, whose attention had already wandered from a story she'd heard a hundred times.

"Was she impressed?" he asked.

Preston caught up her hand as she gave an amused snort. "Not a bit of it," he declared with a laugh. "She'd jus' jumped twice as high herself. But she was impressed by the great long scorchin' I did to my left calf."

"Impressed isn't the word I used at the time, Preston Browne," she scolded. "Nor the one I'd use now if it weren't for the littles here. Silly old fool."

He chuckled. "I was a silly young fool then, but you married me anyway, didn't you?"

"I did." She squeezed his hand, then waved at Jemmee to pass little Preston over to her, before shading her eyes with one hand. "Well, hello there, Linton

Kray, don't you look official?" she said as the Fair Master strode over, his blacksmith's apron trimmed in yellow fringe.

"Thanks Ellie. My granddaughter sewed it on for me. Hey, Preston. Nice to see you both again."

"Hey, yerself," Preston acknowledged.

"These all your grandbabies?"

"Yup. Every last one, an' that pile of puppies over there. This is our newest, little Abbie."

Linton chucked the baby under the chin, smiling as she made a grab for his fingers. "She's a pretty wee thing. Got eight myself and two on the way," he said proudly.

"They're a comfort as you get older. How's your Jillian?"

"Good. She's over at the stone toss gettin' our Hollen ready for his first ever competition."

"I saw him. He's a fine-looking lad."

"He is that. Takes after his ma." Linton straightened. "Well, it's nice to see you both again. The street hasn't been the same without you." He turned to Hektor. "You ready to concede that tug-of-war match yet?"

Hektor smiled back at him. "Nope. Hey, Pat, hey, Jamie."

He nodded as the two burly watchmen headed for the area where the tug-of-war teams were warming up.

"So, you got 'em off shift, huh?" Linton noted. "How'd you mange that?"

Hektor pointed to the large beer tent in the center of the grounds. "Publican Rell felt she would make more money bringin' all her goods an' staff here instead of splittin' them over two sites, so she's closed the Awl and Tongs up for the evenin'. With no tavern, there's no need for Watchmen."

"Always said you were the clever one," Linton said grudgingly. "Good thing I laid a bet with Lee that you'd get 'em back. What?" He widened his eyes in mock surprise at Hektor's expression. "You figured I didn't believe a Watch House Sergeant could run circles around any Captain to get what he wanted? Afternoon, Captain Torrell."

The others turned to see the Iron Street Captain and four other men coming toward them.

"Good afternoon, Fair Master Kray," Captain Torrell said formally. "May I present Captains Rilade and Guthers of the Breakneedle and Water Street Watch Houses respectively, and my dear friend, Captain Elbert, late of Lower Devine. Gentlemen, this is my Sergeant and his family. We've just come from escorting Daedrus to the fair. I understand that he is to drop the flag at the tug-of-war."

"He is that," Linton agreed.

"We're looking forward to watching the competition," Captain Rilade added.

"Won't save your lot from their comin' mud bath," Linton chuckled. "No disrespect to the Watch; a fine bunch of lads they are, but Tay an' Ted are more than a match for Pat an' Jamie, whatever their size, an' Aiden couldn't beat my boy, Jared, in a game of marbles."

"Good thing we aren't only relying on them then, isn't it?" Hektor replied.

Linton followed his gaze to where Hamil and Prest were stripping down with the rest of the Watch House team.

"Who're they?!" he demanded.

Aiden gave him a smile completely devoid of warmth. "Our cousins."

"They ain't Iron Street."

"They are," Daz replied, a dangerous glint in his eye. "Born an' bred."

"Well, they ain't Iron Street Watch."

"Oh, I think you'll find that they are," Captain Torrell said, his upper class Breakneedle Street accent even stronger than usual. "Attached to the Iron Street Watch House for the duration of the Rose Fair."

"You wanna concede our win now, Fair Master?" Aiden asked, glancing past him to the sudden flurry of activity around the bookmaker's stall.

Linton scowled. "Not by half. We'll see you on the pitch in an hour. Bring yer towels."

He stalked off, already shouting to his team, and the Captain smiled.

"I think it's high time the Iron Street Watch gave the Iron Street smiths a nice mud bath, don't you think?" he asked. "My friends and I have sponsored six roses apiece from Flower-Master Greenfields, and I expect them to grace the Duty Sergeant's desk by tonight."

Aiden showed his teeth. "They will," he promised.

"Good man." The Captain turned. "We'll take our places now, I think, yes?"

With the others in agreement, he nodded to Preston and Elinor and took his leave.

"Jus' remember you're a Browne as well as a Dann," Daz said to Aiden a few minutes later as the entire family made their way, en mass, toward the bleachers, "an' we never quit until the job's done."

"Not likely something I'd ever forget," Aiden answered. "Hey Daedrus! Thanks for coming," he called as he took his place at the front of his team.

"I wouldn't miss it for the world, my boy," the retired Artificer replied. "Honored to have been asked. Now where is that flag, Mern?" He turned to the boy at his side, who pointed silently at his pocket. "Oh, yes, of course. Are all of these people your family, Hektor?" he continued. "My, my, there are a lot of you. Now who is who?"

It took some time to make all the introductions, but eventually, Mern drew the older man toward the pitch and the rest took their places on the bleachers. The crowd hushed as sixteen men took hold of the long length of hemp stretched over the ditch. Daedrus fumbled in his pocket for a moment, then pulled out a brightly checkered dishcloth. One hand on Mern's shoulder to steady himself, he lifted it into the air, paused a moment to enjoy the sight of every eye glued to his every move, then flung it to the ground. The crowd roared as Linton and Hydd began to scream orders at their respective teams.

An hour later, as Ismy tucked her arm in his, Hektor took a deep, contented breath. The evening sky was a deep, dark blue, the setting sun a streak of pink and orange against the clouds, the air redolent with the scents of flowers and the sound of music and laughter. It was as perfect a Midsummer's Dusk as could be asked for . . . made that much more perfect by the earlier sight of seven smiths and one butcher going headfirst into the mud.

The Maralud Comes
A-Knocking

Stephanie Shaver

"Who sends gifts on Sovvan?" Herald Wil asked.

"A madwoman, that's who," Herald Lyle said.

"Lyle."

Lord Grier ignored their banter, studying the box instead. It had arrived at Baireschild Manor this morning. No one knew its origin, it had simply . . . *shown up* on a kitchen table next to a bowl of wyncrisp apples, accompanied by a foreboding note: *Happy Sovvan, Lord Grier. Your beloved sister, Madra.*

Grier prepared to open it, armored in a leather coat, gloves, and special spectacles. They gathered in his apothecary, the wisest place to examine any gift from his "beloved" sister, his audience watching from behind a shield of thick metal.

"I still don't understand," said Khaari, the Kal'enedral Scrollsworn. "What is Sovvan?"

"Sovvan is a holiday for ancestors," Wil said from his chair. He'd not yet fully recovered from his last encounter with Madra. Worse, her poison had seemingly stripped him of his Gifts and ability to communicate with his Companion, Vehs. But he'd prevented a war in Valdemar, and thanks to Grier, he hadn't died. It helped that before Grier had taken on the mantle of

Lord Baireschild, he'd been a Master Healer of some renown.

"Sovvan is when we light candles for the dead," Lyle said. "*Midwinter's* when we get festive. Good food, lots of presents, dancing. . . ."

". . . dressing up in a skull and cloak," Grier said, "chasing children around until they give you treats. . . ."

"You *what*?" Lyle sputtered.

Grier chuckled grimly. "It's a Baireschild Midwinter tradition. And there's a *reason* I head for Haven and leave the country traditions back at the manor. Anyway, Khaari—Midwinter and Midsummer are the seasons for giving gifts. Sovvan is . . . more retrospective," he said. "Madra's up to something." He picked up a long, slender knife. "Ready?"

Three voices murmured assent.

Grier pulled up the stiff collar of his coat. "Here we go."

The plain, square box came tied with a piece of twisted green twine, but other than that it looked entirely unassuming. The card had clearly been written under less than favorable conditions—dirt smudged the paper, and the ink had run.

Grier cut the twine and used the knife-tip to flip open the lid.

No explosion. No cloud of smoke. Adders did not spill out.

A swath of black velvet trimmed in silver nestled inside, atop which rested a single white candle. A little card tied to the candle read *Herald Wil*.

His mouth went dry.

"Did she send us roses?" Lyle called.

"No," Grier replied. "A threat."

"I'm not going back to the quarry, right?" Lyle asked as they filed back into Wil's room.

"You're going back," the older Herald said. "The armory needs to be destroyed."

Grier started mixing Wil's afternoon tonic.

"But what if she—"

"Listen to me, Lyle. Dismantling the armory is our priority, period. And yes—Khaari is still going with you. Someone needs to record this. If your report is accurate, then Madra's weaponry had only one goal. She meant to kill *Companions*. That should terrify Selenay."

"*But, Wil—*"

"'But, Wil' nothing. You're both going."

"There's a lunatic with a giant flying construct out there threatening *your life*," Lyle said. "One of us should stay."

"No, Khaari should take Vehs," Wil said, "finish her diagrams, and come back fast."

"You want her to take your *Companion*?" Lyle said.

"Well, I don't want her taking Aubryn. *Someone's* got to stay and protect Ivy." Wil smiled wryly. "I'm still convalescing."

"Or you would be, if you'd take your tonics," Grier said, looking pointedly at the cup in his hand.

Lyle just gaped.

Wil pinched the bridge of his nose. "Exactly what is Madra going to do, Lyle? Mount a full-scale attack on the manor? This is—a distraction." He waved a hand at the air. "We're leaving for Haven soon anyway. Isn't that right, Grier?"

"My hope is someone in Haven can better help you than I." He swirled the cup. "Are you going to take this or not?"

Wil took the tonic from him, but he did not drink.

"Well, *that* at least sounds like a step in the right direction," Lyle said. "The cousins would love to be done."

"I know I say it every time," Wil said, "but truly, they saved the realm."

"And they know it." Lyle chuckled. "Think the Herald Captain could award them a mercenary's commission for all they've done?"

"I can speak to the Greater Council about it," Grier said. "But only if Wil drinks that gods-be-damned tonic."

Wil downed it in one gulp. "Spicy."

"I added beesbalm syrup after you complained last time," he said.

Lyle raised his brows at him. "Look at you, swinging your lordly might." He stood up with a groan, his knees creaking. "All right, back to the mines."

"Dismantle everything, Lyle," Wil said. "And don't die doing it. Okay? Madra is tricky. I'm honestly more worried about you than a bloody candle with my name on it."

"Yes, yes. Stay safe. I know. Bright Havens, it's like we're on Circuit together again."

Wil sighed. "Except now I'm old."

"Oh, come now," Lyle said. "You were old then, too."

"Get out."

Lyle doffed an imaginary hat and danced out the door.

"He *is* Lelia's twin, isn't he?" Grier said.

"Seems more like it with every passing year," Wil said.

"Has anyone seen Ivy?" Khaari asked.

"If she's not in your tent, she's either in the kitchen or with the Companions."

"Ah." Khaari nodded. "So good that she has a . . . *stable* place to be."

Grier and Wil stared.

"Did you—" Grier said.

"Was that—" Wil said.

"Gentlemen," Khaari said, "Kal'enedral *never* pun. Now excuse me, I must pack." With a smirk, she stepped out.

Alone with Wil, Grier turned to him and said, "I'm sorry—"

"Don't." Wil held up a hand. "I don't hold you accountable for your sister's actions. Not when I owe you my life. Just do me a favor." He lowered his voice. "Protect Ivy. She's what matters."

Grier nodded. "Like my own."

"Good." Wil pointed to the door. "Now get out."

In her life, Ivy had known many beds. Boxbeds, stable stalls, sturdy Palace canopy beds, and one carved magnificently by her grandfather, but the beds at Baireschild Manor had a feature she'd come to love—she fit under them.

Best of all, Lady Drusillia tended toward the kinds of duvets that slopped over and dragged on the floor. Ivy didn't know why—it got them all dusty—but it meant that looking *under* the bed required lifting the covers. Most people didn't bother.

So when she wanted to be somewhere she shouldn't be, she went under the bed.

"It's safe, Ivy," Wil said.

She rolled out from under her father's bed, bouncing up to sit beside him.

He brushed dust out of her hair. "Won't be awake for long. What shall we read?"

She had a book in hand—one of the many from Milord Healer's library. Cuddled up beside her father, they recreated their old, familiar microcosm of warmth and security. As they read, he pointed to words and she sounded them out—mostly.

"Your reading's getting better," he said, closing the book.

"Thank you," she said.

He kissed the top of her head. "Gonna sleep now. I love you," he said. "Don't forget to lock the door."

"I won't, Dada," she said.

She opened the door carefully, peeking out to make

sure no one was in the hallway. Then she opened it fully, and for *just* a moment she thought she heard—something. Like little nails clicking on the stones. But the darkness that aided her departure also prevented her from seeing whatever made the noise. She strained her ears, but she didn't hear it again.

She focused on locking the door with her father's key, and the odd noise soon slipped her concern. So long as it wasn't a person, she didn't care. A manor like this teemed with small living things. Pantry cats took care of many of them.

Besides, she'd overhead a great many things, and she needed to say goodbye to Khaari.

Most nights Ivy did not sleep in her assigned room. She picked other places, like the stables, or down in the wagons and tents.

Now those options seemed to be narrowing.

The cousins had taken the wagons to the quarry with Lyle, and Khaari would soon follow, though her tent remained: a squat structure of brown and dark blue out in a nearby field. What it lacked in color, it made up for in practicality and comfort. She had a little traveling desk for her writing and ample pillows and blankets.

A box and two cards currently occupied the desk. Khaari studied them intently, peering at them with a little piece of glass.

"Will you sleep here tonight, child?" she asked as she worked.

"Without you?"

"I'm leaving the tent, so you're welcome to it. Just don't—"

"Touch anything on your desk, I know." Ivy shrugged. "Maybe. Or with Aubryn." She scowled. "Wish I could sleep in Dada's room."

"Ah, Milord Healer is still keeping you away, eh?"

Ivy screwed up her face, affecting a haughty voice. "Little girl, you shouldn't be here. The tonics I give him and you have a nice room and Drusillia picked all the curtains and blah blah blah."

Khaari laughed. "You do a good impression of the long-haired lord, *kechara*."

Ivy puffed a little. "Thank you." Then she deflated. "My room gets so *cold*. And I miss him. But I should be grateful." She smiled shyly. "Aubryn says so, at least."

"Maybe Aubryn should stay there, then." Khaari locked the box and cards into a drawer on her desk. "I should be going."

"Will I see you again?"

Khaari paused in the way that meant an Adult Was Thinking Carefully About What To Say Next. "You know why I am here, yes?"

Ivy nodded. Madra. The Bad Lady her Dada had been chasing. And there had also been some . . . thing calling itself "Lord Dark."

"That task is still mine. I had hoped your father would pursue what you call 'Lord Dark' with me . . ." She glanced away. "Perhaps I'll join you going to Haven. Perhaps not. The prey may rest, it may dream. Best to catch it then."

"But you don't know where they went."

"True." Khaari brushed her braids back over her shoulder. "But—a thing as big as Lord Dark doesn't have many hiding places, nor can it go unnoticed for long."

"What is Lord Dark anyway?" Ivy asked.

"A construct. An abomination. I suspect your Madra woke it. I intend to return its bones to sleeping, once and for all."

Ivy shivered. "What's a con—"

"If I stay and answer your questions, I will never get

to the quarry!" Khaari said, half-scolding, half-laughing. "Time for this when we make our slow way to Haven. *So slowly*, I might add, for I have seen how Drusillia packs."

Ivy wrinkled her nose. She didn't know much about Lady Baireschild, but of her children she knew plenty. They liked to throw forks at her head at dinnertime. Like a lot of noble families, children of a certain age dined separately from the adults, so no one stopped the teasing.

Still, it didn't feel right, complaining. Lord Grier had done a great kindness, saving her father's life. Better to avoid than complain.

Another night eating kitchen scraps. At least they were *good* scraps.

Khaari hugged her, and then Ivy once more found herself alone, wandering across the field back to the manor, where the windows glowed bright but cold.

Grier routinely rose before his wife on those rare occasions when they slept in the same room.

Like her children, Drusillia was a product of an arranged marriage and an arranged life. They hadn't married for love, and they hadn't grown into it. But they at least respected each other. And she respected that he had a seat on the Queen's Greater Council to fill.

A seat I should be filling right about now, Grier thought. He opened his eyes to the weak morning light coming in through the diaphanous bed curtains. Usually, they'd be in Haven by Sovvan. Not this year. Not with a half-dead Herald in the house.

On this morning he woke to Drusillia beside him, her red hair spilling over a naked body pleasantly softened by three seasons of childbearing. He ran a light finger over her hip. She sighed and rolled over, yanking the duvet up.

"It is *much* too early for that, milord," she said into her pillow.

Grier chuckled. "Good morning, milady."

"At least get me a pot of milk tea first."

Instead, Grier left his wife drowsing, heading downstairs to check on his patient.

He unlocked the door, saying, "Good morning, Wil!"

From the bed, he heard a faint wheeze of protest.

Grier pushed open the curtains. "We're going to hold off on the tonic until after breakfast. Maybe take a stroll. Sound good?"

The wheeze turned into a wet, gurgling gasp.

At that moment, Grier's nose picked up on a smell. A mix of stale sweat and urine. And—

Smells like death.

Grier turned around.

Light streamed in through the open window, giving him a full view of Wil. The person he had left last night didn't look a thing like what he saw today: jaundiced, diaphoretic, laboring to breathe.

"Hellfires," Grier hissed, running over and ripping off the soaked covers. Wil had lost control of his bladder sometime in his sleep. His eyes didn't respond to light, his skin felt clammy, and his body raced with fever. Grier's Healing touch indicated a raging infection—no, something *worse*.

Grier yelled at a passing servant, "Get Lukas! Tell him to get my kit! *Now!*"

Lukas, his steward, would know what he meant.

There would be no leaving for Haven now.

"I for one cannot *wait* to leave for Haven," Trudi said.

"Oh, you city folk," Adrande said, huffing as he slid loaves of bread out of the oven with a massive bread peel.

"Yes, us *city folk*," Trudi said, rolling her eyes.

The adults were so busy talking they didn't notice Ivy stealing half the apple bowl.

"Milady all packed?" Adrande asked, shuffling the loaves onto a rack over on the sideboard.

Trudi snorted. "Milady's been wearing last year's dresses for a week. She'd drive the coach herself if milord would let her." She leaned against a table as she gossiped, lazily stirring a cup of milk tea. She had her back mostly turned to Ivy, which meant no one had eyes on the apple bowl. The wyncrisps easily fell into Ivy's palm, then her smock pocket.

"Well, if you wait much longer, you're wintering here."

"Gods, no. You *country folk* and your Midwinter traditions are atrocious."

"Aw, you don't like the ol' Maralud?"

"No one likes the Maralud!"

Adrande laughed. Ivy had no idea what they meant by their lively exchange, but it meant one more apple. She started to reach out—

One of the kitchen cats hopped up on the table and mewed at her. She froze, then batted at it. The cat recoiled, confused, then mewed again. *"Go away!"* she whispered furiously, and she snatched an apple quickly as the cat stepped forward and tried to get a headrub in.

Ivy counted her plunder. Six. It seemed like a good number.

"Ivy!" Adrande said, his voice cracking across the kitchen.

She started, then adopted the most innocent expression she could muster.

"Do you know where the butter crock is in the pantry?" he asked.

She nodded and ran off, relieved she hadn't been caught. Not that she'd be punished. Cook would know *who* she meant the apples for. The fun came in not getting caught.

Her feline companion trotted behind her as she fetched a lantern and hauled open the door to the pantry. There were two pantries in the manor: one above and one below. Above was meant for temporary storage and the cavernous below-ground one for longer term. She ran down the stairs, found the crock, and delivered it to Adrande.

"Can I go?" she asked.

"Yes you—" he said.

She ran out before he could finish.

"They won't let me see him," Ivy said, passing apple after apple to Aubryn.

:Why not?: She could hear the Companion, even though she couldn't directly talk back to her as her uncle could and her father used to do. She didn't know why. She wasn't Chosen or anything. Aubryn told her not to worry about it, so she didn't.

"I don't *know*." She slumped on her hay bale. "I can't even *sneak* in."

:Perhaps the Healer wants to make sure your father is extra rested. Have patience.:

A tear trickled down her cheek, but she gulped and nodded. "Wait, wait, wait. What do we do when we wait?"

:Go for a ride?:

"It's too cold." She scratched Aubryn's withers. "Can Companions read?"

:I think we should leave that as something you do with your father.: She nibbled the second to last apple out of Ivy's pocket. *:Why not the kitchen?:*

"I'm sick of the kitchen." She smiled up at Aubryn, holding the last apple. "There is this locked room in the south tower . . ."

The Companion eyed her warily. *:You shouldn't be going into locked rooms.:*

"So . . . turns out . . . Dada's key *worked* when I tried it on the door. . . ."

The Companion stamped her hoof. *:Ivy!:*

"It's just full of old furniture! And . . . um . . ." She lowered her voice. *"Toys!"*

After a long, judgmental minute, the Companion leaned forward and nipped the apple away.

:Don't. Break. Anything.:

The thing about rooms you weren't supposed to be in is that they were always the room you *wanted* to be in.

The storage chamber was as she remembered it: full of dusty cupboards and canvas-covered furniture. No one had touched the chests full of toys. Ivy found wooden swords and shields in one trunk, button-eyed dolls in another. Hobbyhorses leaned in a canister.

Armed with one of the swords, she set up a battlefield of dolls, imagining herself at the first war of the Border with Hardorn. In this version, it was Ivy alone who stopped Ancar's demons. She waded into the button-eyed masses, swinging her wooden sword two-handed and—

Pop! One of the doll's head flew off across the room.

She ran after it, dodging around canvas-draped furniture, and as she lunged around a set of end tables she stopped—because the polished walnut wardrobe before her *wasn't* covered, and its intricacy stole her breath. Inlaid white ash created scenes of wintertime: delicate snowflakes, leaping stags, holly boughs, and—oddly—pouncing gryphons.

She lifted the latch and pried open the door. It swung open on oiled latches, revealing its contents.

A monster crouched inside.

She wanted to scream. Instead fear clutched her throat, overwhelming her so that she stood paralyzed and blinking up at the horror looming over her.

And then she realized—this was no monster. This was something of mortal construct that hung from hooks inside the wardrobe. Tentatively, she reached up and touched it. It swayed softly, creaking in the quiet. The beaked skull regarded her somberly, the mantle of black and green feathers gleaming against the heavy crimson cloak.

"You're a false-face costume," she said, her fear vanishing in a delightful shiver. She knew this well. The cousins sometimes played at this.

Ivy closed the wardrobe and presently left the tower altogether, now more certain as to why this room had been forgotten.

"You look a sight," Drusillia said as Grier dragged himself into the bedroom to slump in a chair.

"I do?" he whispered.

She walked out into the antechamber, returning with a decanter. He waved it away. "No spirits, please."

"Have you eaten?"

"Lukas put a loaf of bread and cheese in me."

"Impressive. What's wrong?"

"Everything. I—I think he's stabilized, but. . . ." Grier passed a hand over his face. "I don't know. Last night Wil was fine. Something's gone horribly wrong."

Drusillia's face went still. Then she picked up a glass and poured herself a cup of claret. "Is the Herald dying?"

Grier clutched the bottom of his face, staring off into the distance.

"Yes."

Her knuckles whitened. "Grier, if you're about to tell me we're delaying our departure *again*—"

He blinked. "Excuse me?"

"—I'm not waiting any longer. We should have left *weeks* ago. The passes will close, and we'll be *stuck* here."

Grier stared at her. "I'm . . . *very* tired. Maybe I didn't speak loudly enough. Herald Wil is going to die. Did . . . did I say that part? Did you hear me?"

Drusillia drank her claret. "I heard you."

"Really? This is what you care about?"

"You wear Green. I understand your devotion to that. But you have a realm-wide commitment to the Greater Council. So, yes. This is what *I* care about."

"Okay." Grier blinked. "Then, uh, go. And while you're at it, please take Ivy with you." He put his head in his hands. "I don't want her to watch her father die horribly."

"Take her?" Drusillia looked at him, confused. "We can do that?"

"Yes?" Grier spread his hands. "Wil hasn't regained consciousness and probably never will. Her uncle is off at the quarry. Who's going to make decisions for her? That Companion? Do you know what it will do to her, seeing her father die like this?" Something flickered in his brain as he talked, but he was too tired to sort it out.

"Fine. We'll escort her to Haven and let the Heraldic Circle sort out what to do with her. And you'll—?"

"I'll stay," he said, quietly. "I trust you and Lukas can manage the Greater Council in my absence. I'll . . . write instructions." He passed a hand over his eyes, anticipating the long night ahead of him.

Drusillia looked pained. "You take on too much."

"I'm trying to save his life. Or at least, minimize his pain."

"At least you'll get to dress up for the villagers this Midwinter."

He glowered at her. "Really?"

"You know I jest." She finished her claret. "I seem

to be a thorn in your heart tonight. I'll sleep in the Rose Room."

"You aren't—"

"Good night." She kissed his cheek, lips sweet with honey and spice, and he found himself alone by the fire.

He thought of the white candle. Three nights to Sovvan.

We underestimated her, he thought.

"Ivy!"

Ivy started from her daydream, clutching her cornbroom. She'd been thinking about her father and how'd she'd like one visit, just one.

This time there was no Trudi and no apples. No cats, either. She hadn't seen a cat in the kitchen in days.

Adrande waved dough-covered hands. "I need the walnut crock."

"In the cellar?" she asked, casting a dubious eye at the open doorway.

"G'awn. Not like the Maralud is down there waiting to eat you up or something."

The more I hear about this Maralud, the less I like it, she thought.

Still, orders were orders. Down the steps she went, lantern swinging in her hands.

She got halfway down the steps when she heard— something. Like little nails clicking on the stones.

Ivy paused. A gulf of emptiness separated her from the kitchen's warmth and the oppressive darkness below.

It's a rat, she assured herself, aiming her lantern at the source.

The light licked over a shape, and what she saw did *not* look like a rat.

It snarled silently at her, frog's eyes wide and angry. It only stood there a moment before it sprang off into the darkness on bowed legs.

She ran up the stairs and into the kitchen, shrieking, *"The Maralud!"*

Grier delivered the bad news to Lukas and Adrande in his study the next morning.

"Do you mind?" he asked.

Adrande looked pleased. "You know how I feel about Haven, milord. The reasons are miserable, but you're doing me a favor, the way I see it."

"Then it's settled. Go let your underchef know about her temporary promotion." He turned to Lukas as the cook hustled off.

The tall steward folded his hands in front of him and sighed. "I wish you'd let *me* stay."

"Drusillia will need you to run the household in Haven. Who can you spare here? I'll need help with the Herald."

Lukas inclined his head. "I know precisely who and how many."

"Thank you. Also, have you seen Ivy?"

Lukas pursed his lips. "The kitchen, perhaps?"

"I'll check."

"Milord, you shouldn't have to do that. I can—"

"I have to check on her father anyway. It's all right." Grier smiled tenderly. "You have always been a good and faithful friend, Lukas. Take care of my family."

"Take care of yourself, milord."

Wil's illness had reached a stalemate; since the initial deterioration he hadn't gotten worse . . . but he hadn't gotten better. His fever stayed constant. He took no food and showed no signs of awareness. His hair had turned brittle and white. Grier poured what he could into him, and by the end of the day he seemed to improve, but by the next morning he'd be back to square one. Grier kept a servant stationed at his side constantly to freshen him. And to keep Ivy away.

She mustn't see him like this. With that thought in mind, he set out to find her.

Not in the kitchens. Why is she never where she should be? he thought as he started searching through the expanse of the manor. Three stories and two towers, though surely not the south tower, as it was locked tight. Still, it would take candlemarks to visit every room, and she could be anywhere.

Outside, he could hear voices shouting and the creak of wheels. He watched from one of the few unshuttered windows as the Baireschild coach rolled out.

She should be in there. So should I.

And his sister should never have tried to kill a Herald. Grier's eyes skipped over to the stables.

The Companion. The quarry.

Vehs.

Grier moaned. "I'm an idiot."

Grier marched into the stable, his words echoing through the mostly empty structure. "I need Vehs back."

Aubryn leveled a pair of stern blue eyes in his direction.

"Wil is dying. His Companion should be here."

She took a step forward, shaking her mane in what he thought might be anger, though not directed at him.

"Help me, Aubryn. Where is Ivy?"

She shook her mane again and blew a furious whinny.

Grier pointed out the open doors. "You don't understand—I'm doing this for her own good. It isn't too late to catch up with my family. If you can find her—"

The Companion turned around, presenting her rump.

"She's already watched her mother die. Don't let her watch him die, too."

Slowly, the Companion turned back around.

"Please," Grier said.

With measured, stately steps, the Companion walked out of the stable and out the doors. Then she pointed with her nose toward the manor.

It took him a moment to figure out what she pointed at. When he did, he swore.

The costume in the wardrobe didn't scare Ivy anymore. She even admired it. The sturdy construction, the intricate embroidery around the hem of the clever cloak that concealed the wearer. She couldn't wear it—much too bulky and heavy—but she could imagine it would fit well on Milord Healer or her father.

She heard the door to the tower open and started, heart pounding. She looked around quickly for a place to hide—under a canvas, in a chest—but before she could, Milord Healer came around the corner, straight to her.

"Ivy," he said, and stopped when he saw what she'd found.

"Milord," she replied, meekly.

"The Maralud," he said, his eyes on the bird-skull mask.

Her eyes widened. "*That's* its name?"

"Her name."

"The Maralud's a *girl*?"

"Once, the Pelagirs extended deeper into Valdemar than they do now." He ran a finger down the costume's deep crimson cloak. "The Baireschild family has held these lands . . . a long time. Our oldest Midwinter tradition is meant to scare off the things that come out of the hills during the cold months. *The Maralud comes a-knock-knock-knocking*, as the song goes. You're supposed to feed her, or she'll gobble you up."

Ivy's eyes widened.

"Except she doesn't," Grier said, gently. "She's . . . a

good monster. The kind of monster that's meant to only gobble up the bad things."

"I—thought I saw her," she said. "But if *that's* what she is, then I didn't see her at all." She put her chin in her hands. "I don't know *what* I saw, now."

Grier looked at her sharply.

"What did you see?" he asked.

"In the cellar," she said. "I think it was a . . . comb-stuck."

It took him a moment. "Construct?"

She nodded. "I called it the Maralud, though, and Cook said that I was being silly." She scowled. "I told Lukas, but he just wanted to put me in the coach. And then Aubryn said to stop telling your folk anything because you wanted to take me away, so I hid."

She *didn't* add that Aubryn had also said she was going to send for *real* help. She figured Grier didn't need to know about that.

Grier regarded her a long moment and then said, "Show me."

Adrande lit the wall lanterns as they descended the cellar. Grier brought a shillelagh from his great-grandfather's collection, a comforting weight in his hand.

"This is a waste of good oil," Adrande muttered.

"Humor your lordship," Grier said.

The cellar spanned a generous three-quarters of the manor's floorplan, cool and cavernous. A series of shelves ran along the walls, and barrels and more shelving created neat aisles throughout. Cool air came in through shafts that had been dug into the rock, keeping the whole chamber at a constant temperature. Thanks to Adrande, Trudi, and Lukas' efforts, the supplies were kept tidy and organized. They were also the only people—outside of Grier and Drusillia—with keys.

The perfect place to hide, assuming you could get in.

They moved aisle by aisle, and only when they got to the second to the last aisle did they find the pantry cats.

Adrande swore. Ivy made a small sound.

They lay curled on their sides, claws extended, stiff and cold. Grier crouched down to examine them, cautious not to touch anything.

Their fur had turned brittle and white.

"Milord!" Ivy whispered, pointing her lantern light.

Grier looked up. Squatting like a frog above them on a shelf sat a bug-eyed monstrosity about the size of a small dog. It had fully articulated hands and legs, and slick, pebbly skin.

It peeled back its lips and hissed, lifting one greenish-gray hand to block out the light.

Then it leaped off into the darkness.

"Are we safe?" Adrande asked, as Grier locked the pantry.

"We should be. It can't get out—"

He stopped.

It can.

The many, many shafts cut into the rock. He turned around, mind racing. His eyes went to Adrande.

"You fought at the Border?" he asked.

The cook nodded.

"Catch." He tossed the shillelagh at him. "We'll—"

At just that moment, two figures strode into the kitchen, dusty and sweaty from a long ride.

"You understand what kidnapping is?" Lyle spat the words through gritted teeth as Ivy ran over to him. "Regardless of what happens to Wil, she's *my* niece."

"Lyle!" Grier said. "Right now isn't the time—"

"I think you have time to talk to us, *milord*," Khaari said, stroking Ivy's hair. "We rode very hard to talk to *you*."

"There's a construct in the cellar!" Ivy said excitedly. "And it's not the Maralud!"

That got their attention.

"There's *what*?" said Lyle.

"You heard her," Grier said. "If this thing isn't responsible for Wil's sudden illness, I'll eat Adrande's butter crock."

"How big is it?" Khaari asked. "Can we catch it?"

Adrande shuddered. "Ain't getting *near* that thing."

"It's about the size of a dog," Grier said, holding his arms out. "Why?"

She rubbed her chin. "Describe it in detail. If we can corner it . . ."

As she spoke, something in Grier's brain lit up. "Maybe find something that it's afraid of. Something custom-made to frighten the things that come out of the Pelagirs."

She cocked her head. "Do you know of such a thing?"

Grier nodded. "I might."

It came at night because, inevitably, someone fell asleep.

It only needed a moment. The humans often left the door open when they aired out the room or changed Wil's bedclothes, and so it waited—and then shot through the gap, sliding under the bed or into the hallway.

At night, it need only bide its time for the watching human to nod off. They always did.

It hadn't meant to kill the cats, but they'd been a nuisance—their hissing, their *claws*. One touch had put an end to that. It only had two explicit orders: deliver the box and death to the one named Wil. But not a fast death, no. As close to the Night of the Candles as it could get.

And it knew that night came soon, so—

The construct snuck into Wil's room early tonight. The encounter in the cellar meant it needed to act fast.

Still, it waited under the bed, biding its time for the right moment, knowing not to rush. It had little in the way of a mind, and no other weapons save for its poison, so waiting did not bother it.

At some point the door to Wil's room opened, and someone came in. Low voices murmured. And then, softly, "He's passed."

"Milord?"

"Herald Wil has died," the voice said, and the construct jolted as if electrified. *Yesyesyes,* it would have sung, if its creator had made it with vocal chords. "Help me. We'll move him to the cellar for now."

The door opened. And in that moment, the construct peeked out from under the bed.

It seemed safe. . . .

It shot out in a flash.

Something stepped into the doorway, skull-headed and feathered and crimson. Prey recognized apex predator and for a moment the construct thought *GRYPHON GHOST!* and cowered.

And then darkness dropped down, trapping it.

"The Maralud," Khaari said, holding up the horse-sized skull in bemusement. "Do you know, I don't think this came from a normal bird?"

"I've often wondered," Grier said. "But not too hard."

"Your ancestors built a custom on interesting times, I'll wager."

"Well, their interesting times aided ours," Grier said.

The black metal box with the construct inside rattled from time to time, emitting angry hisses. In Grier's apothecary, Khaari, Lyle, and Grier gathered round.

"Lord Dark surely commanded this," Khaari said. "But Madra sent it. They're working closely, it seems."

"What . . . *is* it?" Lyle asked.

"Hm. The name is—I think it would translate to

poison-frog-little-thing. They secrete a toxin on their skin. They must touch you." She nodded to Grier's gloves. "You were wise to wear those."

"And why aren't we squashing it?" Lyle asked.

"Because *it* knows where Madra and Lord Dark are."

They gave her startled looks.

"Once I open this box, its first action will be to go back to them," she said.

"Oh," Lyle said. *"Oh."*

"I think Wil should stay dead for now. He needs time to recover."

Grier nodded. "And you?"

"I will not rest this winter. Lyle, will you join me?"

Lyle shook his head. "Once I'm done with the quarry, I need to go back to Selenay with this."

Khaari nodded. "Then alone I go."

"Khaari—"

"It's all right. I'll find them. I won't necessarily engage." She winked. "I'm not Wil."

Lyle suddenly looked embarrassed. "Grier, about that kidnapping accusation, I'm—"

Grier cut him off. "No apologies, please. *I'm* sorry I didn't think sooner to have Aubryn reach out to your Companion."

Lyle looked relieved, then worried again. "Wil . . . will he . . . ?"

"Now that he's not being poisoned nightly? His odds are better. But so much damage has been done. . . ." Grier took a deep breath. "Time will tell. Let's hope Midwinter is a happier holiday."

In a dusty tower, the Lord of Baireschild remembered.

She loved these dolls, these books. He touched the chests he'd packed away ages ago. His own children never played here. They hadn't been interested in these cracked and ancient things.

He opened the old wardrobe and looked again on the Maralud. *She loved wearing you, too.* She'd always been angry that only the men got to dress up in the costume on Midwinter. Their parents had been strict about that.

Grier had promised her that *he'd* let her wear it once the mantle passed to him, but he'd never gotten to follow through on it. She'd become Madra before he'd become Lord Baireschild.

I guess you found your own monster to court, he thought.

"Going to be a real honor, having you wear the mask this year," Adrande said, huffing slightly from climbing the tower steps. "Ready, milord?"

Grier nodded. "Let's get it over with."

Down in the Great Hall, the remaining manor staff and locals from Solmark came to dinner for Midwinter, Wil and Ivy among them. The Herald looked like a ghost come to the feast, his Whites hanging loose and his head shaved. What hair grew back came in white. He ate like a horse, though, and he even smiled at the Maralud's antics.

Grier ran around the room, clacking the articulated jaw of the Maralud's skull, and the children squealed and laughed, tossing knotted ribbon "treats" at him and patting his nose for good luck. They sang around the Midwinter hearth, and Grier stamped his boots, specially shod in iron so they clattered on the tiles.

Later, the costume once more stowed, he sat beside the Herald and casually set a single white candle down in front of him.

Wil's white eyebrows lifted. "You Baireschild folk are rotten at gift giving, you know that?"

"Just wondering what we should do with it."

Without a moment's hesitation, the Herald picked it up and flung it into the roaring hearth.

"To hell with it," he said. "It's just a bloody candle. *Holidays.*" Wil snorted. "Did Lelia ever tell you about Midwinter . . . ? No? Well, let's just say holidays have not been kind. Know what I celebrate, Grier?"

Grier shook his head, amused. "Tell me."

Wil pointed to where his daughter danced. "Her birthday. *That's* a holiday I'll gladly celebrate, year after year."

Grier raised a glass to him. "Happy Midwinter anyway, Wil. To your health."

Wil raised his back. "Is there beesbalm in this?"

Grier laughed. "Will you ever drink it and find out?"

Herald and lord clinked glasses, as nearby the children danced and sang: "*The Maralud comes a-knock-knock-knocking. . . .*"

Seeing the Truth
Angela Penrose

Herald Josswyn heard the murmur of conversation as he approached the south salon of his ancestral home. Freshly washed and changed, he paused in the arched entryway and got his first glimpse in a long while of the people inside.

His sister-in-law Vannilyn, the Baroness Sellkirt, had a bit more gray in her hair, which wasn't surprising since she was . . . fifty-six, he was pretty sure. There were more lines in her face, but her smile was the same. Her simple gown was of beige wool with green embroidery around the edges, nothing ostentatious, despite being a Baroness.

The one who drew his gaze, though, was Delinda Sand, who sat under a window directly across from him. Delinda and he had run wild as children and been best friends until their parents betrothed them, to their dismay. Dash had Chosen him in time to avert disaster, and she'd happily married Ruban Sand two years later.

She caught sight of him immediately and broke off what she was saying. "Joss! You're home!" She rose and crossed the polished floor of the salon, her light blue gown rippling behind her. Like his sister-in-law, Delinda had some gray in her hair, just a little at her temples and

a bit right at her widow's peak. Little lines framed her
shining gray eyes, and just seeing her made him want to
go out and steal a bull, or hide a farmer's wagon, or glue
all the pruning knives together—all of which they'd
done at least once, as children determined to be a plague
upon their parents and neighbors.

Delinda came and clasped his hands tight. They
grinned at each other, and he imagined she was remembering the same mischief.

"Dash still keeping you out of trouble?" she asked
with a teasing smirk.

"It's his entire job," said Joss with a laugh. "Luckily,
he's very good at it."

"I've no doubt you'd have been eaten by a Change-
Beast long since if not for him."

"Most likely," said Joss, still grinning.

In his mind, Dash said, *:I'll not let you forget that,:*
and Joss sent him a mental laugh.

Vannilyn touched his arm and said, "Joss, it's so
good to see you. How long do we have you for?"

He gave his sister-in-law a hug, then a kiss on either
cheek. "It's wonderful to be home. I've four days free. I
was passing by Trevale on the Trade Road, and since
I was near, I wanted to spend the Spring Fair at home.
I hope more of the family will be here?"

"Yes, and they'll be delighted to see you. Jessamine
took her whole clan over to visit Verity Callan, but
she'll be back soon."

Jessamine was Joss's only sister. He hadn't seen her
in almost four years, and he was looking forward to
catching up with her and meeting a new great-nephew
whose name he couldn't recall.

He said, "I imagine Joris is off on some business?"

"One of the presses broke," said Vannilyn. "I forget
the name of the piece that snapped, but everyone's

quite concerned. I'm not sure why—we won't be pressing any more grapes for months."

"Specialized pieces can take a long time to acquire," said Joss. He gave her a shrug, then turned to the other person in the room and said, "Ruban, it's good to see you again."

He clasped hands with Delinda's husband, who gave him a nod and an, "And yourself," in return. The man was stout and bluff, with a broad face and leathered hands. His father had been a glassmaker with a good head for business, and when Ruban Sand had taken a fancy to Delinda Carboy, and she'd fancied him back, both families approved. Since the death of Delinda's parents, Ruban and Delinda had managed her family vineyards quite well.

The four of them sat and exchanged news for a bit, Joss updating them on the goings-on in the capital and around the kingdom, and the three locals telling him the gossip of the wine country.

When the news began to run dry, Delinda leaned forward and said, "I'd like to ask you about something." She looked away, and he saw her cheeks go a little red. "It's silly, I know, but Perran, my youngest, wants very much to be a Herald. He has no interest in either vintning nor glassmaking, but he's an excellent rider and quite skilled with a sword and bow for his age. He's fifteen, and he's been talking about being a Herald since he was small. I was wondering, maybe it's some kind of sign? Is there anything we could do for him? Perhaps a trip to Haven, put him in the way of some of the Companions . . . ?"

Joss sighed. He always hated getting these questions, and had never thought to get them from Delinda.

"That's not how it works, I'm afraid," he said, his voice gentle. "The Companion Chooses. There's nothing anyone can do to influence that."

"I know that of course. But still, I was hoping there was something . . ."

"It might happen. But if a Companion does Choose him, he or she will come and find him, you needn't worry about that."

She laughed and said, "Well, of course. Dash found you, after all." She sighed and looked at him again. "I just worry about Perran. He has his heart set on it, and it's just not something you can predict or work toward."

"No, unfortunately it's not." Joss searched for some way to turn the conversation and asked about her other sons. Carwin, the oldest at twenty-six, was helping his parents run the winery and had apparently inherited his father and grandfather's head for money and management. Coltrey, the middle son at twenty-two, was a handsome young man—according to his mother—and focused his attention on random studies. He wrote poetry for whichever young lady had his interest in a given week, and that made him popular.

Vannilyn turned the conversation to the coming Fair, which was what they'd been discussing before Joss arrived. As the Baroness, Vannilyn was responsible for organizing the event, and Delinda was her chief helper. Joss promised to assist however he could and was assigned a number of brute-force-and-ignorance type tasks.

The Sands finally made their goodbyes and left, and Vannilyn went off to check on dinner.

Joss went out to the stable to make sure everything was to Dash's liking. Young Unwin the groom had indeed pampered his Companion to shining perfection and was going over all his tack with a thick, knitted pad and a jar of saddlesoap when Joss came across him.

The stable was of gray stone and oak, as were most buildings in the neighborhood. It smelled strongly of fresh straw and only faintly of horse dung. It was dim but airy, and Dash had been given a roomy box stall. The swinging door was propped open so he could go out to the paddock whenever he wanted. There were four mares out there already, which was fine—horses to a Companion were rather like dogs to a human—but that meant the paddock gate couldn't be kept open.

:*It's fine,*: said Dash, sidling up next to Joss. :*I can hop the fence whenever I want. Tell Unwin not to panic if I do?*:

Just as Joss was letting Unwin know that, yes, Dash could hop the paddock fence without much effort, and that was fine, a ruckus approached from behind a cluster of oaks that hid the stable from the side of the house. Joss recognized a sharp laugh—Jessamine was back.

She spotted him and cantered over, then hopped off her gelding to give him a smothering hug. "Joss! It's so good to see you!" She leaned around him and called, "Dash, hello!"

"Hello, Jess," said Joss. He smirked and added, "Sorry I missed your birthday. You're terribly spry for an old lady who's hit the half-century mark."

She punched him in the arm hard enough that he was sure he'd have a bruise for days. "Brat! Just wait, two more years, and it'll be you! Let me go change into a proper gown before Joris sees me and goes spare— then we can catch up until dinner."

"Later, then," said Joss. She gave him a quick kiss on the cheek and strode off to change out of the linen trousers she insisted on wearing for riding. It made perfect sense to Joss, who saw women in trousers all the time. Joris was a stodgy lump, though, always had been, and was too concerned with how things looked.

Half an hour later, he and Jessamine were out on the back patio, which had a beautiful, wide view of the soft, rolling hills covered in narrow rows of green vines, with the occasional house or winery or shed scattered here and there, and puffy dark green oaks filling in the hollows and ravines.

Jessamine was telling him about her friend Verity's granddaughter, a girl named Alisse. "It's such a shame," she said. "The girl is only seventeen, and clearly with child. Verity is sure she has no regular young man, and she refuses to say who the father is. Even if she's determined not to marry him, his family should at least take some responsibility for the baby."

"If she doesn't want to marry him, that might be the trouble," Joss pointed out. "Her parents can't try to march her to the altar if they don't know who to march with her."

"I suppose so," said Jess. "It's still too bad."

Joss nodded but said, "It is, but I'm sure she has her reasons."

Dinner was loud and boisterous, with fifty-two at the big tables in the dining hall. In addition to Jessamine's family, their brother Jarvin had come with his wife, one of his sons, the daughter-in-law and three grandchildren. Joris' son Jevan, the second heir to the Barony, lived at the manor with his wife and two children, and Joris' two daughters had come home for Spring Fair and brought their own families.

Vannilyn's end of her table were all children over ten, of which there were quite a few. The younger ones were eating in the nursery under the supervision of what was likely not enough maids.

Joss found himself the center of a crowd of children after dinner. He was pelted with questions, demands for stories, and requests for rides on Dash.

"Hardly anyone ever rides a Companion other than the Herald," he explained as gently as he could. "But I happen to know there are at least three ponies in the stable, so I'm sure you'll all get to ride while you're here."

"It's not the same, Uncle Joss!" Jevan's daughter Jassilyn complained. She was twelve and got excited enough about horses, let alone Companions.

"You're right, it's not. But it'll have to do." He ruffled her fair hair, which was in two long braids, but had a cloud of loose, curling hairs that'd escaped her plaits and seemed to be trying to escape her head all together. Jassilyn wasn't the neatest of young girls, but Joss figured she had plenty of time for all the Young Lady business later.

The next day began in a buzz of activity. Vannilyn was ruthless about drafting everyone capable of working.

She spent the early morning with Delinda, then they both descended upon the Fair Meadow and got everyone busy. Joss spent the day hauling barrels and timbers and rolls of canvas and putting up stalls and tents along with other men from the neighborhood.

Vannilyn and Delinda went dashing back and forth across the meadow, supervising and giving instructions, both together and separately.

Joss wanted nothing more than to head across the meadow, sneak up behind Delinda, and stuff a handful of grass down her back, as he'd done over and over when they were children. She'd gotten him back with beetles or caterpillars, and once she'd emptied a leather pouch of ants on his head. The scurrying, biting little things had gotten all over him and into his clothes; he'd been covered with itchy red bites for over a week.

She'd apologized about that and swore she hadn't realized they bit quite so badly. Most ants in the neighborhood didn't. Her mother had made her come every morning and clean his horse's stall out for a month, and Delinda had only grumbled about it a little bit.

That had been when they were children, though. Joss grinned at the memory, but left the grass alone.

Late that afternoon, when Joss was standing next to a water barrel getting a drink, Delinda approached. "How are you doing?" she asked.

"Fine. It's warm, but Vannilyn has nothing on our Armsmaster when it comes to cracking the whip and making folks work, so I'm somewhat accustomed."

Delinda laughed and nodded. "We've made good progress. We'll have a wonderful Fair opening tomorrow, if the weather cooperates."

"Leave some milk out for the pishkies just in case," Joss said with a teasing grin.

She laughed again and said, "I just might!" Then leaned to look around him and shouted, "Nevis! You drop that mudball this second and get back to work!" She glared at a young boy across the field who was hurrying away, his shoulders hunched, by the time Joss turned round to look; then she huffed. "At least it wasn't a pouch of ants."

Joss threw back his head and laughed. "I was just thinking about that earlier! You were such a wild little beast back then!"

"We both were, don't try to deny it! I'm sure all our sneaking and plotting and running and climbing and adventuring about is what made you a good Herald!"

He laughed again and nodded. "Likely so."

She gave him a pishkie grin, then turned and bustled off to whatever was next on her list, and Joss jogged over to help three men lugging a huge iron grill across the grass.

The sun rose the next day on a drizzly morning, but the rain stopped during breakfast, and by the time Vannilyn dashed off to fetch her cloak, even the grass had mostly dried.

Folk gentle and common, wealthy and poor, gathered on the Fair Meadow by noon. Vannilyn stood upon a wooden platform decked with painted canvas and draped with flower swags and made a speech about how love bound family and friends and communities together. She introduced a trio of minstrels who'd be playing during the festival, then declared the Fair open.

Joss had always loved the Spring Fair. He wandered among the vendors' booths, looking for baubles to give as fairing gifts. Vannilyn had mentioned on the way to the meadow that the adults in the family had long since arranged for each child to get a token.

There were fifty-four of them, she informed him. If all the adults tried to give something to each child, they'd beggar the family, and those who lived at a distance would have to hire wagons to get all their baubles home. Therefore the limit, and Joss was much relieved.

He ended up buying hair ornaments for Jessamine and his sisters-in-law, an embossed leather wristband for his brother Jarvin, who wore that sort of thing all the time, and a carved wooden pen for Joris, who'd likely appreciate something businesslike.

One of the vendors had a headscarf with lines of tiny embroidered ants trailing all over it. He laughed and bought it to give to Delinda.

The sun set and the dance music began. Children ran about in the dark, playing hide-and-find in the shadows, while mothers put babies down to sleep in baskets, and the youngsters who weren't quite children anymore vanished into the dark for some privacy.

It was late enough that some families had bundled up their children and headed home, when a slow and halting shadow came out from between two trees. Joss only noticed her because he had a habit of noticing everything. He was about to dismiss her when she suddenly cried, "Mama!" and staggered across the grass, throwing herself into the arms of a sturdy woman standing near one of the closed and draped booths.

Joss whispered apologies to his dance partner and moved toward the young woman and her mother.

"Perda, Perda, what happened?" The older woman guided her daughter over toward a torch, then gasped. "What happened? Who did this?"

"I want to go home, Mama." Perda sobbed and clung to her mother. She had a blackened eye and a split and bleeding lip. Her skirt and bodice were disarranged, one of her underblouse's sleeves fouled in the armhole of her bodice; she looked as if she'd dressed in a hurry and with no care at all.

Joss felt his jaw tighten. He straightened up and looked around, marking the people present one by one, looking for anyone who seemed furtive, anyone who was trying to leave by himself. No one stood out.

He approached Perda and her mother, and said, "What happened, lass? Tell us, and we'll make it right as much as we can."

Perda shook her head violently, refusing to even look at Joss.

He stepped back and let her mother tend to her— holding her, rubbing her back, whispering to her. Finally the girl stopped crying, sinking deeper into her mother's embrace. Joss caught her mother's eye, and the woman nodded.

He stepped near again and said in a low voice, "Perda? I'm Herald Joss. Please tell me who hurt you? I want to keep him from hurting anyone else, and only you can help me do that."

Perda sniffled and turned her head, looking up at him.

She wasn't a pretty young woman, but Joss knew that had little to do with this kind of assault. Her features were blunt, and she'd likely have her mother's jowls in another twenty years, perhaps less. She was sturdy built, short and stout, as many from this area were. She'd be capable of hard work every day, and that was valued among the folk, even if it wasn't the fairy-story image of a princess.

Perda stared at him, her expression fearful and somewhat dubious. He repeated, "Please?"

"It was Coltrey," she whispered. "We were in an oak grove, talking and such, and I kissed him a few times. But he wanted more, and I didn't want to. I said no, but he wouldn't listen! He just . . . he's stronger than me. He made me. I didn't want to, I swear!"

She started crying again and buried her face in her mother's shoulder once more.

Joss closed his eyes hard and took a deep breath, then turned and went to find Delinda. He wasn't looking forward to the conversation they were going to have.

Delinda wasn't hard to find, and Ruban was right near her. Joss drew them both aside and said, "A young woman has made an accusation against Coltrey. I need to speak with him. Do you know where he is?" Joss wasn't sure he'd recognize Coltrey, not having seen him in some years.

"What kind of accusation? What rubbish is this?" Ruban glared at Joss, his hands fisted, and made no attempt to modulate his voice.

Joss, firmly in Herald mode, looked Ruban in the eye and said, "She's been beaten up some, and he forced himself upon her."

"Rubbish! The girl's deluded, or she has some grudge against Coltrey!"

Joss said, "That's as may be. If he didn't do this, I'll confirm that, and we'll find out who did. But I need to talk to Coltrey."

Ruban scowled and leaned forward, but Delinda gripped his wrist and tugged him toward her. Her voice lowered, she said, "Arguing will just stretch this out. We'll help Herald Josswyn investigate, and Coltrey will be proven innocent all the sooner."

Ruban huffed and looked down at the grass. Joss saw him take a deliberate breath, then another, before nodding and stepping back.

Delinda released his wrist and turned to Joss, saying, "I saw him go behind the pie tent a time ago," then strode off.

Joss followed her into the darkness with Ruban trailing behind.

Behind the large tent where the pie competitions were held, a group of youngsters was sprawled out on the grass, gathered in the flickering light of a small fire.

"Coltrey!" she called. "Are you here?"

After a pause, one of the boys near the fire said, "He's not here, Mrs. Sand. He went off to meet a girl a while back."

Joss saw Delinda's jaw clench. She nodded and said, "Thank you. Which direction?"

The youngsters looked at one another, then pointed.

It took some searching, but they eventually found Coltrey on the edge of the Fair Meadow, on his way back from wherever he'd been.

"Coltrey! Where have you been?" called Delinda.

The young man looked up, his eyes wide. "Mother? I was, well, walking."

"Alone?"

He squirmed. "No?"

"Who were you with?"

"Mother!" He looked shocked and embarrassed. "I can't—I mean, I'd rather not say!"

Joss squeezed Delinda's shoulder and stepped forward. "Were you with Perda?"

"Perda?" He looked even more confused. "No."

"Perda!" Ruban was right there of a sudden, his anger bubbling up. "That sow is claiming that my son forced her?"

Coltrey yelped, "Forced?!" but his father barreled on.

"He could have any girl in the neighborhood! Only an idiot would think he'd want to touch Perda!"

Joss became aware of a crowd gathering behind them and gave a mental groan. "That's enough of that," he said, projecting all the authority he could at Ruban. "This is easy enough to settle. I'll Truth-Spell Coltrey, and we'll know for certain."

"You're not casting any magic on my son! It's an insult to even suggest he might have done such a thing, and to that girl!"

Joss kept half an eye on Coltrey, expecting him to relax at least a little at his father's declaration, but instead the boy said, "No, do it. If we can settle this right now, then why not?"

"No!" Ruban stepped between Coltrey and Joss, glaring like he was willing to throw a punch to defend his son. Delinda said, "Ruban!" but he scowled at her.

"I won't shut up, and I won't let this bastard cast his magic on my son. I care about his reputation, even if you don't."

"Ruban! That's mad! Coltrey says he wants to be Truth-Spelled! He wouldn't say that if he were guilty!"

"Of course he's not guilty! Someone is trying to drag our name in the mud! That girl bears some grudge, or someone put her up to it, someone—"

"Ruban!" Delinda got right up in his face and glared. She was small but fierce, always had been.

Coltrey stepped up and touched Joss's arm. He whispered, "Mother will win, she always does. Let's get on with it."

Joss nodded and took a few breaths, relaxing his

mind before beginning the rhyme. He pictured the Vrondi, the foggy wisps summoned by the spell. Over and over, until Coltrey's head glowed blue.

"Were you with Perda this evening?" Joss asked.

Coltrey said, "No." The blue glow remained, clear and steady.

"Have you ever lain with Perda?"

"No."

"Have you ever forced yourself upon any woman?"

"No."

Well, that was clear enough. Although it left more questions.

"There," snapped Ruban. Delinda had indeed, it seemed, won their argument, but they stood an arm's length away, and Ruban was still glowering. "He's innocent, as he said before. You'll leave him be now."

"I shall," said Joss. "Thank you, Coltrey." Joss nodded to the three before walking off, back across the Meadow to where he'd left Perda and her mother. The girl was standing in the circle of her mother's arms, but no longer leaning into her. She seemed a bit more aware, a bit more sure of herself.

"Perda? Would you mind if I cast a Truth Spell on you, and had you repeat for me what happened?"

She looked up at him, shrinking just a bit. "Will it hurt?"

"No, not at all." He gave her an encouraging smile, and she nodded, moving a step away from her mother. Half the neighborhood had followed him and they all circled up around Perda, her mother and Joss. He tried to ignore them and cast the spell once more.

When the blue glow appeared around Perda, he said, "Go ahead, tell me what happened, just as you did before."

She glanced around, then locked her eyes on his face. "I was by some oaks with Coltrey. We were kissing and such, but he wanted to keep going, and I didn't want to. I told him no, but he forced me."

The blue glow stayed steady. Every word was the truth.

Joss said, "Thank you, Perda," and ended the spell.

The crowd muttered and shuffled, and he heard a few curse words. Before he could think what to do next, another young woman stepped forward and said, "He forced me too. I didn't think nobody would believe me." She looked at Perda, and suddenly they were hugging and sobbing on each other.

The new girl was thin and bony, with a receding chin and unfortunate teeth. Joss could understand why she'd been hesitant to step up; so many thought only pretty girls were raped, especially by handsome young men.

Another girl stepped forward. "And me. Last fall, at the Fair." She went up to Perda and the other girl and put her arms around them.

After a long pause, another young woman stepped out of the crowd and said, "And I." Her waist was thicker than it should have been, and Joss was suddenly sure that this was Alisse, Verity Callan's granddaughter. She walked over to the other girls and was absorbed into their huddle of sorrow and comfort.

Joss's mind whirled. So many! So many stepping forward, at this time and place. There were likely more who weren't present or couldn't quite scrape up their courage. Someone was stalking the young women of the neighborhood like a sandlion stalking a flock of goats.

And they were all young women, not yet twenty, any of them. Joss imagined Jassilyn cornered in the dark and instinctively brushed a hand over his hip where he had a blade strapped under his tunic.

Slowly and thoroughly, Joss thought. Do it right.

Over the next half hour, he separated the girls and bespelled each one. They were all speaking truth.

By the time he was done, bystanders told him the Sand family had left, taking Coltrey with them.

Fine. It was late, and there was something deeply amiss, something besides the obvious. Coltrey hadn't attacked Perda, and Joss suspected he hadn't attacked the others either. But they were all sure he had. Joss needed to think on it.

He knew where to find the boy, and he could pick up the mess tomorrow.

The next morning, Joss was up before the sun. He'd had all night to puzzle out the situation, but so had everyone else. He could easily imagine some angry brother or father stewing all through the night, then getting up early with a hardened resolve to punish the villain and be done with it. Joss was determined to get ahead of any would-be heroes.

A vineyard was a kind of farm, and farmers rose early. If he set off with the dawn, he'd arrive at Delinda's house in time for breakfast.

:Any ideas?: he asked Dash, while hauling out saddle and bridle.

:A few. No good ones,: said Dash.

Joss sighed and nodded. *:One—someone has figured out how to defeat the Truth Spell. Unlikely. And catastrophic if so.:*

Dash tossed his head in agreement. *:Two—Coltrey is two-minded, and the mind you spoke to honestly has no recollection of assaulting the young ladies.:*

Joss grimaced while tossing Dash's saddle on. *:I didn't think of that. Let's hope not. It's unlikely anyway, terribly rare. Three—someone disguised himself well enough to pass as Coltrey in the most intimate situation.:*

:Possible,: said Dash. *:Someone already of the same build and coloring. And if he carried out his attacks in the dark?:*

:Still a huge risk.:

Joss finished tacking up Dash, mounted and headed off down the drive.

They went in silence, Joss fitting facts together this way and that, trying to see some obvious answer he'd missed. The sun was just rising over a vine-rowed hill when he took the turn past a shallow, bubbling creek.

Before he was halfway to the house, he heard scampering feet and a voice calling, "Herald Josswyn? Wait!"

Dash stopped, and they looked back to see a younger boy who looked rather like Coltrey running up the drive toward them.

:Someone likes early morning walks,: Dash observed.

:He might be coming home from a tryst,: said Joss. *:He looks young enough to think sneaking out with his sweetheart is a grand adventure.:*

"Good morning!" called the young man. "I wanted to talk to you yesterday, but I never got a chance."

"Yes?" Joss mustered a smile for the boy. "And who are you?"

"I'm Perran Sand!"

Ah, that one. Joss really didn't want to deal with the boy's dreams at that moment, but before he could come up with a polite excuse to leave, Perran was babbling at him.

"I'm going to be a Herald! I've seen it! That means I have Foresight, right? That's a Gift, and only Heralds have Gifts. I'm a great rider, and I'm the best archer my age, and I even beat a lot of the older kids. I'm good with a sword, too! I've been having lessons since I was little! I'm going to be a Herald! You can see it too, can't you?"

Joss opened his mouth to explain how things worked to the boy, but then, all of a sudden, he could see it. He got a wavery vision of Perran in Whites.

:Did you see that?: he asked Dash. *:That's . . . I've never had a hint of Foresight before.:*

:I didn't see anything,: said Dash.

Joss looked at Perran. Yes, that was what he'd seen—Perran in Whites.

Wait, that was exactly what he'd seen. Perran, as he was right then, in Whites.

That was impossible. Perran was only fifteen. Even if he were Chosen that very day, he'd spend years in Grays, and he would look very different by the time he got his Whites.

Joss looked down at the boy and said, "I'm not sure. I thought I saw something, but it was a bit hazy. How strange!"

Sure enough, the image came again, brighter and stronger. And because he was watching for it, Joss felt the tickle of Mind-magic.

It was Perran.

:It's a kind of Mindtouching,: said Dash. *:He's making you see what he wants you to see.:*

Joss felt a cold knot in his gut, but he made himself smile down at Perran and said, "Well, let's go talk to your family, shall we?"

Perran beamed up at him and happily led him up to the house.

Most of the adults were awake when Perran led Joss into the dining room where breakfast was laid out on the sideboard.

"Joss?" Delinda wore a loose morning dress and her hair was bundled into a hasty bun. Her face was pale with dark smudges under her eyes, as if she hadn't slept well.

Ruban stood up and glared at Joss. "It's early for calling. What do you want?"

"I'm going to be a Herald, Father!" Perran was bouncing up and down on his toes. "Herald Josswyn saw it!"

"What?" Ruban looked back and forth between Perran and Joss and Delinda, shocked silent.

"I do want to talk about what I saw," said Joss. He looked around at the assembled family before looking back at Ruban. "But I'm afraid it wasn't quite what Perran wanted me to think. Your son is Gifted, Ruban. But the way he uses it, he's never going to be Chosen."

Ruban said, "What?" and Perran said, "No!"

Another man who looked to be in his midtwenties or so, and had a younger version of Ruban's face, stepped up and said, "I'm Carwin, Perran's oldest brother. What's he done?"

"Your brother has a Gift that allows him to project images into other people's minds," said Joss. "He can make them see what he wants them to see. He tried to convince me I was 'seeing' him as a Herald, but he showed me himself as he is, a young boy, in Whites. That would never happen. But it clued me in to what he was actually doing."

He gave Perran a hard look and said, "This is the young man who assaulted all those young women. He gave them the image of his brother Coltrey doing it. The girls were all telling the truth last night, as they saw it. But Coltrey spoke true when he denied assaulting Perda. Both truths cannot be true. The young ladies told the truth as they knew it, but their accusations of Coltrey were memories planted in their minds by Perran when he assaulted them."

Perran turned to run, but his brother grabbed him by the arm and said, "You're not going anywhere. You stand right there while the Herald casts his spell."

Carwin kept a tight hold on Perran's arm while Joss cast the spell yet again, and his parents watched in silence, leaning on one another.

Joss took the spell all the way to second stage, certain

Perran wouldn't speak unless compelled. Then he asked, "Did you force yourself on Perna?"

Perran grimaced and struggled but finally spit out, "Yes!"

Joss went through the names of the other young women. The boy answered yes to each one.

"Did you make them all think it was Coltrey raping them?"

"Yes!"

Ruban staggered back to the table and sat down heavily in a chair, his face pale. "Now what?"

"He'll be punished by the local authorities," said Joss. "Your brother."

"Yes, the Baron administers the Queen's justice in this region. But there's one thing I need to do before we dump this in Joris' lap." Joss had never done this before, had hoped he would never have to, but he knew how, and it had to be done. "No one who abuses a Gift is allowed to keep it. I'll be removing it right now."

Perran started screaming and struggling, but his brothers held him while Joss did what he needed to do.

The rest of the Spring Fair was an odd mixture of subdued and giddy. Most of the neighborhood was glad to have a rapist found and punished, but at the same time, they were shocked that it happened.

Perna's mother sought out Joss to thank him, but Perna herself was keeping to home. Joss suggested a Mindhealer. Her mother agreed to think on it.

The rest of Joss' visit with his family was awkward. His family and Delinda's were close; all the adults and most of the older children felt the discomfort. When Joss packed up and saddled Dash, it was with a sense of relief.

:*It'll have blown over by next time we're here,*: said Dash.

:*Perhaps,*: said Joss. He wasn't sure; he had a sick feeling that his friendship with Delinda would never be the same, but he was willing to wait and see.

:*I did forget something, though. I found it while I was packing up.*: He pulled a long blue ribbon out of a saddlebag and started braiding it into his Companion's mane. :*Happy Spring Fair, Dash. I love you, and this is a token of it.*:

:*I love you too, Chosen. You did the right thing, and I'm proud to be your Companion.*:

A Darkling Light
Phaedra Weldon

"But, Manou," Twill said breathlessly as she and her best friend climbed up the side ladder and into their favorite hiding place since childhood. The Hold was a hive of loud voices, laughter, and music, while the smells of roasted meats, vegetables, and spices filled the chilled autumn air. Harvest Fest was under way, the Hunt had started early that morning, and the first spoils celebrations were underway. "We have to light the Sovvan fires tonight."

"I know that!" Manou huffed as he pulled and pushed his rounded figure up the stairs behind Twill. They were the same age but not the same size. Twill was reed thin, with a mass of curly red hair, a round cherub face and bright green eyes. Manou's skin was darker, and he tanned while Twill freckled. Manou was also a half a foot taller and, obviously, rounder. "And that's not a we. I'm not part of that." He gave an exaggerated shiver on the ladder. "That's you and Jaques. Not gonna catch me out tonight in the dark."

Manou was the Hold Lord's youngest son. Having a different mother than his older siblings, the baby of the family stuck out, not just in his size and his love of food, but in his lack of interest in everything except lore.

Where his older brother and sister were being groomed to take over running the Hold, Manou studied lore of any kind, and every Harvest Fest he reminded her that as of midnight last night, the veil between the worlds of the living and the dead had begun to thin, and soon their spirits would walk among the Holderkin.

Dumb Suppers were being prepared in every household, ready to pay respects to those who had passed during the year. Decorations hung from doors and windows, balconies and store fronts. Cornstalks and bales of wheat straw covered every corner. Even the horses wore bridles woven with orange, yellow, and red leaves.

Twill scooted into their little spot, an alcove overlooking the back gate of the Hold. Most of the year storage boxes took up residence in the alcove, but they had all had been removed. When Manou's dark hair popped up from the ladder, she stood and pulled him the rest of the way up and in, and he slid on his belly across the stone.

"You really need to lay off the honey pastries, Manou," she said as she plopped down, winded. "And I thought you said if I ever got Chosen, you'd go with me." She winced at the whine in her voice. The lighting of the dark during Sovvan Night was supposed to be an honor, but among the Hold children, the stories of ghosts and strange sounds in the dark had turned it into something terrifying.

His face was red and sweat dotted his brow. "Well, I thought I might. But given my father wants me to help my brother guard the stables, I should stay home."

Twill glared at him. "He said no such thing."

"He did too!" Manou set his lips into a thin line. "We've had three horses go missing, and some of the supplies in the shed."

"And it just so happens the stables aren't that far

from the kitchens. The only thing you're gonna do is eat more pastries. You're just scared."

"So are you." His eyes widened. "Oooh. Did you hear about the missing child at one of the southern Holds? Said he went out to light the windows, and there was a scream . . . and then they never found him! I heard the spirits took him back to their side of the veil."

"Stop . . . it." Twill turned and pulled a burlap sack from beneath a blanket.

"What's that?"

"The brazier. I have to light it from the bale fire and take the light forth." She sighed and slumped forward. "If I just didn't have to go outside the Hold walls . . ."

"I know." And he patted her back. "Maybe you should bring your bow. I hope the spirits don't take you, Twill. I'll be very lonely—"

Twill perked up when she heard other voices set apart from the drone of the Hold's activity. She held up a hand and moved on her hands and knees to the edge of the alcove. A couple of the town's Elders and two soldiers were just below them, gathered in a circle.

Manou looked over the edge as well. "Why—"

Twill slapped her hand over his mouth and shook her head. She wanted to hear what they were saying.

She recognized Lord Dorwind by the gray hair at his temples. Next to him stood Lord Ellis, the lore keeper. There was Captain Roth and a soldier she didn't know. The fact they were gathering at the back gate, below the alcove, alarmed her. It was a secret meeting.

"—arrange for a search party," Lord Ellis was saying.

"In the middle of the Hunt?" Captain Roth shook his head. "Too dangerous. Those participating could shoot someone looking for them. The only way a search party could work is to cancel the Hunt."

"That will not happen," Lord Dorwind said. Twill

always thought the man looked like he smelled something bad. "So far the Hunt is going well, and we need the blessing for the winter. We can look for them after the celebration starts."

"After?" Lord Ellis looked shocked. "What if something terrible has happened? What if there is an investigation?"

The group lowered their voices to where Twill couldn't hear them, and then the group moved away through the back gate.

Twill sat back and looked wide-eyed at Manou. He returned the stare, and neither said anything for a few minutes.

"Twill . . ."

"Yeah?"

"I'm scared for you. Someone's gone missing. But they didn't say who."

Twill nodded stiffly. "I can't believe Lord Windbag won't go look for them."

"You think he knows a ghost took them?"

"It's still daylight, Manou." At least, that was the excuse Twill told herself. "Spirits can't take you in daylight, right?"

"You heard them. They just took somebody from this Hold. And they were in the woods! It's not even night yet."

All the color drained from Twill's face.

The two friends spent the remainder of the day scouting out all the houses in the Hold, as well as the ones along the route designated by Lord Ellis. The candles were in place, and if there was a window without a candle, Twill put one where it should be. If she and Jaques split up the route, and they started just before it got really dark, they could be back in the safety of the Hold within an hour.

This realization made her feel a little better as she dressed for the approaching festival. Her mother braided her hair, weaving in yellow leaves. Twill wore a dark green shift over her festival best, hoisted up the sack with her supplies, put her bow and a quiver of arrows inside, and headed to the main square. She didn't know if she could actually defend herself with a bow against spirits, but she'd try if she had to.

Her confidence was shattered when Lord Ellis met her there and told her Jaques wouldn't be lighting the windows with her that night.

"Where . . . why not?" Twill blurted out.

Lord Ellis's expression worried her, especially when he glanced at the main gate as the last of the Hunt parties came through. Cheers and music greeted them, and Twill looked in their direction as well. She assumed the Hunt for the blessing had gone well . . . but it looked odd not to see a Herald about with his magic horse. Or even better, a Herald who sings! Yet none had arrived, and she assumed none were coming.

And what about the missing person? Where was he? Or she? Was anyone out looking for them?

Then an idea came to her, and the hairs on the back of her neck rose. "Lord Ellis." She tugged on his robe. "Where is Jaques?"

"He's been detained. No need for you to worry." He was answering her, but he was also looking in the opposite direction, his gaze locking with Lord Dorwind. "Just . . . do the best you can." Then he looked down at her.

"Is it okay if I go ahead and start lighting them now?"

"Oh, no . . . no, no, no. It has to be when the sun has fully set. Only then can the light dispel the dark."

"But—"

"Ready yourself. You can do this, Twill." And then he was gone, walking away from her and the stare of Lord Dorwind.

"Hey, Twill!" Manou came running up, huffing and puffing the whole time. He was dressed in his festival best as well and looked more like a satin pincushion than a Hold Lord's son. "Guess what?"

Twill held back her tears. "It's Jaques."

"Huh?"

"The missing person. It's Jaques!"

"How did you know?" Manou blinked at her.

"Lord Ellis didn't say it, but Jaques isn't going to help me. The only way he wouldn't would be if he was taken by a Spirit. Oh, Manou . . ." She dropped the bag and put her hands to her face. "I'm so scared." And then what Manou said got to her. "How did I know? You knew already?"

"Yes. Kitchens are the best place to hear stuff, Twill. I told you before. You wanna know what's happening, go sneak a pie." He looked around. "Apparently some of hunters saw spirits in the woods. White, floating things. Jaques was out hunting with his father, and he disappeared. They found his horse an hour later, but they haven't found him."

Twill grabbed his upper arms. "They saw spirits?"

"Yes. Ow . . . you're hurting me."

She released him and looked up at the darkening sky. The fires were being lit around the Hold, and she was pretty sure she'd already missed the lighting of the bale fire. "Maybe if I just hide, they won't know the windows aren't lit."

But Lord Ellis found the two friends as the sun went down. Manou was chosen on the spot to accompany Twill on her journey. He protested as Twill lit the brazier and held it up on its pole as Manou lit the darkened windows inside the Hold. Holdkin cheered as the light spread.

And then it was time to leave the safety of the Hold. No one paid much attention as the two of them stepped outside and into the woods. There was too much revelry happening in the square as meats that had been simmering all day were cut up and served with seasoned vegetables and fresh bread and butter.

"It smells sooo good," Manou whined as they approached the first house and he lit the candle.

"The quicker we get this done, the quicker we can get back in there."

"No way. We're not splitting up." He shook his head.

In truth, Twill didn't want to split up either, but she did want to get done as fast as possible. Running would be good, but Manou didn't run. "You do know they save the best pieces and large portions for the light bringers."

That got his attention. "They do?" He started moving faster. "Let's go!"

There were twenty houses to be lit in all. Twill had counted them several times during her run. They managed to light eleven of them before the wind picked up and the sky cleared, revealing the bright full moon. It illuminated the path ahead as they neared a clearing.

The sound of a branch snapping made Twill stop in her tracks. Manou, following behind her, plowed into her back, and she nearly dropped the brazier. "Ooof . . . why'd you stop?"

"I heard something." She held the light away from them and tried to see farther ahead.

"Twill—"

"Shush. I can't see anything with this light in my face."

"Twill, I think—"

"Manou, can't you be quiet?"

"I see a spirit!" he shouted at the top of his lungs.

That got her attention, and she spun around to see what he was seeing.

It was there . . . just through the trees in the hazy dark, under the moonlight. It was white and moving slowly, the way spirits were said to move.

"Twill . . . let's run."

"It'll catch us."

"Not if we run fast!"

"Ssh." She slowly set the brazier on the ground, careful not to let it tip over and spill the hot coals. Twill opened the bag and removed her bow and quiver. Manou watched with wide eyes as she nocked an arrow and slowly brought the bow up to aim at the moving spirit.

"You can't kill a spirit!" Manou hissed.

"It's coming right for us. You think we can outrun it?" She said as she pulled the arrow back, watching her form, praying she could at least distract it.

"We should run!" Manou hissed.

There was a shout somewhere in the dark. The sound startled Twill and she released the arrow. It whizzed through the air toward the spirit—

But it was gone.

"You killed it!" Manou whispered.

"No . . . I don't think . . . did you hear shouting?"

"Yes. It came from over there." He turned in the opposite direction. "I say we stop now and head back and say we lit everything. I mean, it's windy . . . we can just say the wind blew them out."

"No . . ." Something about the situation felt wrong to Twill. Yes, she'd seen the spirit. But now it was gone. Had she actually struck it? Was that possible? Either way, she had to retrieve her arrow. She'd only been able to fashion ten that passed her bow instructor's approval. "I'm getting my arrow. Come on."

Manou made a noise and grabbed the bag and brazier as Twill moved through the trees toward where she was sure she'd last seen the ghost, her bow out in front of her. She didn't have another arrow nocked, but if something did pop up—

Her foot connected with something solid. Twill stumbled and then fell forward as Manou yelled her name.

She'd lost her bow, but still had her quiver strapped to her back as she righted herself onto her backside and . . .

"What . . ." Manou said as he appeared between the trees. "You killed a spirit!"

At first, she thought the same thing. A figure lay still on the ground beneath her. Twill scrambled off of it, her rough hands catching on the soft fabric of its clothing . . .

Clothing?

"Manou, shine the brazier over here."

"Oh, good plan. Banish the Spirit with the light of the bale fire."

That wasn't exactly what she had in mind. She just wanted to see what she'd tripped over. Nothing she knew of in the forest should be this soft.

It was a man. A young man, with long dark hair that obscured his face. He wore a set of white clothing, all the way to his boots. A wide, dark stain marked his left shoulder. Twill stood and pulled the pole of the brazier closer to see.

"You hit it!" Manou said excitedly.

"That's not my arrow. Look at the fletching. I don't use a red cock feather."

There were shouts again, this time closer than before. Twill pressed a finger to the man's neck and felt for a pulse. "He's alive, but unconscious. Looks like he hit his head."

"Spirits are male?"

"Manou, this isn't a spirit. Look at the leathers. He's a Herald. And he's been shot."

"A Her—" Manou squatted down to see, nearly banging Twill in the head with the brazier. "What's a Herald doing out here . . ." He slapped his free hand to his face. "My father said the Herald was late."

The Queen's Heralds were always invited to the Harvest Festivals. Twill could remember years with and without them. Sometimes they were Bards, and the music was always fun to listen too. This year she'd been so wrapped up in her own fear that she'd not even noticed whether there was a Herald or not.

"But who shot him?"

"They're gonna think you did it."

"I did not! That's not my arrow!"

"I hear something over there!" came a male's voice in the dark.

Manou dropped the brazier and Twill scrambled to make sure it didn't set the forest floor on fire. "You think they shot him? Maybe they thought he was a spirit too?"

"I don't know," she hissed. Her fear of seeing spirits and being taken was now replaced with the fear of being accused of shooting a Herald. "Can you see who it is?"

"No. But they can see the light, I'm sure."

Twill used the bag to move the brazier to a spot beneath a copse of still-green bushes. With the light half hidden, she could see into the clearing just beyond the trees. There were three shadows approaching, one of which looked familiar to her. "Manou . . . I don't think they're from the Hold."

"I recognize one of them. I've seen him with Lord Dorwind before. And he's not from our Hold." Manou's voice dropped. "He's one of the ones my Father thinks is stealing horses."

Twill looked back at them. "They're getting closer. Run back to the Hold and get your father. Get anyone. Tell them someone shot the Herald."

Manou nodded, his head bobbing back and forth on his neck as he dashed with unusual speed back in the direction they'd come.

If she was smart, Twill knew she should run too. But there was an injured man next to her. And not just any man . . . a Herald! But if he really was a Herald . . . where was his horse? The beautiful white one she always admired from a distance but was always too afraid to get near.

"I see a light!" one of the men shouted. "If he's alive, I'll finish him."

That last statement proved to Twill that these men were not here to help. She nocked another arrow and sat as still as possible as the one who spoke came close . . . and when he was close enough, she released. The arrow sang true and struck the man in the center of his chest. He cried out and fell back, but he didn't get back up.

In the back of her mind, her inner voice was screaming at her, you just killed someone! But she couldn't let that make her freeze. These people were bad. And there were two left. And she was scared out of her mind. More so now than ever. Just thinking of spirits taking her made her want to laugh at the absurdity, when it was the cruelty of people in this world she should fear the most.

"He ain't dead!" one of the others shouted.

She nocked another arrow and waited. But no one else appeared in the misty moonlit forest. She whirled around when she heard a noise and released the arrow. It clipped one of the men as he approached, and he fell back.

Twill couldn't get another arrow nocked fast enough as the last of the Herald's attackers ran at her. He held an ax in his hands and held it high, ready to cleave her and the wounded man into pieces. But she managed to ready the arrow and she still held up the bow, knowing the ax would remove her head. She wouldn't be fast enough, and then she would become one of the spirits on Harvest Fest.

She would die trying to save one of the Heralds of Valdemar.

Something blurred past her, over her, and landed its front hooves into the chest of the attacker. She heard the crunch of bones as the man fell back and the white horse landed beside him. He still struggled to move, and the horse reared up and came down on him once again.

Until he was quiet and still.

Having just seen a horse murder someone, Twill started to back away from the Herald, her bow in her hand, the arrow fallen away. When it turned and focused its iridescent blue eyes on her, she froze.

This . . . was one of those magic white horses.

She looked at the Herald.

This was his magic white horse!

The horse lowered its head as she calmly stepped forward and nuzzled the Herald's neck and cheek. He made a noise, and Twill was pretty sure she heard the horse sigh.

Then, to Twill's amazement, the horse slowly bent down on her knees, and then on her belly as she moved herself around her rider.

:Child, move him close to me, please.:

At first Twill wasn't sure where the voice came from, but she stood and started pulling the Herald into the horse. The horse grabbed the Herald's sleeve with her teeth and pulled him up onto her shoulder. His hair fell away, and Twill blushed when she saw his handsome face, though it was bruised. Blood dried on one side where he had struck his head.

:He will recover, thanks to you.:

"Me? I didn't do anything."

:You turned your fear into strength and protected him so I could reach him. For that, I owe you my thanks.:

Twill felt herself blush. She wouldn't even consider until later on that night that she could hear a horse talk. "What happened?"

:We were on our way to your Harvest Festival. Darren spotted some suspicious activity and discovered these three stealing horses with the aid of someone in

*your Hold. But when we gave chase, Darren was struck
and fell from my back. I was caught by one of the men
and placed in a corral. I broke free to find him. And
your light brought me here.:*

"My light?"

She pointed to the softly glowing embers in the brazier. *:You brought the light into Sovvan Night.:*

"TWILL!"

Manou's voice echoed in the dark, and Twill could
hear the horse laugh, but she didn't say another word
to Twill.

The Herald was taken into the Hold and treated by
the physician. Manou and Twill were given extra special
treats, as well as the best of the food the cooks could
find.

It came to Twill during the celebration that it was
Jaques and his father who were helping those three men
steal horses, and taking a cut for their troubles. Jaques
was caught and ran off, and it was him they had been
searching for earlier in the day.

But the best part of the night was the moment Darren, now patched up and wearing simple hold clothing,
was guided by his Companion (as Twill was corrected
when she retold her story and used the word horse) to
the center of the festivities. Darren, with the help of
the Companion, bowed to Twill and Manou.

And the next year, the two of them volunteered to
light the candles in the darkened windows.

A Midnight Clear
Mercedes Lackey

Kettleford was one of those Borderland villages just barely large enough to qualify for the name. There were only nine houses, five on one side of the road, four on the other. There was a watering trough and a well in a widened spot in the middle of the road. There was no inn, though the sign of a shock of wheat above the door of Old Taffy's house and the presence of a couple of benches on either side of the door would inform anyone passing through that they could get beer and something like a meal there. The locals would all gather in Taffy's parlor every night for a drink and a chat, and perhaps a game or two.

Each house had a little cottage garden where folks grew their vegetables, but for the most part, people here hunted or trapped, with a couple of those who knew what to look for supplementing their income by gathering rare herbs and dye-plants. There were hides and furs staked out in various stages of curing in every yard and on every bit of wall, even though it was the dead of winter. Some of the hides were of odd shapes, or very peculiar patterns or colors. This was the edge of the Pelagiris Forest, after all, and strange things prowled the paths; creatures whose furs were highly desirable just for their rarity, weird patterns, or outré colors.

Tonight, it being Midwinter Eve and all, it was not at all surprising that the village was frosted with snow. Not buried ass-deep—no, it was only about ankle-height, the road having been cleared between Kettleford and the last village on Vixen and Vanyel's circuit, and it was about halfway cleared to the next village on the circuit. This was nothing her tall hunter Brownie and Vanyel's neat-footed Companion Yfandes could not handle, even if the road wasn't cleared by the time they moved on. And rightfully, Vixen and Vanyel, Healer and Herald, should have been sharing the Waystation—or at least, Van should have been out there—rather than being here in a house in the village itself. But Kettleford had no disputes among the nine families living there; they only needed to hear what news there was, and besides, it was Midwinter, and none of the villagers would stand for the Herald spending this holiday all by himself in an isolated Waystation.

So they had celebrated Midwinter right here, and Van had good-naturedly left off his Herald's Whites in favor of one of his presents, a local outfit of heavy knitted tunic, deerskin trews, and peculiar, very heavy socks that pulled up to mid-thigh over the trews, worn stuffed into boots. Vixen had the same, and was very glad of it. And here they were, sharing a hearth with the local herbalist and supplier of milk-and-all-things-chicken, Matya.

Matya was the sole holdout among the hunters, although her husband had been one of them when he was alive. She raised herbs, chickens and rabbits, and had three cows. The entire hamlet got their butter, eggs, and cheese from her, as well as their pot-herbs. She was no kind of Healer, though; herbs for the kitchen, herbs for tanning, and herbs for dyeing were her specialty. In season, she'd get at least a visitor a week from all over this area to trade for what she produced. And when she felt like it, she'd go into the forest with a trapper to collect wild herbs and plants that were medicinal, culinary, or produced remarkable colors.

Matya's cowshed was spacious—big enough for a half-dozen cows, though she only had three now. There was more than enough room for Brownie and the Companion. And like every building here, the word "shed" was something of a misnomer; it was built like a fortress, all of stone, with tiny windows that had heavy shutters, and a stout slate roof. Even the chicken coop and the rabbit hutch were built in the same solid way. It wasn't safe, otherwise. This was the Pelagiris Forest, after all. The cowshed locked from the inside as well as the outside; ever since Van and Vix had arrived, Matya had left it up to Yfandes to lock hoofstock up from within once everyone had been coaxed into the shed with grain and hot mash.

Matya's cottage consisted of two rooms with a loft. One room—just big enough for her bed—was where she slept. The other served every other purpose. The loft was over the bedroom. The floor was wood, for warmth; half-logs laid in sand and pegged together, gaps filled with a combination of sawdust and glue. Matya had once told Vixen proudly that her husband had laid it himself, not wanting his bride to have to cope with a pounded-earth floor.

There was a little table, three half-log benches, one corner was a kitchen with a pantry, a cupboard, and a stone sink, and that was all the furnishings Matya wanted or needed. Well, until Midwinter, that is. There was now a handsome chair with back and seat-cushions of stuffed fur patchwork. Van had commissioned the chair and Vixen the cushions, and had had it brought here just in time for the celebration. Matya was clearly enjoying her gift.

Vanyel and Vixen had put their bedrolls up in the loft. They were both sitting with Matya at her hearth, sipping mulled cider with so many herbs in it that even Vixen couldn't identify what they all were. Whatever, it was tasty, and something so complicated Matya only served it on occasions like Midwinter Night.

Midwinter Eve, of course, had been last night. The big village feast had been today, and all three of them were feeling stuffed and more than a bit sleepy.

"I'd better find someone to heal soon, or all this food is going to stay on my hips," Vixen groaned. "What was in that pie?"

"Simple recipe. Butter, sugar, nut-flour, and whole nuts," Matya said complacently.

"That good?" asked what looked like a knitted hassock beside the fire.

"Very good, Harmony," Vixen replied. "Much, much too good. So good I'm afraid it might be illegal."

The hassock giggled, stuck out eight spindly, stocking-covered legs, rotated, and looked up at Vixen from four jewel-like eyes peeking out from among the knitting. *"Vixen happy!"*

"When you talk to someone, Harmony, you say *you* instead of their name," Matya chided mildly.

"All right," said the sweater-encased spiderling. *"You are happy, Vixen!"*

"Yes, Harmony, I am," Vixen said, reaching out lazily to pat the spiderling's knitwear-shrouded abdomen.

As promised, last spring, Vixen and Vanyel had made a point to be at Kettleford when the giant Pelagiris spider, Melody, had come out of the cave she had been hibernating in. But she hadn't been alone. It seemed that her last, huge meal—a monster that had attacked the entire village—had triggered something in her, and she had laid eggs before she slept. They'd incubated all winter long, and in the spring eight spiderlings had trailed their mother out into the strange, bright world.

Vanyel had immediately given them voices too, but at first what they produced had been little more than baby-babble, as one might expect. But it was sweet and tuneful baby-babble, so eventually the villagers had given them all musical names. Harmony, Rhapsody, Madrigal, Allegra, Celesta, Lyra, Nocturne, and Vespers. Like their mother, they were all female. Like their mother, they went to work freeing the village of pests, pretty much eliminating all the mice, rats, and rabbits that tried to feast on the gardens or anything else outside. They were hunting spiders rather than web-spinners, after all, and they could move very quickly indeed on those eight little black legs. Anything trying to poach from the gardens hadn't stood a chance.

By the time Melody and six of her offspring went out, caught and ate huge meals, and squeezed themselves back into the cave to sleep, it was almost time for the first snow. But two of the spiderlings, Harmony and Rhapsody, had elected to spend the winter with their humans. Melody had assured the villagers that the spiderlings would be all right as long as they stayed warm, and the village had set straightway to knitting round covers for their round bodies and stockings to attach to the covers to keep their legs warm. Each cover had a pocket on the back that a flat, warmed stone could be slipped into.

Because the knitted "garments" were made from unraveled sweaters with too many holes in them to mend, they were not patterned so much as composed of unmatched stripes and blobs of shades of brown, gray, a little cream, and black. And when the spiderlings

hunkered down by the fire and pulled all their legs in,
they looked almost exactly like hassocks. Fortunately,
everyone knew not to sit on them.

And the spiderlings made themselves very useful to
the hunters of the village by eating the animals that
had been trapped for fur rather than fur *and* food.
Like their mother, they would inject their prey with
venom from their fangs. In a candlemark or two, every
bit of flesh, fat and organ inside the skin would be liquid. The spiderling would suck it out, leaving only the
valuable fur and bones without all the mess and labor
of skinning the beast. This made everyone in the village very happy.

Another accommodation that had been made for
them were passageways that extended between the upper windows of all the houses, so the spiderlings could
travel from house to house without having to move on
the ground and wait, chilling, for people to answer the
door. The household cats had also discovered these,
and they apparently regarded this as a long-needed
solution to treating the entire village as one, single, cat-
feeding entity. Some of them had grown rather plump
as a consequence.

On the other hand, midnight romps were now gener-
ally confided to these passages, so only the people sleeping in lofts—usually children—were the victims of
hurtling cat-balls in the night. And Harmony and Rhapsody were very good about helping with that problem; if
someone really did not want to be pounced on during
the night, one of them would weave a non-sticky net
over the entrance to the passage. The cats did not like
the feeling of these nets and would retreat.

The spiderlings might be hunters, but the webbing
they produced was also proving very useful. The hunters used it to affix heads to arrows and spears, prelim-
inary to more permanent attachment like metal bands

or glue. Someone discovered that the spiderlings could produce tiny, sticky dots of the stuff that held seams and hems together much better than pins. There were a dozen other similar applications of the stuff, and the spiderlings loved participating in human doings.

"It must be close to midnight," Vixen said lazily, and was about to add, "I think I'm going to bed," when Vanyel interrupted her with an upraised hand.

"There's someone out there!" he hissed.

:Yfandes!: she Mindspoke, because Van would be too busy counting noses out there to warn her. *:Get out of the shed now!:* Only then did she ask, "How many?"

"Two dozen," he said grimly. "Too many for us to take with everyone scattered among the houses and half of us a bit the worse for drink."

"Warn them not to fight, tell them we'll take care of this," Vixen told him—not at all sure *how* they would do this, but certain that fighting back was going to end in Kettleford people dead. "You lie down on the hearth; Matya, wrap up his leg like he broke it. Harmony, Rhapsody, you get up into the loft and pull your legs in so you look like cushions. Don't move until I tell you."

The spiderlings were *fast,* and a good thing too; they were up in the loft, and Matya had just finished wrapping Vanyel's leg, when the door crashed open and three heavily armed men wrapped in half-cured furs shoved inside.

Vanyel looked up at them with a faintly puzzled, dazed expression. "Oh hello!" he said, wiggling his fingers at them. "I'm sorry, I ate the last of the bacon-pies."

This was not the greeting the bandits—they were without a doubt bandits—had expected. The stared for a moment, jaws dropping open. Van smiled vaguely.

"What the hell's going on here?" roared a voice from

behind them, and a fourth man shoved his way into the room. The lamps flickered in the cold breeze from the door, and the fireplace flames thrashed madly. The fourth man was dressed the same as the others, and looked about the same—unkempt beard, hair, moustache all varied colors of brown and blending into the fur around his face. But it was clear from the way the others acted that this was the leader. "I told—" He, too, stopped in his tracks, taken aback by the three people who were *not* shrieking at the tops of their lungs and cowering away from the intruders. "Who're you?"

"For god's sake, shut the damned door!" Matya snapped, and once again caught off-guard, one of the underlings obeyed her. "I'm Matya. This is my sister Morya, and this is our stupid nephew Ifan, who managed to break his leg dancing at the Midwinter Feast. Who the hell are you?"

"Oh hello!" Van repeated, and wiggled his fingers again. "I think I'm going to lie down now." And he suited action to words, quite as if four obvious miscreants armed to the teeth had not broken through the door a moment ago.

"I'd like a cup of whatever he's drinking," said one of the bandits. The leader smacked him in the back of his head with his open hand.

"We're not here for a festival, idiot!" the leader barked. "Tie them up and get to it."

The leader left. The remaining three looked at each other doubtfully for a moment, then tied Matya and Vixen up and began a methodical rummage through the kitchen. It was obvious immediately what was going on; they were here to take everything food-like and portable. And anything of value too, probably.

"Just behave yourselves and nothin's gonna happen to ya," said one of the men, as he stuffed a ham into his pack and followed it with some random jars. Matya's teeth ground audibly.

Vanyel, seemingly asleep, was watching them through slitted eyes. :*Plan?*: She "heard," the "voice" sounding like it originated between her own ears. Vanyel's Mindspeech, as she knew well, was strong enough that he could read just about anyone's thoughts, and be heard even by those with no Mindspeech themselves.

If you can blind them all, Harmony and Rhapsody can jump them from above, and you can get the third one, she suggested.

:*I like it. Tell me when the spiders are ready.*:

Vixen adjusted her thoughts to the odd "level" where the spiderlings thought—Mindspeech, as far as she could tell, was a lot like sound. Some things were too low or too high for humans to hear, unless you had Animal Mindspeech, which she did.

And as soon as she had done so, Harmony's distressed thoughts broke in on hers. :*They're stealing the food! They're going to leave everyone to starve!*:

:*Not while we're here to stop them,*: she told them. :*Move slowly and carefully to the edge of the loft. One of you take the leftmost one, one take the rightmost one. Vanyel will take the one in the middle. When I tell you, drop on them, bite them quickly, and leap as far as you can away! In fact, get into the loft! They can hurt you quite a lot if they hit you!*:

Actually, she was afraid that a blow from a fist from one of these men would kill a spiderling. A blow from a weapon certainly would. She turned her attention toward Vanyel, who nodded slightly as one of the invaders found the honeycakes and began stuffing them into his mouth.

"Hey!" the second said, smacking the back of the first one's head. The third reached for the container where they were stored. And that put them right in line for the eager spiderlings above.

"Now!" she shouted.

It was all over in a flash. Van rose from his "bed," a stick of firewood in hand, and bashed the one in the middle so hard the stick broke, and she definitely heard the distinctive sound of a broken skull. Harmony and Rhapsody dropped down on threads of silk, bit one of the men in the face and the other in the back of the neck, and were back up in the loft before either man could scream.

They *did* scream, though, a horrible sound that started in terror and agony and ended in a gurgle as the spiderlings' quick-acting poison hit their brains. They collapsed beside the one Vanyel had hit.

"I have 'Fandes ambushing any singletons she finds by herself," Van said grimly as he stripped the dying men of weapons, then cut the women loose. "So far she's got two. So that's five down. Shall we repeat this in the next house?"

"It worked before," Vixen agreed. *:Girls, take the walkway to Taffy's house and stay in the loft and tell us what's going on.:*

There was a faint scuttling sound as the spiderlings headed down the wooden tunnel to the next house. *:There's one, two, three, four, five, six, seven here,:* said Harmony, counting them out. *:They're drinking Taffy's ale because they can't carry it.:*

Vixen relayed this to Vanyel, who pursed his lips, considering it. "Let's leave them there getting drunk; they'll be easier to handle. Send the girls to the next house."

But Vixen didn't have to. They were already on the way. And before she could tell them what to do there, Rhapsody called out *:There's only one! We'll get him!:*

:No!: she exclaimed, but it was already too late.

:We got him!: crowed Harmony.

:Stay where you are for now,: she cautioned. *:Tell Cannar and his family to get into hiding and leave the door open. You hide too.:*

:Yes!: There was a pause, then, *:Cannar doesn't understand why you want to do this, but they are slipping out the door and going to hide in the tanning shed.:*

"Well, that should keep them safe enough. No one with a working nose is going in the tanning shed," Vixen muttered. Vanyel nodded, and the two of them slipped out the door just in time for a flicker of movement at Cannar's house to tell them the last of the littles was out and on the way to the shed. And it was pretty obvious why no one had reacted to the screaming. It looked as if pretty much all of the raiders were converging on Taffy's house. Word of where the beer was must have spread.

"Tell the girls to check all the other houses but Taffy's, and if there is only a single person there, to take him out," Vanyel whispered. "'Fandes just got another one.'"

Vixen relayed the order, adding to it, *:Don't forget, you're not as strong as a human, and if they hit you, they can hurt you very, very badly.:* The girls were young, though . . . she had misgivings that they'd take her seriously. *The young always think they are immortal.*

They slipped around to the back of Matya's house and hid in the bushes on the other side of the garden wall. There was a fair amount of shouting going on outside of Taffy's house now—it sounded as if the leader had discovered his men were drinking rather than looting, and was not pleased about it. They huddled in the shelter of the bushes in the snow, and Vixen was just glad she was wearing that nice, warm costume that she'd been given for Midwinter. *I bet Van's glad too . . . if he'd been in Whites, he'd be dead already.*

:We got two more!: crowed Rhapsody. *:Guntrun's family is out and safe!:*

"Enough!" roared a voice from Taffy's house. "Kolgar, Yan, Renfri, Lun, Jarri, Sulma—get yer asses back in that house, and if ye touch another drop, I'll chop off yer drinkin' hands myself! The rest of yew, back to th' houses I sent yew to!"

"We slip in the back of Taffy's," Vanyel whispered. "We overpower them—"

"No, we go get Cannar and Cannar's wife and eldest son. Then we get Guntrun and his two hellcat daughters. We arm them from whatever we can find out there, and *then* we slip in the back of Taffy's," she hissed at him. "I'm a *Healer,* you idiot, not a Guard!"

She heard Vanyel take in a breath as if to retort, but he wisely kept his mouth shut. *They don't call me "Vixen" for nothing. . . .*

Instead, he slipped away from her. She stayed put after fetching the two axes from where Matya kept them hidden in the woodpile. After all, she wasn't trained in moving silently the way he was, either.

:Harmony, can you nip back into Matya's house and get some knives? I'll be at the back door.: Van had grabbed his sword on the way out, but she had nothing. She eased up to the back garden door and waited until she heard a faint little three-note "song." The door opened a trifle, and three big kitchen knives slid out through the crack.

:Our venom sacs are empty,: Harmony said mournfully as she skittered back to Matya.

:That's all right. Hopefully you're done now. Just stay in hiding with Matya.: Vixen picked up the knives, then went back to her hiding place and listened to the muffled sounds of houses being ransacked and waited.

It wasn't long until Van was back with seven more people. Guntrun's wife evidently wasn't going to be left out of the action.

"Are you armed?" Vixen asked.

"Not the way we'd like," grumbled Cannar.

"I have two axes and three knives, who wants them?" she asked.

By common accord, the twin girls got the two axes; the knives went to the two wives and Cannar's son. Vixen got Cannar's wife's frying pan, which was exactly the sort of thing she wanted in her hands.

"Now we go in the back door of Taffy's," she whispered.

The brigands were not as drunk as she would have liked, but they were drunk enough that the nine of them overpowered and trussed them up without a lot of trouble. They freed Taffy and his family, who armed themselves with the weapons of their captors, and passed spares around.

"Now the odds are even," Van proclaimed grimly. "Don't kill anyone you don't have to—"

"What if I have'ta kill *all* of 'em?" Taffy demanded.

"You *don't,"* Van corrected him sternly. "Now come on."

He turned and opened the door. And stopped abruptly.

A babble of voices erupted behind him, wanting to know why he had stopped, but Vixen felt a cold chill coming over her. Whatever this was . . . it wasn't anything good. . . .

"SHUT UP!" roared a voice—that wasn't Vanyel.

Silence fell.

"That's better," said the voice, deep and harsh. "Now alla yew come out, slow-like, hands i' th' air. Don' make any quick moves."

By the time Vixen made it out the door, there were only a couple of other people behind her. And given what she'd heard, she was completely unsurprised to see at least a dozen fur-clad, bearded brigands facing them with bows drawn, backing another fur-clad, bearded brigand who had Kaylie's oldest daughter Liliana in a choke-hold, with a knife to her neck.

She edged along the front of Taffy's house to the right side of the group as the last two villagers emerged from the door. *:Harmony, I have an idea. Go to Matya's house. Tell her this—:*

"Ye see what's gonna happen here," the brigand chief said through a smirk that exposed a mouth full of bad teeth. "Ye're gonna put everythin' ye ain't wearin' down, an' one uv m'men'll collect it all. Then ye're gonna let 'im tie ye up. Then ye're gonna tell us where all th' good stuff is."

And then he's going to have us killed, Vixen thought—angrily. But she didn't have any time to think of anything more, because at that moment, Matya emerged from her cottage, a large bundle in her hands. The villagers all tensed. They certainly recognized what looked to the brigands like a lumpy pillow covered in knitted wool.

"Hey! *Hey!*" the brigand chief yelled, as his men got his attention directed toward Matya. Liliana winced as the knife scored her neck. "Hey! Ol' woman! Stop right there! Show me whatcha got!"

"Ain't nothin' much," Matya whined, in a thin, reedy voice. "On'y—*this!*"

And she tossed Harmony at him.

Now all the brigand saw was something the size of a lamb with *far* too many legs flying straight at him through the air. And the instant he grasped that, he started screaming. So did his men, all of whom were torn between shooting the monster and putting as much distance between it and them as possible.

So he didn't see Rhapsody speeding across the distance between Matya's door and his leg. But when she sank her fangs into his calf, his screams went into the soprano range, and he forgot he was holding Liliana as he simultaneously flailed at Harmony and tried to defend his leg from Rhapsody.

So Liliana slammed her heel down on the instep of the leg that hadn't been bitten and rammed her elbow into his gut, then ducked under his arm and ran for the protection of her friends.

Meanwhile, Vanyel and the others hadn't been standing around; the instant Matya threw Harmony, they charged the brigands.

The brigands were handicapped by the fact that Harmony and Rhapsody were moving as only swift hunting spiders can—here, there and everywhere—and biting whenever a leg came within fang-reach. They were utterly terrified of the spiderlings, and paying very little attention to their human attackers—in fact, most of them were trying to break off and flee.

The villagers had no such handicaps.

It was all over very quickly.

All of the surviving brigands had been tied up and stowed in Taffy's empty barn.

The chief, however, was dying, slowly and very painfully. Vanyel looked down at him, writhing in the snow, as Vixen came up to him with Harmony cradled in her arms. *"I guess I had some poison left after all,"* the spiderling said, without a particle of regret in her voice. *"Can we eat the dead ones?"*

"No!" Vanyel said, as Vixen, Matya, Taffy, and Gudrun all replied *"Yes!"* The Herald looked at their faces searchingly, then sighed painfully and shrugged. "All right. . . ." he began, reluctantly.

"Yay!" Harmony replied, and wriggled to be let down. She and Rhapsody sped to Matya's cottage, one of them stood on the other one's back to reach the latch, and they let themselves in.

"Help . . . me. . . ." the brigand leader croaked, looking up at Vixen.

"Sorry," she said, making sure she didn't sound sorry at all. "I don't know anything about the spider poison. Can't help you."

"Can't, or won't?" Vanyel hissed.

"Bit of both. All I know is that it dissolves you from the inside out, fast. Don't know how to counteract that, and wouldn't if I did." She twitched an eyebrow at the Herald. "Not all Healers are goody-goody do-gooders who believe everyone is worth the effort of saving in the first place, and in the second, it would take a lot of experimentation to find a cure, *if* one could be found. So unless you're proposing that I have the girls bite some more of the prisoners so I can do that experimentation—"

"No!" Vanyel replied, and shuddered. "No." They moved away from the dying man, who at this point was weakening rapidly, his convulsions reduced to spasms and his screams to whining moans. "I've sent 'Fandes with a message to the Guard Post. They're going to need wagons for the prisoners. It's a good thing the road is cleared in that direction."

Vixen stopped. "Give me one," she told him.

Van whirled, face white. "What? No! I told you no experiments!"

"Not going to experiment. Going to send a lesson so no one messes with Kettleford again," Vixen replied. "Give me one and bring him to Matya's cottage."

"But that's where—" Van began . . . then understanding dawned on his face. "All right, I'll pick the youngest, and most likely to have a revelation that this is not a business he should be in. I'll meet you there."

When Vanyel entered the front door with the bound young—less bearded—man stumbling in front of him, Vixen and Matya were waiting, with the spiderlings—

stripped of their wooly coats, abdomens swollen to twice the normal size with their meal—standing between them and the husks that were all that was left of the first two brigands that had been killed.

"So," Vixen said, her voice as hard as steel, "You recognize these two?"

"Two *what?*" the young man asked, eyes on the spiderlings, voice breaking.

Vixen reached down, grabbed one of the skin-sacks by the hair, and held it up to him, face toward him.

"These!" she said, shaking it at him.

He stared, mouth agape. "That's—that can't be—Oh gods, I think I'm going to be sick!" He turned green.

She threw the skin-sack at his feet. "Focus, you idiot!" Vanyel snapped, grabbing his shoulder and shaking him. "Now you listen to me! You see those spiders? *They're* what did that to your *friends*. There are six more of them. They guard this village. And if anything gets past *them*—" He brought his face in very close to the brigand's. "We call their mother."

"*Aye!*" chirped Harmony. "*Mama is* big! *She ate four cows once!*"

The brigand went from green to white. "Hellfire, it *talks!*"

Vanyel shook him again. "I said *focus*. Now, you are going to fold up what is left of your friends, you are going to take them to whatever shithole you idiots are using for a camp, and you are going to show the rest of your friends *exactly* what happens to people who decide to take on Kettleford. Do you understand me?"

"Yessir! Yessir!" the brigand babbled.

Vanyel cut his hands free, and threw a sack at his feet. "Start folding and stuffing. And give me your gloves."

After an interval interrupted only when their captive had to throw up a few times, the young man stumbled

out into the darkness, gloveless, bearing only one of
the sacks the brigands had brought with them contain-
ing the remains.

"Why no gloves?" Vixen asked.

"So he won't be able to start a fire or improvise a
weapon," Vanyel explained. "All the more motivation to
get him to his camp quickly. That was a very good plan."

She gave him a slight bow, and looked down at the
spiderlings. "Can you two eat something that's been
frozen?"

The spiderlings looked at each other. "I don't know,"
Rhapsody admitted. "Mama didn't say anything about
that. Just not to eat anything that's too old."

"I'm on it," Matya said, as Vanyel went a little white
again. "I'll have the corpses stored in Taffy's barn.
When the girls get hungry again, we can thaw one and
they can try it carefully." She glanced over at Vanyel
and grinned. "What? They were no damn use in life,
they might as well be in death." And with that, she
hiked out the door in search of those who were cleaning up the mess.

Harmony yawned, showing her fangs. *"Sleepy."*

"Me too," Rhapsody agreed.

"It's just about midnight, you should be," Vixen
agreed. "Go on, go take your spots. I'll wake you if
anything important happens."

The spiderlings climbed the wall and settled themselves in their favorite place, next to the chimney, where
the heated stone would keep them warm all night.
Vanyel watched them lash themselves in place with a bit
of spider-silk and shook his head.

"What?" Vixen asked.

"They're adorable. And they can go from adorable
to bloodthirsty killer in the blink of an eye."

She laughed at him. "So can I. So can your friends,
the Hawkbrothers."

He shook his head. "Maybe there's something wrong with me for liking that part of you."

"Maybe," she replied, and patted him on the back. "Or maybe you recognize that *everyone* has that in themselves, under the right circumstances, but what you like is that we're honest enough to admit it."

"That . . . and you know where I sleep," Vanyel retorted. "I intend to stay on your good side!"

She broke into honest laughter. "Good enough," she agreed. "And speaking of that, let's grab a piece of that butter cake and go to bed."

"You're full of good plans tonight," Van admitted.

And so they did.

About the Authors

Dylan Birtolo resides in the Pacific Northwest, where he spends his time as a writer, a game designer, and a professional sword-swinger. He's published a few fantasy novels and several short stories. On the game side, he contributed to *Dragonfire* and designed both *Henchman* and *Shadowrun: Sprawl Ops*. He trains in Systema and with the Seattle Knights, an acting troop that focuses on stage combat. He jousts, and, yes, the armor is real—it weighs over 100 pounds. You can read more about him and his works at www.dylanbirtolo.com or follow his twitter @DylanBirtolo.

Jennifer Brozek is a multitalented, award-winning author, editor, and tie-in writer. She is the author of *Never Let Me Sleep* and *The Last Days of Salton Academy*, both of which were finalists for the Bram Stoker Award. Her *BattleTech* tie-in novel, *The Nellus Academy Incident*, won a Scribe Award. Her editing work has netted her a Hugo Award nomination as well as an Australian Shadows Award for Grants Pass. Jennifer's short-form work has appeared in Apex Publications and in anthologies set in the worlds of Valdemar, *Shadowrun*, *V-Wars*, and *Predator*. Jennifer is also the

Creative Director of Apocalypse Ink Productions and was the managing editor of Evil Girlfriend Media and assistant editor for Apex Book Company. She has been a freelance author, editor, and tie-in writer for more than ten years after leaving her high-paying tech job, and she's never been happier. She keeps a tight schedule on her writing and editing projects and somehow manages to find time to volunteer for several professional writing organizations such as SFWA, HWA, and IAMTW. She shares her husband, Jeff, with several cats and often uses him as a sounding board for her story ideas. Visit Jennifer's worlds at jenniferbrozek.com.

Brigid Collins is a fantasy and science fiction writer living in Michigan. Her short stories have appeared in *Fiction River, Uncollected Anthology Volume 13: Mystical Melodies*, and *Chronicle Worlds: Feyland*. Books 1 through 3 of her fantasy series, Songbird River Chronicles, and her dark fairy tale novella, *Thorn and Thimble*, are available in print and electronic versions on Amazon and Kobo. You can sign up for her newsletter at https://tinyletter.com/HarmonicStories or follow her on twitter @purellian.

Ron Collins is the bestselling Amazon Dark Fantasy author of *Saga of the God-Touched Mage* and *Stealing the Sun*, a series of space-based SF books. He has contributed 100 or so stories to premier science fiction and fantasy publications, including *Analog, Asimov's,* and several editions of the Valdemar anthology series. His work has garnered a *Writers of the Future* prize and a CompuServe HOMer award. His short story "The White Game" was nominated for the Short Mystery Fiction Society's 2016 Derringer Award. Find current information about Ron at typosphere.com.

Hailed as "one of the best writers working today" by bestselling author Dean Wesley Smith, **Dayle A. Dermatis** is the author or coauthor of many novels (including snarky urban fantasies *Ghosted*, *Shaded*, and *Spectered*) and more than a hundred short stories in multiple genres, appearing in such venues as *Fiction River*, *Alfred Hitchcock's Mystery Magazine*, and various anthologies from DAW Books. "The Price of Friendship" is her fifth story in a Valdemar anthology. She is the mastermind behind the Uncollected Anthology project, and her short fiction has been lauded in year's best anthologies in erotica, mystery, and horror. To find out where she's wandered off to (and to get free fiction!), check out DayleDermatis.com.

Michele Lang grew up in deepest suburbia, the daughter of a Hungarian mystic and a fast-talking used car salesman. Now she writes tales of magic, crime, and adventure. Author of the *Lady Lazarus* historical urban fantasy series, Michele also writes urban fantasy for the Uncollected Anthology series.

Fiona Patton was born in Calgary, Alberta, and now lives in rural Ontario with her wife, Tanya Huff, an assortment of cats, and two wonderful dogs. She has written seven fantasy novels published by DAW Books and close to forty short stories. "The Rose Fair" is her 12th story in the Valdemar anthologies, the 10th to feature the Dann family.

Angela Penrose lives in Seattle with her husband, seven computers, and about ten thousand books. She's been a Valdemar fan for decades and wrote her first Valdemar story for the "Modems of the Queen" area on the old GEnie network back in the 1980s. In addition to fantasy, she writes SF and mystery, sometimes in combinations. She's had stories published in *Loosed Upon the World*, *Fiction River*, *The Year's Best Crime and Mystery Stories 2016*, and of course *Choices*, the last Valdemar anthology. Find links to all her work at angelapenrosewriter.blogspot.com.

Kristin Schwengel lives near Milwaukee, Wisconsin, with her husband, along with the obligatory writer's cat (named Gandalf, of course), a Darwinian garden in which only the strong survive, and a growing collection of knitting and spinning supplies. Her writing has appeared in several previous Valdemar anthologies, among others. The nucleus for "A Midwinter's Gift" started with the idea of Herald families. What might happen when everyone expects a child to be Chosen, and he or she is not?

Growing up on fairy tales and computer games, *USA Today* bestselling author **Anthea Sharp** has melded the two in her award-winning, bestselling *Feyland* series, which has sold over 200,000 copies worldwide. In addition to the fae fantasy/cyberpunk mashup of Feyland, she also writes Victorian Spacepunk and fantasy romance. Her books have won awards, topped bestseller lists, and garnered over a million reads at Wattpad. She's frequently found hanging out on Amazon's Top 100 Fantasy/SF author list. Her short fiction has appeared in *Fiction River*, DAW anthologies, *The Future Chronicles*, and *Beyond the Stars: At Galaxy's Edge*, as well as many other publications.

Stephanie Shaver lives in Southern California, where she is gainfully employed by Blizzard Entertainment. When she's not doing things for them she's probably writing or catching up on sleep. You can find more at sdshaver.com, along with occasional ramblings on life and pictures of food she's making for herself and her family.

Growing up in the wilds of the Sierra Nevada mountains, surrounded by deer and beaver, muskrat and bear, **Louisa Swann** found ample fodder for her equally wild imagination. As an adult, she spins both experiences and imagination into tales that span multiple genres, including fantasy, science fiction, mystery, and her newest love—steampunk. Her short stories have appeared in Mercedes Lackey's *Elemental Masters* and Valdemar anthologies (which she's thrilled to participate in!); Esther Friesner's *Chicks and Balances*; and several *Fiction River* anthologies, including *No Humans Allowed* and *Reader's Choice*. Her new steampunk/weird west series, The Peculiar Adventures of Miss Abigail Crumb, is available at your favorite etailer. Find out more at louisaswann.com.

Elizabeth A. Vaughan is the *USA Today*-bestselling author of fantasy romance novels. She has always loved fantasy and has been a fantasy role-player since 1981. You can learn more about her books at writeandrepeat.com.

Elisabeth Waters sold her first short story in 1980 to Marion Zimmer Bradley for *The Keeper's Price*, the first of the Darkover anthologies. She then went on to sell short stories to a variety of anthologies. Her first novel, a fantasy called *Changing Fate*, was awarded the 1989 Gryphon Award. Its sequel, *Mending Fate*, was published in 2016. She is now concentrating on her short story writing. She also worked as a supernumerary with the San Francisco Opera, where she appeared in *La Gioconda, Manon Lescaut, Madama Butterfly, Khovanschina, Das Rheingold, Werther,* and *Idomeneo*.

Phaedra Weldon grew up in the thick, atmospheric land of South Georgia. Most nights, especially those in October, were spent on the back of pickup trucks in the center of cornfields, telling ghost stories, or in friends' homes playing RPGs. She got her start writing in shared worlds (*Eureka!*, *Star Trek*, *BattleTech*, *Shadowrun*) and selling original stories to DAW anthologies before she sold her first Urban Fantasy series to traditional publishing. Currently, her published series includes Zoe Martinique Investigations, The Eldritch Files, The Witches of Castle Falls, and the upcoming urban fantasy series, The Dark Backward.

About the Editor

Mercedes Lackey is a full-time writer and has published numerous novels and works of short fiction, including the bestselling Heralds of Valdemar series. She is also a professional lyricist and a licensed wild bird rehabilitator. She lives in Oklahoma with her husband and collaborator, artist Larry Dixon, and their flock of parrots.

MERCEDES LACKEY
The Elemental Masters Series

"Her characteristic carefulness, narrative gifts, and attention to detail shape into an altogether superior fantasy."   —*Booklist*

"Putting a fresh face to a well-loved fairytale is not an easy task, but it is one that seems effortless to the prolific Lackey. Beautiful phrasing and a thorough grounding in the dress, mannerisms and history of the period help move the story along gracefully. This is a wonderful example of a new look at an old theme."   —*Publishers Weekly*

"Richly detailed historic backgrounds add flavor and richness to an already strong series that belongs in most fantasy collections. Highly recommended."   —*Library Journal*

To Order Call: 1-800-788-6262

www.dawbooks.com

DAW 23